Taste of Death

Vampires of Sanguine
Book 2

Sophie Ash

Content warnings

- Mentions of bullying and abuse
- Mentions of chronic medical conditions (asthma and a heart murmur)
- Mentions of suicidal thoughts
- Depictions of depression
- Mentions of toxic family dynamics
- Scars from physical trauma
- Bloodplay/blood in sexual situations

To anyone who has ever felt unworthy.

Life, although it may only be an accumulation of anguish, is dear to me, and I will defend it.

-Mary Shelley, **Frankenstein**

Prologue

Amy

I knew the exact moment I died.

It felt like a weight lifted off of me. Muscle and bone, breath and life were no longer burdens for me to shoulder. I was free from a body and all the sensory inputs of the surrounding world. Nothing hurt. No anxiety gnawed at me. It was a beautiful feeling to be released from it all.

Despite no longer having lungs, I could only describe dying as the freshest, sweetest breath of air.

Despite no longer having eyes or ears, I had some awareness of the world around me as I left my body.

My best friend in the world, Tavia, knelt at my body's side. She pressed her ear to the chest of that empty vessel, her eyes squeezing shut as tears fell. Her hands moved frantically back and forth from the wrists to the neck, searching for a pulse that would never come. Her mouth twisted into a grimace as she sobbed.

I felt her grief, her heartbreak, like waves of heat. Her pain poured out of her, filling the air, the spaces between molecules where I currently was, somewhere in space above the body I'd once lived in. I wanted to hug her, to reassure her like she'd done so many times with me. But when I reached for her, trying to wrap my arms around her or wipe at a tear, I passed right through her.

"I'm so sorry, Tav. It's not your fault."

She didn't hear me. I had no voice to speak with, but it seemed important to say. Our home had been attacked by vampires even though the ruling clan was supposed to protect us. Strangely, we'd been attacked in broad daylight. It was supposed to be impossible, but it happened. So many people had been injured. I couldn't have been the only one that died.

Tavia hadn't been here, so Robin must have used my secret cell phone to call her. Tavia had done so much for me before leaving to become a vampire's blood pet. I never got the chance to tell her what an amazing friend she was.

I jokingly called her my bulldog. Tavia was strong and fearless, always putting herself between me and someone who wanted to push me around.

But she would have been no match for the vampire who gutted me like prey and drank my blood. The crazed monster would have killed her. So this time I was glad she was too late.

The memory of the attack was already distant and fading, like how a vivid dream becomes hard to grasp after waking up. I remembered the pain and horror in the moment, but now it was like sand through my intangible fingers.

I couldn't see Tavia anymore; she was so far away. Or maybe it was me floating away, my soul or consciousness disintegrating now that I no longer had a body. What was my name again? Who had I been?

I was losing myself and that was okay. I'd become the

oxygen from a tree, a breeze through someone's hair, the pauses in someone's laughter. Hopefully that someone would occasionally be Tavia, and she'd be comforted by some sense of knowing that I was with her.

With no body to fight with, no muscles to clench or anything to grasp with, I simply let go. If I had eyes, I would have closed them. Serenity washed over me, like the calmness and peace of floating on my back in a lake on a summer day. Death was a part of life. It was beautiful, and it just *was*.

My consciousness, my sense of self, of *me*, was on the verge of blinking away, when something changed.

All at once, the sense of floating, peaceful calm compressed. I couldn't describe it any other way. If the particles of my soul had been spreading out, carried off by the wind, they were now being gathered and shoved into some kind of container.

I could feel things now, actual sensations as if I had a body again. A soft, fine sand shifted gently under my feet. I blinked as if I had eyes and could see the rough shape of a landscape spread out in front of me.

There were mountains in the distance and a sun in the sky. No, not a sun. The moon? This celestial body had a rocky surface, and the landscape was dark as if it were night. But the light reflecting down from this moon was an eerie red, as if shining through blood.

"Where am I?"

I heard no sound from myself or the strange world surrounding me. Oh God, was this Hell?

Movement in the corner of my vision prompted me to turn, where I saw a figure... dancing? There was no music but the motions looked rhythmic. Ritualistic, even.

The figure was bathed in the strange, red moonlight. It

looked feminine, but moved so fast that I couldn't be sure. It was barefoot and barely dressed at that. It wore a mask or some kind of headdress with a skull and long feathers. Stripes of white and black paint covered its body from head to toe in a pattern I couldn't trace. A long necklace reaching down to its waist was the only thing making sound, reminiscent of a hollow clacking noise like bones.

The dance was passionate, hypnotic. Whoever this person was put their whole body and energy into it. Fingers stretched outward, feet stamped and kicked, and the figure's long spine rolled fluidly like a wave. They carried on like I wasn't even there.

But when the dance ended, the figure stopped, opened its eyes, and grinned at me as if it knew I had been there the whole time.

Long fangs jutted up from the figure's top and bottom lips, and its eyes were blood-red. I could see that it was feminine in shape, with breasts and flared hips. The long necklace was a chain of small skulls.

This was a vampire, one that nightmares were made of. I'd never seen one as horrific as this.

Despair filled me. I really was in Hell, but why?

The figure spoke in a language that I'd never heard before, filled with rolling, harsh syllables. And yet I understood every word.

"You are not dead yet, human girl. My blood is in your veins and you are not finished."

She brought a palm up as if to shove me, never making contact, but I felt the force of it all the same.

I fell backward as if I had mass, a body. The weight of muscle, bone, breath and life, came over me like I was shouldering a backpack. It all rushed back. Aches and pains, anxieties and fears.

My mouth opened to cry out, but the rush of air in my lungs was too overwhelming to make any sound. It felt like I hadn't taken a breath in days.

I was no longer dead.

And I was no longer human.

Chapter 1

Amy

Two weeks later

I hugged the pillow tighter to my stomach, as if more pressure would soothe the cramping and aching. It felt like my stomach was trying to fold itself into one of those little paper triangles Tavia and I used as kids to write notes to each other. Menstrual cramps times a hundred.

Not even crippling depression could make me ignore how hungry I was.

"Amy?" A gentle hand came to my shoulder. I knew without looking that Bea's brow was furrowed with concern. "Amy, I don't think we can put this off any longer."

I ignored her and squeezed the pillow tighter, shutting my eyes against the waves of pain rolling through me. It didn't matter if my eyes were open or not. I always saw myself in that mirror when I woke up.

My blue eyes were set in black, no whites to be seen. Fangs grew longer when I was most hungry, like now. There was an inhuman smoothness to my face, and I was never going to be able to see the sun at its peak brightness again.

And yet I couldn't even call myself a vampire. Vampires were born, just like any other living creature. They were powerful and they ruled this world.

I was something else. A *brusang*. A freshly dead human brought back to life with a vampire's blood.

Tavia had done this to me, which was precisely why I'd barely spoken to her in the past two weeks.

"I'm going to get Tavia," Bea said in her sweet, gentle voice before her hand lifted away.

Like me, Bea was a brusang. In the few moments I'd been lucid and not drowning under the surface of my depression, I learned that she'd been turned about twenty years ago. One vampire had attempted to murder her, and another had saved her life by giving her his blood.

It was apparently some heroic thing he did; I wasn't entirely sure. The guy who saved her was now imprisoned by another vampire clan, serving a life sentence.

My situation was not anything nearly as romantic. A horde of vampires attacked Sapien, my home and the only all-human settlement in the vampire-ruled territory of Sanguine. It was broad daylight and the attacking vampires were hopped up on some drug that allowed them to be unharmed by the sun's rays. And that wasn't the only strange thing.

They didn't just drink people's blood—they mauled us like animals. Several people died, myself included. Why was I the unlucky one to be brought back?

The answer was Tavia, or more specifically, her vampire mate, Cyan. She was so overcome with grief at my death that she begged him to give me his blood. Apparently the turning process for a brusang had roughly 50-50 odds of being successful.

Lucky fucking me.

I heard Tavia's heartbeat before her approaching footsteps. That was the weirdest thing, hearing heartbeats as clearly as any other noise people made. For the first few days, I thought heartbeats *were* footsteps.

"Ames?"

She stopped a few feet away. How pathetic I must have looked from her perspective, rotting on a couch, wrapped in blankets and pillows.

Not that it was anything new for me. Even when I was human, I felt pathetic. I had been born six weeks premature with an underdeveloped aortic valve that gave me a heart murmur. I also had lifelong asthma. What a combo.

As a result, I'd always been smaller and weaker than average. Tavia was three years younger than me, but at ages seven and ten, we'd been the exact same height. When we became adults, she grew tall and strong, while I remained kid-sized. On a good day, I was a whole five feet tall.

Most of the time, I had been glad Tavia was always there for me, shouting down childhood bullies when I felt faint or couldn't breathe. But there were still times that I felt seeds of anger. Not entirely at her, but just once I wished I had the chance to stand up for myself.

"Amy." Tavia moved closer. She stood over me, but never touched me. "I'm sorry, but you *need* blood. It's been two weeks and I'm not gonna tiptoe around the subject anymore. We're taking you to the blood bank. If we have to drag you, we will."

She reached over and clutched the blanket I was cocooned in. I promptly shoved her off, hearing her stumble slightly at my inhuman strength.

"Don't touch me. I'm going." My throat rasped with a burning hunger.

———

I GOT DRESSED IN... something. I was too damn hungry, or maybe too dead on the inside, to care what I looked like.

Tavia's boyfriend, or blood mate, rather, met us in the corridor outside of Bea's place. Cyan was probably attractive; most vampires were. He had buzzed dark hair, angular bone structure, and red eyes. Tavia was certainly obsessed with him. But I couldn't bring myself to notice him more than the lamps on the walls or staircase going up to the main floor.

"Hi Amy." Cyan smiled, probably trying to convey friendliness. "It's good to see you."

I didn't answer, didn't engage at all. Tavia squirmed at his side like she wanted to tell me off for being rude.

Do it, I challenged her in my head. *Say something to me that isn't a hollow fucking apology.*

It was Cyan's blood that brought me back to life, that made me this creature with black eyes, fangs, and a gnawing hunger for blood. My best friend's lover's blood was inside me. It felt perverse for some reason, wrong in a way I couldn't explain. Not least of all because neither of them asked for my consent first.

If they had, I would have said no.

"Ready?" Bea's smile looked convincing, at least. Over the past two weeks, she had been genuinely friendly and warm. There was an adorable pixie vibe to her, if pixies had aquamarine eyes set in black and mini vampire fangs in their smiles.

I nodded and went to walk beside her, moving past Tavia and Cyan without a second glance.

My body moved on autopilot, the hunger pains easing slightly as we left the vampire compound and set out onto the street. It was nighttime, but I still had to blink to adjust to the outside sights and smells.

There were *so* many smells. I wrinkled my nose and rubbed it, resisting the urge to sneeze.

"You'll acclimate to all your new senses after some time," Bea said. "I know it's overwhelming. I swear I sneezed for a week straight right after I was turned. But I'm pretty sure we don't get allergies. At least, I haven't met any other brusang who have them."

I grunted out a noise of acknowledgement. Everyone told me I would get used to this new existence, it would just take time. Time to adjust to a nocturnal schedule. Time to get used to drinking blood. Time for my new superhuman senses to acclimate. And the best part was I had all the time in the world with my new eight-hundred-year-plus lifespan. Time was so great. Time healed all wounds. Time was the most precious currency and I was now a rich woman.

Blah blah blah. Fuck time. I never chose this. I'd trade all this fucking time in a heartbeat to get my humanity back.

"Can you pick out that spicy, woodsy smell? It's coming from there." Bea pointed to a small building that had the word *DARAKT* painted across the front windows. "Those are the cigarettes Thorne is always smoking, the ones that make red smoke."

"Is it red because they're smoking blood?" I asked, my lip curling.

"In powdered form, yeah. But it's not just blood. There's a bunch of different herbs mixed in to give it different flavors."

We passed the smoke shop and I got a strong whiff of thick, spicy smoke. It wasn't terrible, I had to admit. Back home in Sapien, some people grew their own tobacco either for personal use or to sell in the human world. I never could smoke due to my asthma, but I always did enjoy the smell of the dried, harvested leaves.

"Do vampires get lung cancer?" I wondered.

"Nope, neither do brusang," Bea said. "Our fast healing counters any damage done to our lungs."

That made me wonder if I still had my asthma or heart murmur since being turned. I hadn't felt faint or short of breath since I woke up to my new existence. But then again, I'd spent most of my time in a near-vegetative state on Bea's couch. This evening stroll was the most physical activity I'd had in two weeks.

"That's a great restaurant." Bea pointed to another building labeled *Carnassian's* in an elegant script. "Tavia and I have gone there a few times. Great menus for whatever diet you have."

The place was bustling with activity, every seat filled and wait staff hustling from table to table. Large windows opened up to the street, and string lights lined the outdoor patios.

Bea pointed out a few more places as we walked, with me only taking mild notice. Our journey ended at a square white building that reminded me of human-world clinics or small hospitals. The side read *Blood Bank* in large red letters, and *Receiver Entrance* in smaller letters.

Inside felt like a hospital reception area too, clean to the point of sterile, with a front desk and chairs for people to wait in.

I dropped into a chair like a pile of laundry, letting Bea

handle things at the front desk while pointedly ignoring Tavia and Cyan easing into chairs next to me.

The front desk person gave me a short form to fill out and told me that I would have a human tech assisting me. I didn't know why it mattered, but also didn't argue.

Tavia leaned closer to me and I fought the urge to hiss at her being in my personal space.

"Do you want me to come back there with you?"

"No."

I sensed her flinch in my peripheral vision. "Okay, but maybe Bea can? Just so you won't be alone."

Wouldn't it shock her to know that being left alone was exactly what I wanted?

"No."

That seemed to send the message clearly enough and she leaned away from me.

A human woman called my name soon enough and led me through a door behind the front desk. She was dressed in maroon scrubs and carried a file folder, just like any nurse would. If I didn't know any better, I'd thought I'd be getting a checkup in the human world.

"My name's Rebecca and I'll be assisting you with your feeding today." She opened the file folder and scribbled a note on my paperwork. "I understand this is your first time at the blood bank?"

"Yes," I sighed, wishing for this whole ordeal to be over with.

Rebecca glanced at my form and then at me with her eyebrows slightly lifted. "You were turned two weeks ago?"

"Yeah."

"So generally, we recommend brusang take blood at least once a week. The amount depends on your caloric needs and other factors such as your height and weight. You may also supplement with rare or raw meat or a bone marrow mash, but that isn't sustainable for the long term. Since your body is human in origin, you do need calories from human foods as well. Everyone is different, but we like to start with a baseline of one blood meal per week, and a human meal at least every other day."

She stopped talking and I continued to stare blankly.

"Okay," I said finally.

Rebecca's brow pinched, her face showing something like pity. "Did you have any questions?"

"No."

She sighed and set aside my paperwork, lacing her fingers in front of her. "I can tell this isn't an existence you wanted. You're unhappy, maybe even resentful of whoever turned you, and that's valid. I've met a lot of brusang and I promise what you're feeling is completely normal."

I blinked, not expecting the validation.

"My job is to make sure you receive the right kind of blood so you can remain alive and healthy. That's just the first step, but it's a huge one, Amy. I know you're resisting because drinking blood from a live person will solidify the fact that you're no longer human. It's scary and it's emotional."

"I don't want to do it," I whispered. It was the first time I admitted it in actual, real words. Any time Tavia or Bea brought up giving me blood, I ignored them or told them to leave me alone. "I don't want to. Please don't make me."

Rebecca gave me a sympathetic look. "I understand, Amy. But you need it to live. Just like breathing air, drinking blood is necessary to your survival. And someone loves you so much they cheated your human death. This is a second chance."

She sounded like Tavia now. I remembered her

anguished, tear-streaked face when I woke up from death. *I'm so sorry. I just couldn't lose you, Ames.*

My anger flared back to life. "I never asked for this. No one bothered to ask me if I *wanted* this."

The hotter my anger burned, the longer my fangs grew in my mouth, which pissed me off even more.

Rebecca nodded dutifully. "We have people here you can talk to as well. A listening ear might help you work through these feelings."

"No, thanks." Unless she had an empty room for me in which to scream and throw things, I wasn't interested.

The nurse nodded and then looked at her watch. "Well, my shift ends in two hours and those hunger pains are only going to get worse if you don't feed. But ultimately, it's up to you."

I almost laughed. Finally, she wasn't bullshitting. All the pitying looks, not just from her but everyone, the tiptoeing around me, the platitudes of *everything takes time*... I was sick of it all.

But I was also really, really hungry.

I didn't want to drink anyone's blood, but I also wasn't ready to give up. I was still here, after all. Pissed off, depressed, and betrayed, but I was here. I couldn't feel any of those things as a corpse.

And despite the depth of my anger at Tavia, she was still my best friend. I couldn't bring myself to hurt her, to make her feel responsible if I allowed myself to waste away. She already blamed herself for the first time I died.

I did want to process these feelings. I needed an outlet for this anger. But to do that, I needed to live another day.

"Let's get this over with," I said to Rebecca.

Chapter 2

Amy

I followed Rebecca into a small room that looked like a typical doctor's office. In the middle of the room was a light blue folding screen, the type of thing you would use to divide a room for privacy. A round hole about the size of a large grapefruit was cut into the screen about waist-high from the bottom.

Two people spoke softly on the other side of the screen, and I saw slight movement through the hole.

"Go ahead and have a seat." Rebecca gestured to a chair next to the divider on our side of the room. I sat down while she went to speak to the people on the other side.

"Hi there, sorry for the wait. Just want to double check a few things. We've got a brusang who's feeding for the first time, so you may experience some irritation while she learns how to bite. Is that okay?"

"Yeah, that's fine." The answering voice was masculine. Curiosity got the better of me and I leaned forward in the chair to peek through the hole.

"Please don't look through the divider." Rebecca's voice was sharp. "The blood bank operates on anonymity for the safety of our donors. If you don't abide by this, we will blacklist you from using our services."

I straightened, placing my hands in my lap. That actually made a lot of sense and it was embarrassing that I almost screwed up so badly. "Sorry."

Rebecca gave me stern glances while she and the nurse on the other side compared notes and charts. Matching up a blood donor and recipient seemed a lot more involved than I thought.

"All right, here's what I can tell you." Rebecca returned to my side. "You indicated 'no preference' on your form where it asked about the species of the blood donor. Since this is your first feeding, we've paired you with a human. Their blood will be the least shocking to your system. Everything else is more of an acquired taste." She shuffled some papers around. "You disclosed your sexuality and gender as heterosexual female, so your donor is a heterosexual male. We aren't always able to pair up compatible sexual orientations, but the feeding experience tends to be more enjoyable when preferences are a match."

Rebecca closed my folder. "And that is all you're entitled to know about your donor. I'll remind you, if you try to find out any more detailed information such as names, addresses, or what they look like, you will not be permitted to use blood bank services. Understood?"

"Yeah, got it," I said. "Will I have the same, uh, donor every time I come in?"

"Sometimes that can be arranged if you both come in on a regular schedule. But if you're just walking in, we pair you with who we have available at the time. We have no shortage of human donors, but in some cases we'll have to pair you with a female. This won't affect the quality of the blood you receive. Donors are regularly tested to ensure their blood is the healthiest possible."

"You sound like a babe," came the male voice from the other side of the screen. "If you want to keep meeting up like this, I'm so down."

Rebecca's eyelid twitched like she was suppressing an eyeroll. "If the donor wishes for their identity to be known to the recipient, they can of course volunteer that information on their own."

"I'm game if you are," my anonymous donor piped up.

"No thanks, I'm good." The words came in a rush. I barely had a handle on myself in this new life. Navigating flirtatious attention from some guy was the last thing I needed.

"All right. It was just an idea," he huffed, sounding affronted.

"Shall we get the feeding started?" Rebecca suggested.

"Yes, please."

My fangs ached with the need to pierce through warm flesh. My donor's heartbeat became the loudest sound in the room, speaking directly to the aches in my empty stomach.

He stuck his forearm through the hole in the screen. Rebecca took his wrist with a gloved hand and swiped over the blue veins with a cotton pad. The sharp scent of alcohol burned my nose, but that was hardly a deterrent. I leaned toward those pulsing veins, so damn hungry I couldn't stop myself.

"Wait, wait."

Rebecca put her body between me and the donor's wrist, and the growl in my throat was not a sound I thought I was capable of making.

"Oh, shit." I covered my mouth with my hand, pulling back in horror. "I'm sorry, I don't know why I—"

The human nurse just gave me a knowing look. "I really wish you would have come to us sooner. You're on the verge of starving."

I wanted to stand up, get in her face and threaten her to move or she'd become my next meal. At the exact same time, I was horrified that I wanted to do that to her. My hands curled around the edges of my chair because of what I might do.

"Let me feed." My voice was tinged with a growl. "I'm afraid I'll hurt you if you don't."

Rebecca, to her credit, did not look afraid in the slightest. She stood squarely in front of me, and it made me wonder how many threats she'd received from starving brusang and vampires while working here.

"I'm going to put a numbing gel on his wrist so that you don't hurt him," she said calmly. "And then I will let you. His vitals are being monitored on the other side, and if it seems like you're taking too much, we will forcibly remove you if we must." She let out a wobbly breath, betraying some of the nerves she was good at hiding. "Other than that, follow your instincts. They'll tell you what to do."

"Okay." My teeth clenched with restraint, fangs practically stabbing into my lower lip. "Numbing gel first. Don't kill him. Got it."

Rebecca moved quickly, applying the gel and checking in with the donor to make sure he was comfortable before allowing me access to his wrist.

I was horrified and screaming internally at what I was doing, what I'd become. But the scent of his blood was too overwhelming, my hunger too great to stop. I took his forearm and brought my mouth to his wrist.

My lips were sensitive, moving over his skin to find

where his pulse was the strongest. When I found it, I didn't hesitate, and let my fangs sink in.

The first taste that hit me was the numbing gel. It was gross enough to turn my stomach, and the smell overpowering my nose didn't help. I almost pulled away, but then that first mouthful of blood hit my tongue.

It was...fine. Not as bad as I was expecting. Slightly thicker than water but almost as tasteless. The aches in my stomach and throbbing in my fangs began to ease, a clear signal that this was what my body needed. Blood was the source of strength and vitality, the way to survive.

In a way, this felt natural and made sense. But I couldn't ignore the part of me that was freaking the fuck out.

Oh God, I'm drinking blood. I'm drinking blood from a person, a fellow human! This is wrong, this is gross, I could kill him. This isn't me. I don't want this. I never wanted this. Oh fuck, I'm gonna be sick.

My stomach heaved just as I ripped away from the man's wrist. I stood up and made it to the sink just in time to vomit everything I'd just swallowed. I had only taken a couple of mouthfuls, and still I dry-heaved after my stomach was empty. Hunger cramped my insides again, along with disgust and despair.

"You all right? Want to take a break?" I heard Rebecca's voice, followed by the slight weight of her hand on my back.

Ignoring her, I turned on the faucet and rinsed my mouth with water in an attempt to rid myself of the taste of blood and numbing gel. I couldn't get over how the blood tasted almost like water. It wasn't supposed to taste like that. This was wrong, so wrong.

"Hey, why don't we—"

I shoved away the hands that tried to comfort me and tried to return me to sitting down, and pushed my way through the door. There were too many voices, too many heartbeats and too many walls. I needed space and fresh air.

Eventually I made it through the lobby and out the front door. The noise of Tavia's voice filtered through my racing thoughts, but her words didn't register. She was probably demanding to know what happened, what was wrong and where I was going. She was always hovering, always in my space. How did I never notice before?

I screamed, trying to drown out all the noise in my head, all the thudding heartbeats and smells. Why couldn't I have just a moment of fucking peace?

Heading down the street, I turned into a narrow alley, which dumped out into another busy street filled with restaurants and clubs. Tons of people were out, mostly red-eyed vampires, but I saw a few brusang like me and even some humans.

That was the biggest shock, seeing humans out here enjoying themselves among the vampires like this was also their home, their neighborhood. In Sapien we didn't have much contact with vampires, despite living in their territory. We prided ourselves on not assimilating to their culture, not becoming their food and pets. Sapien was the last stronghold of humanity, and I had once been proud to be a human surviving with other humans in a supernatural world.

Now I couldn't keep from staring as a vampire woman with a purple tinge to her red eyes yanked on a human man's shirt collar, smirked, and snapped her fangs in his face before kissing him. And he kissed her back like the air from her mouth was all he needed to breathe.

How did his mouth not get cut up by those fangs? The man's expression was dreamy and blissed-out when the kiss ended. His tongue darted out to catch a speck of blood on his lip, and the vampire's tongue soon joined his. Then the near-pornographic kissing started all over again.

I turned back the way I came, not ready to attempt navigating crowds. Not with all those heartbeats, all the noises and smells. It felt like the perfect storm for a panic attack.

While meandering the quieter streets and alleyways, I brought a hand to my chest to feel my own heartbeat. It was there. I definitely wasn't undead, a walking corpse like the human-world portrayals of people turned by vampires.

The rhythmic thumping behind my sternum was strong, steady. I only felt my heartbeat elevate at my freak-out over having someone's blood in my mouth. Never once since my turning did it ever feel *too* fast, to the point of dizziness and breathlessness.

If becoming a brusang was what it took to fix my heart murmur and my asthma, well, that had to be a cruel joke, right?

"Shit." I stopped walking and looked around me for the first time in several minutes. I'd been so eager to get away from Tavi and Bea, away from everyone, that I didn't keep track of where I was going.

This street was quiet, and darker than the vibrant downtown area. I couldn't have walked very far, but this area looked older, with cobblestone roads instead of paved asphalt. The buildings were taller and made of aged brick. I couldn't even see the lights of the blood bank or any of the restaurants.

I scratched an itch on my hand as I turned around a few times, trying to decide which way to go, or if it would be worth it to knock on any doors and ask for directions. I didn't even know how vampires viewed brusang. Was I equal to them? Or some kind of subjugated class? My panic heightened to a new level and I suddenly wished Tavi and

Cyan were near. I didn't even know if I was in danger or not.

"Shit!" I inspected my hand as the itch worsened to a burning sensation. There was a red, raised area on the back of my palm between my thumb and index finger. And it was spreading toward my wrist and across my knuckles.

What could this be? Had I been allergic to that guy's blood or something? But then why wasn't my throat swelling up?

"Are you lost, miss?"

I whirled around at the voice, taking in the tall, finely dressed figure standing under a streetlight. The light gave his long hair a yellow sheen but as he came closer, I noticed it was more silver.

The hair color was unique, especially for such a young-looking face. But there was no mistaking his eyes—the deep, ruby red of a vampire.

His pupils dilated, and I noted the slight flare of his nostrils as he approached. He was scenting me. Like a predator. So I did what any self-preserving prey animal would do.

I turned tail and ran.

Chapter 3

Amy

If anything could be compared to feeling like a rat in a maze, it would be this. I ran through streets and alleyways, taking turns at random. It seemed like a good idea to shake the vampire, but what did I really know? This was his territory.

But there was a chance I'd end up back by the blood bank, where Cyan would protect me from this guy. Right?

My lungs started to burn, as did my eyes, my itchy hand, and even my lips. Fucking hell, what was happening to me?

Everywhere I went were more cobblestones and tall, bricked buildings. Where the hell was that nightlife district? I couldn't even hear other people anymore.

I slowed to a walk to rub my eyes and realized both hands were itching now. When I looked up, I noticed I'd come to a dead end.

A tall, brick retaining wall loomed up in front of me, gently curving around to form a semicircle.

"If you're done running, would you like to come in for some blood?"

I whipped around and instinctively backed up toward the wall. The silver-haired vampire stood with his arms crossed, blocking my way out.

"I don't want anything from you. And you can't take from me either. You don't have my consent!" My back hit the wall. I was cornered, but I refused to cower.

The vampire's head jerked back, his expression somewhere between shocked and amused. "Little brusang, even if I wanted to take from you, there's barely a drop in all your veins. You're starving." His head cocked to the side as if to inspect me from a different angle. "Were you turned very recently? No wonder you're a feral little thing. Getting light rash too."

"Getting...what?"

"Does your skin feel like it's itching and burning?" When I said nothing, he pointed to the sky on the horizon behind him. "Sun's coming up in an hour or so. Your kind is more tolerant than mine, but you need blood badly. You have no defenses left."

Oh God, how could I have forgotten about exposure to the sun? I'd been inside, with artificial light and no windows, for two straight weeks. And he was right. The eastern sky was a quickly lightening navy blue. Already the burning was getting unbearable. What would happen to me once that blazing ball of fire was fully risen?

As if sensing my distress, the vampire said again, "You may come in for blood. And to stay overday, I suppose. There's no adequate shelter around when the sun's out. Then you can go on your merry way tomorrow at dusk."

Like hell I was going anywhere with a stranger.

"No." I shook my head, putting on my bravest face despite leaning all my weight against the wall. The burning sensation was so persistent, I wasn't sure I'd be able to stand on my own. "I'm not going to your house. I don't even know you."

"Well, we're technically already here." The vampire looked like he was trying not to smile.

"What?"

"You're in my courtyard." He pointed at a building just outside the semicircle of the retaining wall. It was at least three stories tall, with stone steps leading up to two wooden doors with heavy bronze knockers affixed above the wrought-iron handles. "That's the main house." His arm swept across his body to point in the opposite direction. "That's my garage." It was a simpler, single story building with a wooden overhead door.

"So if you insist on staying glued to that wall, the best I can do is set up a shade canopy out here. It'll be painful, but as long as you stay out of direct sunlight, you'll live." He shrugged. "Probably."

My teeth ground against each other through the pain. It felt like my skin was on fire. "And if I come inside with you?"

The vampire's expression softened. "You'll have full protection from the sun, a blood meal, and a room to rest in. That's it."

"You're not a creep?" I demanded. "Or a...I don't know. Are there vampire serial killers?"

"I'm sure there are." He gave a full-on smile and despite the fangs, I felt no sense of threat. "But I'm not one of them. Or a creep. At least, no one has accused me of such."

"Why are you helping me?"

"Well I can't shove you off to someone else because everyone is already turning in for the day. And you're going to be dead on my literal doorstep in, oh," he turned to glance at the sky, "forty-five minutes, probably. So my options, and by extension yours, are quite limited. Wouldn't you agree?"

It seemed crazy, impossible even, that going with him was truly the only thing I could feasibly do. I wanted to run and scream for help, find Tavi and let her protect me like she always did. But the burning all over my skin was already so bad and getting worse. And I was so weak, I could barely stand without assistance.

None of this made sense to the human me. But my new reality meant that I needed to drink blood and avoid the sun. And this silver-haired vampire was my best chance of getting those things.

He seemed tired of waiting for a response and turned toward his door, a note of regret in his expression. "I have to get inside. Best of luck to you, little brusang."

"Wait."

I stepped away from the wall and felt a thousand tiny pinpricks of fire on my feet. Then I was falling, gravity pulling me down to crash against the cobblestones.

The hard punch of stone against my face never came. I was lifted away instead, the distance between me and the ground increasing as I was carried.

"I've got you. Temkra, you weigh nothing. When did you last feed?"

"My name's Amy, not Tenka, or whatever you said." Everything still hurt, but the burning sensation felt a bit soothed, like I had been wrapped in a cool, wet towel.

"All right, Amy." The vampire chuckled and I felt the vibration of sound against my cheek. "My name is Novak. Temkra is our goddess. I was swearing, not calling you by her name."

"That's a mouthful." My body rocked with each of Novak's steps and I was suddenly *so* tired. My eyelids shunted closed and couldn't seem to reopen. He might as well have been rocking me to sleep.

"It can be. We're in my house now and I'm going to put you down on a settee, Amy."

"'Kay." All at once, my entire backside was supported by the softest cushions I'd ever lain on. From ankle to nape, I was supported by clouds.

Novak's arms slid away from me, and I didn't realize how much I liked the feel of them until they were gone. But from his scent and the volume of his voice, he was still near.

"Lourna, can you bring the salve for sun exposure? And prepare a guest room, please. Thank you."

I turned my head on the pillow and inhaled, seeking out that warm, comforting scent I couldn't quite place, but wanted to bury my nose in.

"Amy?" Gentle fingers moved hair off my forehead. "I'm going to give you my wrist. I'm well-fed, so take as much as you need—"

"No." I shook my head, scooting toward the back of the couch as my eyelids flew open in panic. Novak sat on the floor next to the loveseat, a bewildered expression on face.

I wasn't sure why it was a detail I noticed, but this close, his hair looked like platinum silk spilling over his shoulders.

"No," I repeated. "Not from the wrist. I... I know I need blood, but not like that. It freaked me out last time."

"Ah. Okay, well." His smile looked uncomfortable, pasted on for the sake of politeness. "The other best places to feed from usually require a degree of... intimacy."

I scooted even farther away. To his credit, he did not move in any closer.

"Aren't there any non-intimate places that aren't the wrist?"

Novak's eyes lit up and he straightened. "Hold that

thought." With effortless grace, he stood and walked out through a wide, open doorway.

Now that I was alone, I could finally take in my surroundings. Well, try to, anyway.

"Fuck me," I whispered, eyes roaming all over the details of the elegant, high-ceilinged room.

The walls were a dark forest green with a subtle damask pattern. Built-in bookshelves painted in the same green covered one wall from floor to ceiling. The crown molding was bronze, as were the legs of the furniture, the coffee table a few feet away, and tons of other accents and small details.

It felt like I'd been transported to a movie set, a historical drama from the Victorian period or something. Only nothing looked fake and prop-like. Everything was real, and looked incredibly well-crafted.

This guy was rich, and obviously so. Blood 'til Dawn, the clan that Cyan was part of, was the ruling clan of Sanguine, but they didn't look wealthy. They rode motorcycles and wore beat-up leather jackets. Their compound was simple, no frills. Above ground, it looked like a small warehouse. The biggest extravagance was the stripper pole in the great room.

How did Novak live in a place like this and not be considered royalty?

"Here you are." He returned a few minutes later, holding a crystal glass filled with a dark red liquid. "Better drink it fast. Blood doesn't keep well when exposed to air."

Novak held the glass out to me and my eyes went straight to the thick bandage wrapped around his forearm that wasn't there before.

"Jesus Christ, were you trying to amputate yourself?" I stared at the glass, which wasn't small and nearly filled to the brim with blood.

He gave me a bored look. "We heal at a rapid rate so yes, I had to cut myself pretty deeply for this much blood. I'm fond of having two hands though, so not quite amputation level. But I'll be completely healed by dusk and this way, you won't have to put your mouth anywhere on my," he inhaled sharply, "on my person."

With slow trepidation, I accepted the glass from him and just stared at my reflection on the dark surface of his blood.

"Do you need anything else?" he asked dryly. "A curly straw, perhaps?"

I wasn't sure if he was trying to be funny, but a short laugh burst out of me anyway. "No, thanks. But, um, do you have to... watch me?" I had barely glanced up to meet his eyes when he started backing out of the room.

"Of course not. I'll see how your room is coming along and return to check on you later. I can have my chef prepare you some solid food as well, if you'd like. She's human, but knows the brusang palate very well."

"Oh no, that's not necessary." I tried to sit up taller without spilling my glass of blood. The longer I stayed, the more I wondered how embarrassed I should be. With rooms like this, a chef and housekeeper presumably, who was this guy? Some kind of vampire prince? He certainly talked like one.

"It's no trouble at all. Jo will be thrilled to work on something new." Novak gave a slight smile, showing only a hint of fang. "Please just drink up and relax. I'll be back shortly." He turned and walked out again, leaving me alone with this cup of blood and the fancy wallpaper.

I stared at the glass of blood, trying to decide if I'd drink it or not, when a human woman in her forties walked in, carrying a small jar.

"For your skin," she said with a polite smile as she set the jar on a side table, and left the room before I could say thank you.

I set aside the blood on the same table, grateful to have a distraction as I unscrewed the jar and took an appraising sniff. The substance inside was creamy and white, like lotion, and smelled faintly herbal.

The moment I swiped my fingertip through it, instant relief came to that sore, itchy spot. I gathered more of the lotion and rubbed it everywhere that had hurt, sighing with relief at the coolness.

Once that was done, my attention returned to the blood. The hunger pains had returned, but at least the burning sensation all over my body had gone. My instincts screamed at me to chug down the blood, to lick every drop until the glass was clean. But I hesitated, remembering the watery taste of the anonymous donor's blood and how I had freaked out. The heat of his skin against my lips, the pulsing of his open veins directly into my mouth. It had been too much all at once, and I shuddered at the memory.

Novak was clever to bring me a glass. Without even knowing why the feeding process had freaked me out, he eliminated those aspects. I had been a human for twenty-seven years; I could totally drink from a glass. I could pretend it was juice, or one of Tavia's wines.

Bringing the glass toward my nose, I took a tentative sniff, lifted my face away, then sniffed again. Novak's blood even smelled a little bit like wine in a way I couldn't place. Something sweet with a little bit of a bite to balance it out.

"Ow." Something stabbed my lip, and I brought my hand up to realize it was my own fang. They were longer than they'd ever been before, and pulsed with a dull, insistent ache.

I had been stalling, working up the courage to drink the blood of some strange vampire from a glass that probably cost more than my old house. But right then, I had forgotten why I hesitated at all. Novak's blood was rich and full of vitality that I so desperately needed.

I brought the glass to my lips and drank deeply.

Chapter 4

Novak

A knock came to the ajar door of my office. "Yes, come in," I said, not looking up from the handwritten notes I was poring over.

"The guest room is ready, sir."

I looked up to see Lourna, my human housekeeper in the doorway. "Thank you, Lourna. Did you check in on Amy?"

"I did, sir. She drank her fill of your blood and appears to be in a healing sleep."

My eyebrows shot up at that. The little brusang obviously hadn't been in good shape when I found her, but to fall into a healing sleep she must have been worse off than I thought.

"Should I try to wake her and take her to the guest room?" Lourna asked.

"No, that's all right. I'll take her myself. You go ahead and take the rest of the day off."

Lourna hesitated by the door. "Jo said to tell you she's prepared a whole board of bites to eat if Amy wants solid food. We don't know what she likes, so there's a variety. It's wrapped up in the fridge."

I smiled at that. I was older than my human staff by a good two hundred years. And yet these two women in their forties were more motherly than any vampire matriarch I'd ever known. "I appreciate it, thank you."

Lourna took her leave, and I spent a few minutes organizing the papers on my desk before heading down after her. After closing the study door behind me, I paused at the wall mirror on the landing to make sure my clothes weren't rumpled.

Old habits never truly died, especially when vampires didn't reach adulthood until the age of one hundred. My mother hadn't fussed at the invisible creases in my shirt, hadn't threatened to drain the human staff dry for their incompetence at pressing clothes in well over a century. And still, I couldn't stop checking myself over before going downstairs.

That was all it was, a habit that refused to die. It had nothing to do with wanting to look presentable to the strange little brusang in my sitting room.

It wasn't like Amy tried to make herself presentable. The poor thing had been trying to end her own life, most likely. Incidents of self-harm and suicide were higher in brusang than other populations. Many of them didn't adapt well to their new vampiric traits and considered themselves monstrous.

That showed how highly they regarded us full-blood vampires, which was not at all.

I wondered what Amy's story was, if she was someone's human blood pet who begged to be turned in order to match the lifespan of her *verakt*, her protector. A lot of naive humans did that, fell in love with the vampires who fed on them and proposed being turned so they would have centuries together.

Of course, any vampire who agreed to such a thing was a massive piece of shit, because a human had to be near death for the turning process to work. And then, it only worked about half the time.

Amy was one of the lucky ones to be alive.

Once down the stairs and on the first floor, I smiled at the sound of Jo's whistling as she tidied up the massive open-concept kitchen. Happy humans always expressed themselves in the most amusing ways.

At the entrance to the front sitting room, I paused to take in a passed-out Amy splayed out on the settee. A blanket covered her legs, probably Lourna's doing. The empty glass of blood sat on a side table.

She already looked healthier, with color in her cheeks and more softness to her face. Everything about her had been brittle and sharp out in the courtyard, from her limbs to her tongue. She had been defensive but fragile, like a cornered animal caught in a trap.

"What happened to you, little one?" I wondered aloud.

She had been clearly starving, but there was a fierceness to her. A clear will to live. And yet she seemed put off at the idea of taking blood from a wrist, the most benign of all places. At least the glass idea seemed to work.

I clicked my tongue in self-chastisement as I entered the room. It was disquieting to watch her sleep from the doorway while creating a narrative in my head, and I intended to keep my word to her about not being a creep.

Scooping under her back and knees, I lifted her limp form off the sofa and secured her against my chest. She was still light in my arms but there was more heft to her than before, which was a good thing. A sign that my blood was doing its job of replenishing much-needed nutrients.

Amy's head rested on my shoulder, her cheek nuzzling my shirt. Her hand even curled into the fabric from where it rested on her stomach. Despite her stirring, she didn't wake from the healing sleep. Her eyes were shut and moving behind her eyelids.

She wasn't likely to hear me, but I spoke to her in a low voice anyway. "I'm taking you to the guest room. Rest as long as you need, no one will disturb you."

A soft sigh escaped Amy's lips and her head fell back slowly. If she'd been awake, I'd assume she was trying to look up at me. I looked down just as her head came forward, and felt her lips brush my neck just above my shirt collar. And like the strike of a match, my body reacted.

"Fuck." I groaned at the lengthening of my fangs, the pulsing ache in my upper jaw, and my own heartbeat elevating in a sudden rush.

"Hmm... " Amy mumbled in her sleep, her lips gently mouthing over the blood vessel in my neck over and over. Not quite kissing or biting, but just... lazily tasting. She was still hungry, her instincts taking over as she slept and seeking more sustenance.

There was no fear in her motions now, no hint of the pinched look of disgust from earlier. But she was also unconscious, with no idea of what she was doing. If she did know, she would probably be horrified and press herself against a far wall like she did in my courtyard.

Her lips were soft, and it had been a long, long time since a woman nuzzled my neck before helping herself to my blood. I'd forgotten how sensitive the area was, how the warm contact made me crave physical connection.

But I was not about to take liberties with an unconscious brusang, no matter how good her mouth felt.

The prepared guest room was open, smelling like fresh
linens and cut flowers. Lourna had even set an arrangement
of red roses, poppies, and dahlias on the nightstand.

Fighting to ignore the soft mouthing at my neck, I
hurried across the threshold and toward the bed, where I
placed Amy down as gingerly as I could.

Breaking the contact between her lips and my skin was
far more difficult than it ever should have been.

Lourna had the foresight to pull back the blanket and
duvet, so Amy lay on the crisp, freshly washed sheet. After
a few moments' hesitation, I picked at the battered laces on
her shoes, sneakers of some kind, and removed them from
her feet. Her socks were worn thin and the left one had a
hole just beneath her big toe. I made a mental note to ask
Lourna if she had any extra pairs she wouldn't mind
donating.

I placed the shoes on the floor next to the bed, then
pulled the blanket and duvet up to Amy's shoulders.
Humans were more sensitive to cold temperatures and
vampires tended to keep their homes cool. I didn't know if
brusang had that same sensitivity, but figured she'd push the
covers down if she got too hot.

I left the room before I started to think and wonder too
much. It would do no good to stare at the sleeping woman's
lips and reimagine them on my neck.

A FEW HOURS LATER, I sensed Amy's movements from her
room. My study was only two doors down the hall, but I'd
been too distracted and bleary-eyed to focus on the data in

front of me. I had no problem sending my focus out of the room though, hyper-alert to any stirring or weight on floorboards in the guest room.

The moment those sounds came, it was like a shot of adrenaline. I stood from the desk, alert and poised. *She needs more blood,* my instincts screamed at me.

As if I could forget the soft brush of her lips on my jugular. But I knew that once she was awake, Amy would not be receptive to feeding from my neck. With that in mind, I went to the liquor cabinet in search of a clean glass. With a quick slice of a letter opener against my forearm, I prepared her next blood meal.

Once the glass was filled and my wound closed, I made my way down the hall and knocked at the closed guest room door. My pulse spiked, almost to a frenzied level as I waited for a response. I didn't have female guests often but this level of nerves was unusual, even for me.

"Uh, come in?" Amy called hesitantly from the other side.

I turned the knob and stepped inside to find her sitting up against the headboard, her knees bent toward her chest and the comforter pulled to her chin. She was wide-eyed, apprehensive, but also looked much more alert and healthy.

"Hi." I hesitated near the foot of the bed. "Did you sleep well? Are you cold?"

"No. I, um... " She relaxed, stretching her legs out in front of her. "I mean, I did sleep well. I'm not cold. I just didn't know where I was."

"One of my guest rooms. Seems you needed the rest."

Amy's eyes darted all over, from the ceiling to the rugs to the antique furniture. "*This* is a guest room?"

"One of the more spacious ones, but yes." I approached

the side of the bed slowly and set the glass down on the nightstand. "Some more blood, if you would like it."

Her dark blue eyes immediately went to the healing cut on the inside of my forearm. "Doesn't it hurt when you do that?"

"Not really. I don't know, maybe a little." I closed my fist to make my forearm flex. The wound was slightly sore, but hardly anything noticeable. "Vampires are so used to biting each other in various places, I don't think we have many pain receptors when it comes to surface cuts and bleeding."

"What time is it?" Amy scooted to the edge of the bed and carefully picked up the glass of blood.

"About six in the evening. In another hour or so, I'll be able to escort you home."

Amy's shoulders drooped, her spine curling into a slouch. It hit me then that she might not have a home, that as a human she might have been killed, revived as a brusang and then abandoned. That certainly explained her gaunt appearance from before.

It didn't happen often. Most humans were respected as equals these days, but some vampires held onto outdated beliefs that they were nothing but livestock for us to feed on.

"Do you have somewhere to stay?" I tried to ask the question as delicately as possible.

"Yes, I do." Amy straightened, then took a long deep drink of my blood.

A satisfied warmth filled my chest and abdomen as I watched her drink. She may not have been at my neck or wrist, but my instincts were pleased that she found nourishment from my blood.

"I have somewhere to go, it's just not the best living situation right now," she went on.

I felt a flare of protectiveness that I didn't know was in me. "Are you safe there?"

"Yes, it's nothing like that. Just a difficult situation with my best friend." Amy finished the glass, leaning back to take every last drop.

"I'm sorry to hear that. Is that why you were out by yourself last night?" There was so much more I wanted to know, like why she had been nearly starving. Surely this friend's situation couldn't be good if she wasn't even feeding properly.

"Yeah, I needed some space. My friend has always been like a mom to me. I love that she's always had my back, but she can be kind of overbearing, you know?"

"Sure. My mother was like that too." I swallowed the next words on the tip of my tongue, which was offering to let her stay here if she ever wanted space from this "friend." That was probably overstepping into creepy territory. And besides, this woman was a stranger to me.

"Can I ask a potentially weird question?" Amy chewed her lip, her small fang poking out.

"Sure." Having a stranger in my home was already weird enough as it was. How bad could a question be?

"Why does your blood taste so good?" Amy looked at the empty glass in her lap. "It's so much better than the blood I tried at the blood bank. I want to lick the whole damn glass, but that would definitely be rude." She glanced up shyly. "I am really new to all this, in case it wasn't obvious."

Keeping my expression neutral was difficult while I fucking glowed on the inside. No one had ever paid such compliments to my blood before, and I was more pleased than ever. Inviting her to stay didn't seem like such an outrageous idea anymore.

"It's probably because you were on the brink of starvation," I reasoned. "You were so deprived of essential nutrients that almost any blood would have tasted like the fountain of youth. When was the last time you fed, anyway?"

Amy set the crystal glass on the side table, spinning it slowly to watch the dim lamplight catch the intricate cuts and etching of the design. She was stalling.

"Well?" I pressed.

She returned her hands to her lap, again looking shy, if even embarrassed.

"Technically, that initial glass of your blood was my first feeding. The first successful one, anyway."

My mouth dropped open in shock. "Are you fucking kidding me?" I was raised to not say foul words in front of women, but I couldn't stop myself. "You *never* had blood before mine? How long have you been a brusang?"

"Two weeks." She gnawed her lip again, her small fangs like kitten teeth. "I had gone to the blood bank right before I ran into you. My friends took me there to receive blood and I just... couldn't do it."

"They waited *two weeks* after your turning to get blood in you?" I scoffed. "Some friends."

"It wasn't their faults," Amy protested. "It was mine. I had a... a really difficult time after I woke up. I felt betrayed. I was depressed. They tried to help, but I did nothing for two weeks but melt into a couch and eat a few slices of jerky. I kind of hoped I would... " She trailed off, waving a hand through the air. "You know. Die again."

"But you didn't actually want to," I filled in.

"No." Amy sighed wearily. "It's still hard to accept that

I'm... this. Not really human anymore, drinking blood to survive. But I want to live. My best friend wanted me to live. So that's something, I guess."

"It's more than something. Choosing to live is everything."

Amy frowned. "What do you mean?"

"Being alive isn't the same as living. Braindead people are alive. They have inflating lungs and a beating heart, the two necessary functions that determine the difference between being alive and being dead. But they are not *living*. They don't have lives. See the difference?"

A smile tugged at Amy's lips, her nose wrinkling. "What are you, some kind of vampire doctor?"

I laughed dryly. "I'm a scientist, of sorts. But you get what I'm saying, right?"

"I think so," she mused. "I might not have been braindead, but I definitely wasn't living those first two weeks."

"Right. Some people are just alive. They exist. They go through the motions. But living is a choice. It has to be something you want more than just being alive. You're more than a functioning heart and lungs." I picked up the glass from the side table, noticing the residual warmth from her fingers. "I'm glad you've decided to live, Amy. That you want to live a life, even if it's different from what you imagined for yourself."

Her lips twitched with a smile, her gaze lowering to the blankets over her legs. "Thanks, Novak. I think you're the first person who's put it that way for me."

"Sure."

An awkward silence followed, and it dawned on me that I should probably get the hell out of her bedroom. "Well, I'll let you rest until sundown."

"Wait." On my retreat to the door, Amy gripped the

covers like she wanted to throw them back. "Is it okay if I get up and I dunno, stretch my legs? I feel wide awake now, like a crazy amount of energy compared to before."

"Oh, yes. Of course. I can show you to the kitchen if you're still hungry. My chef prepared some solid bites. Or I can provide more blood, whichever you prefer."

Amy curled in on herself, drawing her legs and shoulders up, hiding a smile behind her knees. "Your house is so nice and I just realized how filthy I am. Any chance I could have a shower?"

"Absolutely. Through there." I swept my arm toward the attached bath. "I believe my housekeeper left a change of clothes too. Take as long as you need. I'll be two doors down when you're ready for the tour."

"Thank you." She sighed, tilting her head to rest her cheek on her knee. "Thank you so much, Novak."

I nodded curtly before turning to leave the room. As I let the door shut behind me, I wondered when I suddenly became Mr. Hospitality.

Chapter 5

Amy

This Novak guy seemed to have a limitless supply of hot water. I wanted to soak under it forever, and had to constantly remind myself that I was a guest, and not a particularly welcome one. He couldn't have been thrilled at having to scrape my dying form off the cobblestones, cut himself to feed me, and then provide me with a bed and shower.

I had either run into the kindest, most patient wealthy vampire in existence, or one with ulterior motives trying to lull me into a false sense of security. But so far, he hadn't seemed creepy at all.

Eventually I forced myself to shut the water off, and the chill that crept in was not entirely unwelcome. It crept along my skin like a physical touch, alerting all my senses.

I felt better, mentally and physically, than I had in weeks. The crushing sense of despair over my turning wasn't entirely gone, but it felt lifted away slightly. Removed from me, so that I at least had space to breathe, to just be.

The aches and pains of my hunger were gone, and I actually felt sated. Comfortable, satisfied even. I felt... good.

As long as I didn't look in the mirror.

Seeing fangs in my mouth and my blue irises surrounded by black always came as a shock. A slap in the face to remind me that I was neither human nor vampire. At least vampires had power and status, but my black eyes set me apart as something other. I was too human to fit in with those with red eyes and that dangerous allure. And now too strange and inhuman to ever be accepted by the people of Sapien.

But what really sent me spiraling wasn't on my face, but on my abdomen.

Yes, my skin was now airbrush-smooth and any wounds would heal without a single scar, but the scars from my human life were frozen in time. Including the ones from the attack that killed me.

The massive bathroom was full of mirrors, so it was hard to avoid looking at myself as I grabbed a towel, but I managed it. I didn't want to look down at my body either, so I closed my eyes as I dried off. Novak's impossibly soft, luxurious bath towel trailed over the jagged scars running from my navel to my sternum.

I only opened my eyes after securing the towel around me, and let out a shaky, relieved breath. Depression spiral avoided, for now.

Still avoiding contact with any mirrors, I slipped into a pair of dark pants and a cream-colored sweater I found in the guest room's dresser, then went off to find Novak.

I stuck my head out in the hallway and looked both ways before stepping out cautiously. The decor out here was just as dark and luxurious as the two other rooms I'd been in. The far side of the hallway was a balustrade creating a waist-high border on this entire level of the house. Stretching on tiptoes, I leaned over the barrier to see the main floor below.

There was the room where Novak had first put me, right off the intricately carved front door and a foyer with some kind of mosaic tile pattern in the floor.

I kept one hand on the railing as I walked slowly toward the glow of an open door, which I assumed was where Novak waited for me. My gaze could barely soak in every detail before being pulled to admire something else. A massive chandelier hung in the center of the ceiling, directly above where the staircase ended on the first floor.

I had seen old movies on the random TV channels we'd pick up from the human world, and of course I'd read romance novels about dukes and princes of faraway lands, but never in my life had I ever known such wealth was actually possible.

Hesitating at the entrance to Novak's office, I studied him from where he sat behind the massive wooden desk. His brow furrowed as he examined some papers, one elbow propped up on the desk's surface while that hand rubbed his temple. Was he that tired while talking to me in the guest room? Did he even sleep at all while the sun was up?

He looked up after a moment, and I didn't know which exactly caused my breath to catch in my chest—the striking red color of his eyes or the way his handsome features lit up at the sight of me.

"You look refreshed." He leaned back in his chair, rolling his shoulders. "Feel better?"

I nodded. "You look... busy."

Novak chuckled and lifted his hands in a sheepish gesture. "The work never stops, I suppose. Shall we go downstairs?"

"Can I ask what you do? It seems you're very uh," I glanced around the lavish room, "important."

He gave a slight smile as he stood and rounded the desk. "How important I am varies depending on who you ask."

"I'm asking you."

Novak paused several feet away from me, a respectful distance, but still close enough for me to pick up his scent. I almost found myself leaning forward for a closer appreciation of whatever that delicious cologne was.

"I am unfortunately more important than I ever would have preferred to be," he sighed.

"That tells me absolutely nothing."

"You should probably get the hang of being a brusang before finding out what my role in Sanguine is." The smile he gave was tight, more like a grimace. "As with all vampire clans, there are a few centuries of history to take into account." He gestured toward the open doorway. "After you."

I turned, heading for the stair landing. "Which clan are you part of?"

Novak inhaled sharply, his strides slightly ahead of mine as we took the stairs together. "My clan is called Rathka's Order."

"Does your whole clan live here? And who's Rathka, an ancestor, I take it?" My fresh burst of energy seemed to have dialed up my burning curiosity as well.

"No. Aside from my household staff, I live alone. And Rathka is a deity, the younger brother of Temkra, our goddess. Some say Rathka's our first ancestor, but that's where history and legend sort of bleed into each other to where you don't know which is truth or myth. But my clan and family line have embodied his ideals going back many generations."

"Oh, wow. So everyone in your clan has their own place? Are they all like this?" I gestured toward the chandelier above us.

Novak chuckled. "We have a few homes like this but no, not exactly. My clan's situation is... complicated."

"Oh, I'm sorry." We made it to the bottom of the stairs and I gave him a rueful look. "I didn't mean to ask personal questions, that was rude of me."

"It's all right." Novak headed across the foyer and I followed him dutifully. "It's refreshing to hear a lot of direct questions, actually. As vampires get older, we tend to assume and infer a lot. Once you reach a certain age, you think you know everything."

He led us to an open-concept kitchen with a huge, dark marbled island and matching cabinetry.

"There's a human saying about assuming."

"And that is?" Novak opened two large doors that I realized was a refrigerator designed to look like the rest of the cabinetry.

"When you assume, you make an ass out of you and me."

Novak laughed so suddenly that he nearly dropped the wooden tray covered with foil. He recovered quickly though, and placed the tray on the island. "That's clever. I like it."

All kinds of tantalizing smells hit my nose as he peeled back the foil. Vinegar, salt, spices, plus traces of blood and muscle.

"Help yourself." Novak pushed the tray toward me. "My chef made it for you."

My mouth watered. "All this for me?"

It was an assortment of bite-sized meats, all beautifully arranged and prepared in different ways. Marinated, smoked, seared, and even some pieces that looked raw with just a touch of seasoning.

"I'm not too familiar with human food," Novak said. "But she said this is all suitable for humans if you're not fully adjusted to eating like a brusang yet."

"It looks too pretty to eat," I admitted, eyes roaming over the display.

"Oh, don't worry about that." Novak scoffed. "When Jo wants to put on a presentation, you'll know." He pointed to the red cubes of raw meat. "I know that one. This is mukrot."

"Oh yeah, muck-rot. I totally know what that is."

His smile was roguish, but not cruel. "A mukrot is a livestock animal that can drop limbs and regenerate them. Kind of how lizards can grow their tails back."

I stared at him. "Are you pranking me? I've never heard of such a thing."

"They're kept by Marrowers underground, who harvest bone marrow and meat from the discarded limbs. It's a very popular food among vampires, and can substitute for blood in a pinch."

"Uh-huh," I said, still skeptical.

"You can dip it in this." Novak's finger moved over a small condiment bowl that looked like applesauce. "It's a bone marrow mash from the same animal. I eat it at least once a week. It's my favorite."

"So you do eat things besides blood?" Feeling brave, I picked up one of the red meat cubes and swiped it through the mash.

"For pleasure, not necessity." He grinned at me from across the island. "Otherwise I'd have no need for a chef at all, would I?"

"I guess not." I popped the morsel into my mouth and

my eyes went wide at the rich flavors that exploded on my tongue. A little spicy like ginger, with a buttery consistency that melted in my mouth. "Holy shit, that is really good!"

"Told you." Novak took one for himself before pressing away from the counter. "Try everything, don't hold back."

Everything on the board was delicious in its own unique way. It made me wonder if my taste buds had become enhanced along with my other senses, because I couldn't remember human food being half as flavorful as everything here.

And yet none of it compared to Novak's blood.

The cut inside of his forearm was a barely noticeable pale scar now. I noticed it anyway because Novak had pushed his sleeves up past his elbows. The fabric creased and wrinkled just below his biceps, and it added a rough-ness to his aristocratic look.

A roughness that was very appealing, I realized. He had good blood vessels in his forearms too, surrounded by corded muscle.

While my hunger was sated, my fangs tingled at the thought of the blood coursing under his skin. Blood that was refreshing as water from a wild spring, and more delicious than Tavi's homemade wine.

The sound of metallic clanking startled me, jerking my gaze away from Novak's forearms as I searched for the source of the noise.

"It's the automatic shutter system," he explained. "When all sunlight is gone, the windows open up."

"Oh, right. Most of your house isn't underground."

"I do have a basement for emergencies, but no." He gave me a wry look. "How could my ancestors show off our wealth and prestige if we didn't build upward so everyone could see?"

"You know, I keep wondering if you're vampire royalty." I popped another flavorful meat cube in my mouth. "And you're not exactly disproving my theory."

"We've had our go of that in the past." Novak rested his forearm on the counter, leaning against the edge. "It never lasted, though. My family's never been, let's say, diplomatic enough, to be the ruling clan for any amount of time."

"You seem very diplomatic," I observed. "Philanthropic, even, with the way you take in ragged, starving brusang off the streets."

"Don't give me too much credit. You were the first." He took another bite from my tray, slicing it deftly with his fang. "And probably the last."

"Am I that horrible of a houseguest?" I said it as a joke, bringing a hand to my chest in fake shock. But I cringed while waiting for the answer. Novak had been more than hospitable to me, while I must have been a major inconvenience to him. Now with the sun down after I'd been here all day, he had to be dying to kick me out of his house.

"Not at all," he said lightly. "You've made my day far more interesting. But," his smile bared the tip of one fang, "I can only handle one insatiably curious brusang at a time. So don't go telling your friends about how philanthropic I am."

"And share these snacks?" I held my hand out over the tray. "Share your blood? Hell no."

Novak laughed, but it sounded forced and I wondered if I overstepped. The truth had slipped out before I'd fully realized it.

I felt possessive over Novak's blood. The thought of anyone else taking from him sent a twist of discomfort in my gut. And not only that, I felt possessive of *this*. The time we were spending together, just eating and bantering in his glorious kitchen.

He was probably hundreds of years older than me, and wealthier than I ever thought possible. Someone like him should have made me feel smaller, less than. But being with him like this felt so casual, even comfortable. He leaned against the counter lazily, with his sleeves rolled up, getting creases in his shirt, while he grabbed snacks with his fingers and patiently entertained my stupid questions without any ridicule.

Whatever *this* was, it was nice. It reminded me of when Tavi and I stayed up all night talking about anything and everything. Those moments were the most special ones. There was something about talking until dawn about the dumbest topics that made a friendship feel unbreakable.

But with how things were between me and her now, I questioned how true that really was.

All I knew right then was that I liked talking to Novak, and in my short time of knowing him, I felt like I could be myself with him.

Even while I was in the process of figuring out who "myself" was.

Novak rapped his knuckles on the marble counter, angling his head so that his gaze shifted to the now-open windows. "I suppose we should get you back home."

"Oh, yeah." While I was romanticizing our one conversation, he'd probably been hoping I'd take the initiative to leave myself. So much for not being a shitty guest. "Of course." I pushed away from the counter, resisting the urge to grab one last bite from the tray. "I'll just grab my clothes from the room upstairs."

The grand staircase was an easy climb. So easy that I pushed myself to go faster, enjoying the speed and power that could have only come from Novak's blood. I kept up my pace once I hit the landing, jogging to the guest room to collect my clothes. It felt good to move, good to push myself even slightly.

On my way back down the stairs, I wondered what I'd do for my next serving of blood. Was there any chance Novak would let me come back? Or would I have to force myself back to the blood bank?

He waited in the foyer, wearing a long coat that matched his waistcoat and trousers, his hands encased in black leather gloves.

"Ready?" he asked.

"Oh, you don't have to come with me. I'll find my way back." My smile came nervously. I wanted nothing more than to stop being an inconvenience to him. "You've done too much for me already."

"Nonsense. I'll see you home safely." His look was impish as he gave a final tug on his gloves. "Besides, we both know there's a chance you'll end up in my courtyard again."

I forced out a laugh. *Oh, he definitely doesn't want me here.* "That's true. Your guest room is too nice and your snacks too tasty. Work on making those shittier if you want to be left in peace."

Novak bared a fang in a slight smile but didn't respond. "Where are you staying?" He opened the front door and gestured for me to go first.

"With Blood 'til Dawn." I walked through and waited for him to close up. "Do you know—"

He didn't move from his spot next to the open door, but it was his expression that cut my words short. His lips curled into a snarl, and his eyes were alight with shock and something else. Anger, or maybe even malice.

"What did you say?" he hissed.

"Uh, Blood 'til Dawn?" I swallowed.

"Are you serious?" Novak snapped out of his frozen

state, closing the door behind him as he joined me outside. "Or are you joking?"

"Serious." Although I started to wish I wasn't.

"You're staying with the ruling clan of Sanguine?" Novak's gaze narrowed, his eyes like two red lanterns in the dim light of dusk. "How did that happen? Did one of them turn you?"

"Yes," I sighed. "My best friend's mate did."

"Mate?" he repeated. "Like a blood mate?"

"Um, yes?" I frowned. "I don't entirely know what that is, but they're having this big ceremony in two weeks."

Understanding dawned on Novak's face. "That's right. I've heard that's happening." He glanced at me again, his expression cool and remote. "That's your friend you're having trouble with? She's having a mating ceremony with Cyan of Blood 'til Dawn?"

"Yup, that's her."

"I see."

I'm glad you see because I am in the fucking dark, buddy.

The kind, casual Novak I'd been speaking to was gone. This vampire was closed off, a cold and stiff aristocrat. He didn't even meet my eyes as he started down the cobblestone street. "Let's get you back before they send out a search party."

I hurried to match his stride. "Let me guess. There's a long and complicated history between your clan and Blood 'til Dawn?"

He huffed out a mirthless laugh. "More than you can imagine, little brusang. And none of it is good."

Chapter 6

Amy

My short walk with Novak was nearly silent, but as we approached the single-story building that was the garage entrance to the Blood 'til Dawn compound, the urge to speak my mind grew overwhelming.

Summoning courage I didn't know I had, I turned in front of Novak to block his path.

"I just want to say thank you, sincerely. For taking me in from the sun, the room, your blood, the food, everything. Whatever your history with them is," I flung an arm out toward the garage behind me, "it doesn't take away from the kindness you showed me today. I won't ever forget it and I'm... I'm glad I met you, Novak."

He met my eyes for the first time since we left his house, but remained silent for several long seconds, his expression unreadable.

Finally a crack showed in that cold exterior, and I saw the tip of one fang bared in a slow smile. "I'm glad I met you too, Amy. It was... " he paused, his smile fading as he searched for a polite word. "... nice having your presence in my home."

What a word choice. I had a feeling that *nice* was anything but a compliment.

"I'll miss your probing questions," he added teasingly. "I'll have to encourage my staff to ask more. Or else I'll be explaining my family history to the walls."

"Well, I mean we might still see each other around, right?" I couldn't suppress the hopefulness in my voice. "We live close enough to each other."

Novak ducked his head, swiftly stepping around me to walk up to the garage's side door, where he pounded his fist three times. "That's not likely to happen, I'm afraid."

The door opened before I could ask why, and then things happened too fast for me to track. There was a snarling noise, and then Novak was being dragged inside by two fists gripping his jacket.

"Novak!" A rush of sudden, instinctive urgency took over me. He was mine and something was attacking him, taking him from me.

With no time to dwell on that thought, I followed him through the door, my vision red and my fangs long and snapping. Not to feed, but to use as weapons.

Novak was pinned to the wall by two other vampires. They braced their hands against his shoulders and elbows, their grips unrelenting.

"What the fuck are you doing here, Novak of Rathka's Order?" a third vampire asked coolly, hanging back. I recognized him as Thorne, the head of Blood 'til Dawn. From what little I knew, he was essentially the king of vampires.

"Get off of him!" I snarled at the two restraining Novak, who wasn't even fighting back. "Let him go, you psychos!"

They ignored me while Thorne moved in and began

searching Novak's pockets. At his slightest flinch, one of the vampires braced his massive forearm against Novak's throat.

"Don't touch him, you animals!" I cried. "He just walked me over here. What the hell is your problem?"

Two more people rushed in from the house, and I knew by scent alone that it was Tavia and Cyan. They did nothing to stop the assault while the big vampire said to Novak, "Try anything, Rathka's Bastard, and I'll crush your fucking windpipe."

Novak, to his credit, did not look threatened or the least bit afraid. "Noted," he drawled.

I, on the other hand, couldn't compose myself to the same degree. How could I when Blood 'til Dawn was treating him like a criminal?

"You guys are crazy! Let him go! He didn't do anything!"

"Amy, you don't know what his kin have done to us," said one of the vampires pressing Novak to the wall. "They almost killed Cyan."

My attention turned to Tavia, who was looking at Cyan like the sun set and rose on him. "Is that true?" she asked, glancing at me for a moment before returning her gaze to him. "*His* clan were the ones who injured you that night?"

I wasn't sure what Novak's clan had to do with the last twenty-four hours, or why he was currently being restrained because of what other people had supposedly done.

Cyan kept his gaze fixated on the only innocent vampire in the room, as far as I was concerned. Even if he wasn't physically holding Novak down, he was complicit by just standing there and doing nothing.

"Yes. Thorne and I were attacked by the remnants of Rathka's Order that night," Cyan confirmed. "Novak here is the only of them left who isn't a cannibalistic monster."

"A title I'm happy to carry," Novak said wryly.

Was I hearing things right? They were suspicious of him because he was the last of his clan who was... a normal vampire?

Before I was turned, Tavia had told me about Cyan getting injured while out on a patrol. She'd been very general without many details, but we'd heard stories about monstrous vampires since we were kids. Mindless, blood-thirsty creatures who were more likely to maul someone to death than simply drink blood.

Not unlike the vampires who had attacked our settlement and killed me.

"I'm sure you are, Cursed One." Thorne stepped away, apparently finished with the patdown. "The only question that remains is what were you doing with our brusang?"

"I'm not *yours*," I snapped. "I'm not anyone's."

Thorne turned his menacing red eyes to me. If it weren't for the fear that flashed through me, it would have been fascinating to note how dangerous his gaze seemed, despite being the same color as Novak's.

"You're considered the kin of Cyan's blood mate," the clan leader said. "That makes you ours. Our kin, our family."

"I did nothing but provide her shelter from the sun, along with blood and a meal of meat for sustenance." Novak answered Thorne's question calmly. He never responded to the Cursed One moniker, which had to be deeply insulting. "Nothing inappropriate or untoward occurred."

"She was with you all day?" Cyan went stiff, his eyes narrowed.

"*She* is right here," I interjected. "And yes, I stayed at Novak's house. But nothing happened, just like he said." I returned Cyan's stare, daring him to insinuate anything else.

"You took blood from him?" Tavia asked.

My gaze snapped to hers, and she startled as if she didn't expect my reflexes to be so fast. She looked worried, even a little betrayed. And I had to admit, deep down, I got a little thrill out of disappointing her. I felt like a teenager rebelling against an uptight mother.

"Yeah, so? That's what I do now, don't I?" I put on a wide, exaggerated smile so that she'd see my fangs. "Thanks to you."

Tavia swallowed and lifted her chin. "You were just so uncomfortable at the blood bank. I didn't think you'd take from a stranger."

"Novak isn't a stranger to me; he's a friend." I wasn't entirely sure if he would agree with that, but it felt right to me. Plus, I couldn't resist throwing another barb in Tavia's face. "He helped me, *actually* helped me when I needed blood, rest, and to get out of the sun."

"Amy, you don't know him," Cyan said. "You don't know the history between our clans."

For fuck's sake. I was beyond done with hearing "clan history" as the excuse for mistreating people right now in the present moment.

"Whatever *he* did, which sounds like absolutely fucking nothing, it doesn't warrant you treating him like a criminal just because he walked me here." These vampires might have been the ruling clan, but that didn't mean they weren't assholes. I crossed my arms and lifted my chin to give Thorne my best glare. "Let him go. Right now."

For all I knew, I was breaking thousands of vampire laws by making any kinds of demands for Novak, but I was past the point of caring. He hadn't done anything wrong, and my blood boiled hotter every second they kept their hands on him.

"It's all right, *akra*." Novak rolled his head along the wall to look at me, that small smile showing a glint of fang. "I'm used to this from my Blood 'til Dawn neighbors. Par for the course."

I opened my mouth to argue, to tell him that didn't make it okay to treat him like this. I certainly had no bias for this clan, not even with Tavi basically marrying into them. But Thorne stepped forward, his gravitas soaking up all the attention in the room.

"Here's what's going to happen, Novak of Rathka's Order. We will let you go, undisturbed. But you will not take this brusang or anyone else of our clan into your home. You will not see her again, period. I think that would be best to keep the peace among our kind, don't you agree?"

Fuck no, I do not agree.

But the question was not directed at me. I had no power here, as Thorne made abundantly clear. And anyway, the choice was entirely in Novak's hands.

His expression hardened, gaze falling on me without saying anything. I couldn't even begin to wonder what he was thinking, what kind of history or politics his mind ran through to decide his answer. From the moment he was dragged inside, it was obvious this wasn't just about me staying at a stranger's house. Something bigger was at play here, something more than him and me.

And yet my breath caught in my chest as I waited, hoping for a certain answer. Or even just a sign, the hint of a smile or some expression crossing his face that signaled he wanted to see me again.

When several seconds passed with him saying nothing, Thorne pressed once again.

"Might I remind you that Blood 'til Dawn is the ruling clan of Sanguine. While your ancestors may be spinning in their graves at that fact, it is still a fact."

"Are you saying this is an official clan decree?" Novak's voice roughened slightly, the ease and humor gone.

"I'll make it one if I have to," Thorne said. "But if you're such an honorable, noble male, we won't have to resort to that, will we?"

Novak glanced at me one more time, and my heart sank at the cool mask across his expression. "No, we won't."

"So you agree to never set eyes on this brusang again?"

No.

"I do."

Satisfied, Thorne gave a slight nod to the two vampires, who released Novak from his pinned position on the wall.

Novak straightened his waistcoat and adjusted his sleeves, truly looking like a prince compared to Blood 'til Dawn with their scuffed boots, faded jeans, and leather jackets.

My instincts surged at the sight of him. I wanted to rush over and hug him, to feel the reassuring pulse of his jugular under my lips. I wanted to put my body between him and the others and bare my fangs, challenging them to come through me if they wanted him.

At the same time, I knew all those urges were wildly inappropriate for someone I just met. Maybe my vampire side wanted to protect the blood source I liked the most. That had to be it—some kind of animalistic survival thing.

I kept those instincts reined in as Novak gave a final smoothing of his waistcoat and a curt nod in my direction. "Take care, akra."

That word. He'd said it twice. What did it mean?

With that, he strode out the side door into the street

without so much as a glance to anyone else. I watched him go, wishing with all my heart that I could go after him. But I knew Blood 'til Dawn would stop me, and I didn't want to be pinned to the wall like he had been.

A sudden touch made me flinch, and my head jerked to see Tavia with her hand hovering over my shoulder.

"What?" I snapped.

She drew her hand away and moved closer to Cyan. "Just glad you're back. Glad you're okay."

This passive side of Tavia was almost as infuriating as her overbearing side. If I snapped at my best friend, she snapped back. Fights weren't common between us, but one of Tavia's defining features was that she didn't back down. Who was this person who acted afraid of me now that I had bigger teeth?

She cast her eyes aside, holding onto Cyan's arm like a good, dutiful little wife. Not even a year ago, she gave a guy a black eye and cursed up a storm because he was trying to steal a batch of her wine.

Apparently I wasn't the only one who had changed. But at least I hadn't changed for a man.

I went robotically into the house with no destination in mind. My need to be away from Tavia and all of *them* carried me through the communal great room and down the stairs to the underground corridor where all the clan members had suites of rooms where they slept during the day.

Nothing's changed, I realized when I entered Bea's apartment and collapsed into the same sofa I'd rotted in for the past two weeks.

I felt exactly the same as when I was first turned into this... thing. Angry, resentful. Ugly. Wishing I could crawl into a hole and disappear.

A light clicked on and then a soft voice called out, "Hey, Amy?"

"Sorry, Bea. Now's not a good time." I rolled into the couch cushions, bringing my legs up to curl into a ball.

There was a sigh, and then I felt the weight of someone sitting next to my legs. "I'm sorry. I know you've had a rough couple of weeks, but I really need to talk to you."

I turned slightly and looked up at her. Somehow, Bea's looks and style fit the brusang features perfectly. She had a bit of a goth vibe with straight black hair, blunt bangs to her eyebrows, and she wore predominantly black clothes and silver-toned jewelry. Tonight, her lipstick was a darker shade of red. All that combined with her delicate bone structure and adorable button nose? The small fangs and black eyes were natural accessories to her overall look. She looked born to be an alluring, vampiric creature.

Jealousy flooded me, but I forced it down because Bea had always been polite and sweet. It wasn't like she was preternaturally gorgeous to torment me.

"What did you want to talk about?"

She chewed her lip in a nervous response. "I understand things are tense with you and Tavia right now, and I don't want to exacerbate that. But it has been a couple of weeks, and don't get me wrong, I've been happy to help you. It's just that my place isn't set up to be shared by two people, and it's starting to feel a little, um, cramped in here. I haven't had any real privacy in a bit, so... "

Bea trailed off, but I knew what she was saying. Her apartment in the Blood 'til Dawn compound was a studio. Rather than an actual bedroom, her sleeping area was separated from the living area by a half wall. Aside from the small kitchenette and bathroom, there wasn't much space.

And now she wanted me out.

I sat up, and her blue-green eyes went round with guilt. Shit, she felt really bad. Bea was just too nice. We were alike in that sense. Or at least we had been, until I'd become a ball of bitterness and depression.

"I'm really sorry, Amy. I just want to get the living room tidied up and—"

"No, don't be. I'm the one that should apologize. I've taken over your place, overstayed my welcome." I rubbed my face, feeling bone-deep exhaustion settle into me. "It's just... I don't know where else to go."

Bea hesitated before speaking. "Tavia and Cyan have an extra bedroom."

I snorted. "Any chance I can get my own place? Maybe a little studio like this?"

"I believe there are some vacant suites, but you'd have to ask Thorne."

Ask the asshole clan leader who forbade me from seeing Novak ever again? Yeah, right. It sounded like becoming roommates with Tavia and Cyan was my only option. Great.

I stood, hesitated, then gathered up the blankets and pillows that had been my bed and home for the past two weeks. "I'll get this stuff washed and then return it. Sorry again, Bea. I should've realized."

"Oh no, don't worry about it. Put that stuff down, you've got enough on your plate." She yanked the bedding from my arms and dumped it back onto the couch, then gave a sympathetic squeeze of my shoulders. "The beginning of being a brusang is hard. Really fucking hard. It's so alienating feeling like you're not human, but also not a true vampire. But it does get easier, I promise. And I am here if you need anything, seriously. Come back over and have some tea with me whenever you want."

I looked at her face, her flawless skin and bright eyes set in black. The only imperfection I noted was the scar across the base of her neck, and it did nothing to detract from her beauty, or her sweet, cheery demeanor. She definitely wasn't a woman who struggled to look at herself in the mirror.

"When?" I asked. "When does it get easier?"

The optimism in her expression faltered a little. "Well, everyone is different. And coming to terms with being a brusang is not a linear path. But for me, it was about five years before I really accepted who and what I was."

Five *years*? I didn't know whether to hysterically laugh or cry.

If I was being deeply honest with myself, I wasn't sure if I would last that long.

7 Novak

THE MONSTER STARED at me with unblinking red eyes, its pupils the size of pinheads. Black blood vessels crisscrossed over the entire eye like spiderwebs. It was hunched over, but the same height as me, its skeleton an elongated, twisted form of what it once was.

"Are you going to cooperate today?" I kept my eyes on it while sterilizing a small scraper tool with isopropyl alcohol.

The creature never answered when I spoke to it, not with words anyway. But in the fifty years I'd kept it captive in my basement, I never kicked the habit of trying to have a conversation. Once upon a time, this had been a vampire after all. A person.

I approached the barred cell, holding the scraper tool down next to my thigh, and earned a hiss of warning from the monster.

"I just need a few skin cells," I said, as if I could reason with it. "I need to see if there are any changes from last week." *To see if you've gotten any better.*

This task felt futile. Who was I kidding? Everything felt futile. Over a hundred years of trying to find a cure for the madness that plagued my clan and nothing to show for it.

But I couldn't stop. What would be the point of anything then? What if I was on the brink of discovering the cure?

I pushed back my sleeve, exposing my forearm. The creature's eyes dilated at the sight of my flesh, its jaws parting with a whine like a dog.

I took advantage of the distraction, jabbing the scraper through the bars to drag along the creature's side. It roared in response, its rank breath hitting me in the face like a sucker punch. Just as I pulled the scraper back, the monster lunged for my exposed forearm.

"Shit!" Pain shot up my arm like a hot brand. Usually I was good at keeping out of reach, but I was off my game today. Distracted.

Backing away from the cell, I glanced at my forearm where it had gotten me. Four scratches from its filthy claws puffed red and throbbed with a pain that I knew would linger. Healing would take longer than a normal wound, an ever-present reminder of how I'd fallen short in this endeavor.

Turning my arm to show the creature its work, I asked, "Satisfied?"

Saliva dripped from its near-skeletal jaws. The skin over its bones had become so thin and brittle, I could see the shape of its gums and all its teeth, not just the fangs. Bony-fingered hands wrapped around the bars of its cell, those animal-like claws preventing a tight hold.

The creature was covered in dirt and filth. At this point, it was impossible to tell if it was wearing any clothes or had been male or female. It was hunched over, misshapen. There wasn't a shred of the proud vampire it had once been. Not anymore.

"Are there any of you still in there?" My voice was heavy with despair. "Do you know who you are? Do you even recognize me?"

The creature let out an anguished, hungry roar. It had been for over fifty years. But considering that it would only be satisfied by vampire or human flesh, I wasn't exactly inclined to give it regular meals.

I stared at the edge of my scraper, not entirely hopeful that I got viable skin cells through all the grime and filth. Not for the first time, I wondered if it would be better to put this creature out of its misery.

Before I could follow that train of thought, the intercom on the wall beeped. I dropped the scraper into a sterile plastic bag and turned away from the monster to answer the call.

"Yes?" I released the button and waited for a reply.

Lourna's voice crackled through the speaker. "Sorry to interrupt, sir. You have a call on your office line."

"Who?" I pressed, knowing it couldn't be good if she was hesitant to tell me.

"Baros of Carpe Noctem."

"Fuck." I let my forehead touch the wall, letting out an exasperated breath before pressing the button to answer. "Did you tell him I'm unavailable?"

"I did, and he insisted on waiting for as long as it took. He made vague threats about coming over unannounced if you didn't get back to him."

My eyes closed and I breathed out more curses in English and Vampiric. "Fine. I'll be right up."

I let my forehead linger on the wall for another beat before peeling off my nitrile gloves and dropping them in the hazardous waste bin. Without looking back at the monster, I left the cell room and entered the small clean room that acted as a buffer between the basement and the rest of the house.

I spent several minutes scrubbing my hands and the scratches on my arm. Like a human, I'd have to clean it well several times daily to avoid an infected wound. But I'd been scratched and clawed so many times at this point, I knew I was immune to becoming the same as that creature. Apparently I was the only one. And that was the big fucking mystery at the core of all these experiments and tests.

Everyone in my clan, all of my bloodline except for me, had either died or become *that*.

It started slowly. The first case happened probably before I was born, nearly three hundred years ago. Some of my earliest memories were of an adult uncle and cousins expressing a craving for flesh, not just blood. They attacked human staff at first, and then fellow vampires. When they could no longer be reasoned with, they were locked up. And they slowly became just like the creature in my basement.

One by one, over the course of a couple centuries, Rathka's Order succumbed to what most called Rathka's Curse. The illness was unexplainable and unstoppable, taking adult males, females, and children. Mostly from my clan, but a few others fell to it as well.

Until there was just me.

Well, and the expectation of finding the cure and restoring Rathka's Order to its former glory. I didn't earn advanced degrees in microbiology, bacteriology, and immunology just for the fun of it.

After washing my arm thoroughly, I patted it dry, applied an ointment, and then a bandage. It would be a week or longer before the skin was like new again, unless I took blood from an especially strong source.

My thoughts turned to my recent brusang visitor, Amy. She seemed to like my blood. Would she ever return the favor?

I dismissed the thought just as quickly as it came. Blood 'til Dawn forbade us from ever having contact again, and I wasn't about to piss off the ruling clan any more than they already were. Besides, Amy had been so skittish about feeding that she couldn't even take it from my wrist. She definitely wouldn't react well to my taking from her.

Her presence here, brief as it was, had been a welcome shake-up to the monotony of my life. Her curiosity and the calm, steadying force of a new heartbeat in my senses made that day pass far too quickly. But I had to accept that small stretch of time for what it was—an anomaly. An outlier.

Her time here would be a fond memory to cherish, considering I had precious few of those.

I finished cleaning up, placed the baggie with my used scraper in the mini fridge to examine later, then punched in the door code to enter the main house.

I dreaded every step up to my office, and still arrived there too quickly, the red light on my desk phone blinking ominously.

Sinking into my chair, I pressed the button defeatedly and brought the phone to my ear. "Baros. Good to hear from you."

"Novak, hello." If the head of Carpe Noctem knew I

was lying through my teeth, he wouldn't give it away. "It's been a while, so I wanted to touch base. Maybe revisit your thoughts on the offer I proposed."

"Ah, right." My molars ground against each other. "It slipped my mind, I'm afraid. I've been tied up with... you know, trying to keep a handle on things."

"Of course, I understand. All the more reason to produce an heir," Baros said smoothly. "It's impossible to establish a strong clan with one person. You need offspring. My daughter is free this evening, actually. Why don't you come by for a drink and some darakt? You can sample her blood as well."

My throat and stomach tightened. "I'm afraid I can't. I have a... "

"Listen." Baros's tone grew hushed. "It's not just my daughter I'm offering. There're signs that our benevolent ruling clan is losing its grip."

I frowned. "Blood 'til Dawn?"

"That name should be a curse," Baros spat. "But yes, they're weakening. The time to start planning is now."

"Planning?"

"Yes! To regain our seat as ruling clan." He sounded so excited, I could almost hear the spit flying from his mouth. "But I can't do it alone. And if you play your cards right," he added, "I wouldn't be opposed to Carpe Noctem and Rath-ka's Order as joint-ruling clans."

The idea was completely absurd, but seeing that my clan was considered on the verge of extinction, it was also intriguing enough that I wanted to hear more.

I didn't like Baros as a person, nor did I like his father when he was the head of Carpe Noctem. But our clans had been allied in one way or another since their inception during the war with the werewolves. When my clan members began succumbing to Rathka's Curse, Carpe Noctem was one of the few clans to seek healers across Shyftworld. At least publicly, they had sympathy for my suffering kin. Everyone else, Blood 'til Dawn included, believed my clan deserved to be wiped out.

And if I took a good, hard look at the facts, I might even agree with them.

But until I found a cure, I was all that was left. If Carpe Noctem was offering me a lifeline, I had to at least consider it.

"I can see you in an hour," I said.

———

THE BRUSANG BUTLER at the Carpe Noctem estate frowned when I dismounted my motorcycle and removed my helmet. I could afford a car and driver, but always hated the confined feeling of a car. Why waste the money when I could feel the rush of wind with no walls around me?

"I'm sorry, sir. I don't believe we have any valets who can drive a... " The butler made no attempt to sound apologetic, holding his tongue as if any variation of the word "motorcycle" could not be uttered in polite company.

"You can leave it. I won't be staying long."

I flashed a smile. The butler gave me a strained one in return. His brown irises looked almost golden set in the black sclera that denoted him as a brusang.

Seeing him made me think of Amy again, how candid she had been about her struggles with the turning. Did this butler have a similar experience? Or did he embrace the chance for a new life with vampiric traits, even if there was only a fifty-fifty chance he'd survive the change?

"Of course, sir. Please." The butler's tone was clipped, formal with no nonsense as he stood aside, leading me into the house with an outstretched arm.

"Thank you, um, what's your name?"

He closed the front door before striding ahead of me. "I have no name. If I am performing my duties correctly, you will have no need to address me. This way, please."

"Well, shit," I muttered, following after him. I couldn't even imagine how traumatic it must have been to have his whole identity erased.

Like most vampire homes, the majority of Carpe Noctem's estate was underground. The nameless butler led me to an elevator on the far wall and we took the ride down together silently.

The doors opened smoothly a minute later to a room that was somehow both cozy and cavernous. A chandelier hung from an impossibly high ceiling over a set of plush red couches, loveseats, and armchairs. Red smoke wafted lazily from the low table in the center, and conversation echoed from the three figures perched on the furniture.

"Novak, come in!" Baros gestured me over, a fat dark cigar pinched between his fingers. "Join the party. Drink? Smoke?"

"Sure, thank you." I eased down into one side of the loveseats next to Baros, who was in one of the armchairs.

"Have you met my second, Mazor?" Baros indicated the male vampire sitting in the armchair across the table from him.

"I have not, it's a pleasure." I dipped my head toward the other vampire, who gave me the signature slimy Carpe Noctem grin in return.

"And of course you know my daughter, Inessa."

The female vampire sat perched on the loveseat across

from me. Her gown was covered in tiny black and red jewels that flashed and glittered with her subtle movements. If she walked or danced, she'd look like some kind of gothic disco ball. Already I was craving the dark soothing tones and soft lighting of my own home.

"We actually haven't met before, but I'm charmed." I put on a smile that I hoped was polite enough. "It's a pleasure to finally meet you."

Her smile was soft in return, heavy lashes fluttering low over her pale skin. "The pleasure is mine, Novak of Rathka's Order."

The nameless butler appeared before me, holding out a shallow wooden box filled with an assortment of cigars. I chose one at random. Smoking was not my thing, but darakt, a mixture of powdered blood and herbs for flavor, was the one substance that united vampires of all walks of life. And my rudeness would be noticed if I refused one.

Working-class vampires usually bought darakt cigarettes by the pack, often sticking to their favorite brand or flavor. People like Baros paid a premium to have his own custom blends made with only the finest quality ingredients.

After my cigar was lit and I was situated with a glass of wine, Baros got straight to business. "Did you hear about the attack on Sapien, the human settlement?"

"Just rumors." I held the red darakt smoke in my mouth before blowing it out, trying to save my throat from the burning. "Nothing substantial. But it doesn't make sense. Blood 'til Dawn took their sacrifice, did they not?"

The human-only settlement of Sapien remained free of vampire influence due to an arrangement called the Half-Century Selection. Every fifty years, Sapien chose one of their own to give to the ruling clan, usually as a blood pet. In exchange, vampires were not permitted to feed on anyone in Sapien, and certainly not attack them. The ruling clan was supposed to enforce this.

"They did." Mazor leaned forward, his expression gleeful. "And yet an attack happened anyway, just weeks later. A few humans died. Almost a dozen injured."

My wine glass paused on its way to my mouth. Was Amy among those who had been badly injured? Or even died? She never explicitly mentioned being from there, but the timing lined up.

"Do we know who attacked them?" I mused.

"Wish I did." Baros sighed. "I would have invited them to this table. Any enemy of Blood 'til Dawn is a friend of mine."

"I've heard rumors trickling in about crazed monsters. Just a horde of them running in and tearing the humans apart. Sounds like your kind of people, eh, Novak?"

Mazor laughed while I gave a tight-lipped, clenched smile. "Those with my clan's affliction are hundreds of miles away from the human settlement. They're mostly in the forests and mountains of the Crown. I heard it was Marrowers who had been slipped draitrium, but Blood 'til Dawn is certainly keeping a tight lid on it."

"Because they're embarrassed," Baros declared. "Whatever happened, it makes them look weak. They're hoping it blows over, but we've been waiting for an opportunity like this." He shot a grin at his daughter. "Haven't we, akra?"

"Of course, Father."

The three words sounded rehearsed, like they were all that she was allowed to say. She never met my eyes when I glanced at her, and I found myself feeling sorry for her. Like the butler, like so many others, she was just a tool for her father's whims.

"Do you ever miss the Crown, Novak?" Boras blew a red smoke ring. "I loved visiting your family's home out there when my father took me. It was glorious. Even as your guests, we felt like kings."

I took a long swallow of wine. The Crown estate was, by all accounts, my home. I was born there, grew up there. It was the seat of my family's power, when we had power. It was also the place of so many nightmarish memories before, during, and after my bloodline succumbed to their incurable madness.

"I miss the wild beauty and fresh air of the country, sometimes," I said. "But I do love the convenience and liveliness of the Heart."

Boras's eyes flashed. "What if we took your ancestral home back from Blood 'til Dawn?"

I stared at him, not understanding. "Took it back? They're the ruling clan."

"Not for long, if we get our way." A slow grin spread over his face.

"Not if they keep losing their grip," Mazor added. "Not if they fail to stop us."

I looked between the two vampires, an increasingly sinking feeling taking root in my gut. "What exactly does Carpe Noctem have planned?"

"We're going to unseat Blood 'til Dawn and resume our place as ruling clan," Baros said. "And there can be a spot for you as well, Novak."

"How exactly do you plan to do this?" I asked. "My bloodline is all but wiped out. Blood 'til Dawn are fighters, and they're crafty. Carpe Noctem may have resources but respectfully, you've never been a warrior clan. Blood 'til Dawn isn't going to give an inch without a fight."

"They're weakened, as I said. And from what I hear,

they have a soft spot for the young. They adopt juvenile vampires frequently, taking in strays."

"So?"

Baros turned toward his daughter, paused when he looked at her, then returned his greedy gaze to me. "Impregnate my daughter with your heir, and move back to the Crown estate to restart your bloodline."

My throat tightened and dried out like I'd inhaled too much darakt. "You're serious?"

"Very. The Crown estate is a fortress. Your progeny will be safe. Blood 'til Dawn won't storm the building while a pregnant female is inside. They will already be at a disadvantage."

"I fear you may underestimate how much they despise my bloodline." The memory of being pinned to the wall, searched, and questioned came to the forefront of my mind. All of the snarling, disgruntled clan males were hazy in my recollection. The only clear face I saw was Amy's, her fury at my treatment and how she stood up to Thorne, demanding that he let me go.

The memory made a smile tug at my lips. No one, not even anyone in my clan, had ever been so furiously righteous on my behalf. I hoped Amy's friend realized what a gem she was.

"No matter how much they despise you, they will not harm a child or a pregnant female," Baros insisted. "They will be cautious, and we'll use that to press an advantage."

I cast a glance toward his mostly silent daughter, wondering how she felt about being essentially used as a meat shield.

"You stand only to benefit from this, Novak," Mazor said. "You'll win your ancestral home back, be closely connected to the next ruling clan, and have an heir to repopulate Rathka's Order."

"Only if the child is a male," Baros piped up. "If it's a female, you'll have to try for another, naturally."

His daughter shifted uncomfortably. Nothing prevented a female from becoming an heir and taking over a clan. Baros was just an antiquated bastard, and a callous one, to say that right in front of his daughter.

"Well, this all sounds very... ambitious," I hedged. "I'll have to give it some thought."

Baros laughed as if I'd made the most hilarious joke he'd heard in his life. "What is there to think about? You need an heir. We need to crush Blood 'til Dawn. Nothing could be more simple."

At my core, I didn't want to be involved in this scheme. For all his faults, Thorne was much smarter than Baros, had the support of nearly all of Sanguine, and a lot more firepower. If a rebellion was on the horizon, my money was on Blood 'til Dawn keeping its crown.

On top of all that, I didn't want to impregnate some woman who was a stranger to me, and the Crown estate could rot into a pile of rubble for all I truly cared.

But... what else was I doing with my life?

I was the last of a disgraced, fallen bloodline, spending my waking hours poring over a century's worth of collected data and notes. Yes, I was trying to find a cure, or at least the root cause of what befell my clan. But after years upon years of running into dead ends, I was tired.

And I was lonely.

What was I even trying to prove anymore, and to whom? My kin were all dead or mindless monsters with a bottomless hunger for live flesh. Even if I did find a cure and reverted them back to their original states, would they be grateful? Would they even care? Would the monster in my basement embrace me? Or would everyone be just as dismissive toward me as they had been before?

Baros would never expect me to love or commit to his daughter, and likely, neither would she. But I knew I could treat her well, better than her father easily, and provide her with everything she needed. At the very least, we could live harmoniously. Maybe something like love or affection could grow over time.

And if she did become pregnant, I would love that child fiercely, and with absolute certainty. Male or female didn't matter; I would adore the little vampire I helped to create.

My own family had not been loving. I was a second son, an afterthought to my older half-brother, who was my father's heir. The two of them made it clear that I would never measure up, least of all because I was quiet and book-ish, unlike the proud, brash warriors that made up our clan. Only my mother showed me any semblance of love, and she was taken by Rathka's Curse while I was a juvenile.

Having a child might be my only chance to wholeheart-edly love someone, and to have someone love me in return.

Inessa held out a delicate, pale wrist toward me. "Will you take my blood? And see if my taste is to your," she paused, lowering her lashes demurely, "your satisfaction."

I didn't really want to, but my hands were tied. Like with the darakt, to refuse would be considered a slight against Carpe Noctem. And if I was actually going to make a child with this woman, even if there was no relationship between us, I would have to touch her at some point.

Turning toward her, I slid to the end of the couch until her arm was in my reach. "It would be my honor." I glanced at Baros. "With your father's permission, of course."

"Please, proceed." Baros waved a hand at us before turning to Mazor, their heads bent in conversation.

Inessa shifted toward me, her eyes downcast as if in deference. Visually, she was attractive enough, but the silent, obedient females were never my type.

If I were able to choose a long-term partner, I'd want an equal, along with a friendship that was also passionate. Someone to talk to about anything that came to mind without fear or judgment. Someone who could challenge me and stimulate my mind just as much as they would accept all of my idiosyncrasies.

But with the constant shadow of Rathka's Curse hanging over my head, I wasn't exactly swimming in prospects. Still, I could certainly do worse than Inessa of Carpe Noctem.

Leaning over her wrist, I murmured in Vampiric, *"My gratitude for the gift of your blood."*

My lips skimmed over her pulse, finding the ideal spot to drink from before I let my fangs sink in.

I had no expectations of how Inessa's blood would taste. Among fellow vampires, the flavor was as unique and varied as the individuals. And yet when hers hit my tongue, I came away feeling almost disappointed. There was nothing *wrong* with her blood, but it tasted rather... bland. Almost as flavorless as a human's.

I drank just under a handful of swallows, as much as would be considered polite, then unlatched my fangs. Then, just to be extra polite, I lingered over her wrist, closing the puncture marks with small swipes of my tongue.

A soft smile was the only change in Inessa's expression when I lifted away.

"Did my blood satisfy you, Novak?"

I forced my lips into a returned smile. "Very much. Again, I'm grateful."

She brought her hands to her lap, eyes lifting slowly under heavy lashes. "Then I look forward to our union, and the future we will create."

Her blood settled uncomfortably in my stomach, like a bad wine.

"As do I."

Chapter 8

Amy

Finding Novak's house was much easier the second time around, although I couldn't fully explain how I got there. It wasn't like I knew my way around any better than the first time. I wondered if it was his blood somehow leading me back to that delicious source for another taste.

I wasn't especially hungry, but the prospect of tasting Novak's blood again was partially what spurred me to slip out of the Blood 'til Dawn compound that night. The other parts, such as his beautiful home, the simple, easy conversation, and the pressing *need* to get away, were just as significant. But going out for blood was a convenient excuse if I needed one.

I didn't tell anyone I was leaving, nor did anyone ask where I was going or try to stop me. Tavia was giving me space, as she would put it, but I knew she just didn't want to deal with me. The other Blood 'til Dawn vampires seemed to feel similarly, which was just fine by me.

There were other people who wouldn't treat me like I was a bomb about to go off. At least, I hoped there was.

I reached Novak's house without incident and used the heavy brass knocker on the door to announce my presence.

A thread of insecurity coiled through my chest as I waited. What if he didn't want to see me? I could have made an epic mistake by coming here. Thorne forbade us from seeing each other, but no one at Blood 'til Dawn seemed to actually care much about what I did. And no one seemed eager to explain all this complicated vampire clan history they alluded to all the time.

The door opened to reveal a human woman who looked to be in her mid-forties. She wore a white chef's jacket and the furrow between her brow softened when she saw me.

"Well, look who came back around." A wide smile came to her face. "What can I do for you, Miss Amy?"

I was taken aback that she knew my name. Novak must have told her. "Hi. Um, nice to see you again. Is Novak home?"

"He's not. He stepped out for a bit."

Before I could feel any shred of disappointment, the chef widened the door and stepped aside to let me through. "Come in and wait for him. He shouldn't be long. I'll fix you something."

"Oh no, that's okay. I don't want to impose. I just wanted to see if he was home."

"Nonsense. I think he'll like the surprise." A smirk curved her mouth. "I'm Joanne, by the way. Call me Jo. I don't think we formally met last time."

"Nice to meet you, Jo. Your spread was incredible last time. Just delicious."

She beamed with pride. "I'm glad you liked it. I'm playing around some more and could use a taster. Between you and me, vampires have no palates for actual food. Come in."

"Well, as long as I'm not intruding—"

"You got cement blocks on your feet, girl? Get in the damn house."

Her sharp tone surprised me, but the smile softened it. Seeing as she left no argument, I crossed the threshold, chuckling sheepishly.

"Lourna!" Jo hollered as she closed the door and crossed the foyer. "We've got a visitor!" To me, she pointed at the kitchen island where I sat last time. "Sit. You like pastrami?"

"I don't think I've ever had it," I admitted, sliding onto a stool.

"Ah." Her dark eyes lit up like she understood something. "Never ventured out to the human world, huh?"

"A few times, not a whole lot. My community was pretty self-sufficient, but we went to the human world once every few months for supplies. The closest place to us was a little town in Oregon."

"Oh yeah, you're from that little humans-only settlement in the Ribs, right?" Jo squinted. "What's it called?"

"Sapien," I said. "Yep, the last settlement in Sanguine is still run by humans, for humans."

"How'd you end up with the... ?" Jo drew small circles in the air, indicating my eyes, probably.

My throat tightened. I'd avoided talking about it until now, but couldn't exactly dance around the subject with Jo's blunt questions.

"Our settlement was attacked and they got me." I shrugged, as if I could feel casual about such a thing. "Someone was able to call my best friend, and she came to help. She'd been chosen as the sacrifice for the Half-Century Selection, so she brought Blood 'til Dawn with her. She begged her mate to bring me back and," I shrugged again, "here I am."

Jo whistled as she swiftly sliced through a large cut of meat. "That's some wild shit right there. Must be hard."

"Thanks. I... You know, I'm figuring it out. Where are you from?" I was eager to get the subject off of myself.

Jo glanced up with a grin. "New York, baby. Born and raised." Her accent made it sound like *New Yawk*.

"Really?" It was actually rare that I met a human from the human world. "How did you end up in Sanguine? And as a chef for a vampire?"

Almost everyone in Sapien had been born there. All we'd ever known had been a world of vampires, shifters, witches, and magic that the vast majority of humans didn't believe in. My old home has prided itself on preserving human culture and community. Unlike other humans who had found their way into this world, we didn't conform to the world of the supernaturals. We remained independent and had done so successfully for centuries. The thought of Sapien made me incredibly homesick.

"There's an entrance to this world at Niagara Falls. Almost twenty years ago, my drunk dumbass fell into the Niagara River. It was so fuckin' cold and I thought I was gonna die. But I was okay with it, you know? My life was a fuckin' mess." Jo took out a loaf of bread and began slicing it. "Felt myself sinking, drowning. I must have gotten right under one of the falls because it felt like I was getting the shit beat out of me. Next thing I know, I'm washed up on the shore of this serene, mountain lake. The water was as smooth as glass." She turned to get more items out of the fridge and laughed. "Definitely not New York."

"Where were you?"

"The Crown, north part of Sanguine. That's where Novak's clan is from. And I was lucky enough to run into him while he was up there, doing science or whatever he does." She cackled again as she placed slices of cheese on the bread slices. "This poor man must have lost his shit seeing a soaking wet and filthy stumbling human around. But he took me in, patient as a saint while I lost my shit over vampires being real, then gave me a home and a job. I've been here ever since."

"Wow. Have you never wanted to go home?" I asked.

A few days before the attack on Sapien, a woman from the human world, Heather, had stumbled upon our settlement in a similar way. All she wanted was to go back home. She disappeared one day, assumedly back to her world. I wondered if she ever made it back and was okay.

"Nah." Jo brought the two bread slices together in a towering sandwich. "I love New York, but my old life woulda killed me if I'd gone back. I got a second chance here, kind of like you." She plated the sandwich and placed it in front me. "Eat up. Tell me what you think."

"What is it?" The bread was light brown in color, the sliced meat bright red and tender.

"Pastrami on rye. It's a New York staple. Loved by humans and hopefully brusang." Jo's smile was slow, confident. "Cured the meat myself. Go ahead."

I took a bite, chewed, and moaned at the flavors hitting my tongue. The combination of salt, fat, and spices was perfect. The cured meat sated the bloodthirsty part of me, for now. I would need blood soon, but this would hold me over in the meantime.

"Oh my God, Jo, that's so good!" I'd barely swallowed the first bite before taking another. "Novak is so lucky he found you."

Jo laughed, a sound I was enjoying the more time I spent with her. "His tastes leave me limited, but I've missed making human food. I'm glad there's someone else to enjoy it now."

I just swallowed the last bites of the sandwich when I heard a rumbling outside that grew increasingly louder until it seemed to be right outside the front door. There was no mistaking that sound—a motorcycle engine.

My heart jumped into my throat and I froze. Did someone from Blood 'til Dawn find out I was here and come to get me?

"Ah, speak of the devil." Jo appeared calm as she took my plate and wiped down the counter. "Sounds like the boss is home."

The sound cut off abruptly and a few minutes later, the heavy front door swung open. Novak's footfalls echoed over the floor, long strides eating up the space between each step, which came to a slow stop as he entered the kitchen.

He was still dressed immaculately with black trousers and a matching waistcoat over a white long-sleeved shirt. Again, his sleeves were rolled up past his elbows and he held a black leather jacket in one hand. His long, silver-blond hair was disheveled, a little wild. It suited him extremely well, like he was born to be aristocratic and a rebel.

"Um, hi." I swallowed. "Again."

"Hello." He turned and hung up the leather jacket on a coat tree just outside the foyer. "Didn't think I'd see you here again."

My whole body tensed like a rabbit about to bolt from a predator. "I can go."

"Right after you've eaten? No, stay." Novak tugged his leather gloves off as he meandered toward the island. "I'm just surprised, that's all."

Jo's back was turned, but I swore I heard a snickering, "knew it," under her breath.

Novak's eyes slid toward her with a suspicious gaze. Before he could ask any questions, I blurted out, "I didn't know you rode a motorcycle."

His gaze returned to me, amusement dancing in his red eyes. "Well I can't let Blood 'til Dawn have all the fun, can I?"

The smile grew across my face before I could stop it. "Definitely not."

He reached the edge of the counter and braced his palms wide on the dark marble. "And should I be concerned about them crashing through my door at any minute?"

"I don't think so." I shrugged and wiped my hands on a napkin. "I'm not worth the trouble."

"Why do you say that?"

I paused before answering. He looked genuinely baffled as to why I wouldn't be a priority to Blood 'til Dawn.

"I'm just not anybody important. They don't know what to do with me, so nobody cares if I stay or go."

Novak curled his fingers and tapped his knuckles gently on the counter. "A vampire clan is supposed to look after all its members, both immediate and extended."

"They're also busy preparing for the blood mate cere-mony," I pointed out. "So again, I'm not a huge priority at the moment."

"Ah, that's right," Novak said like he'd forgotten.

"Are you going?"

"I wasn't planning on it."

"I don't blame you," I scoffed.

A smile tugged at the corner of Novak's lips. "Aren't you going? It's a big day for your friend, right?"

"I don't think I have much of a choice."

Novak pulled out the stool from under the counter and sat down. He seemed closer to me, resting his elbows on the marble surface and leaning in slightly. "Are you still angry at her for bringing this change upon you?"

I sighed, tilting my head back to admire the pendant lights hanging from the ceiling. "I don't know. Honestly, I'm tired of feeling mad at her. I'm tired of feeling depressed and resentful of what I am now, but I'm not ready to completely forgive her yet." I folded my arms on the counter, speaking aloud the thoughts forming in my head. "And I feel bad because I know she feels awful over what happened to me. She's my best friend and I don't want her to suffer." I frowned. "But she's found the love of her life and is perfectly happy in Blood 'til Dawn, so it's not like she's suffering that much."

"Relationships are complicated," Novak said with a sympathetic nod. "Especially our longest and closest ones. Sometimes it's the people we love most who hurt us more than we ever thought possible."

When I looked at him, it was impossible for my gaze not to travel up the length of his exposed forearms. Jesus, since when did I become a forearm fetishist?

"Sounds like you speak from experience," I mused.

He laughed dryly. "Yes, and I don't have many regrets, but one of the big ones is holding onto a lot of unresolved feelings toward my family. And as you can see," he lifted and spread his hands out with a wry expression, "they're all gone. I can't even say I loved everyone in my clan, but it's... haunting to have resentments and old wounds never be resolved. You don't want that." He brought his hands down and straightened. "Even with a nearly thousand-year life-span, you never know when Temkra will take you to eternal rest."

It was good advice that I was taking very much to heart. But my brain snagged on certain details.

"So, what Cyan said the other day, about your clan being monsters?"

Novak's eyes closed for a long moment and he nodded. "It's true. We started noticing it a couple hundred years ago. No one knows for sure, but I believe it's a disease, possibly viral in nature. Most people call it Rathka's Curse. But all of my clan succumbed to it, except for me. They're... unrecognizable, impossible to reason with. And yes, they've been known to cannibalize." He let out a short scoff. "A good example of being technically alive but not living a life. They may as well be dead. They're certainly not vampires, or even people, anymore."

"Holy shit," I breathed, staring at him in shock. "Novak, that's terrible. Are you saying they're out there but you can't help them in any way?"

He ran a hand through his hair, suddenly looking exhausted. "Hasn't been for a lack of trying. I've dedicated the last hundred years of my life to finding a cure. But nothing so far has worked. As far as most are concerned, I'm the last of my line."

A hundred years. I couldn't imagine being completely alone for that long. How could he stand it? I assumed he was single, but maybe I was wrong. Whichever the case, his relationship status definitely wasn't my business. Although once the thought crossed my mind, I was suddenly insatiably curious to know.

A mirthless smile crossed his face as he watched me. "Are you questioning your decision to show up unannounced to my house?"

"No. I mean, I'll go if I'm bothering you. I don't want to

be a nuisance, but I just... That's so awful, Novak. I can't even imagine losing everyone."

"You're not a bother at all." He paused as if he were going to say more but decided against it. "And you might as well know what the story is with my clan. All of Sanguine knows, so now you're in the loop."

He tried to sound nonchalant, but it couldn't have been easy to talk about. That coldness from before had returned, and I wondered if it was a mask he put on to shove down his emotions. If that was true, maybe he didn't intend to seem so callous when we parted at Blood 'til Dawn's compound.

Or maybe I was just desperately looking for a connection that wasn't there.

"I'm really sorry about your family," I said. "And that you never resolved things with them. You make a good point. I know Tavia's heart was in the right place when she had me changed, I just... "

To my surprise, Novak leaned toward me and gently knocked his shoulder against mine. The contact was one thing that sent my skin flushing with heat, but the scent of him was something else. That warm, masculine fragrance invaded my senses and hit my brain like a drug. I felt my fangs lengthen and kept my lips firmly clamped shut to hide them.

"I'm sure it would mean a lot to her if you attended her mating ceremony." Novak was apparently unaware of his effect on me. "As in, willingly and happily supporting her."

The words left my mouth before I could fully comprehend what I was asking.

"Will you come with me?"

Chapter 9

Norak

I had never known many brusang. My family didn't believe humans were worth turning. They were barely people in my parents' eyes. Humans were too fragile, too short-lived, and multiplied too easily, just like simpler animals. They were good for a quick, emergency blood source and little else.

I used that lack of knowledge as an excuse as to why I was so drawn to Amy. My house staff gave me a better understanding of humans, but Amy, with her mix of human and vampire traits, was so utterly fascinating.

Did she know that she ran her tongue along her fangs while listening to me talk? Like she didn't know what to do with them. It drove me wild in ways I hadn't felt in years. I certainly hadn't felt this wound up while sampling Inessa's blood. Quite the opposite, actually.

On my ride home, all I could think about was taking a shower. I wanted to wash my mouth and my body, and I hadn't even lain with Baros's daughter yet. But the thought of fucking some stranger for the sole purpose of creating an heir make my skin feel coated in grime.

Such an agreement wasn't even uncommon among vampires. Our long lives meant that offspring were rare, and romantic relationships didn't always produce children. Sometimes outside arrangements were made. Such things had always been strange to me, even if they were normal to everyone else.

However, those feelings of grime and mild disgust vanished the moment I saw Amy sitting and eating in my kitchen like she belonged there. She was a breath of fresh air and a welcome distraction from Baros's scheming. She was so petite that her feet gently kicked in mid-air. My chef, Jo, suddenly busied herself when I appeared, but I'd seen that secret smile. She and Amy had been talking like they knew each other.

Amy looked right at home here, and that didn't bother me in the slightest.

She asked me a question while I was admiring how bright her irises looked set in their black depths. Her eyes looked like distant galaxies, holding infinite worlds within. She was so lucky to not have the boring red irises that all vampires had. It was only after that thought that her question registered in my head.

"You want me to come with you to the Blood 'til Dawn mating ceremony?"

She chewed her lip nervously. "Well, yeah."

I pulled in a breath, imagining Amy on my arm while surrounded by the ruling clan who wished my bloodline extinct. Oh, it would be satisfying to see them squirm. Almost as good as seeing her at my side, proud and defiant against their expectations.

On my exhale I said, "I don't think that's a good idea."

Amy's face fell and I mentally added disappointing her to my short list of regrets.

"It's not that I wouldn't *like* to. It's just very likely that I wouldn't be allowed as a guest," I amended.

Amy frowned. "I thought all of Sanguine was invited, since blood mates are such a rare occurrence or whatever."

"It is. The whole territory will be celebrating, and I'm sure Thorne would permit ninety-nine percent of vampires to attend as your plus-one." I smiled wryly. "But that would definitely not include me."

"But what if... " Amy got a devious look on her face that sent a rush of sensation through my fangs. "Do you think they would ask for your name if I said I had a plus-one?"

"Why?" Suspicion laced my tone.

Her eyes flashed with mischief and the tips of her small fangs peeked out through her smile. "What if we just showed up together?"

"I mean no offense, but that sounds like a terrible idea."

"Or a brilliant one," she retorted. "Come on, what are they gonna do? Haul you away and cause a scene at the wedding of the century?"

"I don't know, they might."

"No." Amy shook her head emphatically. "They want this to go off without a hitch, right? As long as we don't cause trouble, why would they? Cyan wants the day to go flawlessly, and so does Tavia, of course."

"Amy," I sighed. "You haven't known them as long as I have. This could go very badly."

"Listen, I know Tavia and she's got Cyan by the balls. He worships the ground she walks on. If she lets us come, Cyan will make sure it happens."

"Cyan isn't the head of the clan," I reminded her. "Thorne is."

"Thorne's not the one getting married. Mated, whatever." Amy waved her hand flippantly. "In human weddings, the bride is the one calling the shots. It's *her* day. The groom's job is to make sure she's happy and that she gets the day she wants."

"Okay. Fair enough," I hedged. "But how do you know Tavia will allow us to attend together? As Cyan's blood mate, she's fully entrenched in Blood 'til Dawn, who see me as an enemy. What if she orders to have me removed?"

Amy shrugged and picked at the crumbs of her sandwich before answering. "If she wants to save our friendship, I don't think she'll refuse my wanting you there."

I watched the side of her face, noting how her eyes refused to meet mine. "That's a bit manipulative, don't you think?"

Amy shrugged again, feigning nonchalance, but I could tell she wasn't entirely comfortable with the idea.

"Pulling something like that is more likely to drive a bigger divide into your friendship than repair it," I said. "Why do you even want *me* to come with you?"

She laughed like the question was ridiculous. "I mean, why not? I like talking to you and you've been really nice to me. You don't treat me like they do, always tiptoeing around me like I'll explode into glass shards at any second. And all the pitying looks." She closed her eyes and shook her head. "It feels like you're my only real friend besides Tavia, and she's all wrapped up in Cyan now. I just... don't want to feel alone during the ceremony."

Amy finally turned her head and looked at me, her expression open and vulnerable. "I'm sorry if that's weird and too much since we just met, but it's the truth. I know you and Blood 'til Dawn don't get along, and I don't mean to be manipulative. I just want a friend at my side while I support my other friend during her big day. That's all."

My thoughts almost turned to, *this poor woman*, but I

quickly shoved that away. She didn't want pity. She needed someone at her side, meeting her where she was as she figured out this new life. And for some reason, Amy wanted that to be me.

It had been a long time since I felt like I had a real friend as well. And I liked Amy for all the reasons she seemed to like me. It was honestly a relief to meet someone who didn't have any preconceived notions of me based on the past actions of my clan. I still couldn't believe how steadfastly she defended me while I was being searched and questioned, fearlessly demanding my release. No one, not even anyone in my own family, stood up for me like she did.

One small fang dragged across her plump lower lip and my skin heated at the memory of her mouth on my neck when we first met.

"So?" she prompted, utterly unaware of the effect she had on me. "What are you thinking? Will you come with me?"

I propped an elbow on the counter and rubbed my forehead. There were hundreds of ways this could go wrong, but maybe a few ways it could go right. She needed me and I wanted to be there for her. Walking untouched among Blood 'til Dawn would be an added bonus.

"Let's do this," I said. "Talk to your friend, Tavia. Tell her that you want to bring me."

Amy's face scrunched up like she smelled something rotten, and that told me plenty how she felt about my idea.

"Handle it however you want." I raised my hands. "Ask for permission to have me as a guest, or simply inform her that I'll be your plus-one. But I'll feel a lot better about attempting this if she has a heads-up. And," I grinned, "it forces you to communicate instead of trying to deceive her."

"Yeah, no shit." Amy rubbed the bridge of her nose. "And if I'd rather not?"

"Then I'm not going."

Her glare was adorable. "Seriously?"

"Yes, that's my one condition. The bride deserves to know who's crashing her big day, does she not?"

Amy groaned, dropping her head into her hands. "You're the worst."

"That's a funny way of saying I'm such a good friend, trying to repair your relationship with your other friend."

"Shut up." Her head popped back up, a wry smile tugging at her lips. "Fine. I'll talk to her."

"Excellent. Let me know what she says. Do you have a phone?"

Amy straightened, patting her pockets. "Oh yeah, I do. I always forget I have it on me. We didn't have personal phones in Sapien."

So she *was* from there, and had probably been in the attack. It didn't feel appropriate to bring it up while we talked about phones, so I filed the information away for later.

"That's surprising," I said, taking my phone from my pocket. "We're permanently attached to our devices out here."

"I can see why. Text messaging is so much fun. It's like passing notes."

Trying to keep my smile hidden, I saved Amy's number as she recited it to me, then sent her a bat emoji so she would have my number.

She squealed when the message popped up on her screen. "How do you get other emojis? I only have the basic smiley faces."

"It should be an option on your keyboard. Here." I held

my palm out and she placed the phone in my hand with no hesitation.

Time ceased to exist as I showed Amy various features on her phone, including the camera and the few mobile games we could poach from the human world. She proceeded to take no less than a dozen blurry selfies of us, and I showed her how to attach photos to the contacts in her phone. Of course, she chose the least flattering picture of me to save to my number, but at least she looked cute in the photo.

She was in an incredibly tense game of Snake when I felt fatigue settle over me like a heavy cloak, and a warning itch creeping up my spine. Glancing up, I noticed for the first time we were alone in the kitchen. Jo must have left ages ago.

And if the clock was correct, dawn was only an hour away. Fucking Temkra, had Amy been here all night?

"Amy."

"Mm-hmm." Her eyes were locked on her phone screen, fingers directing the snake around its own body.

"It's almost dawn, akra." I nearly bit my tongue. That was the third time the endearment had slipped out. "I should take you back."

She paused the game, blinking as she looked up. "Oh wow, it feels like I just got here." A frown pinched her brow. "I'm sorry, I didn't mean to stay so long."

"Don't be," I insisted. "I'm... glad you came over."

Her smile was warm—at least it made me feel warm—as she slid off the barstool. "Me too. Thanks for letting me hang out, Novak."

"Of course." I awkwardly slid off my own stool. "Let me get my coat."

"No, it's okay." Amy held up a hand. "I know my way better now. You don't have to walk me."

"And let you walk alone? Absolutely not."

Amy's hand dropped, her face hardening. "I don't want to see them harass you like that again."

I waved a hand through the air. "How they treat me doesn't matter—"

"Yes, it does." She stood firm, her expression determined. "You deserve better than that, Novak."

It had to be the first time anyone told me I deserved better, and I was struck dumb by the declaration. After knowing me for barely two days, she was so certain that Blood 'til Dawn treated me unfairly? What had I done for Temkra to bless me with someone so loyal?

"Even if that were the case," I said, still trying to recover from my shock, "I don't want you walking back alone. Maybe I can see you off at their door from a distance."

"And if they catch you watching me from across the street or wherever?" she pressed. "You'll look even more suspicious than if you just walked up with me."

"Well, we need to come up with a solution before the sun rises." I glanced at the windows, knowing the lightproof shutters would fall into place at any minute.

"We can take her."

Our heads turned at the same time, finding Lourna and Jo sitting near the bottom of the stairs.

"Blood 'til Dawn doesn't know we work for you." Jo tapped her temple. "And even if they did, they don't harass humans. We can make sure she gets there safely."

"You're sure?" I asked. "Isn't their compound out of your way?"

"Eh, barely." Lourna shrugged. "I gotta swing by the market anyway."

It was a kind offer. They seemed to like Amy, and had no problems withstanding the sunlight.

I looked at Amy. "Would you be all right walking home with them?"

"Yeah, definitely." She nodded and glanced at the humans with a grin. "Maybe I can sweet-talk Jo into giving me her pastrami recipe."

"Ha! Fat chance, girly. You gotta come to the Rathka house if you want to be fed right."

All of the women laughed and I felt the tightness in my chest ease. I trusted them, and Amy would be in good hands.

"Before you go." I touched Amy's elbow and leaned in to speak low in her ear. "Do you need anything?"

"No, I don't think so." She spoke at normal volume, a look of confusion crossing her face. "What do you... Oh."

I held out my unbandaged forearm and closed my fist, flexing my wrist back to make the veins pop under the thin veneer of skin. Amy's demeanor instantly shifted. Her pupils dilated and her lips parted as her fangs fully descended. She looked ready, wanting. Hungry. I wished for nothing more than to find a private room and let her take all she needed from me.

And I wasn't necessarily talking about just blood.

I could also see her hesitation, the nervous swallow and the furrow in her brow, and knew acting on those instincts would be a bad move.

"I'll get a glass for you to drink from."

I left her side to round the counter and bring a glass down from the cupboard. She was no longer starving and wouldn't need a huge amount, so I settled for a half-pint and went looking for an appropriate knife.

When I turned, searching in the island drawers, a

distinct scent hit my nose. Feminine and musky, a little sweet, and coming from directly across the island. The scent was distantly familiar. I recognized it but couldn't quite place it. When it finally hit me, I nearly stabbed myself in the palm with the knife I'd found.

Amy was aroused.

By... me?

I whipped around, turning my back to her without daring a glance in her direction. My heart kicked up a furious beat in my chest and I knew she could hear it, which only made the situation worse.

She couldn't be feeling that way toward me. Maybe she was... just horny in general?

Whichever the case, I focused all of my willpower on not turning around for another lungful of that sweet perfume. That would become a slippery slope to running my nose along her neck, which would lead to tasting her blood. And that opened all kinds of doors that would intertwine hunger and sexual cravings in all kinds of messy ways.

Especially since she made it clear we were only friends.

And she was technically part of an enemy clan.

Rational thoughts and resisting my urges did nothing to calm down my cock, which thickened and pressed almost painfully against my zipper.

I liked Amy, but I had no delusions about this becoming any deeper. She was lost and needed a friend who wouldn't take advantage of her.

Even if she became comfortable enough to feed skin-to-skin, and deeper feelings grew, I was on the verge of creating an heir with Inessa of Carpe Noctem. Amy deserved better than a guy who would leave to actively impregnate someone else.

But I was getting far, far ahead of myself.

I slashed the knife across the inside of my forearm, cutting deeper than necessary. The quick flash of pain cleared my head and deflated my erection, thank Temkra. My pulse slowed as I held the wound over the glass, my self-control returning. When the bleeding slowed and I turned around, Amy was frowning.

"What?" I set the glass on the island and pressed a clean dish towel to my forearm.

"I just hate that you have to do that." She drew the glass of blood closer and lifted it to her lips.

"Do what?"

"Hurt yourself." She swallowed a deep drink and pointed at the glass. "So that I can have this."

I shook my head. Her concern for my wellbeing was as strange as it was satisfying. This woman had a talent for making me feel all kinds of warm, unfamiliar things.

"I told you it's not very painful. And I don't mind."

"Still, I don't like it." She drained the glass in two more large gulps and set it on the counter. "But thank you for your blood, Novak."

My response was automatic, which should have worried me. But the Vampiric phrase flowed like water out of my mouth like it was the most natural thing in the world.

Amy smiled, as if the sounds of the Vampiric language pleased her, even if she didn't understand the words. "What does that mean?"

"It means, feeding you is a pleasure." I grabbed the glass and took it to the sink. The English version sounded like it was trying too hard, so I felt compelled to add, "It's just something we say after giving blood. It's polite."

"Oh." She lingered at the far end of the counter, even

though Jo and Lourna waited for her in the foyer. "What's that other word you've used a few times?"

"Which one?" I asked, even though I knew perfectly well.

"Akra? Am I saying it right?"

"Perfectly." I grinned. "And it doesn't mean anything exactly. It's... your name," I lied.

"My name?"

"It's how Amy would be pronounced as a Vampiric name."

Her eyes lit up. "Oh, I like that." She stuck her hand out toward me. "Nice to meet you. I'm akra."

You certainly are.

I fought to keep a straight face as I shook her hand, the gesture strange and extremely human. "Well met, akra."

Amy giggled and turned away, throwing me a glance over her shoulder. "I'll let you know what Tavia says about the ceremony."

"Okay. Get home safe." I watched her head for the front door, struck by a sudden sense of longing. She was leaving and I didn't want her to go. "Text me when you're home," I called out.

"Okay!" she called back. "Sleep tight, sweet dreams!"

I already knew my dreams would be sweet if I went to bed thinking of her. But the reality was so much sweeter, and I'd be counting the hours until she was here again.

The three women chatted among themselves before the door closed and cut off all sound. As soon as they left, only the gentle hum of electricity could be heard throughout the house.

I was alone again, and perhaps for the first time, I really didn't want to be.

Chapter 10

Amy

The Blood 'til Dawn compound was quiet when I snuck back in, and the sun was just starting to peak over the horizon. Not a single living thing stirred as I crossed the great room, descended into the underground corridor of rooms, and crept to my bedroom in Tavia and Cyan's apartment.

I got into bed and took out my phone, the screen lighting up the windowless darkness of the room. Feeling like a teenager writing to a high school crush, I typed out a text.

> I'm home. Thanks again for letting me hang out tonight.

His reply came moments later.

> Glad to hear it. And let's do it again sometime. :)

I grinned so hard that my cheeks hurt as I hit the power button and turned to put the phone on the nightstand. I was really, really happy that I met him, to the point of feeling giddy. He was so cute and wickedly funny. On top of that he was smart, kind, and encouraged me to work things out with Tavia, despite being part of an enemy clan.

"Oh God." Even though I was alone and in the dark, I groaned and covered my face with the duvet.

I had a massive crush on Novak. I liked him, and I also *liked* him.

What was I supposed to do about this? Even if Tavia and I repaired our friendship and she allowed me to bring him to her ceremony, she'd never support anything more between us.

And anyway, who was to say that he felt similarly? He was the last in a bloodline to an ancient clan and I was a nobody brusang. For all I knew, he was betrothed to some other vampire from a powerful clan.

We were friends. That much was clear. I was probably some kind of charity case to him. I'd nearly starved to death on his doorstep and still couldn't bring myself to bite another person. Except...

Except I almost did tonight. I'd wanted to.

When he flexed his forearm and made his veins pop like that, it awakened a hunger I hadn't yet felt at that point. I didn't just want his blood—I wanted my mouth on his skin and to feel his on mine in return. I wanted to taste *him*, not just drink the hot fluid in his veins.

The feeling came over me so quickly, and then I was noticing everything about him. His broad back, the round shape of his shoulders. His collarbones just barely visible at the unbuttoned top of his shirt. I noticed his lips, his eyelashes, his fingers, even the shape of his ears. And naturally, I noticed his neck.

I didn't just notice, but wondered how sensitive it was. Would he react to a nip on his Adam's apple? Would his head fall back with a moan if I trailed my lips from his jaw to his shoulder, searching for that perfect spot to pull from his vein? Would he touch me if I straddled his lap to drink from his neck?

All of those thoughts, and even more inappropriate ones, ran through my head while he cut his arm and bled into a glass to feed me. The guilt of that was what sobered me. I stood there, lusting after him, while he hurt himself so that I wouldn't be hungry.

Such a contrast definitely put our differences into perspective. Novak was sweet, selfless, and shrugged it all off like it was no big deal. Me? I was given a second chance at life, then wallowed about it and pushed away my best friend.

Sleep overtook me to thoughts of Novak and Tavia, and wondering why they chose me. Those two deserved better, but while they had me, I might as well make the effort to be better.

———

I woke up after the longest, deepest sleep I'd had in weeks. My body felt stiff, and I stretched with a groan. I couldn't even remember the last time I had slept so well.

After slipping out of the immensely comfortable bed, which I had to admit was miles better than Bea's couch, I looked at the time on my phone.

"What, really?" I rubbed more grit out of my eyes and blinked to stare at the time again.

It was almost sunset, which meant I'd slept the entire day.

And I felt... good. The most refreshed and energetic I'd felt since being turned. If I'd known blood could make me feel like this, I might have come around a lot sooner.

I left the bedroom not knowing what to expect, and my heart did a little stammer when I saw Tavia pouring a cup of coffee in the small kitchenette.

She startled when I came out, almost spilling the pot. "Oh! Hey."

"Hey," I returned. "Good mor—er, evening, I guess."

"Evening." She continued to stare at me for a few seconds like I was a stranger who magically appeared in her home, which I suppose I was. "Want some?" she gestured toward the coffee maker.

"Sure, thanks." Desperate for no awkward silences, I piped up, "Cyan not up yet?"

"No, he won't be conscious until after dusk." Tavia poured a cup for me and placed it on the counter.

"Thanks." I approached to take the coffee and lifted it toward my mouth.

"Might not want to drink it yet. It'll scald your tongue."

For a few moments, I warred between letting the warning go or snapping at her for treating me like a child. Tavia seemed to notice too, and she grimaced.

"Sorry," she said, eyes lowering. "Trying to break the habit of... you know."

Always protecting me, I thought.

Remembering that I was making an effort to do better, I set the mug down with a sigh. "It's okay. I would have regretted that sip."

Tavia nodded and there it was, that awkward silence I'd been trying to avoid. I stared at my cup, wishing I could drink just so I'd have something to do besides standing here like this.

In all our years growing up together, I'd never felt this with her. We were always jabbering about something, and what little silence we did have, it was always calm and comfortable.

"So." Tavia broke the silence first. "You sleep well?"

"I actually did. Might be getting the hang of this nocturnal thing yet." I glanced up from the counter and attempted to smile at her. *See? Effort.*

"Lucky," she grumbled. "Took me over a month and I still don't fully have the hang of it."

I only nodded in response, silently speculating on things I was sure she didn't want to say out loud. Like my quick adaptation to sleeping during the day was probably a result of no longer being fully human. I wondered if Novak's blood had anything to do with it too. I felt like a brand-new person since last night.

"Anyway, you're looking better," Tavia said, her gaze roaming over me. "Healthier, for sure."

"Thanks," I said, choosing not to volunteer any information right then. She was clearly trying to fish it out of me.

"Good sleep really does wonders. You look alert, refreshed."

"Mm-hmm." I chose that moment to pick up my coffee, carefully blowing across its surface before taking a tentative sip. It was perfect, just hot enough to bite but not burn.

"If I may say, you even look," Tavia took a long pause and I wondered if she would really go there, "well-fed."

I set my coffee down and looked at her squarely. "You want to ask me, so just come out with it."

To my surprise, she retreated. "No, sorry. I'll admit I'm worried. But you're clearly alive and well, and I said I'd give you space. If you want me to know anything, you can tell me. But I know I've been too pushy and overprotective, so I'll just leave you be. Sorry, Ames."

She picked up her coffee and made a beeline across the apartment, heading toward her and Cyan's bedroom. Part of me was relieved to be left alone without any awkwardness or prodding, but I also knew it was on me to start repairing things.

"Wait," I called to her. "I'm sorry too."

Tavia stopped and turned slowly to face me. Once I had her attention, I kept going.

"I'm sorry for how I've been acting since, you know, all of this," I gestured around my face, "happened. This change has been a lot to deal with, but I shouldn't have lashed out at you. I know you meant well. I've always known that. And I was more cruel and entitled than I ever had the right to be. I hurt you, Tav, and I'm really sorry about that."

She went eerily still as she listened, then took a long pause before saying softly, "You have every right to be angry with me."

"Sure, I'm not denying that." My palms wrapped around the steaming mug. "But I didn't have to treat you like I did. I didn't have to rot for two weeks on Bea's couch and lash out when you tried to help. I could've handled my anger better."

Tavia paused for a few moments before hesitantly approaching me again. "I appreciate you saying that. And I could've handled myself better too. I'm sorry for being over-bearing."

I nodded. "My behavior didn't make you worry any less. I get it."

A tentative smile touched Tavi's lips. "Do you want to sit?" She held an arm out toward the couch.

"Sure." I followed her lead and felt tension draining out

of me as I relaxed into the couch cushions. We weren't all the way fixed yet. I still had to drop the Novak bomb on her, but this progress felt good.

Tavia remained standing, looking nervous. "I... I got something for you." She flushed, as if embarrassed.

I stared at her, confused. "What do you mean?"

"Just a little gift. Wait here." She went into the bedroom, moving quietly, and returned with a canvas tote bag, which she held out to me.

I accepted the bag, noting the weight as I set it on my lap. When I peered inside, the threat of tears pricked my eyes.

"You got me knitting supplies?" I lifted the skeins of wool yarn, my fingertips already buzzing with satisfaction at the soft material. There were so many different colors, including my favorite shade of blue. A pair of knitting needles were already set in an inner side pocket. At the bottom of the bag, underneath all the yarn, sat a book of patterns.

"Not everything has to change," Tavia said softly. "I remember how much you loved knitting. When I first moved here, it was my winemaking that kept me sane."

"Thank you, Tav." Emotion filled my voice as I carefully refilled the bag with yarn. "This is really nice and thoughtful. And you're right. I can't wait to make something."

Knitting was my favorite hobby aside from reading, and yet I'd hardly given any thought to it after being turned. Without realizing it, Tavia had given me a part of myself back, one of the few pieces of my human life that I found genuine joy in. Already, I was eager to hold the pair of needles in my hands and get into that soothing rhythm of manipulating yarn into something beautiful.

"You're so welcome. I can't wait to see what you do." Tavia laughed a little awkwardly as she took a sip of coffee. "So, back to your well-fed look. Did you end up giving the blood bank another try?"

I took a deep breath, my heart suddenly beating like a drum. Telling her the truth could undo this tentative peace we'd just found. But lying would only have bigger consequences later. And Novak was right. She had the right to know who would show up to her mating ceremony.

I also had to be honest with her if I wanted any chance of our friendship being repaired.

"I went to Novak's house again, and took his blood," I said in a single breath.

Tavia's eyes widened, her mouth going slack. "You *what?!*"

"I would also like to bring him to your ceremony as my guest." I closed my lips against the urge to say, *if that's okay with you.* Whatever permission she gave regarding the ceremony I would honor. But my friendship with him did not require her approval.

"Amy!" She hissed out my name and immediately glanced at her closed bedroom door, as if expecting Cyan to burst out any moment. "Are you crazy? Thorne forbade any contact between you two!" Her expression changed, concern pinching her brow. "Did he seek you out?"

"No, Novak didn't do anything wrong." I straightened, firming up my tone. "I sought *him* out. I went to his place and he wasn't home, so his chef let me in. And I just kind of hung out until he got there."

"And you stayed there all night?" Tavi whispered.

"Nothing happened," I insisted. "We just talked. And he gave me blood before I left."

"Amy... " Tavia shook her head, clearly disappointed. "Why?"

"I like him." I shrugged. "He's nice and easy to talk to." His blood was also the best thing I'd ever tasted, but I wasn't ready to admit that to her yet.

"He's an enemy of Blood 'til Dawn," Tavia pleaded. "If Thorne doesn't want you seeing him, it has to be for a good reason."

I rolled my eyes. "Apparently it's a reason so good, no one can tell me what it is. Novak has been nothing but kind to me. I consider him a friend."

"Just a friend?"

I licked my lips, remembering the taste of his blood and all the lustful feelings I'd been having right before drinking it. "Yes."

Tavia shot me a look like she wasn't buying it. "And you want to bring him to my mating ceremony. Why? They could kill him on sight!"

"Not if you don't let it happen," I argued. "And I want him there because I don't want to be alone while you're up there."

"You won't be alone. Bea will be there."

I sighed. "Don't get me wrong. I like Bea, and I appreciate everything she's done to help me as a fellow brusang. But she's *your* friend. I'm sure I'll get there with her eventually, but Novak is the first friend I've made here on my own."

Tavia groaned, dropping her head into her hands. "Even if I want to say yes, this is going to cause trouble with the clan. It won't put Cyan in a good light."

"Who says the clan has to know? Until he shows up, of course."

Tavia dropped her hands and gave me a withering stare. "You know I can't do that. I can't convince Cyan to do that."

"Why not?" I challenged. "I just want Novak as my plus-one. It's not like I'm trying to sneak him into the compound for clan secrets or whatever."

My best friend sighed as her head fell back. "I don't know, Amy. This feels like it's inviting so much more trouble than necessary."

"Novak will behave himself. He's just going to sit with me. As long as Blood 'til Dawn doesn't act out, there will be no trouble."

Tavia leveled her gaze on me again. "You're so different now. I used to be the troublemaker, and you were the peace-keeper. What happened?"

"I guess things change when you're sacrificed to a vampire and I wake up from the dead as one."

She huffed out a soft laugh over a sip of coffee. "Yeah, I guess you're right."

Nothing was said for a few minutes, and after some deliberation, I decided to lift the biggest weight sitting on my chest.

"Look, I miss you," I said. "I miss... how we used to be."

Tavia's smile was tinged with sadness. "Me too. I feel... responsible for fucking up our friendship."

"Well I certainly didn't help." I took a deep breath. "I'm really happy for you and Cyan. Seriously, I'm glad you two found each other. I know things will never be exactly the same between us, but I still want us to be... you know, good."

"Thanks, Ames. That really means a lot." Her smile brightened. "I want us to be good too."

I steeled myself with another breath. "I'm excited to watch your ceremony. I can't wait to be there and support you. But Novak is important to me too. It would really mean a lot to me if you allowed him to come."

Tavia sighed again, but there was noticeably less exasperation in the sound. "I can't promise anything, but I'll do my best to convince Cyan."

My heart soared with relief. "Thank you, Tav. I appreciate that so much."

"He better be worth it," she grumbled with another soft smile.

"He is," I said. "I think if you got to know him, you would really like him."

"I do hope I get that chance." Her smile widened. "Who knows, maybe this gesture will go toward healing whatever centuries-long grudges the two clans hold against each other."

"Wouldn't that be nice." I sipped more coffee, relaxing for the first time since we started talking. "So, blood mates. What's that like?"

Tavia laughed softly, a blush darkening her neck and cheeks. "Oh my God, how do I put it into words? It's the craziest, most intense feeling of *rightness* I've ever felt. It's so passionate and strong, but secure and solid too. It's always there, which is comforting, but it's exciting too. It's constant butterflies mixed with this deep knowing that he's devoted to me and will never stray." She paused, laughing again. "Does that make any sense?"

"Sounds like romance novel stuff," I teased, then cackled at the look she tossed my way. Tavia had never been a romance reader, while I devoured hundreds of those pulpy paperbacks long into the night. Thinking about those books made me realize they were my only possessions that I missed from my previous life. They were so much fun to flip through and escape into.

"You might be right," Tavia admitted with a dreamy grin. "I can't believe this is my real life sometimes. That he's really mine."

"What does blood mates mean exactly? Is it something about your blood in particular?"

She nodded. "So it turns out my blood is like, custom-made for Cyan. That's how I think of it, anyway. My blood fits all of his nutritional needs perfectly, so that flips some kind of switch in a vampire's brain. It makes me taste especially good to him, and all other blood will taste terrible, like vomit-inducing. It's some kind of vampire survival thing that keeps them hooked on the blood that will benefit them the most."

"Wow." I didn't know what to expect, but it definitely wasn't that. "So it's actually scientific."

"I guess so."

"I have so many questions." My fingers flew to my temples. "What if you find a blood mate but you can't stand that person? What if the blood mate dies? What if you're gay but your blood mate is an opposite sex person, or vice versa?"

"I don't know entirely how it works." Tavia laughed, her blush deepening. "But I will say, between Cyan and me, there was a strong... chemistry. Not just blood, but you know."

"*Sexual* chemistry." I shimmied my shoulders and waggled my eyebrows until Tavia snort-laughed. Finally, our old dynamic seemed to be finding its way back. One of my favorite parts of our friendship was how unabashedly silly we could be together.

"Not *just* that," she said once recovered. "But just... regular chemistry, you know? He was easy to talk to. We got along as people just existing together, you know?" She grinned dreamily again. "If your blood mate is out there, I hope they make you feel the exact same way."

"It does sound nice," I admitted. "But it's super rare, right?"

"Oh yeah. Bea said the last one was twenty years or so ago."

I nodded, sinking into the couch cushions with my hands around my coffee mug. As lovely as it sounded, I had no expectations of such a thing happening to me.

The night of Tavia and Cyan's mating ceremony was a full moon, bathing all of Sanguine in silver light. Rather than the Blood 'til Dawn compound, the ceremony was being held out in a public square.

The entire territory was invited to witness and celebrate, although the public was kept at a distance behind a roped-off perimeter guarded by Blood 'til Dawn members. After checking in with guards, invited guests were allowed inside the perimeter where about a hundred chairs had been set out before a raised dais.

Blood 'til Dawn seemed to be taking security extremely seriously, and shooed away many people who asked about having a seat closer to the couple. After most of the inner seats were being filled, the public began crowding around the perimeter, and I noticed some people climbing onto rooftops and balconies to watch.

My heart was fluttering with nerves as I took a seat in the farthest row from the dais, closest to the street where Novak said he'd be approaching from. For the first time, I started to have doubts that this would work. The Blood 'til

Dawn guards were turning people away with efficiency, informing onlookers that if they weren't on the guest list, they weren't permitted entry.

I didn't know if Novak ever made it to the guest list. Tavia talked to Cyan, but that was all I knew. She'd gotten so busy in the last week getting fitted for her gown and preparing for the ceremony that we hadn't had time to discuss it much. I assumed the plan was still in place because she never told me otherwise. She would find a way to tell me if it wouldn't work, right?

In order to not alert suspicion, I opted to not visit Novak's house in the week leading up to the ceremony. We texted every night though, and talked on the phone a couple of times. Finding new messages from him were my favorite moments of the week. Hearing my phone chirp or feeling a buzz in my pocket sent my chest fluttering.

But texts and calls were nothing compared to seeing him in person, and I found that I missed him. Least of all because it had been just over a week since I last took his blood, and the hunger had become a constant, gnawing ache.

I'd fantasized about his blood the last couple of days, which always turned into fantasies of *him*. I wondered what his body looked like under those fancy clothes, how well those strong forearms could hold me.

I was dying to see him, and yet incredibly nervous because of how much my crush on him had grown. I had to keep my attraction to him in check, had to keep reminding myself that my fantasies would stay purely in my head. Even if Novak did somehow return my feelings and desires, he was basically a vampire prince. Forget out of my league, he was out of my whole damn universe.

My phone buzzed with a message and I hurriedly checked the notification.

Coming down the street now. I'll be there in five.

My already frazzled heartbeat kicked into overdrive as I typed out a reply.

Okay, I'm right next to the checkpoint.

An agonizing four minutes later, I heard the perimeter guard let out a gruff, "What the fuck are you doing here?"

Gathering all my courage, I stood and headed in his direction. With an inward groan, I realized it was Rhain posted to this spot. He was the massive vampire who had his arm against Novak's throat.

"I was invited," I heard Novak say.

"By who?" Rhain demanded.

"Me."

Rhain whipped around, his expression confused as he stared into the air above my head.

"Down here." I smiled as the huge vampire's gaze slowly lowered to meet my eyes. Sure, I was shorter than most people on a good day, but compared to him, I was an absolute pipsqueak. "There you go."

Rhain's glare softened only a fraction, and he at least had the decency to back up so as to not loom over me. "I'm sorry, but he's not permitted."

"Yes, he is," I chirped. "Tavia said I could invite him."

"Tavia is not the head of this clan."

"It's her ceremony. She's the one giving up her human life to spend centuries with one of your kind. Are you telling me she has no say over the guest list?"

Novak's eyes bounced between us, his mouth tense like he was fighting a smile.

With a frustrated noise, Rhain pulled out his phone. "Give me a minute. Don't fucking go anywhere." He walked a few feet away, leaving Novak and me to stare at each other with matched wide-eyed expressions.

"Cyan, it's Rhain." The big vampire turned around, keeping us in his narrow-eyed sight as he muttered into the phone. "Got a small problem with your mate's brusang friend... huh? Don't tell me you're... Are you fucking with me? Cy... " Rhain's glare hardened even more as he listened. "You're sure about this? What if... fuck, fine. Okay." He ended the call so abruptly, I wondered if he broke his screen. "Stay where we can see you," he said to Novak. "And if you try anything, even breathe weird, you're out of here, Rathka's Bastard. Understand?"

"Completely." Novak grinned as he entered the perimeter and paused to dip his head at Rhain once he was past the barrier. "Thank you for your hospitality. I'm sure it'll be a beautiful ceremony."

Rhain just snarled and turned his back, resuming his post.

"Oh shit, we did it!" Once we were out of earshot, I was practically squealing. "But Jesus, you didn't have to antagonize him."

"Ah, he makes it too easy. Couldn't help myself." Novak's smile softened, his eyes darkening as he took me in from head to toe. "You look beautiful, akra."

Heat rushed from my belly to my cheeks. I was borrowing one of Bea's dresses, one that she had to hem thanks to my height, otherwise it would be dragging on the ground. But the top fit me nicely, giving me a bit of cleavage and accentuating my waist. The dress was a cornflower blue with sparkly black accents. Tavia blurted out that it matched my eyes when I tried it on, and while she meant it as a compliment, I wasn't sure how to feel about that.

When I was human, I always thought my eyes were pretty, my best feature even. Now, I was just getting over the shock of seeing my blue irises surrounded by black. I was so self-conscious of them because they made it abundantly clear that I was neither human nor vampire.

But when Novak called me beautiful right then, all the insecurity melted away and I felt radiant. It was the first time a man had told me such a thing and meant it genuinely. I knew Novak wasn't trying to flatter me, trying to manipulate me with the hopes of getting something later.

"Thank you." I hoped those two words sounded humble and gracious and not like his compliment was the highlight of my whole week. "You look handsome, very dashing."

He shoved his hands in his pockets, rocking back on his heels to look down at himself. "I clean up well, sometimes."

His charcoal waistcoat was embroidered with a subtle pattern, making him look elegant and refined. Even under his jacket, I could tell how well everything fit him, tailored to his form like a glove. Meanwhile, I was in a borrowed dress that reflected how strange my eyes were.

Suddenly I didn't even feel deserving enough to be standing next to him, let alone being his date.

"Should we find a place to sit?" Novak offered me his arm, oblivious to the downward turn of my thoughts.

"Oh, sure." I slid my hand around his bicep and let him lead.

The stares and chatter were in full swing as we found our way to a row of empty chairs. I could feel the eyes on us as we walked, hear the whispered conversations but not all of the words. Logically, I knew it had to do with the fact that he was here at all, a rival clan member in enemy territory, and whatever history that entailed.

But a small part of me was paranoid that they were whispering about me, wondering why a nobody brusang was on the arm of such a handsome vampire.

"Here should be good." Novak allowed me to sit first before lowering next to me. "In plain sight of everyone who wants to murder me, but far enough away that nobody feels threatened."

He spoke sarcastically, but I knew there was truth to his words.

"Is now a good time to tell me why Blood 'til Dawn hates you so much?"

A long silence passed, and I thought he would ignore the question entirely. As he watched people fill the seats in front of the dais, he said, "My clan did awful things to Blood 'til Dawn." His gaze turned toward me. "That's the objective truth, not one of those two-sides-to-every-story bullshit. A lot of people suffered. That's why many vampires are glad Rathka's Curse wiped out my bloodline." He leaned in closer, his breath tickling my ear. "Some even think I wrought the Curse upon my kin. What do you think of that?"

"I don't believe it for a second." I laughed. "You couldn't bear to see little ol' me starve in your courtyard. There's no way you could wipe out your entire family."

Novak leaned back, chuckling. "It's sweet that you have such faith in me."

"Besides, that makes no sense," I added. "If you cursed your family, why would you be hated if they were so awful? Wouldn't you be a hero?"

He shook his head. "Anyone capable of wiping out a clan is capable of other terrible things. Plus, I came from them." He shrugged. "Who's to say I'm not just as terrible, or even worse than they were?"

"Me." I leaned toward him to whisper conspiratorially. "I think you're a softy under all the big bad rich guy stuff."

Novak's head fell back with laughter. His eyes were bright with mirth and his grin made my heart skip a beat. "You're the only one in the world who thinks that, akra."

"Doesn't mean I'm wrong."

"True enough."

Our attention turned toward the dais as a hush fell over the crowd. Tavia and Cyan stood facing each other in front of a small altar. A third person with long, black hair covered in stripes of black and white paint stood on the far side of the altar, in the space between the couple.

"Who's that?" I asked Novak in a whisper.

"Ruslan," he answered. "His clan is Temkra's Blood. They're very religious, so they're often tasked with doing ceremonies like these."

After being prompted by Ruslan, Cyan removed his shirt and picked up a long dagger. His eyes never strayed from Tavia as he began cutting his own chest with the blade. I could see that he was carving characters, going over scars that were already on his skin.

I wanted to cover my eyes, it looked so painful. But he never flinched, not even as his skin reddened and swelled with each mark.

"Holy shit, what is he doing?"

"Tavia never told you about Blood 'til Dawn and their vows?"

"She definitely never said anything about this."

"Silver is the only material that can irreparably damage vampires and cause scars." Novak angled his head toward me. "Blood 'til Dawn scar themselves with silver blades when they make vows. Makes it a permanent reminder so that you're more inclined to keep your vow. Probably doesn't feel good to break your word and have a lie carved into your skin for the rest of your life."

"Wow, I had no idea." Reluctantly, my respect for Cyan increased a little. He was carving himself up for Tavia like his body was a ritual offering. "What did your clan think of this custom?" I asked Novak.

"Barbaric, naturally." He snorted. "Real vampires break vows, double-cross, and lie all the time. Whatever it takes to come out on top, according to my father, at least."

"But not you?"

Novak was quiet for a moment, intently watching the ceremony. "No. After seeing all the damage lies can do, I don't want to subject other people to that."

My chest warmed as I turned my attention back to the dais.

Cyan's vow to Tavia was now running off of his chest, the markings heading toward his ribs. His lips moved, but his voice was too low to hear. The vow was meant only for her. Tavia's gray eyes were wide, shining with tears of emotion. She worried at her lip, hands clenched in front of her as if fighting the urge to stop the man she loved from harming himself. But she must have known about this custom and that it would be part of the ceremony.

"He really loves her."

I didn't realize I had said that out loud until Novak replied with, "Seems that way."

Once Cyan was finished, Ruslan turned to Tavia, holding out his hand as he said something. She placed the back of her arm in his palm and allowed him to draw another knife across her forearm, letting her blood spill into a wooden bowl on the altar. It reminded me of Novak cutting his arm to let me drink his blood.

The sacrifices we make for the ones we love.

Not that Novak loved me. No way, that was ridiculous. But he did at least like me enough to accommodate my weirdness about drinking blood directly from a vein.

Although the more I thought about it, the more curious I grew. I might like to try drinking from a wrist as long as it was his.

"This blood ritual has always fascinated me." Novak's gaze was riveted to the stage. "Their blood is mixed together in the bowl and some herbs are added, all while Ruslan says an incantation over it. Then she drinks it." He narrated the actions as they happened. "And just like that, her lifespan is tied to his. She will live for centuries. And when they die, it'll be together."

"That's actually really romantic." I watched Tavia's throat work as she tipped the bowl back, swallowing the contents.

"Maybe," Novak mused. "But is it actually blood magic or based in science? Is there some kind of chemical reaction that happens, or is Ruslan truly channeling Temkra's power?"

"Typical male response to romance."

Novak chuckled, the sound dying away as Tavia finished drinking the concoction, the ritual complete. She and Cyan stared at each other for a beat before closing the small distance between them in a kiss that was equally fierce and tender. Cheers and applause erupted as those two became lost in the world of each other.

"They do seem well-matched." Novak's chair creaked as he shifted his weight. "Give them my well-wishes."

"Yeah," I said blankly.

I was oddly entranced while watching Tavia and Cyan. They held each other tightly and kissed, spoke some words, smiled, and kissed again. Cyan's face was reverent, his forehead seared to hers. I was too far away to be sure, but there may have been tears in his eyes. He looked at Tavia like she was a goddess who walked the earth. Like he would devote every breath and beat of his heart to her happiness.

God, how did it feel to have someone look at you like that? To know beyond any doubt that someone loved you that much?

I was happy for Tavia. She had been my biggest defender as we grew up, literally. Bullies pushed me around because of my asthma and how small I was, and she pushed them right back because I was never strong enough to do it myself. She deserved more than anyone to have a partner who fought for her.

But where did that leave me? And would I ever find someone who felt that way about me? My happiness for her fit right alongside the hollow emptiness I felt for myself.

"Hey." Novak nudged his knee against mine. "Want to get out of here?"

I wrenched my gaze away from the dais, turning to him. "Yes, please."

He held out his elbow, prompting me to take his arm. "Let's go."

I hugged my arm around his bicep and together we walked out into the night.

Chapter 12

Novak

"Ever ridden a motorcycle before?"

Amy shot me an apprehensive look as she walked next to me. "No."

"Would you like to?" I dug out my keys, tossed them in the air, and caught them. "The night is young, and it's not too cold."

We walked a few more steps down the cobblestones of the oldest neighborhood in the Heart, approaching my home.

"Okay, fuck it. Why not?" Amy said.

She seemed distracted, maybe a little wistful. She'd been in a cheery mood when I'd arrived for the ceremony, but by the time it ended, she was noticeably more withdrawn. Maybe she thought her friendship with Tavia would take a backseat now that she was officially mated.

From what I gathered, Amy was also a bit of a romantic. Did she wish for a relationship like what Tavia and Cyan had? I mean, who fucking didn't?

A blood mate was rare, but a long-lasting romance filled

with passion, love, and devotion? Before witnessing the ceremony today, I wasn't sure such a thing existed at all.

There was no love between my parents, or even between my father and his primary blood pet. She'd had good genes for breeding, so he fucked her until they made my half-brother. That heir, the golden child, was one of my biggest tormentors.

My mother may have loved me. Our household staff said she was sweet and soft-spoken, but Rathka's Curse took her before I reached adulthood at one hundred. My memories of her were vague at best. My brother's mother made her resentment of me extremely clear. She made sure to let me know how much she hated my existence simply because my father paid attention to another woman who wasn't her.

I pulled my focus from those thoughts as I unlocked my garage door. Dwelling on my past would send me spiraling if I ruminated too much, and I wanted to enjoy the rest of this night.

"Put this on," I said to Amy, handing her my spare helmet.

I waited until her ears were protected inside the helmet before turning the motorcycle on. The initial roar filled the garage before it lowered to a rumble. Amy stood nearby while I did all the initial checks—tires, fuel, fluids. I didn't take the bike out nearly as much as I liked to, so I always made sure it was in riding condition.

Once satisfied it was good to go, I threw a leg over and settled in the seat. "Hop on."

Amy climbed on behind me and placed a tentative hand on my waist. Reaching behind me, I brought her hands forward until they rested on my stomach, her arms snugly embracing my sides.

"Hold tight and lean with me. We'll go fast, but keep

holding on and match your movements to mine. You'll be safe as long as you hold on. Understand?"

Amy nodded, her eyes bright as full moons in the slim opening of the helmet.

I went slowly at first, minding the busy streets full of pedestrians and other riders in the Heart. Everyone seemed to be in a celebrating mood after the ceremony. Businesses and homes threw open their windows, letting loud music blast out onto the street. People danced on rooftops and as they crossed the street.

The celebratory atmosphere was infectious. I wanted to feel it too, but where it was quiet. And with only one person.

As soon as I found an open road heading north, I accelerated with a roar of the engine and tore across the landscape. Amy clutched me tighter with a gasp, and I couldn't help the grin on my face or the leaping thrill in my blood as she pressed against my back.

The wind made her dress flutter behind us, baring her legs that cradled mine. When we got to a comfortable cruising speed my fingers itched to fall to the side, to rest on her knee that gently pressed on my outer thigh. My thoughts weren't even sexual in nature, at least not entirely. I just wanted to casually touch her with no ulterior motives, because she was there.

I wanted to touch her to give her comfort, maybe even seek comfort from her. And something else I realized with the clarity of the cool evening wind whipping at my face: I wanted to touch her like she was mine.

While my grip tightened on the handlebars, Amy had begun to relax. Her hands rested on my hips, her torso leaning lightly against my back. The elevation began increasing as I headed for the mountains, and the roads started to wind.

Amy leaned her weight on me with every turn, just as I told her to. She remained relaxed, even as the roads grew steeper and the turns more harrowing. I knew these roads well and her body language suggested she trusted me. The higher we climbed, the more the temperature dropped, and the only tension I felt from her was an occasional shiver from the cold.

I pulled onto the next available turnout, which just happened to have a spectacular view of the full moon and the forested valley below.

After shutting the bike off, I leaned forward to peel my suit jacket from my arms. "Here, put this on." I held it out toward Amy. "I could feel you shivering."

"Thanks." Her voice came out muffled from within the helmet's padding.

"You can take that off if you want," I said, sliding off the bike. "I'm not about to punt you into the valley."

With a laugh, she removed the helmet and shook out her hair. "Is this our destination?"

I realized I was staring as she smoothed her hair out, and turned to look beyond the guardrail. "I didn't have a destination in mind," I admitted. "I just thought you'd want to get away for a bit."

"Well, this is beautiful." She walked up next to me, swimming in the jacket she'd put on. The moonlight made her eyes shine even brighter, like two galaxies in the cosmos. "Is all of that still Sanguine?" She pointed at the distant mountain range, the contours of the sharp, jagged peaks just barely visible.

"Yes, that's the Crown. The northernmost region of Sanguine. If you head east," I pointed to the right, "you'll eventually run into Vargmore, the werewolves' land. But those mountains are ours."

"What's with the names?" Amy wondered. "The Crown, the Heart. I've heard vampires say Sapien is in the Ribs. Is all of Sanguine supposed to be a body?"

"Yes, actually. We believe Sanguine to be the body of Temkra, our primary deity. The story goes that she lay down and sacrificed her flesh and blood so that her children, the vampires, would have a home."

"Oh." Amy fell quiet for a few moments. "I see. That's really beautiful, actually."

"Sometimes I do forget how beautiful this place is." My gaze remained on Amy's face. "It's nice to be reminded."

"And who is Rathka?" Amy walked forward, approaching the guardrail.

"Temkra's younger brother. He's an opposing force to Temkra. While the goddess is nurturing, patient, loving, Rathka is impulsive, vain, and violent."

Amy turned to look at me, an impish smirk on her face. "And your clan chose to embody him over the goddess?"

"Correct again." I sighed. "Rathka's Order was a warrior clan, but we also enjoyed wealth. Obscene wealth, often to the detriment of other vampire clans. Some believe we took it too far, and that's why Rathka turned his back on us, and cursed us."

"With the sickness that made your clan monsters?"

I nodded. "The Crown region was actually my clan's territory. The fortress I grew up in is just beyond those mountains."

"Do you miss any of it?" Amy asked gently. "Your home? Your family?"

I let out a long, heaving breath. "Yes. I guess I do. I mean, it's where I spent my childhood. They were the people who raised me. We used to be at the top of the vampire hierarchy, and now it's just... me." I frowned, trying fruitlessly to untangle the complicated feelings I'd carried my whole life. "I had everything I ever wanted, but I wouldn't call my childhood happy. I can't definitively say if I ever loved my family. Especially as everyone around me got sicker and I never changed."

"I'm sorry," Amy said. "That must have been so scary and isolating, watching everyone change like that with no answers." She slid her arms underneath mine and looped them around until she was gently hugging my bicep, her head leaning on my shoulder. "If your family knew you've been trying to find a cure all this time, I'm sure they'd be so proud of you." Her head lifted and her voice brightened with hope. "If you discover it, you'll be able to tell them then. Wouldn't that be amazing?"

I smiled in spite of myself. She was so pure-hearted, she had no idea. If my father was still out there, and I cured him of Rathka's Curse, he'd flay me alive with silver knives for allowing Blood 'til Dawn to become the ruling clan, a title he believed belonged to Rathka's Order alone. Of course, he conveniently ignored the historical facts that we'd never managed to hold onto the ruling seat in the few, brief times we'd had it.

"Honestly, I don't know if I'm any closer to finding a cure now than when I started," I admitted. "Part of me wants to throw my hands in the air and give up, but... " I trailed off, once again at a loss to describe my feelings of obligation to my family. I didn't love them, actually hated them most days. But they were my kin, my blood. I owed them the effort, didn't I?

"You still feel the need to be loyal to them," Amy said. "Like a sense of duty."

I looked at her. "Yes, that's exactly it." Her embrace around my arm had loosened, and my fingers found hers to entwine with gently. "Don't tell me your family is like mine."

"My blood family? Never knew them," she said with a shrug. "Sapien's population has been shrinking over the years because so many humans left to live among the vampires. The elders said that's what my parents did. Tavia's too. The whole community raised us. So they're all my family, in a way."

"That can be good and bad." I walked toward the guardrail at the edge of the turnout and stepped over it, leading Amy along by the hand.

When I took a seat, she settled down next to me. We had an unobstructed view now, the massive moon painting the mountains and valley below in silvery light.

"Yeah, it wasn't all good." Amy released my hand to clasp hers together in her lap. "I was... bullied. A lot. The only one who ever stood up for me was Tavia."

"Bullied? Why?" I stared at her, unable to comprehend it.

She was breathtakingly beautiful, clever, and so sweet. Not that cruel behavior toward a child was ever warranted, but it just didn't make sense to me. If I were a human boy, I'd be a stammering, blushing mess every time I talked to her. As a man, I would have been trying to impress her, to court her until she told me off or agreed to be mine.

Like you're trying to do now?

"I was born premature," Amy explained. "So I've always been small for my age and I had some health conditions. A heart murmur and asthma. I never could keep up with other kids my age, so I got ridiculed for it."

"Fuck. That's terrible."

I didn't have the exact same experience but could relate to what she must have felt. My brother and I were constantly thrown into competition against each other, and it was never a fair match. He was forty years older than me, and bigger and crueler in every way.

"As an adult, I still struggled with a lot of things," Amy went on. "Anything to do with manual labor, really. I think people started to resent me because I couldn't push myself as hard to contribute. So I tried in other ways. Cooking, making blankets in the winter, watching children while parents worked." She let out a sigh that seemed to deflate her whole chest. "Don't know if it ever made an impact though."

"I'm certain that it did," I said. "You don't need brute strength to be valuable to a community. It sounds like they didn't appreciate you enough."

She shrugged and laughed lightly. "Whether I was appreciated or not didn't matter to me, honestly. I was always happy to help. It felt like I was doing something important, keeping our human community alive in a vampire-run world."

That was one place she and I differed greatly. All my life, I sought approval from my father and my brother. I thirsted for a single word of praise or pride like a prized drop of blood. Sometimes I wondered if I was still chasing that approval, that acknowledgment that I'd done well by our clan, by trying to find this fucking cure.

Amy's smile faded as her fingers rubbed absently at her throat. "Since becoming a brusang, I haven't felt any of my symptoms from before. No shortness of breath, no crazy heartbeats or feeling faint. I feel physically stronger too. I bet I could do a lot more for them now than before."

"It must be the healing properties of vampire blood," I mused.

She laughed bitterly. "But would they even want me back now?"

"Are you thinking of going back?" My chest squeezed with an uncomfortable ache at the thought.

"I don't know." She sighed again. "Now that Tavia's got a life beyond fighting my battles for me, I have to figure stuff out. I just never thought we'd end up in such different places, you know?"

"She's not going anywhere," I reminded her. "She's still your friend. You two live in the same place."

"I know, it's just different now." Amy laughed. "It sounds silly, but we really were attached at the hip all the time. People thought we were sisters. Now I have to do life without her."

I waited a long time, weighing the pros and cons of my next thought before taking the leap and saying it. "You have me, you know."

Amy reached across her lap and placed her hand in mine. The small touch sent a fire blazing through me.

"Thanks for saying that. And you have me too, Novak."

"Thank Temkra for that." My thumb moved across her wrist, and it was only then I noticed that her veins felt more rigid and prominent than they should have. Almost like tendons instead of blood vessels. Her face looked fine, if a bit thinner than usual.

"Akra, when did you last feed?"

Amy lifted an eyebrow. "When I was last at your house. Why?"

Concern tightened my chest. "That was over a week ago. Why didn't you take blood during the week?"

"I don't know." She pulled her hand from my lap, turning her gaze away.

"Aren't you hungry? Your veins are stiff, have you not been feeling well? You should have told me."

"It's not a big deal," she protested. "I'm a little hungry, sure. But I've felt okay all week." Holding her wrist in her opposite hand, she mumbled something else under breath.

"What was that?"

"I just... I... " She stopped and chewed her lip with her small fangs. "Never mind. It's probably weird and childish."

"Akra, tell me," I urged. "You're new to this; there's no need to be embarrassed." I reached for her hand again, just lightly brushing my knuckles against her fingers. "I would never ridicule you."

Amy slowly opened her fingers, allowing my hand to rest in her palm. She spoke looking down at our hands, in a voice almost too quiet for me to hear.

"I don't want blood from anyone but you."

My chest tightened again, but for a different reason. Pride and affection threatened to burst through my ribcage. She wanted me, and only me. To her, it may have been childish, but to me it was everything.

"Let's ride back," I suggested. "We can stop at a restaurant for a glass, then find somewhere private for you to feed."

Amy looked up briefly, then returned her gaze to our hands. She turned my hand over and gently stroked her thumb across my wrist as I had done to her. I heard the small hiss of breath as she touched my pulse, her fangs growing long and her pupils dilating.

"Can I try without the glass?" She was already lifting my wrist toward her mouth.

Please, yes, I begged inside my head. *Put your lips on my skin. Taste me and take what you need.*

"Are you sure?" I asked with a tight breath.

She unbuttoned my cuff and pushed my sleeve to my elbow. Just the light drag of her fingers on my forearm lit up my nerves like lightning in a storm. She could touch me anywhere and it would be bliss.

"I don't want you using the knife," she said. "I don't like seeing you hurt yourself for me."

"It's not a problem. Don't make yourself uncomfortable for my sake."

"I'm not uncomfortable."

Her lips touched the skin of my wrist in a moment of heightened anticipation before her fangs sank in. The sharp penetration was brief and little more than a scratch, and then her instincts took over. Amy's lips sealed over the wound and she began to pull from my vein.

My eyes shunted closed at the sensations sweeping my body. It had been so long since I directly fed anyone, and I remembered it being pleasant.

But this... This was something else entirely.

Every draw of her mouth was like a caress on my erogenous zones. My neck, my groin, even my lips and ears. I shuddered with sensitivity, desire filling me with aching need. Why wasn't she in my lap? The only thing better than her pulling on my vein would be if her ass pressed against my cock at the same time. Then I could bite the nape of her neck, tease between her legs with my free hand, anything to make her feel just as good as I did.

"Akra. Darling." My fangs throbbed in time with the pulse in my cock, the need for her rendering my words as little more than growls.

Amy's aroused scent bloomed in the air, tangy and floral. Her thighs pressed together, hips shifting in little squirming movements. My forearm pressed between her breasts as she sucked at my wrist. I used my free hand to push her hair from her neck, massaging and caressing her nape as I leaned in. Fuck, she smelled incredible. I hadn't even tasted her yet and I was drunk on this woman. I wanted to drown in her.

"Amy... " Her name left my mouth as a reverent moan, the type of thing I would say at the height of pleasure.

But saying her name seemed to break a spell.

Amy removed her fangs from my wrist and turned her head to face me. I had leaned in so close that her forehead and nose pressed to mine.

"Novak?"

The question in her voice was what sobered me and prompted me to pull back. Sexual need still coursed through me, and her bloodstained teeth and lips did nothing to dissuade it. Those bright, questioning eyes with her bloodthirsty mouth took my breath away and would fuel my fantasies for ages to come.

But she had stopped feeding and my mind cleared of the overpowering lust. I realized what I was about to do—bite her in return, and touch her in ways that were anything but platonic.

Two things she had definitely not asked for, and would certainly erase all trust if I carried out those desires. She felt safe with me and that was not something I intended on changing.

"Have you had enough?" I asked, my voice like gravel.

Amy licked her lips then ran her tongue over her teeth, and it was all I could do to stifle the groan in my throat.

"I think so. Thank you, Nov—"

"Good. Let's get you back." I stood from the guardrail, stepped over it, and hurried back to the bike before I could do anything I regretted.

Chapter 13

Amy

Novak dropped me off back in town, just outside of the guarded perimeter of the blood mate ceremony. He barely said, "See you later," before taking off in the direction of his house.

I could only stare at his shrinking red taillight as he drove away, wondering what the abrupt change in demeanor was all about. One minute, I had his incredible blood in my mouth, my body filled with sensations as we drew closer together. He was leaning in, almost like he was going to kiss me. Or even bite me in return.

And then he pulled away, like getting any closer to me would have been a huge mistake.

Did I want him to bite me? I wasn't entirely sure. The idea didn't completely turn me off, especially if receiving a bite felt anywhere near as good as taking one. It was almost embarrassing how close I'd been to coming. Did he freak out because of that? Could he even tell?

I wandered past the perimeter into the square, where people continued to celebrate Tavia and Cyan's mating. A barrel of wine had been tapped in one area, and people were gathering as if to toast the couple. Tavia and Cyan stood nearby, attached at the hip with beaming smiles and cups filled with wine.

"Go for a little joyride, did you?"

I turned in the direction of the voice and saw a cloud of red smoke before the speaker. Thorne pushed off from the brick wall he'd been leaning on, tossed the remains of his cigarette, and lit up another.

His slow approach made me bristle. "Were you waiting for me to come back?"

"I wasn't sure *if* you'd come back, to be honest." Darakt smoke billowed from his nostrils as he flicked ash away. "Thought I might have to cut the party short to investigate a kidnapping."

Thorne's tone was always dry. I could never tell if he was being sincere or sarcastic.

"And now that I'm here?" I asked. "Are you going to punish either of us for disobeying your order?"

"Did you want to go for a joyride with him?"

"Yes."

"Did he harm you in any way?"

"No, of course not."

"Then I have much better things to do, believe it or not. It's a shame you didn't listen, though. You'll just have to find out the hard way."

"Find out what?" I said, exasperated. "What horrible things his ancestors did to yours, so therefore he must be just as bad? Even though he's his own person and has only ever been kind to me?"

Thorne's expression held mild curiosity as he listened to me speak. "You'll understand after you've lived a few centuries, little brusang. Blood is a powerful substance— that's how it sustains us. And when the same blood flows through generations, you learn to expect the same behavior."

"Humans aren't like that," I argued. "We give people chances. We don't judge someone just because they came from a bad family. People can rise above their circumstances."

"Sure, because humans live for like, two weeks compared to us," he scoffed before taking a long drag. "But you're not human anymore. Don't forget that."

"Tavia still is, isn't she? Even though she'll live as long as Cyan now."

"Hmm, I don't know." Thorne cocked his head, eyes focusing on some distant plane as he pondered. "She's biologically the same, unlike you. But she's still touched by Temkra's magic, bonded by blood and love to a non-human." His red gaze slid over to me, a smirk tilting his lips. "Guess it begs the question of what it means to be human, doesn't it? Will Tavia lose her humanity, whatever that is, as she lives for hundreds of years?"

"No." I shook my head confidently. "I'm certain she won't."

"I suppose we'll see." His gaze turned appraising as he took me in from head to toe. Not in a way that creeped me out, but it definitely took me aback. "You look nice tonight, by the way. A whole world away from where you were two weeks ago. Holding up well?"

"Yes," I sighed, not caring to discuss my mental state with him. "Believe it or not, I'm not actually made of tissue paper."

"Oh, I believe it." He turned to watch the party, a cigarette between his index and middle finger. "What I can't believe is you flaunting a Rathka's Order vampire at a Blood 'til Dawn event. It's not just bold, it's... in poor taste."

I stiffened, my jaw clenching. "I won't apologize for inviting him. He's my friend. He's been there for me, and I didn't want to be alone."

"Friends, huh?" Thorne mocked. "Is that what I saw?"

A large figure approached us before I could argue any more. I thought it was Rhain at first, but this person had gray skin and prominent lower fangs to match the upper set. The sudden memory of huge fangs and yellow eyes hit me like a freight train, panic stealing all the breath in my lungs.

It was the same monster that attacked Sapien.

The same one that killed me.

The monster extended a hand to Thorne, and the two of them clasped forearms in greeting.

"Beautiful ceremony, Thorne. Looks like your guests can't get enough of the marrow dishes."

"They were delicious, Drace. Thank you for coming."

"I'm just glad Cyan finally got his head out of his ass. She's a lovely blood mate."

"Yes, they make a fine couple."

"I'm on my way out. This moonlight is getting too strong for me. Just wanted to pay my respects."

"I'll come to Marrowtown soon. We need to catch up."

"I'll hold you to that, topsoil."

With a chuckle and another forearm clasp, the two of them separated. I'd been frozen in fear during their entire brief conversation, and only when the monster turned his red eyes to me, gave a small nod and said, "Good evening, miss," did the urge to run kick in.

Before I could escape and warn Tavia, Thorne clamped a hand down on my shoulder.

"Easy," he muttered. "You're not in danger. Calm down, little brusang. Your heart's beating so fast, it's vibrating."

"But he... that was... "

"He's a Marrower. Related to those who attacked your home, but he wasn't among them. Drace looks like a scary brute, but he's harmless. Calm. Down."

"How?" I hyperventilated. "How do you know?"

"Because the Marrowers who attacked Sapien were drugged. You remember the yellow eyes? They had no control over what they did. Unlike warmongering Rathka's Order, Marrowers by nature are the most peaceful of the vampires. You are safe, Amy."

His mention of Rathka's Order reminded me of Novak, which was the first step in edging me away from my panic. Eventually, my breaths calmed to the point where Thorne released my shoulder.

"Feel better?" he grunted.

"I... I didn't know they were... " I turned in the direction the Marrower had gone, but he was already out of sight.

"Marrowers keep to themselves. They stay underground for the most part. A couple have topside businesses, marrow eateries mostly. But the best stuff is in Marrowtown." Thorne lit up another cigarette, eyeing me through the red smoke. "You sure you're all right? Not gonna go all tissue paper on me?"

"I always thought of the attackers as monsters but now I feel kind of bad," I admitted. Drace actually wasn't unattractive, despite the initial shock of the big lower fangs. "I didn't know they were just another type of vampire."

"Ah, they know what they look like. The tusks do it for some people. Everybody's got their thing."

"You're sure the attackers were drugged?" I asked. "What if it was some kind of illness, like with Novak's clan?"

Thorne shook his head, smoke billowing around him. "Not the same thing at all. We know this drug, and we're holding the attackers in our compound while they detox. Rathka's Curse is... " He took a long pause. "It's something else entirely, something that consumes the brain. There's nothing left of the person they once were. What they became is fucking nightmare fuel." Inhaling deeply on his cigarette, his eyes narrowed in thought. "Although, to a human settlement that keeps themselves closed off from vampires, they might believe someone afflicted with Rathka's Curse is the same thing as a drugged-out Marrower. Now that's a theory."

I watched him smoke, trying to connect the same dots he was. "You think someone is trying to pin the blame for the attack on Novak?"

"Not saying anything, except that a human from Sapien wouldn't know ass from elbow if that were the case."

"Fine," I groused, turning toward the flurry of activity in the center square. "I don't want to be involved in vampire politics anyway."

Tavia and Cyan were posing for photos, embracing intimately with beatific smiles on their faces. They held mostly still, shifting poses slightly after several shutter clicks.

"We want a kiss!" someone yelled. "Smooch his face off!"

The couple laughed at the cheers and wolf whistles encouraging more daring photos. Then they faced each other, Cyan's grinning lips murmuring something that looked like, "Let's give them something good," before meeting in a passionate, tongue-thrusting kiss.

Fists and wine glasses went up in the air, followed by jubilant cheers and more lewd suggestions.

"They look happy, don't they?"

I had forgotten about Thorne until he spoke. For a

moment, I was just as entranced by Tavia and Cyan's display of love as everyone else.

"Yeah," I answered, trying not to let my jealousy show. "They do."

Thorne's voice came directly next to my ear.

"If you want a chance of happiness like that, forget all about Novak of Rathka's Order. He'll only bring you misery."

Chapter 14

Amy

I leaned over the kitchen counter, my phone in my hands and my text thread with Novak on the screen. I lost track of how many times I'd typed out a message and then erased it.

The ceremony had been days ago, and I hadn't heard a single word from him since he abruptly dropped me off at the square, after I thought we'd had a nice time. Now I was second- and triple-guessing whether or not to message him first.

He'll only bring you misery.

Every time Thorne's words tried to shove their way into my mind, I pushed them back twice as hard. Not even the king of vampires and chain-smoking would make me think Novak was a bad person just because of his bloodline.

"Put your phone away and try this." Tavia shoved a wine glass with a few ounces of red liquid in my face.

I looked up, meeting her bright but hooded eyes. Her hair was up in a messy ponytail, a flush covering her neck, cheeks, and ears. A lazy smile seemed permanently fixed to her face since the ceremony. She looked blissed-out, or more crudely, well-fucked, like she woke up receiving at least five orgasms per day. Considering she was in her honeymoon phase, that probably wasn't far from the truth.

But more than anything, she looked happy and in love.

Obliging her, I set my phone down and picked up the wine glass by the stem, swirling it as I inhaled deeply.

Tavia was a master brewer, vintner, cideress, you name it. If it was fermented alcohol, she knew exactly how to make it delicious and drinkable. It was her biggest contribution to Sapien when we lived there. No one dared to mess with her because they didn't want to be cut off from the booze supply.

For the first time ever, I smelled something off and slightly foul in the wine. Almost a rancid, rotten scent. I schooled my features so as to not offend Tavia.

"Did you try something new?" I kept my tone casual, glad that she was pouring another taste for Bea and not watching my expression.

"I added a little bit of blood at the start of fermentation. It's an experiment, since vampires like to add blood to their drinks. Of course, Cyan can't taste it so I need unbiased, un-blood mated opinions."

"Whose blood, your own?"

That might have explained my aversion. Since Tavia had done the blood mate ritual at her ceremony, maybe her blood smelled off to me because her lifespan was now tied to Cyan's.

Another thing to consider was that I generally wasn't attracted to women. I remembered the sexual rush that came over me when I drank from Novak's wrist, as if I'd ever stopped thinking about it. He'd looked so close to kissing me, to pulling me into his lap and devouring me, and not just my blood.

If he'd have made a move, I would have given in. Enthusiastically. I had never wanted anyone so intensely before. He must have known that, must have seen me squirming as I drank from him. I was on the brink of an orgasm from his blood alone. He could have been... turned off? Weirded out? All I knew was that he stopped everything, took me home, and gave me the silent treatment.

Message fucking received.

"No, it's not my blood." Tavia laughed. "Cyan would have a fit; my blood is only for him. I went to the blood bank and bought a donated bag."

I frowned. Well, there went my theory.

"Is it human?" Bea inquired, taking a sip.

"Dragon shifter, actually."

"Ah, that explains it." Bea smacked her lips. "Just a little spicy. It's really good, Tav!"

"Thanks, Bea." Beaming, Tavia turned to me. "What do you think, Ames?"

"Oh, yeah!" I effused, swirling my glass more aggressively. "Same. It's delicious."

"Yay!" Tavia did a happy little twirl, which I'd never seen her do before. "It's just a test batch, but I'm really excited to jump into a whole new world of flavors with blood."

"Bet you never thought you'd say that." Bea smirked before draining the rest of her taster.

Tavia laughed. "Definitely not."

My phone buzzed with a message and I immediately zoned out of the conversation to read it. When I saw Novak's name, my chest felt like fireworks as I opened his text.

Hey, I'm sorry about how I acted the other night. It's been a long time since anyone fed from me directly and I forgot how intense it can be. I'm sorry if I freaked you out. I just wanted to make sure I was levelheaded before getting in touch.

My fingers hovered over the screen, trying to decipher his message. Words like *intense* didn't necessarily mean he was attracted to me, but they didn't mean he wasn't.

I waffled between full-on honesty or being more coy in my reply. In the end, I decided the full truth was best discussed in person.

You didn't freak me out. We're good. It was intense for me too, but not in a bad way. Can we talk about it more face-to-face? Just so I understand feeding better. Maybe when Jo is whipping up something delicious? :)

Haha, yes. Of course. She works this weekend. I'll let her know you'll be here. :) Any requests?

I'm open to surprises ;)

Just when it comes to food?

"Amy, hey."

I looked up from being engrossed in my phone to see that Cyan, Tavia's mate, had entered the room. I hadn't even heard him come in, but he was across the counter, his arms around Tavia's waist.

"Hey, Cyan."

"Can we talk for a second?" The vampire released my friend and nodded at the couches across the room.

"Um, sure." I stared at Tavia, who shrugged. Her face gave no hints as to what her mate would want to talk to *me* about.

Was it over Novak? His texts sounded like he was starting to flirt with me and I was really eager to get back to my conversation with him. Blood 'til Dawn couldn't track my phone activity, could they?

I followed Cyan nervously to two armchairs at the farthest end of the room. He sat in one and gestured for me to take the other.

"So, what's up?" I did my best to sound unbothered as I sat down across from him.

He said nothing for a few moments, which didn't help my nerves at all. He just watched me with those sharp, red eyes. Brighter and a little eerier than Novak's.

"How are you holding up?" Cyan asked finally.

"With what?"

He let out a soft chuckle. "Must be good, then. I just mean everything in general. The attack, coming to live here, all the adjustments afterward."

"Oh, well... "

My arms instinctively crossed over my stomach. Aside from seeing the Marrower after the ceremony, I only thought of the attack on Sapien when I saw my scars in the mirror.

Since meeting Novak, I felt like I had emerged from a fog. My first two weeks as a brusang were awful, but that almost felt like a different existence. I had been drowning in the grief of my human life, and Novak was my first real breath of fresh air. He made me feel like I could be okay as a brusang.

Now, how to explain it to Cyan without hearing another lecture like the one I got from Thorne?

"I've been holding up okay," I said, giving him an earnest nod. "It was rough at first, but I think it's sunk in now. And I'm just doing my best."

"That's good." Cyan leaned back with a smile. "I'm glad to see you talking with Tavi again."

"Yeah, me too."

"I wanted to pull you aside because we're releasing the Marrowers who attacked Sapien."

A bolt of panic hit me, and a clear memory of that day surfaced. Roaring monsters with yellow eyes and large lower fangs.

"You are?"

"Yes." Cyan's gaze weighed heavily on me. "They've detoxed from the draitrium, and we've confirmed that none were in their right minds at the time of the attack. Someone set them upon the settlement—none of them chose to do it. If you recognize any of them around the Heart, we're confident that they would never intentionally hurt you."

"Oh my God. Thorne mentioned they were drugged."

"That's correct." Cyan sighed. "Now we're tasked with helping on repairs and finding out who drugged them." He lifted a hand. "That's not something for you to worry about, though. I just wanted to make you aware those Marrowers are actually innocent."

"You're helping to repair Sapien?" I asked, an idea striking me like lightning.

"Yeah, the property damage was substantial. And we feel responsible, since our part of the Half-Century Agreement includes protecting the settlement from attacks."

"Do you think... I could come?"

Cyan's eyebrows lifted. "You want to come with us?"

"Well, yeah. I mean, that was my home. Plus, I've been

wanting something to fill my time. I can mend fences, help clean up any debris, whatever you need."

A sense of homesickness filled me. I hadn't seen Sapien in over a month. I missed Robin, who was like a mother figure to me and Tavia. I missed the woods where we'd go foraging, the sounds of roosters crowing in the morning, the community kitchen and the smell of food cooking. I even missed the people, despite knowing few of them cared for me.

"I don't know if that's a good idea, Amy," Cyan said. "Tavia and I snuck you out of there, making them believe you'd heal better if you lived with your best friend. Have any of those humans even seen a brusang before?"

"I don't know, probably not." I shrugged. "But I am still human in a sense, right?"

"Yes." The word was hesitant and drawn-out. "But also no. You're not the same as you once were. And Sapien's humans pride themselves on *not* integrating with vampires. Forgive me for saying this, because there is absolutely nothing wrong with being a brusang, but," he looked uncomfortable, fangs digging into his lower lip, "you might be a little *too* vampiric for them."

My excitement began to deflate. "You think I shouldn't go?"

"That's up to you. If you want to come, we'll be glad of the help. I just know Tavi wants to leave that place behind because of how they treated both of you. It holds painful memories for her." His brow furrowed with concern. "I would hate it if going back dug up old wounds for you."

He was right to be concerned. I wasn't sure how I would have survived if I didn't have Tavia with me. But then again, I never got the chance to find out. If a bully shoved me in a mud puddle, she immediately did the same to them. When a boy stole my clothes when we went swimming, she rubbed poison oak all over his pants before I even knew my stuff was missing.

Who would I have been if I wasn't in Tavia's shadow?

I had stood up for myself more in the weeks since becoming a brusang than in my whole human life. Cyan was right; I wasn't the same as before. But I needed to revisit my past to know how. I couldn't fully articulate why. It was some mix of seeking nostalgia and closure at the same time. All I knew was I needed to go back, this time without my bulldog at my side.

"I would still like to go," I said. "I need to, for me."

Cyan nodded gravely. "All right then. We're buying materials and tools then heading over there next week."

"Thanks for letting me tag along."

"Sure. I just hope they remember your teeth are sharper." He stood with a smirk. "Thanks for talking with me."

Another idea hit me as he started to turn away. "Oh hey, Cyan."

"Yeah?"

"I know you said not to worry, but the drugged Marrowers. You're trying to trace where the drug came from?"

"Yeah. We took blood samples when they got here." He blew out a breath. "Unfortunately, none of us are smart enough or well-equipped enough to do anything with them. I'm sure the properties of the drug can be isolated, which would tell us more. Thorne's reaching out to his sources, but we don't have an on-hand nerd to do any testing. So our hands are a bit tied."

I took a deep breath, bracing myself. "Novak has a lab. He's very, I dunno, sciencey. I'm sure he could help in some way."

Cyan barked out a laugh. "What?" He leaned in closer,

nearly whispering. "Novak of Rathka's Order? You can't be serious."

"I am serious. It's just a suggestion, anyway. Wouldn't hurt to ask him."

"Uh, yeah it would." Cyan gave me an incredulous look. "You're really into him, aren't you? Shit." He lowered his mouth to my ear, actually whispering. "Did he make you his blood pet? Is that why he had to show his face at my ceremony?"

"No!" I jerked away, anger heating my face. "He didn't even want to come, because he knew it would cause friction. I wanted him there. He hasn't even fed from me once, for fuck's sake. If anything, he's *my* blood pet."

Cyan shook his head, casting his gaze around the room before returning to me. "I would not go around making statements like that, if I were you."

"Why not?" I shot back. "He's nice to me, and he doesn't judge me for who I'm friends with."

Cyan's jaw clenched, like he was holding back a tidal wave of things he wanted to say. "Just be careful around him. Rathka's Order, they were not good people. They used my kin," he pointed to himself, "to build armies to fight against the werewolves, while they sat back, safe and warm in their castle in the Crown. Just because we were a poorer, more expendable clan. They had the blood of other vampires on their hands."

My breath stuttered. When Novak mentioned his clan did awful things to Blood 'til Dawn, I never imagined it was something like that.

"I'm sorry that happened. Really I am, but none of that is Novak's fault."

"What's that human saying?" Cyan tilted his head. "The apple doesn't fall far from the tree? Oh wait, there's another one. A chip off the old block, something like that?"

I continued to glare while Cyan shook his head and sighed again.

"Just be careful, Amy. For your sake, I hope he's different. But it's widely believed that his clan was so morally corrupt, Rathka himself turned his back on them."

"You're talking about the sickness, Rathka's Curse?"

"Is it really a curse if all it did was expose their true nature?"

"Novak didn't receive the Curse," I argued. "By your own reasoning, he is different from the others."

"Or," Cyan countered, "he got the worst punishment by having to witness it all. To watch the fall of his clan, the eradication of his family, and be left with nothing."

Chapter 15

Novak

"Come in," I said to the soft knock at my office door.

Lourna cleared her throat. "You have a visitor in the foyer, sir."

I looked up from my data printouts. "Amy?"

"Sadly, no." The human woman looked just as disappointed as I felt. "It's ah, Thorne of Blood 'til Dawn."

"Thorne?" I couldn't hide my surprise at who was essentially the vampire king coming to see me himself.

"I'll be right down, Lourna. Thank you. Offer him something while he waits."

"Of course."

She left and I tried to wrap my brain around what Thorne could possibly want. He had to be pissed about my showing up to the mating ceremony. Naturally, he didn't like me walking freely in and out of his territory. Not that I could blame him, but I would stand my ground.

Without a clan to rally behind me, I had no true power against Thorne. All I had was my dignity. He wasn't going to have me groveling for an apology. And if he really was the just and fair ruler he claimed to be, he wouldn't cut down a man who was already powerless.

Only one thing was for certain. I sure as hell would not let Amy shoulder the blame.

I waited a few more minutes before heading down to the foyer. The scent of darakt itched my nose as I came down the stairs.

"Thorne, welcome," I said as I hit the ground floor.

"You can skip the pleasantries, Novak." His lip curled into a snarl. "You don't want me here and I don't want to waste my time. Where can we chat privately?"

If someone wandered into Sanguine for the first time today and saw him, they never would have believed Thorne to be the head of the ruling vampire clan. He wore a threadbare T-shirt under a well-creased leather jacket, probably a relic from the 1970s. His darkwash jeans were faded to gray, and his leather motorcycle boots were scuffed to hell. He looked like an ordinary working-class vampire from the Heart, maybe a mechanic or darakt manufacturer.

Before they made the challenge to rule and won, the Blood 'til Dawn vampires had been exactly that: manual laborers with humble roots.

"Fine with me. Would you prefer somewhere you can smoke?" I noticed he played with a lighter, and a pack of darakt cigarettes sat in his shirt pocket. Just because he was abrupt didn't mean that I forgot my manners.

"Yes, sir," he sneered with a fake upper class accent to mimic my own. "I would prefer that very much indeed."

I ignored his mocking, and turned to lead him through the house. "This way."

Trying not to be obvious, I glanced over my shoulder and in mirrors to watch him. Not that I believed he would steal anything, but I wouldn't put it past him to spit on my floors. And I'd be damned if Lourna cleaned up any mess he made. Thorne could grab a rag and spray bottle and do it himself.

I reached the door to a small patio just off of the downstairs library, opened it and stepped aside for him. "Choose any ashtray you like. Make yourself at home."

Thorne meandered around the patio, checking out the stringed bulbs offering gentle light, the ferns, small trees, and red-flowered plants lining the perimeter, and the outdoor furniture that Lourna kept in immaculate condition.

"Nice little jungle you got here." Thorne eased himself into the loveseat, choosing the ash tray on the side table that had belonged to one of my uncles. "I want something like this at our compound. It's just that no one seems to have much of a green thumb."

"Most of the plants were my mother's." I sat across from him, downwind from where his smoke would travel. "I'm fortunate that my housekeeper seems to be good at keeping them alive."

"How nice for you. Smoke?" Thorne held out a cigarette toward me.

"No, thank you. What can I do for you?"

He grinned slowly, red smoke curling from the corners of his lips. "Do you have any vices, Cursed One? Or are you too good for any of them?"

I shrugged. If by vice he meant unhealthy obsession, that would be finding the cure to Rathka's Curse. Day in and day out, that was what kept me going for at least a century. But that addiction was becoming more burdensome than thrilling in recent months. There was no longer a high to chase, no hope for relief. Like a long-time addict, I simply kept going because I no longer knew any other way to live.

"Or maybe your vices go beyond darakt," Thorne continued to muse. "Got a sex dungeon in this fancy house? A harem of blood pets you fuck and drink from?"

My expression didn't change despite Thorne's taunting. My dungeon downstairs was anything but a sexual kink. It was my biggest source of shame and mental torment.

"What do you want, Thorne?"

He continued taking his sweet time, settling comfortably on my couch while red smoke billowed around him like a blood aura.

"Did you enjoy the blood mate ceremony?" he asked in return. "It was awfully nice of Tavia's friend to invite you, despite my explicitly forbidding you to see her."

"Is that what this is about, then?" I straightened. "So punish me for disobeying. Just leave Amy alone."

Thorne's eyes narrowed. "I know that she invited you to the ceremony. That she has been coming here to see you. As far as obeying my order, you've actually been a good boy." He flicked the end of his cigarette. "Are you fucking her?"

My lip curled, as did my fists. "No. And don't talk about her so crassly."

"Oh lighten up, for fuck's sake." He finished his cigarette and promptly stuck another one in his mouth. "So, what's got her so interested in you? She like rich boys?"

"I don't know," I answered. "Maybe Blood 'til Dawn hasn't been the most welcoming family, so she's seeking a friendly connection elsewhere."

"Her best friend is part of our clan."

"Her best friend who's been planning the ceremony and spending all her time with her new mate? Yes, I'm sure Amy feels like a priority over there."

"Is that what she is to you?" Thorne's eyes sharpened. "A priority?"

I sighed, feeling exhausted with this pointless questioning. "She's a friend. Someone I've come to care deeply about. When she comes here, I can't bring myself to turn her away. Whatever she's getting from me, it's clearly not available at home. If that's a crime according to Blood 'til Dawn, fine. Punish me however you see fit. But don't come down on her for seeking a friend."

Thorne was quiet for a long while, pensively smoking. "What's your stance on draitrium?"

It was an abrupt shift in topic, but I went along with it anyway. "Draitrium needs to be heavily regulated. It's far too dangerous otherwise."

"Regulated?" he barked. "Why, so the burnt-out husks of bodies don't stack too high?"

"You know there are rare occasions when our kind may be exposed to sunlight, either accidentally or by circumstances that can't be avoided. Small, regulated amounts of draitrium could prevent serious burns or even death. It could save someone's life in the right circumstances, Thorne. You'd rather let them die than take a substance that protects them from sun exposure?"

"Our kind are not meant to live in the sunlight. That is an indisputable fact. It's the one thing that Temkra and Rathka both agreed on." Thorne leaned forward, his fangs bared. "This drug will wipe us out before it saves us. No matter how you try to rationalize its usefulness, you know I'm right."

"You want drae eradicated for good, I take it."

"Of course I do," Thorne hissed.

"How?" I asked. "Seriously, how do you expect to do that without financially ruining Sanguine? It's the basis of our alliance with the dragon shifters. They depend on our business to mine it. What happens to them if the demand dries up?"

"Like I give a fuck about the dragon shifters." Thorne rolled his eyes. "I'm more concerned about the vampire families being torn apart by addiction."

"The addictive qualities are concerning, yes," I agreed. "Which is another reason for regulation. If the draitrium ore is further studied and tested, it can perhaps be bonded to other chemical compounds that will lessen the side effects while keeping the benefits."

"Something you'd love to do, I'm sure. I hear you're something of a scientist."

I shrugged. "It is terrible that draitrium can only be bought through street dealers. Regulation would mean only certain amounts can be purchased, which would reduce the risk of abuse and overdose. If we had them available at medical facilities with licensed professionals handling the dosage—"

"Like your ancestors did to mine?"

The accusation stopped me short. I was foolish not to have seen it coming. Thorne would never actually listen when it came to this topic, or any other probably. Not as long as this stain darkened our history. He was too emotionally close to the subject.

I brought my palms together, working to keep my voice level and calm. One of us had to be. Despite coolly smoking darakt, Thorne was anything but calm. I could feel the deep, seething hatred from across the table like a bonfire.

"My family was wrong to do that to yours," I said. "I was young at the time, and didn't learn of the deception until the aftermath. I truly thought it was an honest mistake.

At the time, I didn't believe my father could be so purposely malicious."

Thorne laughed bitterly. "Not a single point of that plan wasn't made with malicious intent. From the moment Rathka's Order purchased ninety percent of the draitrium coming in, they planned to murder with it. Their own people, other vampires."

"I don't deny that," I said.

"They got my father, Kalix's father and brother, and so many more, hopped up on drae for what? Because it sure as hell wasn't for a surprise attack on the werewolves like they claimed."

I nodded, lowering my head. "Our elders felt threatened by the growing support of your clan. You had the love of the people, and our power was slipping from our grasp."

"An entire generation of vampires wiped out," Thorne continued. "Burned to death by the sun near the Vargmore border. Your clan even pinned the blame on the werewolves, saying they must have been captured and thrown outside in broad daylight. We proved that they lied, and got silenced for it."

"It's abhorrent," I said. "Not only what was done, but the lies and the effort taken to cover it up. I deeply regret that my bloodline and my clan name was ever tied to such actions."

I lifted my gaze to Thorne's, still wondering what he wanted. An apology? I'd give one happily, along with restitution for his clan if he wanted that. I'd never stand by the atrocities my ancestors committed. Whatever proof of that he needed, I would give.

"Did you give draitrium to a bunch of Marrowers and set them to attack Sapien?"

My breath left my lungs like I'd been kicked in the

chest. I should have seen this coming too. Thorne's hatred of me and my clan truly knew no bounds.

"No." My calmness was hanging by a thread. "I had nothing to do with that."

"You sure?"

"Yes." My fangs grew long. Not to feed, but to use as potential weapons.

Thorne's eyes narrowed and he stubbed out his cigarette, for once not reaching for another one. "If you're lying, I will find out. And when I do, I will execute you. Publicly. Rathka's Order will be nothing but a bygone clan, a footnote in history."

"You'd love that, I'm sure," I said through gritted teeth. "But I am telling the truth."

"Right. Because you're so different from the others in your family, aren't you?" Thorne stood, brushing ash off his jeans. "The good, studious, second son. Spared by the Curse." He smirked. "Or cursed to live on? Hard to say."

"I'll see you out." I rose and gestured to the door leading back inside the house.

"I don't trust you with Amy." Thorne went ahead of me, leisurely walking back the way we came. "But we don't restrict personal freedoms in Blood 'til Dawn, even if we don't agree with those decisions. So as much as I hate it, I won't prevent her from seeing you."

"How generous of you."

That was why he wouldn't make it a clan decree, which would have made his order akin to a law. His clan prided itself on individual choice and freedoms, and would lose the support of the people if he started taking those away.

In any case, I wished he'd walk faster. The sooner he left my house, the better.

"If she's got an ounce of common sense, she'll figure it out on her own," Thorne mused, almost to himself.

I didn't reply. Amy had plenty of common sense. What she didn't have was preconceived notions of me based on what my family had done. She didn't blame me for their actions, and that was more refreshing than I realized. It was really damn nice to spend time with someone and let them get to know *me*. Just me, without the weight of my clan's history or reputation on my shoulders.

"Oh, congratulations, by the way." Thorne paused and turned to look at me just as he entered the foyer.

I stared at him, puzzled. "For what?"

He grinned like a shark, teeth on full display. "For your soon-to-be heir with Carpe Noctem's daughter. Rathka's Order just may live on after all."

My blood went cold. "How do you know about that?"

"The working class does have eyes and ears, you know. Even if they don't talk to their employers."

I thought of the brusang butler at the Carpe Noctem estate. His whole *I-exist-to-serve* shtick must have been an act. If I remembered correctly, there was another brusang besides Amy in Blood 'til Dawn. Maybe they knew the butler.

"I assume you've already told Amy, since you two are such *good* friends," Thorne went on, his tone mocking.

Despite my effort to school my features, he saw right through me and his grin became absolutely maniacal.

"Oh, you haven't? That's interesting. Well, I'm sure you'll tell her soon. Unless there's some reason you don't want her to know?" Thorne turned, letting himself out the front door as he said, "It would be a shame if she ended up hearing it from someone else."

"I... Of course I'll tell her," I called out. "Soon."

Thorne gave me one final, slimy smirk over his shoulder. "See that you do, Novak. See that you do."

"God, I love this view." I leaned against the doorway of Novak's office balcony, looking out at the city below and the mountains in the distance. "If I were you, I'd be looking out at this all the time."

Novak glanced up from the mess of notes on his desk, his gaze softening as he smiled. "I never noticed its beauty until you mentioned it. But maybe I'll start appreciating it more."

From my vantage point, he seemed to be looking at me, not at the landscape beyond the balcony railing. I looked toward the mountains again to hide the fact that I was blushing. He was doing that more often, saying things that sounded like he might be flirting, but I could never be sure.

We'd been in his office together for a couple of hours in mostly companionable silence. Before getting up to stretch, I had been working on a knitting project, a throw blanket, in one of Novak's armchairs while he worked at his desk. The silence between us was just as easy as our conversations. I loved that he didn't feel the need to fill quiet moments with the noise of his own voice. The scrapes of his pen, shuffling of papers, and the clicking of my knitting needles were the perfect ambiance to a relaxing evening.

"Take a break, you've been poring over those papers for hours." I went to his drink cabinet and started rummaging around.

"Sorry, am I boring you?" Again, he sounded playful.

"Massively." I closed my eyes halfway and made a long snoring sound.

He laughed, and I drank in the sound like water to a parched woman. "You're the one who showed up and wanted to hang out while I worked."

"And aren't you lucky I'm the most interesting thing in your life?" I pulled out two glasses and a corkscrew. "Want to try Tavia's wine?"

"Sure." Novak leaned back in his chair, stretching his arms above his head with a groan.

I might have let my eyes linger on him for a second too long before focusing on opening the wine bottle. Everything he did seemed to have inherent sex appeal lately. His smirks when he joked and teased me sent my heart racing a little faster. I found myself sneaking glances at his forearms and shoulders so often, you'd think I was raised to believe arms were pornographic.

And it wasn't just his arms, but his hands too. His throat, the crease between his brows. Even the way he walked, full of understated confidence. My crush on Novak was growing out of control and I was helpless to its whims.

After pouring two glasses of wine, I re-corked the bottle and noticed an end table covered in small objects against the far wall. One of the objects was a framed miniature painting of a figure in a barren, red landscape. My curiosity piqued, I went for a closer look, aware of Novak's approaching steps behind me.

The figure in the painting was feminine with long black hair spilling out from a masked headdress of feathers and some kind of animal skull. She was posed in a way that seemed to indicate dancing, wearing a long necklace of skulls, black and white striped paint, and nothing else.

Recognition hit me the moment Novak spoke up. "That's Temkra, our goddess."

"I saw her," I said, recalling the dancing, fanged figure that pulled me back from death. "Before I woke up as a brusang. She spoke to me."

"Did she?" Novak handed me one of the wine glasses as he lowered into a loveseat nearby.

This end of the office was cozier, with couches and ottomans, the drink cabinet, a few messy shelves, and a large window facing the same direction as the balcony. And of course, the end table with the Temkra painting, and a few scattered objects including a small bird skull and an incense tray.

As Novak placed his feet on the ottoman, he didn't look skeptical, but genuinely intrigued that I had seen his goddess, the mother of all vampires.

"What did she say to you?"

I took a sip of wine as I recalled it, thankful that Tavia didn't add any blood to this one. "She said I wasn't dead yet. That her blood was in my veins and I wasn't finished."

Novak's eyebrows went up. "Wow. That had to be a strange experience. Temkra doesn't speak to our kind very often. The recorded instances of it are few and far between."

I stared at him. "You mean, you believe me?"

"Of course I believe you. Why wouldn't I?"

"I dunno, it's just... " I went to sit next to him, propping my feet up on the same ottoman. "Human deities are a lot more intangible, I guess. There are a lot of non-believers because so much rests on having faith. When someone claims to have a special connection to God, the first thing people suspect are delusions. Maybe even a mental illness."

Novak chuckled. "It's not like that with us. Temkra and Rathka are very real, tangible presences in our lives. There's enough proof of their existence that pretty much all vampires believe in them to some degree." He looked at the miniature painting with a pensive sip of wine. "Temkra shows herself to those who pray and ask for guidance. As you can probably tell by the lack of burned incense, I haven't tried to communicate with her in years."

"Any reason for that?"

He shrugged with a small shake of his head. "I don't know. Maybe I feel like she turned her back on me. Rathka did after all, why not her? In any case, there's just nothing I have to say. Mainly I just keep the altar objects because they were my mother's. They're her only possessions I have."

I pulled my legs off the ottoman, sliding my shoes off to curl my feet underneath me on the couch. The position had me leaning closer to Novak.

"Do you remember much of her?"

He sighed, slouching into the couch cushion. "Not what she looked like. Mostly her voice. She sang lullabies to me in Vampiric. And her voice was very soft as she spoke, not just to me but everyone. I get the sense that she was a very gentle person, and that made her an outcast in a very blood-thirsty, aggressive clan."

"That's too bad. I wonder if she was lonely."

"I think she was." Novak nodded. "My father kept a few blood pets. He had his favorite, my half-brother's mother.

And my mother just happened to get pregnant, so she became secondary in the ranking, you could say."

I let my disgust show on my face. "That sounds like a very cold way to think of the mothers of your children."

"It was. There was no relationship between them. Just sex and blood and heirs to continue our lineage." He scoffed. "A whole lot of good that did."

"Well your dad sounds like an ass, but your mother sounds lovely." I rested my elbow on the back of the couch, facing Novak. "It's a shame you didn't have her longer."

"Yeah." He took a long sip of wine. "She was one of the first to succumb to Rathka's Curse, actually. Some of my earliest memories are of her acting strange. Staring at nothing for hours. A craving for meat, and really intense mood swings. Those behaviors were so far off from her normal personality, they had to be early symptoms."

"And the Curse never touched you?" I asked. "It wasn't like you caught the illness and got better, you just never had it?"

"No." Novak let out a dry laugh. "That's the one thing that's baffled me my entire life. The Curse spread like wild-fire; it seemed so contagious. I came into contact with so many of those afflicted, and yet it never affected me."

I paused to sip more wine and think. "I'm jealous of you."

"Jealous?" His incredulous expression made me laugh. "Of what?"

"One," I held up an index finger, "you had a mom, for however brief it was. Two, you must have been born with an iron-wall immune system, while I, as a preemie, had to live in an incubator for the first month of my life because my immune system was shit. And even after that, I had defects."

"There is absolutely nothing defective about you." The way he said it left no room for doubt, and his words warmed me all over.

"I guess that's subjective now. But as a human, I definitely did."

"All right, fine. Are you done humbling me?"

"Never, pretty boy." I pressed my foot against his leg and curled my toes to grip his pant leg.

Novak made an exaggerated show of looking down his nose at my foot. "Remove your toes at once, peasant."

"Peasant!" I cackled, waving my foot in his face. "How dare you!"

He set aside his wine and grabbed my foot, using his opposite hand to deliver a relentless tickle attack to my sole.

I screamed with laughter, kicking and flailing. "No, stop!"

Novak pulled my leg across his lap to more effectively trap my poor foot. His arm wrapped around my whole leg, bicep squeezing my thigh to hold me in place while he continued to ravage light, tickling touches across the bottom of my foot.

"I can't breathe!" Tears squeezed out of my eyes from the force of my laughter. "Stop, I'm gonna die."

At that, he released me, still wearing that haughty expression. "That'll teach you."

"Teach me what?" I struggled to catch my breath, still laughing too hard.

Finally he broke, his face stretching out into a laughing grin. "I don't even remember what I was punishing you for."

"Bravo." I clapped mockingly. "You play a rich asshole very well."

"I learned from the best."

Only when his thumb gently stroked my ankle did I

remember that my leg was still in his lap. My body must have tensed when I felt it, because the movement instantly stopped.

"Do you want me to move?" I asked.

"Only if you want to," he answered.

My leg stayed in his lap. After a few long seconds of silence, his gentle massage of my ankle resumed.

It felt nice. Novak's touch was so light, I knew there were no ulterior motives or expectations. It was sweet and affectionate just for the sake of it.

He switched hands, reaching for his wine nearby. I followed suit and took an indulgent sip of mine.

The silence began to feel heavy. Neither of us were blind to the fact that things were becoming more physical between us. At the same time, neither of us seemed willing to be the one to address it directly. We were friends, yes. But ever since the ceremony, we were dancing around a line that crossed from platonic to romantic.

Novak's thumb circled my ankle bone, his touch moving slightly up my shin. He looked straight ahead at the window with the mountain view. His face looked relaxed, content. Was he happy like this, sitting here with my foot in his lap? Did he like having me around to pester him while he worked?

Or was he thinking of having these moments with someone else? Did he keep me around because I was convenient and available to him? Novak didn't seem like that kind of guy, but that was how guys had treated me back in Sapien. And it wasn't like I had a lot of experience with men.

"So." I took my leg from his lap, curling them underneath me again. "I'm going back to Sapien tomorrow night."

I said the first thing to pop into my head to break the silence.

"You are?" Novak looked surprised. "Permanently?"

"Oh no, just to help Blood 'til Dawn with rebuilding from the attack."

"Oh." It might have been wishful thinking, but he looked relieved. "So you're getting more involved in clan activities, then?"

"I wouldn't call it that. Cyan tried to talk me out of going." I leaned my head against the back of the couch. "Be honest with me. Is it a stupid idea?"

"I can't give a definitive answer because that's completely subjective."

"Stop being such a *scientist*," I whined.

Novak chuckled. "Whatever I say doesn't matter because it would just be my opinion. You're the one going, so what do you think?"

"I don't know. I want to see the settlement and every-one, but I'm nervous."

"I think it's completely reasonable to feel that way." Novak held up his empty wine glass. "This is good. Do you want more?"

"Yes, please." I handed him my glass. "Told you Tavia was a winemaster."

"Is she going with you?" Novak stood and carried our empties to the cabinet to refill them.

"No. I think she'd be perfectly content to never go back," I admitted. "She never liked how they ran things there. Even if she never ended up with Cyan, I think she would have left to live among the vampires eventually."

"And you felt differently?"

Novak's back was to me as he poured our refills, looking even taller than normal from my vantage point. His legs were long and hugged by the dark gray slacks he wore. The shape of his ass was no mystery, leading up to a trim waist and broad shoulders. He turned around with an expectant look on his face, and only then did I remember he asked me a question.

"Sorry, what?"

He smirked, like he knew I was checking out his backside. "You felt differently than Tavia, about Sapien?"

"Oh, yeah I think so. Thank you." I accepted the wine from him, watching as he sat next to me. Was he a few inches closer than before? "I felt more... loyalty to them, I guess? It's pretty significant to be the only human settlement in Sanguine, even if everything wasn't perfect. I wanted to help keep that going, do my part to keep human traditions alive." I sipped from my glass, letting the wine linger on my tongue before I swallowed. "Although lately, I've been wondering if those traditions are even worth keeping."

"You sound like me with my family," Novak said. "It's a tangled mix of feelings, isn't it? To feel that sense of loyalty while also knowing they didn't treat you well."

"Yes, exactly. It's a headfuck."

Novak touched his glass to mine. "To loyalties that headfuck us."

I laughed and accepted his toast. "Cheers." After taking another sip, I added, "Thanks. You get it. I think you're the only one that does."

With a small smile, Novak lowered his arm from the back of the couch. It almost looked like he was going to put his hand on my leg, but he placed it in the space between us instead.

"I just hope your visit goes well, and that you get what you're looking for out of it."

"Me too. I still don't entirely know what that is. Closure? Clarity? No idea, but I just know I need to see it again."

"They better treat you with respect and decency, and not a whiff of fucking bullying. That goes for the humans and the Blood 'til Dawn members you'll be traveling with."

The intensity with which he said that almost made me snicker. "Or else what?"

Novak smiled coldly and I realized he was dead serious.

"Or else they'll contend with me."

Chapter 17

Amy

As it turned out, Blood 'til Dawn owned vehicles other than motorcycles.

Five of us piled into a van with all but the two front seats ripped out. Rhain and Cyan sat up front, with Rhain driving. Laith, a younger-looking vampire with pale blond hair close to Novak's shade, and Desmond, a darker-haired vampire with one chipped, blunt fang, sat with me on the van's floor.

We sat among stacks of plywood, rebar, bags of concrete mix, long two-by-fours, and several toolboxes. There were no seatbelts, but someone had at least welded handles to the van's inner walls. The three of us grabbed for the handles on instinct whenever Rhain made an especially wild turn.

"Temkra save us, he's going to flip the van one day," Desmond muttered.

Laith seemed less bothered being thrashed around. He grinned with every wild turn like he was on a rollercoaster ride.

"Are you excited to see Sapien again?" Laith asked me.

"I don't know if excited is the right word," I admitted. "Definitely nervous but hoping for the best."

"We won't let anyone mess with you. Right, Des?"

"No one will be brave enough to do anything." Des made a dismissive noise. "She's one of us now. Just snap your teeth a little, Amy, and those humans will jump to do whatever you want."

I forced a smile but couldn't shake the dread creeping into my stomach. I didn't want to scare anyone. I wanted them to see me as... *me.* Like when Tavia came back to visit after she was given to Cyan. Robin and I were overjoyed to see her again. Would Robin react the same way to me now, with blackened eyes and sharp teeth?

But if the people of Sapien feared me a little, that might not be so bad. A touch of fear could command respect. They wouldn't mess with me, like Des said. And they sure as hell wouldn't bully me.

I wasn't so meek anymore. If anyone tried to push me, I knew I could push back.

"What will you guys need me to do?" I returned my focus to the real reason we were going, to rebuild. No matter how Sapien saw me, I was going to help.

"Mixing the concrete for the new fence post bases." Des grabbed a wall handle and swore under his breath while we took another precarious turn. "That'll help reinforce everything so nothing can tear it down."

"Works for me."

"And whatever those douchebags up front need," Laith called loud enough for Rhain and Cyan to hear.

Rhain didn't respond but Cyan pretended to rummage in the center console before holding up his middle finger.

Before leaving, he'd asked me again twice if I was sure about coming along. I answered yes like a normal person the first time. The second time, I just climbed into the back of the van and waited for the drive to begin.

Eventually, Sapien's security lights were visible on the horizon, looking like stars or planets hovering closer to us than the rest of the cosmos.

A sense of unexpected relief came over me. Most humans weren't awake at night. How could I have forgotten? We'd be working while everyone was asleep, and might not see any humans at all.

I felt relieved about that, which in itself felt unsettling. It eased my anxiety about anyone seeing me and possibly being disgusted or afraid, and at the same time, reinforced some toxic thoughts about my own self-image.

After several weeks, I still avoided looking into mirrors. I avoided looking at my own eyes or my body whenever possible. Whenever Novak gave me those long looks, like his gaze was drinking me in, I felt torn between wanting to hide and wanting to bask in his attention.

No matter how comfortable I got with him, the fear of rejection lingered. I was convinced that if he looked deep enough—stared into my eyes long enough, or saw me naked —he'd discard me in an instant just like every other guy I crushed on.

It was better that other people didn't see me. Better for me, better for them. Rejection hurt too badly. It was sharp and cut deeply like a sword. From certain people, rejection felt like dying.

Loneliness was at least a slow-creeping, familiar hurt that always hung in the background. I only really became aware of it when I saw a stupidly happy couple together, like Cyan and Tavia. Feeling alone never truly left, but I could eventually grow numb to its constant presence.

So when the van parked and Laith, Des, and I got out, I didn't even look toward the dark, sleepy houses in the settlement. I just helped unload the supplies and waited for further instructions.

The bags of concrete mix were pretty self-explanatory. I had to go to the well in Sapien to fetch water while Des and Laith started digging holes for the new fence posts. Rhain and Cyan went around assessing damage to walls, decks, windows, and roofs. Some things could be patched up quickly. Others needed more extensive repair that would take several trips.

I walked through the quiet settlement several times to fetch water for the concrete mix. It felt different at night, like a ghost town. The Heart was so lively by comparison, and not just because more people lived there. Had I already gotten so used to being nocturnal that a human's daytime schedule seemed strange and alien?

"That's good, Amy. Show that concrete who's boss," Laith said over my shoulder as I stirred the bucket of goopy, gray mix with a stick. "Yeah, work it like that."

"Leave her alone." Nearby, Des hammered a fence post down with a mallet. "She doesn't need your weirdly sexual coaching."

Laith went to him, spreading his feet wide on either side of the post so that it mimicked a six-foot tall, wooden erection.

"Hammer me, Des. Give me that big ol' hammer and whack it hard."

I laughed and Des shot me a look of betrayal. This was their dynamic, I realized. Laith the goofball and Des the grounded, serious one. But even Des cracked a blunt-fanged smirk at Laith's antics.

"I ought to hammer you right in the cranium." Des shoved at his friend's shoulder, and Laith came back to check on my concrete.

"That looks good. Let's fill these holes, shall we?"

I snorted. "Sure."

He looked at me, eyes large and expressing something between panicked and amused. "I wasn't even trying that time, I swear."

"Uh-huh. Sure, you weren't."

Laith grabbed the bucket handle and lifted, carrying it to the row of freshly dug post holes. I followed him, bringing along a broad spade to spoon the concrete in.

"Look, I know I'm a lot," he said, setting the bucket down. "Too much for some people. You can tell me if I'm getting on your nerves and I won't be offended. I'll knock it off." He smiled, looking both sweetly boyish and a little feral. "Not everyone gets it, but there's just something about a well-placed dick joke, you know?"

"I get it, Laith." I shoved the spade into the wet concrete and scooped out a sizable blob. "Now let's fill these holes nice and deep."

Laith's face broke out in pure elation as Des cried out, "No, not you too!"

"Shut the fuck up," Rhain called over from the van. "You're going to wake up the humans."

"Whatever," Laith huffed. "They know we're here, right?"

"Yes. Doesn't change the fact that they're skittish about noises at night."

Working with Des and Laith went smoothly. We hushed our laughter and jokes as much as possible, but still received glares from Rhain on occasion.

On another trip into the settlement for more water, I heard a series of noises coming from one of the trailers. The flimsy door swung open hard, hitting the exterior wall, and it made me freeze like I'd been caught sneaking around.

A man stumbled out wearing nothing but boxer shorts and a pair of slippers. His eyes were barely open, his feet dragging with an unsteady gait like he was drunk. Judging by the smell of him, that was probably true.

He found his way to a bush next to the trailer and planted his feet wide with some degree of effort. I smelled the urine before I heard the splash of it hitting the ground. Wrinkling my nose against the acrid scent, I kept on toward the well to fill my bucket with water.

The guy must have been holding it in for a while because he was just finishing up as I headed back toward the fence line. He did his little shake before tucking himself back into his boxers, and then looked up.

Our eyes met and I recognized him.

Tom Harrison. The guy I lost my virginity to.

When he first started flirting with me, Tavia warned me about him. She told me to be careful and not to believe everything coming out of his mouth. There were rumors going around that he'd placed bets with his friends. One wager was that I'd willingly sleep with him. The second was that I'd tell him I loved him.

I did both.

I fell for it all, hook, line, and sinker. I'd been so swept up in having a guy paying me positive attention for once, giving me compliments and flowers, and actually having someone besides Tavia to stand up for me. He carried on charming me and being a perfect, polite gentleman for weeks. Surely it couldn't be an act.

But I found out the truth when it all came out the morning after we slept together. After a lifetime of bullying, I had no idea that another, deeper level of humiliation existed. Being pushed into mud puddles and laughed at while I struggled for breath felt like nothing compared to that morning.

That moment, naked and vulnerable next to Tom while he laughed, became a glass sculpture inside me. It shattered over and over again for years. Time never seemed to heal me, not when I saw him around all the time. He would give me that knowing smirk, maybe wink, or make a kissing noise, and I'd feel the shattering inside me all over again.

Sometimes, I didn't even need to see him. I'd be feeling perfectly fine, in the middle of a conversation with Tavia, and my mind would just... go there. My traitorous brain pulled the memory like a card hidden up a sleeve, with no rhyme or reason.

I learned right then, staring at Tom in his boxers and my bucket of water in hand, that while vampire blood may have healed my asthma and my heart murmur, it did not heal that delicate glass sculpture inside my chest.

Recognition shaped his expression first, and then abject horror.

The glass sculpture broke.

"What... what the fuck?" Tom stumbled back, blinked, rubbed his eyes, then blinked again.

"Hi, Tom," I said flatly. "Just helping to fix the fence."

"Stay away from me!" He stumbled back some more, this time tripping on something and landing on his ass.

All I wanted to do was disappear into thin air. Maybe rewind time to a few seconds earlier, and I would know to linger in the shadows while Tom stumbled back to bed. Unfortunately, there was no unseeing that expression on his face. And he was now in my direct path to escape. I had no other choice but to approach him.

"I have to go around you," I tried to explain.

But every step I took in his direction was met with horrified screams and frantic scrabbles backward. Tom's eyes were wide, his chest heaving with panicked breaths.

"Oh God, oh fuck, please don't bite me! Please. Someone help!"

He turned on his side and vomited. Probably more an effect of his drunkenness than seeing me, but it didn't exactly make me feel any better.

I hurried past him, the sight of his curled-up form, hands over his neck as he whimpered, "No, please don't," worming its way from my peripheral vision deep into my psyche.

Lights inside trailers and cabins began turning on, muffled sounds of movement and voices coming from inside. Of course Tom's noise would alert people and start a chain reaction of humiliation. I had to join the vampires at the perimeter before anyone else saw me.

A door opened just behind me and I quickened my pace.

"What's going on?"

The pang of familiarity hit me right in the chest and my steps faltered. Robin! She raised me and Tavia, taking on both a big sister and motherly role to us. She'd been the main person I wanted to see. I couldn't pass up the chance to say hi.

I turned toward the sound of her voice, putting on a smile to mask the despair of what just happened with Tom. "Hey, Robin."

She was wrapped in a robe in her open doorway. The changes in her expression were in the reverse order of Tom's. Horror hit her first, and then recognition.

I immediately realized my mistake. My fangs, although smaller than a full vampire's, were on full display when I smiled, and I was standing right under one of the security lights. There was simply no hiding my blackened eyes.

"Amy?" Robin's voice was filled with fear and sorrow. "My God, what happened to you?"

"It's okay—" I started toward her, then stopped abruptly at her resulting flinch and retreat into her house.

She stared at me with the door now a barrier between us, only her head visible. The look on her face was somehow worse than Tom's. I saw fear, revulsion, pity. The jagged glass pieces inside me crushed into thousands of tiny shards, all of them cutting so much deeper than ever before.

Neither she nor Tom had ever seen a brusang before, but that didn't make the looks in their eyes hurt any less.

I wasn't sure how long I stood there when something big and dark blocked my view of Robin.

"We're repairing the damage from the attack as scheduled." Rhain's low, growly voice boomed from directly in front of me. "Naturally, we can only work at night. There is nothing to be alarmed about. We'll be finishing shortly."

He turned and used gentle maneuvering on my shoulders to turn me around as well. With light pressure on my back, he urged me to walk. I became unfrozen somehow and went with him to the perimeter. It was only when he guided me to the van that I realized my hands were empty. Rhain had taken my bucket of water.

"Don't worry about the fence. I'll help Des and Laith finish it up," he said in the softest tone I'd ever heard from him. "Just... have a seat. We're almost done here."

"Okay." I felt like a robot that had been shut down. The

humiliation had reached so deep, the glass sculpture crushed and pulverized to the point of feeling nothing.

Rhain hesitated like he wanted to say something but then thought better of it, and left me there.

So I sat alone, with nothing but Tom and Robin's horrified expressions playing on a loop in my head.

Chapter 18

Novak

I pulled away from the microscope and rubbed my eyes. If I looked at any more tissue samples tonight, I'd surely go blind.

Enough work for tonight. Dawn was an hour away.

I switched off the light on the microscope and stretched my arms overhead as I crossed my office. The bottle of wine in the sitting area tempted me, but it was the one made by Amy's friend. I'd much rather share it with her.

She'd probably be finishing with the Sapien repairs by now. I wondered how it went, if she got what she needed from the visit.

My cell phone lay dark and silent on my desk. Should I text her, or would that be too much? We'd been tentatively crossing more touch barriers lately. I was enjoying our growing closeness, and it seemed she was too. But Amy was still figuring herself out, and I didn't want to overwhelm her.

She never mentioned coming over after finishing in Sapien, but I hoped she would. Even after just a few hours apart, I found myself missing her. A lot.

I returned to my desk, deciding on sending her a casual,

friendly checking-in text, when I heard the doorbell from downstairs.

Hope lit up my chest as I left the office and hit the stairs. I could barely feel my feet, I was practically floating.

"Sir?" Lourna hesitated in the foyer when she saw me coming down.

"I'll get it, thank you."

She smoothed the look of surprise on her face quickly. I never rushed to answer the door. I'd never been excited to receive visitors until recently.

I pulled the door open and the rush of joy at seeing Amy gave me a lightheaded feeling. She had just been here the night before, but it still felt like too long.

"Hey, come in. I was just about to text you."

She walked through, crossing the foyer silently. The poor thing was probably exhausted after doing manual labor all night. She probably needed blood. And maybe another foot massage. Or a shoulder massage. I wasn't picky. I only wanted to touch her and to listen to her voice.

"Are you hungry? Jo said you could raid the fridge, so she left things in there for you. I still have Tavia's wine from the other night if you want to split it. Amy?"

My joy at her presence turned to worry. Something wasn't right. She was never this quiet.

I moved in front of her to see her face. Her expression was completely blank, just empty. Her eyes were vacant, unfocused and off somewhere else.

"Amy?" I took her face in my hands, concern hitching my breath. Even that first day we met, at her lowest possible point, she was expressive. Emotional. Whatever this was, it wasn't her.

"Akra, what the hell happened?" My thumbs stroked over her temples and the apples of her cheeks, trying to pull her attention from wherever her mind was. "What is it? Please tell me."

Dozens of scenarios ran through my mind. Thorne did something, threatened her maybe. Maybe he sent her over here to end our friendship for good. The cruel fucking bastard, I'd kill him for this.

Finally, Amy's eyes focused. She blinked as dark tears started to fill her eyes. Her brow pinched with tension and her jaw clenched, lips wobbling like she was holding back a tidal wave of emotion.

"Novak?"

The pain in her voice broke my heart and fired me up with rage. "Yes, I'm here." A tear began to spill from one of her eyes, but I caught it with my thumb. "Please, you're killing me. What's wrong?"

My questioning seemed to make everything worse. Her eyes squeezed shut, spilling more tears as a great, gasping sob wracked her whole body.

Alarm and confusion rang through me. Amy took my hands away from her face, turning away like she didn't want me to see her, so I pulled her back into my chest. She cried into the privacy of my shirt, the muffled sounds breaking off pieces of my heart one by one. My lips rested against her hairline as I held her, just listening to her sobs as my mind ran wild.

This was so much worse than that first day we met. Back then, Amy didn't know how to cope with her second chance at life. Right now, she was so deeply wounded that she probably felt like she was dying again.

I held the back of her head with one hand, the other running up and down her back. Lourna entered the foyer, looking just as worried as I felt. She opened her mouth to speak, but closed it when I shook my head. Amy needed to feel safe to process whatever happened. For some reason she trusted me, and she didn't need an audience.

"Going upstairs," I mouthed to Lourna before leaning down to whisper in Amy's ear. "I'm going to pick you up."

Amy barely had to move. I just crouched low and scooped her up behind her knees, then took the stairs slowly to not jostle her. She curled up small against my chest, her sobs quieting, though her breaths were ragged and distressed.

On the second floor, I passed the guest room and took her directly to my bedroom suite. The window shutters had closed with the onset of dawn so the room was already dark. After kicking off my shoes, I sat on the edge of my bed and turned to lie on my side with Amy still in my arms.

"I'm sorry... " Her voice was so small and choked with tears.

"Shush. Don't be." I pulled her close, bringing her face to my chest to cry there if she needed to. "You have absolutely nothing to be sorry for. Whoever made you feel this way is the one who should be fucking sorry."

Her body shook with more sobs and hiccupping breaths, but she clung to me like a lifeline. Despair thrashed wildly inside me. I was desperate to know who hurt her this badly, but wouldn't push her to talk until she was ready.

I stroked her back, her hair, her cheek. My touch seemed to soothe her even if my words didn't. The crying seemed to come in waves, slowing for a time before starting up again. I didn't know what else to do besides hold her through it. What I would give to know what she was thinking so I could fix all the hurt.

After some time, she quieted again, pulling in deep, shuddering breaths. I didn't know if all the crying had exhausted her or she had truly exorcised what had caused her so much pain. Whichever the case, I was content to hold her in the dark. It was surely daytime now, but the lack of light in the room gave the illusion of night. Fatigue made me drowsy, but I would not leave her.

"Do you want to talk about it?" I asked after a long stretch of silence.

Amy sighed and the air from her mouth felt like a caress against my throat.

"It's stupid," she said quietly.

"Don't do that." My lips brushed her forehead and before I could overthink it, I pressed a kiss there.

"Do what?"

"Reduce your pain to that word. What you're feeling isn't stupid, it's important."

She let out a dry huff. "Important? Me?"

"Yes, you." I drew back to see her face clearly. Those galaxy eyes were puffy and tinged with red, the dark tear tracks on her cheeks like watered-down ink. "You're important to me."

"Why?" The word came out as barely a whisper. Her mouth formed the word and her bottom lip began to tremble like she was about to cry again. She genuinely didn't know why and that baffled me.

"Because you're strong, curious, and brave. You're so honest and forthcoming. You've dealt with your own life and death with so much grace and maturity."

She laughed bitterly. "I think you have me confused with someone else."

"I don't." I brought her face closer and let another kiss linger on her forehead while I gathered the nerve for what I'd say next. "And you're so achingly beautiful, even when you're sad."

Amy went eerily still for a moment before shoving

against my chest, creating distance between us. "Don't lie about stuff like that. It's cruel."

"What?" I'd struck a nerve, clearly. She was crying again as she shoved me away, but I held onto her straightened and locked arms. "Amy, I'm not lying."

"Just stop, Novak." She tried to roll to her other side, facing away from me but I wouldn't let her.

"Why do you think I'm lying?" I demanded. "I'm ridiculously attracted to you. How could you not know that?"

"How can you be attracted to eyes like this?" She pointed at hers.

I took the opportunity to pull her close again, so close that my forehead and nose nudged hers.

"I love your eyes," I said. "I always think of them as two galaxies. There's so much depth and beauty to them."

Amy's breath shuddered as I wiped more tears. "I was *dead*, Novak. A literal corpse that came back to life. How does that not gross you out? How can you think I'm anything but monstrous?"

"Vampires are already monstrous in the eyes of humans, for one." I stroked my knuckle across her cheek. "Half of Sanguine believes I infected my own clan with Rathka's Curse. If we're going off of what other people think, I'm ten times the monster you are."

Amy blinked and sniffed. "But that's not true."

"Neither is the fact that you're anything but beautiful." I placed a kiss between her brows. "As for the other part, Temkra spoke to you and brought you back. She decided you weren't finished with life. Our goddess *chose* you, Amy." I traced her lips with my thumb. "And I can't help but think she wanted us to find each other."

Amy didn't respond. But she stopped crying, and her

gaze fixated on my mouth, hovering only inches away from hers.

I closed the distance with the intention of making the kiss gentle, comforting. But the first taste of her hit me like the first drop of blood after a long drought. No, she tasted better than blood. Even through the flavor of salt from her tears, she was Amy. Pure and sweet and *mine*.

She went from pushing me to pulling me, her hands diving into my hair as her mouth opened, deepening the kiss. Our tongues surged and explored, our fangs adding a level of pressure that only elevated my desire. She rolled to her back and I followed, refusing to disconnect from her for any reason.

Her body fit below me like she was made for me, warm and responsive. I lowered enough to feel her without crushing her, needing contact with every beautiful swell and curve.

A tiny prick of pain bloomed on my lower lip, and Amy broke away abruptly. "Oh, I'm sorry." She covered her mouth as if ashamed of her fangs, the culprits that nicked me.

I took her hand and pinned it to the side of her head, hovering my mouth just over hers. A drop of blood fell from my lip to hers, and watching her tongue lick it away was almost too much to bear.

"Don't ever apologize for drawing blood," I whispered. "It's what we do, what we're made for. Use those cute little teeth on me all you like. If you want a taste of me while you kiss me, then take it. Take all you need, akra."

Amy turned her face to the side, breaking eye contact, but the bashful smile and lack of tears told me she was feeling better. I kissed her cheek and the corner of her jaw, fighting the urge to move lower to her neck. I would not be able to keep my fangs out of her veins, and she hadn't given me consent to drink from her yet.

"You don't actually think my teeth are cute," she said.

"Yes, I do." I kissed her temple. "They're smaller than vampire fangs and I think they're adorable. I love when you laugh because that's when I can see them most clearly."

I tickled her ribs, earning a bright peal of laughter. She faced me again with that smile that I loved, and some of the brightness in her eyes had returned. Her hand came around my nape and I lowered my mouth to hers, lost in kissing her again.

She licked the already-healing cut on my lip, drawing a moan from deep inside my chest. I wanted her blood and her body so fucking badly. Her pulse hummed in my senses, just as much a comfort as it was a distraction. It wasn't enough. I was desperate to have her across all of my senses, to just drown in her.

But this was not the time to take what I wanted. She needed me to give. I still didn't know what happened in Sapien, but it was abundantly clear that she needed to be seen, appreciated, adored.

Even loved.

"I do have a confession to make," I said when we parted for a breath.

Amy's brow pinched, looking worried. Her hands on my back stopped moving. "Okay. What?" She looked like she was bracing herself for a rejection and that broke my heart.

"Akra is not actually your name in my language." I kissed the bridge of her nose. "It means something else."

"What does it mean?"

"It's a term of endearment, sometimes between family but most often between lovers." I brushed a piece of hair off her forehead. "The English equivalent would be like, darling or sweetheart."

Her brow furrowed deeper like she was confused. "But you've called me that since the beginning."

"I know." I kissed her brow until it relaxed under my lips. "You were dear to me then. Ever since you told off Blood 'til Dawn for searching me like a criminal. Probably before that, actually."

She let out a little snarl. "They were assholes for that."

I brushed my mouth against hers with a chuckle. "There's my akra." Her lips pulled apart with a smile and I kissed her again before attempting a question. "Were they assholes to you tonight?"

I tried to keep my tone light, desperate to keep her from spiraling into sadness again despite the pent-up rage boiling inside me. No matter what, I'd find out who made her cry. I'd find out who made her feel like she was less than divine and undo the damage until she believed it herself.

Amy let out a shaky sigh. "No. They were... nice, actually." Her eyes remained dry when they glanced up at me. "I'm almost afraid to say it, but Blood 'til Dawn might not actually be so bad."

"What?" I fell to my side, clutching my chest as if I were wounded. "Akra, how can you say such things?"

She laughed, rolling into me as she grabbed my hand. I laced our fingers together as I kissed her again, grinning and making her laugh some more. That smile with her adorably tiny fangs was my weakness and I could never get enough.

I also filed away the knowledge that it must have been the humans of Sapien, not Blood 'til Dawn, that caused her tears. And I honestly wasn't surprised. Short lifespans apparently made certain species idiotic.

Amy broke our kiss, resting her forehead against mine as

her fingers dabbed at my shirt. "Sorry for crying all over you and ruining this."

"Yes, it's such a shame." I brought her knuckles to my lips and kissed them. "I don't have any other shirts to wear. Not a single one."

She laughed and shoved at my shoulder. I let her push me over until I sprawled on my back, tugging her down with me. Amy nestled into my side like she was created to fit against me. Her head came to rest on my shoulder with a gentle sigh, her breaths no longer shaking.

"Are you feeling any better?" I kissed her forehead, knowing I hadn't been able to keep my lips off her the moment I started.

"A little." Her hand skimmed across my torso, resting near my opposite shoulder. "Thank you, Novak."

"Always, akra."

Amy's grin started to fade as her eyelids drooped. "Is it morning?"

"Mm-hmm. The sun is rising as we speak."

Her eyes fluttered open and I saw distress in those two galaxies and tears welling once again.

"What's wrong?" I turned on my side, ready and willing to let my shirt catch her tears once more.

She pulled in a shaky breath. "When night returns and we wake up, will you still want me like this?" She wiped at her eyes and sniffed. "Will you still want to kiss me and hold me like you are now? Or is this just... I don't know."

I slid both arms around her waist, bringing her tightly against my torso. "I have been dying to hold you and taste your kiss for weeks. Every night since I first met you, I've been hoping you come over, or that you're already here when I come home. This isn't 'just' anything, Amy. I miss you every moment you're gone, and every moment you're here makes my life brighter."

I kissed her hard, catching her mouth in a tight lock and not releasing until I felt the aching need for air. "So yes, I'll still be here at nightfall, akra. And I'll still want you with every blood cell in my body."

Her eyelids drooped again, exhaustion and nocturnal instincts pulling her toward sleep. "I want to believe you, Novak."

"Believe me. I have never meant anything more sincerely in my life."

She nodded once, lips parting as her eyelids fully closed.

I eased her onto her back, then carefully pulled the duvet and sheets down and back up over her. She was already asleep by the time I removed my damp shirt and settled in next to her.

My nerves were rattled. I still wanted answers. But her breathing and her strong, steady heartbeat slowly lulled me to sleep.

Chapter 19

Novak

Amy was still out cold when I woke up near dusk. I leaned over and brushed a kiss against her cheek, reluctant to leave the bed without her. But she needed rest, and I was already restless.

I dropped last night's shirt and the rest of my clothes in the laundry, then stepped into the shower. The moment I dressed and got out, Lourna was tidying up the bedroom.

"Baros of Carpe Noctem called. He's on your office line," she whispered, tiptoeing around the room so as to not wake Amy.

"Fuck." With being so concerned about her last night, I'd forgotten all about him.

"He called last night as well, but I didn't want to disturb either of you." She glanced at Amy, sleeping peacefully in the center of my bed.

"Right, thank you." I rubbed my forehead, already anticipating what a headache this call was going to be.

"Should I bring her something?" Lourna asked. "For when she wakes up?"

"Like what?"

"Well, humans usually appreciate a glass of water and some painkillers after a rough night."

"Then yes please," I said. "Whatever she needs."

Lourna clicked her tongue, her sympathetic gaze on Amy as she moved around the room. "I hope the poor thing is all right. Will she be staying?"

Fucking Temkra, I hope so.

"I'm not sure," I admitted. "That'll be up to her when she wakes up."

"Don't worry about her, sir. See to your business." Lourna's spine straightened. "We'll take care of her."

"Thank you, sincerely." I gave my housekeeper a grateful smile on my way out of the bedroom. It seemed I wasn't the only one who'd become fond of Amy in the past few weeks.

The walk to my office was too short, no matter how much I dragged my feet. The red light on my desk phone blinked ominously like some kind of evil eye.

With a taut breath, I stood behind the desk and answered the call. "Baros. Sorry to keep you waiting."

"I'm sure." I could hear the aristocratic sneer in his voice. "You seem awfully busy these recent nights, Rathka's Order."

I didn't realize I was at your beck and call, was what I wanted to say. What I actually said was, "I apologize. What can I do for you?"

"Right. I've scheduled Inessa's fertility ritual for the end of the month on the new moon. I trust you'll make it a priority to attend? Seeing as you'll be putting that heightened fertility to good use."

All of the air left my lungs as if I'd been punched in the gut. "The end of the month," I repeated. "So soon?"

Female vampires had a brief fertile period roughly once

per year. Those with the right means and connections could call upon Temkra's Blood, the clan with the closest, most sacred connection to our goddess, to perform a ritual to expand that fertility window. The ritual was said to at least double the chances of a successful pregnancy.

I had pushed away thoughts of my arrangement with Carpe Noctem, but with Thorne's recent visit and now this phone call, I had to face it head-on. The idea of fucking and impregnating a stranger had always been uncomfortable for me, even if everyone acted like the end result was worth it.

But right then, with Amy asleep in my bed and the taste of her kiss lingering on my tongue, I felt downright disgusted.

"Yes, the sooner the better." Baros sounded nothing short of jovial. "Her fertile time last year was during the spring and lasted about three days, so I'm quite confident we're timing the ritual well for optimal results."

If he felt awkward about spilling the details of his daughter's fertility cycle to me, he gave no indication. And optimal results? He sounded like a human breeding an animal for specific traits.

"Baros," I said tightly. "I'm afraid I'm not able to fulfill my end of this agreement. I apologize for going back on my word, but I've thought about it some more and—"

A loud laugh burst from the phone. "Don't be ridiculous, Novak."

"I promise you I'm being quite serious."

"No, you're being foolish. Think about what you're doing."

"I assure you I have. And I've determined that this plan is not for me."

"It's not about what's for *you*, idiot," Baros hissed. "This plan is for our kind, for all of Sanguine. It's about knocking down Blood 'til Dawn until they're buried in the mud where they belong. This is about restoring our clans to their true greatness."

I sighed, rubbing my temple. "I'm sorry, Baros. I don't—"

"Your father was right about you."

My breath stopped, my grip choking around the phone receiver.

"What?"

"You're a disgrace to Rathka's Order," Baros spat. "Just like your father moaned and bitched about all night at clan gatherings. His soft little second son, always reading books, always looking at things under microscopes and clinging to his mother. You never grew up. Not even when your father's legacy was crumbling all around you, could you grow a backbone to save your clan."

I wanted to slam the phone down, to tell him to fuck off with all the cold carelessness of an icy wind. But I didn't. I couldn't. I could only freeze and listen, like I had done all my life.

"Even now when you're the only one left, on the verge of extinction," Baros prattled on, "you can't do the easiest thing in the world and fuck a female! Were you born without a cock too, Novak? What in Rathka's name is wrong with you?"

"Nothing."

The word leaving my mouth was just noise, an automated response to the barrage of abuse coming at me through the phone. It could have been my father, my brother, any number of people on the other end. And I might as well had been a child or even a juvenile with the way I shut down and absorbed all the blows like punches, just waiting for it all to be over.

Logically I knew I shouldn't let Baros get under my skin. But he was already there because he knew exactly how to worm his way into that spot, to become that voice in my head.

"Then you'll do your duty and create an heir." His smugness came through the phone like a bad smell. "You have no other options, son. You must see that. No one else wants to touch your clan's name with a ten-foot pole. Without me, you're ruined. You have nothing now, on the verge of having less than nothing. Keep me as your ally and you'll have something worth living for again."

I thought of Amy, her tears soaking my shirt, the softness of her mouth and the sweet sharpness of her fangs. She didn't care about my clan's name, my history. She came to me when she needed a safe place. Having that trust felt more precious than any power and wealth my clan ever had.

But everything was so new. She was figuring out how to balance her human and vampiric traits. Once she did, she might move on from me or prefer to be only friends. There might be a kernel of truth to Baros's words, and she may eventually see me as spineless, someone too weak to carry the responsibilities of his clan on his shoulders. Plus there was the fact that she was technically part of Blood 'til Dawn, who would love nothing more than to see my bloodline extinct.

I shut my eyes against the building pressure in my temples.

"Do you understand me, Novak?" Baros pressed. "This is your duty. You will attend this fertility ritual and impregnate my daughter because you'll be the biggest disappointment in vampire history if you do not."

"I understand." Those two words were more noise that meant nothing. I just wanted this conversation to be over.

"Excellent." His tone turned pleasant in an instant. "I'll see you at my estate on the new moon."

I slammed the phone receiver into the cradle without any goodbye. I could picture him in the same moment, hanging up the phone gently with a victorious smile on his face. He and my father were like two peas in a pod, happiest when crushing someone's spirit.

Baros's father was similarly cruel, unsurprisingly. I had been secretly pleased to find out twenty years ago that Kalix of Blood 'til Dawn had killed him. A shame that Kalix ended up imprisoned by Carpe Noctem as retribution. Baros certainly loved having him as a prisoner.

Thoughts of murder were running through my head right then. Not that I would act on them, but the walls of my office felt like they were closing in on me. I needed to get out of here before I did something stupid.

I jogged down the stairs and yelled to Jo in the kitchen as I passed, "Need some air. I'll be back." My coat was around my shoulders and my feet hit the sidewalk before she ever replied.

I walked without any destination in mind, just needing movement through my limbs to calm the fuck down and shake Baros's words from my head.

Inevitably I ended up in the Cap, a vibrant, bustling neighborhood within the Heart of Sanguine. The streets were lively, as they always were. Restaurants, bars, and nightclubs were packed. Red smoke drifted on the breeze from the darakt shops and music played from several different directions. In the distance, the bright white building marking the blood bank could be seen.

My mouth dried. I needed blood, it had been a while. I should stop at the blood bank while out. It was there for exactly this reason, for vampires or brusang with no one to feed from.

Despite knowing this, I turned away from the stark white building and headed down a street full of restaurants and lounges. Amy had only ever fed from me. While she hadn't expressed wanting to return the favor, it felt wrong to take from other sources when she hadn't.

We weren't blood pets, mates, or exclusive in any other way. And yet, the thought of any kind of intimacy or touch with someone else turned my stomach. It didn't matter if it was as simple as blood drinking or more involved like creating a child. She was the only one I wanted any shred of intimacy with.

My teeth ground against each other, fangs nearly stabbing into my lower gums. I would not be attending that fertility ritual or doing anything with Baros's daughter, but he would not let go unless I offered him something else. He was dead-set on overthrowing Blood 'til Dawn and wanted me in his back pocket. The trick was getting out of his scheme while still making him believe I was on his side.

The world around me blurred and became white noise as I walked. I had no leverage against him, no clan to support me. All I had was Amy, and that connection was fragile too. If Thorne told her about Baros before I could end the deal, she would absolutely walk away too.

Fuck, why couldn't I have found a cure for Rathka's Curse? At least then I might've had a shred more power against Baros. I would have had the power to say no, at least.

"Hey, it's you."

The voice didn't register until a hand caught my wrist, stopping me in my tracks. I looked to see Amy's friend Tavia sitting with her mate, Cyan, on a patio next to the street.

She had reached across the small loveseat they sat on and over the patio fence to grab me.

"Ah, hello," I said stiffly, unsure why she stopped me.

Cyan's mouth thinned, his hand drifting mostly likely toward a silver dagger hidden somewhere on him. But when Tavia asked, "Where's Amy?" it sounded more curious than accusatory.

"She's at my house," I said. "Sleeping. I just needed to go for a walk." To Cyan, I added, "You know where I live. You're welcome to check on her."

Tavia placed a hand on his chest like she was telling him to back down. "That's not necessary. I just wanted to make sure she's okay."

I turned toward her then, moving closer to the fence and out of the flow of people walking the street. Cyan subtly tugged his mate closer to him, glaring at me.

"She was really upset," I admitted. "Did you see her after she returned from Sapien?" I wasn't sure how much Tavia knew, but it sounded like she and Amy had reconciled. Maybe she could give insight into who hurt her so badly.

"No." Tavia shook her head. "These guys came back without her." She pointed at Cyan with her thumb and gave *him* an accusatory look.

"She asked us to drop her off in the Heart, so that's what we did," he argued. "I figured she was going off to see him." He acknowledged me with a jerk of his chin. "You know we don't like it, but Amy can make her own decisions."

"How did she seem on the way back?" I asked.

"Fine," he threw back. "Maybe a little quiet, but fine."

"What happened while you all were there?" Tavia asked him.

"Exactly what I'd like to know," I said.

"Some humans saw her, like I told you." Cyan addressed his mate and ignored me. "They got spooked, that's all. Pretty much the same reaction to seeing vampires. It wasn't a big deal."

Tavia sighed loudly. "Not to you, maybe. But Amy's sensitive. She's still adjusting to not being human." She looked up at me. "Novak, would you like to sit with us?"

"I'm sorry, what?" Cyan stared at her.

"Cy." Tavia's head swiveled in his direction. "Novak is Amy's friend. She spends more time at his place than with us. Doesn't that make him worth getting to know?"

Cyan didn't flat-out refuse but mumbled something like, "She'll get over it."

"I'll behave if he does," I said, nodding toward the other vampire.

Tavia beamed. "That sounds fair. What do you say, Cy?"

A long moment of glaring and jaw-grinding passed before he finally muttered, "Fine."

I went through the patio gate and took a seat on the sofa across from the couple. "Thank you for allowing me to join you."

"I'm glad I saw you," Tavia said. "You stand out in a crowd with that hair color."

"All of Rathka's Order had that look," Cyan said flatly. "The ghost hair."

"You sound jealous, Cyan." I couldn't help ribbing him, running a hand through my pale blond strands.

Cyan snorted. "Jealous of *you*? Yeah, right." His arm tightened around Tavia's waist, face turning to kiss her temple. The wordless remark was clear. *I have my blood mate, and therefore everything I need in this woman beside me.*

Tavia let out a sigh but leaned into the affection regardless. "Not even five seconds and you two are already shit-talking."

"I apologize. Congratulations on your mating, by the way."

"Thank you." Cyan actually sounded gracious, his hand possessively around Tavia's hip. "There's nothing like finding your person."

I was starting to think *I* had found my person, but with Baros breathing down my neck, a life with her seemed out of reach.

A vampire waiter came over to set a wine glass down in front of me, and Cyan gestured to the open bottle on the table. "Help yourself. Tavi just sold five cases of her wine to this lounge and we're celebrating."

"Thank you, and congratulations, again." I poured myself a modest-sized glass. "Amy brought one of your wines to my house, so I'm already a fan of your work."

"Oh, that's very sweet. Thank you." Tavia blushed and looked a little uncomfortable, clearly not one to bask in her accomplishments. "Five cases seems a little excessive, but it's what they asked for."

"Nonsense, they're already selling it," Cyan told her. "They're going to sell out by the end of the week and ask for twenty next time."

"You're full of shit." Amy groaned, but grinned at his praise.

Cyan turned to me. "I'm planting an orchard for her ciders. Obviously she needs a vineyard and all the right facilities and equipment too."

"That seems like a logical next step," I said. "Let me know if you need an investor. I love to support a good product and new businesses."

The two of them looked shocked. Cyan even sputtered and choked.

"We don't need money from Rathka's Order." He grimaced like he was going sling another tired insult, but a glance at Tavia had his expression softening. "But your generous offer is... noted and appreciated."

"Now that would be a step toward repairing the feud between your clans." Tavia smirked over the rim of her glass. "Blood 'til Dawn and Rathka's Order coming together over some wine, can you imagine it?"

"Don't get your hopes up." Cyan dropped a kiss on her shoulder.

The two of them were so naturally at ease with each other. Comfortable, with a spark lighting up their touches and glances at one another. Their connection was one to be envied.

"Can you tell me anything else about Sapien last night?" I focused on Cyan, since he was with Amy that night. "Who were the humans who got spooked by Amy?"

"I don't know." He ran a hand over his buzzed hair with a sigh. "Some human male. Looked like his blood tasted bad. You know what I mean?"

I nodded while Tavia shook her head with a small chuckle. It was just a feeling vampires had sometimes. Every once in a while, we only had to look at a person to *know* that their blood was shitty.

"The other was an older woman. I think... " He turned to Tavia. "I think it was Robin, the one who looked out for you and Amy."

"Oh no." Tavia's face fell. "If Robin reacted badly to seeing her, Amy would've been crushed. She looked up to Robin. We both did."

"What about the male? Who was he to her?" I desperately wanted to know if he'd been one of Amy's bullies, or significant to her in some other way.

"I don't know." Cyan threw his hands up helplessly.

"What did he look like?" Tavia asked him. "I'm sure I know who he is."

"Like a worm. A really thick one, with bad blood." She smacked his arm and he proceeded to give his best actual physical description of the male. Then Tavia looked at me, anguish and sorrow in her eyes.

"That sounds like Tom Harrison. I hate him with every fiber of my being."

"Why? What did he do?"

Tavia's shoulders slumped.

"He broke Amy's heart."

Chapter 20

Amy

I felt like I was waking up from the dead all over again, only in a much more pleasant way. This bed was the most comfortable one I'd ever slept in, and as I rolled and stretched, I felt so much lighter.

My tears had all run out, and the heavy weight of worthlessness no longer sat like a boulder on my chest. But a flutter of anxiety filled me when I remembered what else happened last night.

Novak carrying me, holding me. Kissing me.

I brought my knees toward my stomach, suddenly self-conscious and worried. How pathetic must I have looked to him?

"Sleep well?"

I startled, flipping over to find Novak in bed next to me. He sat against the headboard, dressed in slacks and a fresh shirt with the sleeves rolled to his elbows. His legs stretched out long in front of him, crossed at the ankles. A leather folio was open in his lap and a pen rested in his hand. Scribbled notes and what looked like scientific equations covered the spread of papers in front of him.

In short, he looked relaxed but scholarly, and absolutely delicious.

"Uh, yeah." I was self-conscious of my hair, my face, the day-old clothes I'd slept in—basically everything. "I see you managed to find a shirt."

Novak grinned and capped his pen. "I searched far and wide to no avail. So I resorted to hand-sewing an old curtain to make do."

"Wow." I gave him a once-over, nodding approvingly. "You are quite skilled with a needle and thread."

"I'd say it's a necessary skill during times of massive shirt famines."

The longer this conversation went on, the harder it became to not laugh. "You know, if the situation is that dire, I'm sure your staff wouldn't mind if you just went without for a while."

Novak's grin wobbled with restrained laughter. "Walking around the house with no shirt? After all the trouble I went through to make this?"

"Just something to keep in mind if I mess up that one with snot and tears. Your sacrifice would be appreciated."

"By just my household staff?"

"No... "

He leaned in closer, ruby eyes bright. "By who else, then?"

His gaze was so intense and I couldn't hold it in any longer. I hid my face in a pillow and burst into laughter. When I felt Novak's weight slide closer and his hand rested on my waist, it wasn't shock that quieted me, but an elated sense of relief.

He hadn't lied, hadn't touched or kissed me last night out of pity or selfishness. He was still here, as he said he would be.

"It sounds like you're feeling better, akra." His voice was every bit as warm and comforting as the bed.

I sighed into the pillow, my breath warming the soft fabric. "In some ways, yes."

"But not in others?"

Moving the pillow slightly, I peeked at him with one eye. "I'm a little embarrassed about last night."

Novak's brow pinched with a frown. "You have no reason to be. I wish I could have done more to ease you."

"What? No." I let the pillow fall away. "Last night, you did more for me than anyone else ever has. Even Tavia."

A smile curled his mouth. "Tavia not much for cuddling and forehead kisses?"

I let out a small laugh. "Well, our relationship was never like that. Don't get me wrong, she's a good listener and we could talk for hours, but when I'm upset she always wants to... *do* something about it."

"You mean retaliate against those who hurt you."

"Yeah." I nodded. "I appreciate a friend who isn't afraid to throw punches or yell at a man twice her size. But that wasn't always what *I* needed, you know?"

"I won't lie, the thought crossed my mind," Novak mused. "I was worried about you, and I wanted to find out who hurt you and make them pay for it." His voice went low, lips curling to expose his fangs. "But you needed me to stay, and that was more important than making some humans piss themselves in fear."

"Hey, I never said anything about humans being the reason."

Novak slid lower to lie next to me, then propped himself up on an elbow. "I stepped out for a bit earlier tonight, and ended up running into Tavia and Cyan."

"You did?" I sat up higher. "Oh God, was Cyan an asshole? He's like that, sometimes."

"No. They were both pleasant company actually." Novak looked at me in a way that made my cheeks heat. "He told me what happened in Sapien. And Tavia deduced who they were based on descriptions. Tom Harrison and Robin?"

I hid my face behind the pillow again. "Great. Now I'm even more embarrassed."

Novak stole the pillow and threw it off the bed. "Those humans should be embarrassed. Not you." With no barrier between us now and his gaze locked on me, vulnerability crept up my spine like a ghostly chill.

"I meant everything I said last night." Novak made no move to touch me again, but his words were like a caress. "You're important to me. I find you breathtakingly beautiful, and... " he paused as if wrestling with himself. "I like having you in my home. Especially in my bed."

My eyes widened. "This is *your*—"

I looked around the room for the first time ever. This was definitely not the guest room I'd stayed in before. The bed was much bigger, as was the room itself. A massive fireplace took over the far wall, with two armchairs and a coffee table in front of it. The windows reached from floor to ceiling, showing a starry night sky and a waning half moon.

"Are you okay with being in here?" Novak asked in response to my jaw-dropped gaping.

"Yeah! I mean, of course. It's just, I thought your guest room was luxurious, but this feels... resplendent."

"You haven't even seen the four heads in the shower."

"Four shower heads?!"

"That's not even the best part." He grinned. "There's a bench built into the wall."

I stared at him. "A bench is the best part?"

"Yes! So you can sit down." He quirked an eyebrow. "A hot shower is supposed to be relaxing. Who wants to be on their feet the whole time? The shower bench is a genius invention."

I shook my head, laughing. "If you say so."

Novak's smile softened. "If you're feeling up for it, I thought we could go out tonight."

"Out? Out where?"

"Just into the Cap for a drink or meal. Get some fresh air. Spend some time together outside of these walls."

"Like a... " I wasn't even sure if I had the guts to say the word. "A date?"

His grin widened and my heart fluttered. "Yes, exactly."

"I'd love to, but I don't have anything clean to wear." I was still in the clothes I'd worn to Sapien.

"We can shop for clothes first, if you'd like. Rack up a bill on Blood 'til Dawn's account, or," he paused, voice lowering, "let me take care of everything."

"You don't mean that." I tried to laugh it off but Novak looked dead serious.

"I wouldn't have offered if I didn't mean it. You can keep sets of clothes here if you want. I have plenty of closet space."

"Why?" I demanded.

"Massive shirt shortage, remember?"

My laugh was a mix of nerves and genuine amusement. "No, I mean why would you offer to buy me clothes?"

His gaze heated. "Is it so hard to believe that I like you and want to see you taken care of?"

I swallowed. "I mean, a little."

He let out a frustrated little growl as he leaned in closer, stroking his knuckles against my cheek. "It should be a fucking crime that so many people in your life caused you to feel that way. If I can't punish those humans, then I'll make you see your worth for as long as you let me." He pressed a kiss to my forehead. "You should be cherished, akra. A few changes of clothes is just a drop in the bucket."

I was too choked up to respond. Novak dropped another kiss on my brow before backing away.

"Go ahead and shower. I'm going to take care of a few things in my office. Come get me when you're ready."

———

"BEEF TATAKI." The vampire waiter at Carnassian's placed the dish in front of me. "And the kitfo for you, sir." He set Novak's food down and stepped back. "Can I get you anything else?"

"This is great, thank you."

"Enjoy, folks."

As the waiter left, I hurried to remove my chopsticks from their paper wrapping. We'd gone clothes shopping for two hours before eating and I was starving.

"Be honest," I said. "Is Jo going to be upset that you're cheating on her with restaurant food?"

Novak laughed, setting a napkin in his lap. "I think she'll understand that I'm taking you out on a date." He extended his hand across the table. "Let me see that."

"This?" I held up the paper wrapper that my chopsticks had been in and he nodded. When I handed it over, he started folding it on the table's surface.

"Plus, as talented a chef as she is, she can't always whip up authentic Ethiopian food when I'm craving it." His attention was steadfast on his paper-folding project as he spoke.

"You actually crave food?"

"I crave tastes and textures. There are more foodie vampires than you might believe."

"I believe it." I picked up a piece of barely-seared beef with my chopsticks and chewed. The meat melted in my mouth, dancing in all kinds of flavors that I had never perceived as a human before. Rich, savory, balanced with a burst of citrus. I could get used to this.

Novak finished folding up my paper wrapper and placed it next to my plate. "There you go, akra."

"What's this?" I picked up the folded paper, which now looked like a small boat with an indent in the middle.

"You can rest your chopsticks on it."

"Oh." Words were lost on me. It was such a small but thoughtful gesture. "Thank you."

Novak had just taken a bite of his food and smiled slowly as he chewed, the muscles in his jaw flexing in a way that shouldn't have been sexy. But then again, I found his forearms and rolled-up sleeves sexy so maybe jaw muscles weren't too far off.

"How's your food?" I asked when I remembered how to speak.

"Good. Do you want to try it?" Novak pushed his plate toward me. "Rip off a piece of that bread, scoop it up, and dip it in the sauce."

I took a bit from his plate and he tried a bit from mine. We talked about food and flavors we liked and didn't like, ribbing each other about our differences in tastes as we enjoyed our meal. It was... easy and light. Fun. Another moment with Novak I wanted to soak up forever and never see the end of.

"How's your research going?" I paused in my eating, resting my chopsticks on the little stand he made for me.

Novak chewed slowly, the muscles in his jaw working hypnotically before his throat bobbed with a swallow. "I think it's coming to an end, to be honest."

"Really? Is that good or bad?" I couldn't tell from his reaction. He didn't seem happy about it, more resigned.

"It's not a cure. So in that sense, it's a failure." He took a long swallow of his wine. "But I was able to isolate the cause of the disease, a virus, and the antibodies. From that, I can make a vaccine to help prevent future cases. But as far as the damage that's already done?" He shrugged and lifted his hands in a giving up motion. "There's no undoing it, from what I can see. Maybe in another fifty years, with more discoveries and advanced technology, it will be possible. At this point though, I think I've done all I can do with the tools at my disposal."

My jaw hung open. "Novak, that's incredible! You've discovered the source and can save lives. I can't believe you sound so disappointed. You've done more work on this illness than anyone else has."

His look was sheepish, like he was taking too much credit despite doing all the work. "I fell short of what I originally set out to do, so it doesn't exactly feel like a victory."

"There's a saying humans have." I picked up my chopsticks, digging into my food once again. "Shoot for the moon. If you miss, you'll still land among the stars."

Novak's mouth lifted at one corner. "Which means?"

"It's a way of saying even if you don't hit your original target, you can still accomplish great things. You made a discovery that will help people! That's amazing and you should celebrate that."

"Thank you. But your saying doesn't make sense because the nearest star is still ninety-seven million miles away from the moon."

"Oh, you get what I'm saying, Mister Scientist. Don't make me throw my cute little chopstick rest at you, I quite like it."

His laugh was warm and throaty, a dangerous combination with the teasing and affection in his ruby eyes.

"Seriously, though. That's an amazing accomplishment and you should be proud. *I'm* proud." I picked up my wine glass and held it out toward him. "To your brilliant mind and your discoveries."

Novak stared at my wine glass for a long moment before silently picking up his own. For once, the highly intelligent vampire with a clever mouth seemed to be at a loss for words. I got the sense that he didn't often hear that someone was proud of him, and I intended to correct that.

"Thank you, akra," he murmured, touching his drink gently to mine. "That is... lovely of you to say."

"My pleasure." It truly was. I sipped my drink, enjoying the sight of him speechless and flustered across the table.

"Enough about me. Tell me about your life as a human." Novak's foot gently curled around my calf under the table.

I brushed off the request with a laugh. "There's not much to tell."

"Nonsense." He tapped the toe of his shoe against my leg. "What did you do? What were your interests?"

"I mean, I tried to be useful in whatever ways I could." I shrugged. "Tending the animals, cooking community meals, making quilts in the winter. I'd help Tavia with her alcohol projects sometimes, even though all the specifics went way over my head."

"You're a caretaker." Novak's voice was warm with affection, his hand finding my knee under the table. "You look after people."

"I guess. I did a lot of reading in my spare time. Trashy romance novels, mostly."

His smile turned into a full-on grin. "My mother loved those books. I still have her collection in the downstairs library."

"You do?" I perked up.

"Would you like to see them?" He removed his hand from my knee and placed it palm up on the table, amusement dancing in his eyes.

"How is that even a question? Yes!" I placed my hand in his and reveled in the warmth of his fingers curling over mine.

"Let me pay this bill then and let's get out of here." Novak waved down the waiter and made a signing motion. The waiter nodded on his way to the kitchen with a stack of empty dishes.

"Thank you for the meal and the new clothes." My thumb rubbed over the veins in Novak's wrist. "You really didn't have to."

"I know, akra." He held my hand between both of his and kissed my fingers. "But I wanted to."

I had never felt so content before. My belly was full. I had multiple shopping bags full of new clothes at my side, and a gorgeous man who seemed genuinely into me holding my hand.

Even Novak's hands and wrists were beautiful, long fingered with prominent veins under his skin. Veins with such delicious blood...

Heat rushed through me at the thought of his blood, and I felt my canines lengthen in my mouth. I wasn't even hungry, but it was the taste of him that I wanted. His skin and the heady, strong pulse underneath. I wanted him in my senses, in *me*. And not just in the sense of feeding.

He'd never taken my blood before, never asked for it. I was beginning to figure out that Novak was too selfless to ask for anything that would benefit himself. At the very least, he would make sure all my needs were met first.

As we held hands, waiting on the check, I saw his pupils dilate when looking at my wrists. I noticed the points of his own fangs poking past his top lip. He tried to be subtle about adjusting his pants, but I noticed that too.

"Novak." My fangs were on full display as I smiled and for once, I didn't care.

"Akra."

My touch ventured higher than his wrist, stroking the long, corded muscle in his forearm. "Would you like my blood?"

He hissed in a sharp breath, then muttered something under his breath before saying, "I would love nothing more." He grabbed my hand and placed a kiss on my wrist. "When we get home."

I squirmed in my seat, biting my lip to hold back my wildly excited grin. The waiter could not come back soon enough.

Chapter 21

Amy

"Your heart is beating so fast." Novak's free hand rested on my lower back as we entered his house. "Are you sure about this?"

"Yes, I'm sure." He set aside my bags, took my coat, and as soon as my hands were free, I toyed with the neckline of the dress I wore to dinner. The dress he just bought me. "I'm excited but a little nervous I think." I smiled sheepishly at him. "It feels kind of like a first kiss, only with less sobbing into the only shirt you own."

Novak's eyes were just as dark with desire as they had been in the restaurant. He wanted my blood, that much was clear. And maybe other things, if the last time I fed from his wrist was any indication. I could hear his heartbeat too, slightly elevated but still calmer than mine.

But I trusted him, and only him, to feed from me. There was no other person I wanted to share this experience with. Maybe I was romanticizing something that was a normal, biological need for vampires, but there was no mistaking the blatant want in Novak's red eyes as he crossed the foyer toward me.

"This is going to be a lot more intense than just a kiss." He took my hand, interlacing his fingers with mine. "If you want me to only take your blood and do nothing else, tell me now." He brought his other hand to my cheek, leaning his forehead down to mine. "Because feeding is not the only way I want to devour you."

"I'm not opposed to that. I just…" A shaky breath left my lips. "Can we go over some things first?"

"Of course, akra." His lips pressed to my forehead, warm and reassuring. "Let's sit down."

He led me by the hand, even though I knew his home's layout at this point and immediately knew our destination.

Novak's home library was a thing of wonder. Floor-to-ceiling built-in bookshelves stuffed with volumes of every size and subject. And considering he had fifteen-foot ceilings, the shelves naturally had rolling ladders.

I actually hadn't spent much time in here since Novak was usually in his study, and I always wanted to be where he was.

"There's my mother's collection." He pointed to a shelf with glass doors, the worn paperbacks arranged neatly inside.

I followed him to a gigantic chaise lounge that could easily fit both of us. "Your mom's books are the only ones behind glass."

He shrugged, wrapping his arms around my waist from behind. "They're all I have left of her, so I want to preserve them. They're important to me." With a soft groan, he eased us down to the chaise together. "Far more important than my family's history, records of battles or wealth or any of that other bullshit."

I spun in the cocoon of his embrace to face him. "You're very sweet, you know that?"

A smile tilted his mouth. "I know that you're the only person who thinks I am."

"Lucky me." My arms looped around his shoulders. "It seems this sweet side doesn't get shown to very many people."

Novak stared at my lips, his gaze slowly running down my throat and across my collarbone.

"I don't want to be sweet to you right now."

My skin tingled with anticipation. "Does it hurt?"

"No." Warm fingers caressed my shoulder and the side of my neck. "From me, it'll never hurt."

I believed him. The weight of his words felt like an anchor. Grounding, solid, and true.

"What does it feel like?"

"Remember when you took from my wrist? It will probably be similar to that."

I swallowed, heat rushing to my face. Aside from kissing him, that was the most physical pleasure I'd ever experienced.

"And if I want to feed from you at the same time? Is that a thing?" I couldn't explain why, but the idea of mutually feeding from each other was incredibly satisfying.

Novak hitched in a breath, his voice going even lower and huskier. "It is most definitely a thing. You can bite me anywhere you wish. Take my wrist, my shoulder, anywhere you can reach. I'm yours to take from, just as much as you are mine."

I nodded, my focus going to the strong, proud column of his throat.

He angled my chin until our eyes met again. "Any other questions?"

His fangs were so long now, dangerous weapons behind extremely soft lips. "No, I don't think so."

"And you're okay with me touching you beyond what's necessary to feed?"

"Yes." I was practically panting already, my leg sliding over Novak's hip. I couldn't imagine wanting anything more. "Yes, I would like to... do more."

"You should probably give me some kind of signal if you want me to stop." His hand slid from my knee up my thigh, letting the material of my dress fall away and expose more skin.

"I trust you," I insisted. "I won't want you to stop."

His hand rested halfway up my thigh, thumb caressing in small circles. "Tell me if that changes at any point, okay?"

I nodded, inhaling sharply when he leaned in to kiss me. He stopped short, and when I tried to close the distance, he held me in place with a firm hand around my nape.

"Tell me with your words, akra."

My pulse beat wildly, lips aching for contact while he hovered a hair's breadth away. He was commanding a response, not giving me what I wanted until I did so. And still, his other hand caressed my leg in small circles with so much tenderness.

"I'll tell you," I whispered, "if I want you to stop."

"Beautiful."

Before I could figure out if he was pleased with my answer or complimenting me, his mouth fitted against mine with delicious, tantalizing pressure. Our bodies shifted as we found a rhythm in the kiss, moving to a reclined but slightly upright position in the chaise. Novak's knees nudged my legs apart, sending my dress higher up my thighs.

Time was lost as I explored his mouth properly, without tears and crushing despair in the way. I traced his fangs with my lips, becoming familiar with those curious points.

"Why are yours so much bigger than mine?" I asked before pulling on his bottom lip.

A laugh burst out of him. "Ah well. You were born human, so I'm guessing there are limits to how big your fangs can be."

"What? No dirty jokes?" I kissed him through my smile. "I gotta say, I am disappointed."

"I'm a little distracted, I have to admit." He turned my face with a gentle nudge of his hand, kissed my cheek, and then the corner of my jaw.

After a kiss below my earlobe, he dragged the points of his fangs down the side of my neck. Goosebumps and shivers wracked my whole body, the anticipation winding me up.

"Fuck, Amy." Novak kissed the juncture of my neck and shoulder, his mouth lingering like he was savoring the taste of my skin.

"Please," I whispered, my heart hammering.

He kissed me there once more, tongue flattening against my pulse. My eyelids fluttered closed, breath caught in my chest as I waited.

I felt two sharp points of pressure, but no pain. The barrier of my skin broke and Novak sealed his lips to my skin, his chest against mine with a gentle weight like a blanket.

He moaned with the first pull on my vein, and the sensation sent my head falling back, my whole body arching into him. I had been feeling good while kissing, but within seconds, I ratcheted up from *good* to *holy-shit-I'm-so-turned-on-and-I'm-going-to-come-if-he-doesn't-stop.*

Each draw of his mouth came with a blast of sensitivity

on my clit, hitting me in just the right way that sent pleasure coiling in me tighter and tighter. He wasn't even physically touching me there, but I felt the rocking shifts of his body, his hips canting forward like he wanted to thrust into me.

Novak kept moaning against my neck, settling more of his weight on top of me until our torsos were flush together. His hand slid up my waist, palming my breast over my dress as he drank from me. My thighs locked around him, holding him in place because every cell in my body never wanted him to leave.

My open, panting mouth felt too empty, too dry. I wanted to be kissing him, tasting his tongue and skin and fangs. Or his blood.

I grabbed his hand that rolled over my breast and brought his wrist to my mouth. Biting into him was as instinctual as breathing, easy as resting my forehead on his chest for comfort. Novak's body jerked when the first drop of blood hit my mouth, and his groans against my neck grew more guttural, animalistic, and desperate.

The taste of him somehow soothed my aches and heightened my senses into a frenzy. My clit was so sensitive, it was near painful. Our hips rolled against each other, chasing pleasure and release. Novak fit so well between my legs, the friction of his hard length adding another layer of dizzying sensation to the pulls of his mouth. He felt so good in every imaginable way. Tender and rough. Safe with a touch of danger.

I came in a heady rush that stopped my breathing for a few seconds, my whole body locking up like I'd been turned into stone. The tension released and I floated on pulses of sensation, my heart kicking against my ribs like a caged bird.

Novak's fangs left my neck, making me shiver as he soothed the bite with his tongue. I did the same to his wrist, a little clumsier, and licked up a trail of blood that ran down his forearm.

His torso lifted away from mine, and I immediately missed it. The weight of him, the press of his body against me was a source of comfort and safety I never knew I craved until now. His forehead rested on mine, chest heaving with his panting breaths.

"Good?" he rasped. "You okay?"

"*So* good." I lifted my lips toward his, tugging him down toward me.

His kiss was warm and indulgent, but he kept his hips away. "I...have to clean up."

My brow furrowed. "What do you mean?"

Was he blushing? His skin had a warm, flushed tint, maybe from my blood. And his smile took on an endearing, sheepish curve.

"You made me feel just as good as you did." He laughed, eyes casting away bashfully. "In terms of... below-the-waist things."

I stared at him. "Below-the-waist things?"

"I came in my pants, okay?"

"Oh!" I swallowed my laughter and must have made a weird face.

"It's fine, laugh. It's your fault, anyway." His crooked smirk returned, knuckles stroking my cheek. "You're so fucking beautiful, my body just couldn't handle it."

His eyes shone with pure adoration and wonder, like I was something to marvel at. But my post-orgasm clarity had returned, along with my self-consciousness. "So, my blood tasted okay?"

"Okay?" He scoffed out the word like it was an insult. "Did you miss the part where I just told you I came in my pants?"

I let the laughter free that time, and he went on.

"Your blood tastes incredible, akra. Sweet, rich, hot, and so velvety smooth. If my tongue could orgasm, I'd be a far bigger mess right now."

His praise was like sunshine to a light-starved plant. I wanted to bask in it for hours, to feel it strengthen me where I had been so weak before.

"You poor thing," I said with a glance at his crotch. "Although I must say I'm flattered."

"You should be. This has never happened to me before." He stood awkwardly from the chaise, but still held his hand out to me like the perfect gentleman. "Come wash with me? We can try out those four shower heads."

I took his hand and allowed him to pull me up, because how could I not? He kissed my knuckles with a smile that was both affectionate and suggestive. We could continue our fun, doing more below-the-waist things, as he put it. I was addicted to how he made me feel, how confident and sexy, but also sweet and considerate he was. He was only interested in doing more with me if I was enjoying it too, and knowing that made me feel safer and more confident than I had ever been with a man before.

I *wanted* to let loose with him more than anything, to be free and uninhibited to enjoy myself and him fully. But I felt like there was a barrier inside me, a brick wall that wouldn't let me cross into that zone. It was the same barrier that blocked me from looking at my body in the mirror.

I knew it was irrational. Novak was attracted to me, genuinely liked me, and some scars on my stomach weren't likely to change that. But fears weren't rational, and I still couldn't get Tom and Robin's horrified expressions out of my mind. If Novak looked at me with any amount of disgust, it would shatter me beyond repair.

Because, I realized at that moment, I was falling for him.

We climbed the stairs together and approached his bedroom, my panic heightening at every step while I tried to think of possible excuses. At the threshold I stopped short, resisting when he walked in.

He turned to me, curiosity on his face. "You all right, darling? You don't have to wait for an invitation to come in." He chuckled, pleased with his vampire joke as he kissed my wrist.

"I just... I already showered earlier tonight." The excuse felt like a lie, a betrayal. "I'm actually a little worn out, so I might just go to bed if that's okay."

"Of course it is." He framed my face with his hands, kissed my forehead, and then brought his lips down to mine.

I sighed into his kiss, which was lingering and sweet. My arms went around his back as I leaned into him. Guilt gnawed at me as he kissed me tenderly again and again. He was so giving and patient while here I was, still holding back.

"Does this mean you're spending another day here?" Novak's gaze was excited, hopeful. It boggled my mind that this perfect man wanted even more time with me.

"Is that okay?"

"You really need to ask?" He kissed me again, smiling against my lips before pulling away. "My closet is through the double doors across from the bathroom sinks. Put your new clothes in there. I should have extra toothbrushes and things in the sink drawers." He kissed me once more, then walked backward with a slight grimace. "I'll join you soon. Things are getting sticky down here."

I laughed and watched him speed-walk awkwardly to his insane four-headed shower. The water ran while I changed into a baggy T-shirt for bed, and his automatic shutters came down to cover the windows with the onset of dawn.

This felt normal in the best way. Easy. How it should be, living with a partner. Lots of kisses and a bedtime routine. I climbed into bed and got comfortable as I waited for Novak.

This would be so perfect if I could let my guard down with him. I pictured it behind my eyelids like a distant fantasy. Being brave enough to let him see me naked, to shed my clothes without a care and see nothing but lust and desire in his expression. In my head, I saw it play out like a movie. Our bodies entwining with no barriers or shyness between us. I saw my lips move, forming fearless words as I told this gorgeous vampire that I was falling hard and fast for him.

But my heart had been battered enough to know that I shouldn't expect fantasies to become real.

Chapter 22

Novak

*A*my is my blood mate.

It didn't fully hit me until I'd been standing under the shower head for a few minutes. The result of my embarrassingly fast orgasm had washed away, and at the first thought of her, my cock thickened and pulsed, already needy for a real touch from her.

Only her.

Her blood was better than anything I'd ever tasted in my life. It was life itself, beautifully bright and vibrant on my tongue. Every swallow felt like a caress from my throat to my groin. I had felt some tingles of arousal from drinking blood before, but nothing like that. Amy had never even touched me directly and yet I'd made a premature mess of myself like I was a juvenile being gripped and stroked by my wildest fantasy.

Amy was everything I never dared to fantasize about because I never thought she could be real. She came to me when she needed safety in a vulnerable moment, defended me because of who I was, not because she was hoping to gain something from my clan's name. She didn't even care about the status of Rathka's Order, or our contentious history with Blood 'til Dawn. This stunning brusang with galaxies in her eyes and kitten fangs cared about *me*.

But blood mates were on a different level than caring for. Her blood was chemically and nutritionally perfect for me and me alone. All other blood sources would taste rancid and foul now that I'd tasted her. My vampire biology wanted me hooked on the one source that was my perfect biological match until my death.

That was absolutely fine with me. Another six hundred years of kissing Amy's perfect neck before I sank into her? Sign me up.

The only question was, did she feel the same way?

I closed my eyes under the shower's spray, the hot water running over me a poor replacement for Amy's fingers. Weeks ago, when she first came to my house, she made a little offhand comment. *Why does your blood taste so good?*

At the time, I chalked it up to the fact that she was starving. Any blood would have tasted like a miracle. But then I remembered scenting her arousal in my kitchen, her little moans and squirms when she took from my wrist the first time. And the fact that she had never successfully taken blood from anyone else but me.

Had our true, physical chemistry been driving us toward each other since the very beginning?

"Fuck." My head tilted back, letting the water rain down on my face. "Temkra, is it really true?"

No answer came from the shower head. If I really wanted an answer from the goddess, I'd have to meditate at my mother's altar in my office. Or consult with a member of Temkra's Blood.

A blood mate. For me, the disgraced second son of an

extinct clan. After centuries of trying to prove myself worthy, it felt too good to be true.

Amy was already in my bed, asleep and breathing deeply, when I turned off the shower and dried myself. I slid in next to her slowly, taking care not to disturb her rest. Once beside her, I couldn't seem to shut my brain off. I was lying in bed with my blood mate beside me, and she had no idea.

Now I had an even better reason to end the arrangement with Baros. Not even he could argue against who Temkra had chosen for me.

But there was still a problem that could get in the way of our happiness. One that had an insatiable hunger for vampire flesh and was currently haunting my basement.

———

My sleep had been fitful and restless, with long stretches of staring at the ceiling and watching Amy lying peacefully next to me. She roused when dusk fell, adorable as she stretched to wakefulness.

"Evening." I slid against her back, kissing her nape as my arm went around her waist.

"Mm, hello." She rolled into me, snuggling into my chest until she found a comfortable spot. "Sleep well?"

I kissed the top of her head. "Well enough. You?"

"Like the dead." She yawned and kissed the space between my collarbones, firing up my pulse. "I should probably call Tavia to let her know I'm alive and well."

Besides a relaxed sigh that sent her melting into me, Amy made no effort to move.

"Are you staying another night?" My hand moved lazily

up and down her back, smoothing out the large T-shirt she wore to bed.

Amy's head lifted, her brow furrowing. "I should probably go, huh? This is what, three straight days? I'm sure you want your space."

I cupped her ass, ran my hand down the back of her thigh until I reached her knee, then brought her leg over my hip. "Do I look like I want space from you?"

Her head went back on a soft, musical laugh and I leaned in to kiss the long, pretty stretch of her throat. I could spend hours just exploring her neck, finding all the tiny blood vessels and sensitive areas that made her gasp.

"I just don't want to overstay my welcome." She kissed my brow, hand sliding around my waist until her fingertips stroked my spine. "Being with you is like staying in a dream I don't want to wake up from."

"You're always welcome here." My thumb rolled circles alongside her knee. "Come and go as you please. If you need space, take it." My lips rested on her forehead. "As long as you come back," I amended.

Her answering smile was slow, coy. Sexy. "As if you could keep me away."

That would have been the right time to spill my secrets, to inform her of the ravenous undead monster in my basement, as well as Carpe Noctem's chain around my neck, even though the agreement was null and void in my eyes. *Also, surprise! I'm literally, biologically, dependent on your blood to survive.*

Amy deserved to know everything and make her own choices based on that knowledge. But right then, wrapped up in each other, in the warmth of my bed, it made the most sense to kiss her and not ruin the perfection of this moment.

She sighed contently into my mouth, our lips moving

with slow, unhurried friction. My eyes closed so I could take her in with my other senses. This did feel like a dream, the best kind. And I wanted to prolong this for as long as possible.

Her leg slid farther over my hip, toes grazing my calf. The closer proximity brought more contact to my thickening cock, the organ trapped between our pelvises as we wound tighter around each other.

Amy made soft, eager noises through our kisses, her lower body beginning to rub against me more insistently. I grabbed her ass and pulled her closer until we were flush, her leg spread wide and my erection grinding against her core.

The friction was maddening through our underwear. I wanted skin-to-skin contact, to see her beautiful naked form wearing nothing but my bite marks. I grabbed the hem of her T-shirt and began to pull it up—

"No, don't!"

Amy reacted faster that I could comprehend, swinging her arm down to stop me from bringing her shirt up. It was so unexpected that the fabric slipped from my fingers.

In an instant, the mood changed. Playful and passionate became tense and guarded. Amy held the shirt down so low, the collar stretched at her neck. Her eyes were wide with panic.

"Darling, I'm sorry." Hesitantly, I reached a hand toward her face. She let me touch her cheek but the stiffness didn't leave her body. "I thought we were... fuck, it doesn't matter. Are you all right?"

She let out a long, slow breath, her body relaxing a fraction. "I... don't like being naked. I didn't mean to freak out, I just... panicked."

Her voice was so small, like she was ashamed.

My mind immediately took off, speculating all the possible reasons why on Temkra's soil she would ever feel that way. Did it have anything to do with that filth of a human male who broke her heart?

One day I'd find out the reason, but now was not the time.

"I'm really not a prude. I just don't like having my top off." Amy grimaced with shame. "I'm sorry. We were having fun and I ruined it."

"Stop. You didn't ruin anything." I leaned in, caressing her cheek as I kissed her forehead, brow, and nose. "It doesn't matter what we're doing. I'm satisfied as long as you're enjoying yourself."

She didn't look convinced. "You're sweet, but you don't have to lie. I know I'm weird."

"I like weird. Especially when it shows up on my doorstep with the prettiest eyes I've ever seen." That finally got the smallest curve of a smile on her lips, and I seized the opportunity to kiss them. "Seriously, akra, I'll never do anything you don't want. Your sense of safety is of utmost importance to me."

A sigh of relief left her lips and her hand wrapped around my nape, fingers tangling in my hair. "Thank you, Novak. You're amazing."

"You are," I breathed into her mouth.

We fell into lazy, slow kissing again, but a thought nagged at the back of my mind. She still didn't fully trust me, and why should she? The whole time she'd been open and vulnerable with me, I'd been holding back. Keeping secrets.

A gust of wind howled and made the house creak. I could imagine the creature downstairs snarling at the noise, dragging his skeletal fingers along the bars of his cell. Talk about overstaying his welcome. I'd kept him here for probably fifty years too long.

But it wasn't like I could set him loose, not even to the deep forests of the Crown. He, like his cursed brethren, would make his way to the towns and villages of that region, following the scent of living flesh.

A nip on my neck pulled my focus back to Amy and her sharp little fangs.

"Where did your mind go?" she asked, softly mouthing at my neck. "Thinking about what a weirdo you've got in your bed?"

I pulled away and leaned back against the headboard, too deep in my fucked-up thoughts to lose myself in her. "You're perfect as you are, akra, but I haven't told you everything about my research. And I should. It's only right for you to know if we're going to be... involved."

She took a long moment to respond to that, blinking slowly. "Okay. What haven't you told me?"

My fingers drummed nervously in my lap. "There's a cursed member of my clan here, in my house. I captured him fifty years ago, and well, he's been here ever since."

Amy stared at me, wide-eyed. "Here? Where?"

"In the basement level. The house is safe. There are multiple security doors between the main floor and his... his cell." I leaned my head back, letting it thunk against the headboard. "No matter how much I told myself that it was to find a cure, that everything would be justified if I could undo the Curse, it doesn't change the fact that I've been holding one of my kin prisoner for this long." My head shook from side to side. "And now that I'm almost certain there is no cure, that the damage is done, I don't feel right keeping him down there. But there's no way I can release him. He's a danger to others."

"Novak." Amy had sat up and was now at my side, her hand reaching for mine. Her expression was calmer than I expected. "Who is he to you?"

My eyes closed and my throat tightened. "He's my brother."

Amy's face fell with sorrow. "Oh, Novak... "

"I swear I was trying to help, to do my duty for Rathka's Order." Once the excuses and justifications spilled from my mouth, there was no stopping them. "All I wanted was to make my clan proud, to be more than a do-nothing second son. I worked for *centuries* to save them, to decode this curse down to its atoms so they would find me worthy of the clan's name. If I cured them all, brought Rathka's Order back to its former glory, that would mean something, right? I didn't even want anything in return. Just an ounce of pride, a single fucking acknowledgment from my father and brother would have been enough. It would have been *everything*."

Amy was silent at my side. If I didn't feel her hand over mine, I would have thought she'd left the room.

"I'm seeing now how delusional I was." I rubbed my temples, suddenly feeling an ache behind my eye sockets. "Even if I had cured everyone, they would have found a way to credit someone else for it, to diminish what I had done. Nothing I ever did made them respect me in the past, so why would they start now? Even if they did give me some hollow appreciation, it wouldn't have been enough. I was *starving* for my father's approval. I would have tried harder, done anything for more scraps."

A bitter laugh escaped me. "Just fifty years ago, I was convinced that all I needed was tissue samples from a live specimen. If I captured one of them, I would be that much closer to figuring it out. I realized it was my brother because of the scraps of clothing left on him, and his signet ring. I had daydreams, fucking fantasies even, of him hugging me after he was cured, telling me he was so proud of me. That he was so grateful to have his mind back, his life back."

I shook my head again. "But that'll never happen. It doesn't actually matter that I'm the last one left because I was never one of them to begin with. That was the one truth they never let me forget."

A long silence followed, and I felt a strange emptiness in the center of my chest. Like the vault I'd kept everything hidden away in was suddenly wrenched open and the contents had taken flight. I was afraid to look at Amy, to read the expression on her face now that my deepest, ugliest truth was out there.

But she had come to me when she was at her lowest, found shelter in my arms, during an emotional storm. I had to trust that she would hold that same space for me.

By the time I gathered the courage to look at her, she was already crawling into my lap. When I opened my mouth to speak, her kiss pressed me into the headboard.

I wanted to kiss Novak until I was all out of breath. I wanted to run down to the basement and yell at his brother about what an asshole and a terrible family member he was. I wished I could go back in time and tell young Novak he was worthy of love and recognition in spite of his shitty family treating him like an outcast.

He needed those words right now, and I could only hope he valued my opinion enough to take my words to heart.

"They were wrong about you," I whispered against his mouth. "So, so wrong. Don't you see? You're better than all of them ever were."

His hands trembled slightly as they held lightly onto my waist. It couldn't have been easy, confessing everything he did just now. He seemed to feel guilty about keeping his brother imprisoned, although he could rot for eternity down there for all I cared. From the sound of it, he'd been a bully. I knew the type well.

"You're such an incredible person, Novak." I held his face between my hands. "You're kind and honest and so selfless. You could've passed me off to someone else that first night we met, let me be another vampire's problem or finished me off by draining the rest of my blood. You encouraged me to repair my friendship with Tavia. You held me all night while I cried without making me talk about it. Fuck, you've spent centuries trying to find a cure for a family that never appreciated you. That speaks volumes about the kind of person you are."

Novak's arms went tighter around me as I spoke, his forehead leaning heavily against mine.

"I'm tired," he admitted in a hoarse whisper. "So fucking tired of carrying all of Rathka's Order on my shoulders. None of them are here to tell me I'm not doing enough, but I hear their voices all the same. Upholding my duty to the clan is what I've been trained to do since birth, and I don't know how to stop."

His head came forward until it rested on my shoulder. I raked my fingernails over his scalp, massaging the tight muscles in his neck.

"You're not alone," I told him. "You have me. And if you need me to hold onto you while you let it all go, I'll be right here. You don't need Rathka's Order. You can choose to free yourself from them."

He leaned his forehead against my neck, arms clamped around me in a tight embrace. "I've never felt like I had choices. I was raised to put the clan above all else, and look where that got me. Trying to please ghosts, and monsters in my basement." His head lifted, brow pressing to mine. "You're the first thing I've wanted selfishly. I want you around for the simple fact that you make my blood sing in my veins."

My heartbeat accelerated, screaming a beat that

sounded like, *Choose me. Be the first and only person who has genuinely wanted to keep me.*

"Nothing bad will happen if you choose to be selfish," I said, trying to keep my voice steady. "No one is here to make you feel guilty about your own happiness. And if your ancestors want to haunt you from their graves for choosing yourself, I'll happily tell them to fuck off and leave you alone."

That earned me a smile and a soft chuckle. "My mother would one-hundred percent say that Temkra brought you to me, and I should never refuse gifts from the goddess."

"Your mother sounds like she was lovely." I kissed his brow. "But what do *you* want? What will make you happiest, Novak?"

A heavy sigh seemed to deflate his whole chest. "I want to let go of the past, to stop giving power to people who don't exist anymore. I think I've wanted that for a long time but didn't know how. Or just never wanted it badly enough." His knuckles stroked my cheek. "Not until you."

"I know it's not easy. It's not exactly the same, but since coming to terms with no longer being human, I've been feeling a lot of the same resistance. The guilt for going against my upbringing. Disappointing people whose approval I wanted, but they never respected me no matter what I did."

The realization hit me like a light bulb clicking on. Novak and I were so different, and yet our struggles were so similar. Every word I told him was exactly what I needed to hear for myself.

"Yes." He breathed the word on a sigh of relief and a warm, lingering kiss. "You understand me exactly, akra. You know what it's like. Fuck, I think you're truly the only person that does."

Our mouths found each other again, giving strength and reassurance that words could not.

"I want you," Novak said when we parted. "I want a life that's my own, and I'm ready for it." He let out a nervous laugh. "It still feels like I'm diving off a cliff, though."

"I know." My arms went around his shoulders. "But it's as simple as making a choice. Choosing one path and leaving another behind."

His next sigh was weary. "It's not quite that simple for me. Not with my brother downstairs."

"Oh, right." Somehow I'd forgotten about that already. His brother just didn't hold space in my mind when it was Novak who needed love and appreciation. "What should be done about him?"

Novak swallowed tightly. "I can't release him. And I can't bear to keep him down there."

The unspoken solution felt like a heavy, weighted presence in the room.

"Do you have a way of making it quick? Painless?" If I knew anything about Novak, he would not want his brother to suffer.

He nodded. "I have a silver dagger. One stab to the chest should be enough. I don't even think they're capable of feeling pain in that state." His fingers laced at the small of my back. "I've killed a few before, in self-defense. He's defenseless, but... " He shook his head. "If there's anything left of Evin in there, he's probably been suffering for decades. To put him out of his misery would be a kindness."

"Do you want me to do it for you?" Maybe it was callous, but I wasn't at all bothered about stabbing a cannibalistic creature who made Novak suffer in his younger years. If anything, it might be cathartic.

"No, it needs to be me. I have immunity to the disease,

you might not. I definitely can't risk you." He leaned back, chest heaving with another sigh. "I have to do it. This is how I bury the past and truly move forward."

"I'll be there with you." My hold tightened around his shoulders, bringing him in for another kiss. "You'll never be without my support." *Or my love.* That last part burned in my throat, not ready to be spoken aloud.

"Amy... my akra." He spoke my name reverently between each kiss, fingers curling into my shirt and holding onto me like I was the only support he needed.

I had never been needed by anyone before, not even Tavia.

"You can do this." I stroked his hair back, my forehead melded to his. "You're so strong, so brave. I know you can do it, Novak."

He huffed wryly. "I think you're the first person who's actually believed in me."

"How could I not? You believed in me, after all."

His hand came to the side of my face, thumb stroking with gentle reverence next to my mouth before he was repeating my own words back to me like a simple truth. "How could I not?"

Our mouths connected again with more passion and fervor than before. Hunger stoked low in my belly, and determination fired me up. I pressed on Novak's shoulders and he leaned back only a few inches before meeting the headboard. My hips rolled in his lap, grinding against him to create sensation and friction that had him groaning.

He grabbed my waist, bucking into me as his tongue surged into my mouth. I kissed him back, but removed his hands from my waist, pinning them at his sides.

"What are you doing?" His eyes were dark with lust, canines long with hunger. "I want to touch you, akra."

"Not right now."

"Why?"

I brought my legs inside of his, kissing his neck with small nips that didn't draw any blood. My mouth skimmed over his collarbones and down his chest, following the sparse pale hairs and long, lean muscles that covered his torso. I scooted back as I drew lower, listening to his accelerating heart and ragged breaths. I reached the waistband of his underwear, and only then did I look up at him to answer.

"Because I'm going to let you be utterly selfish before you complete the hardest task of your life."

He seemed to get the picture when I tugged his boxers down to reveal his cock, thick and long where it rested on his lower belly.

"Amy," he hissed, putting his hand over mine. "You don't have to. I appreciate the gesture very, very much but—"

"I want to." A smile pulled at my lips as I stuck my tongue out, giving a small lick to his broad head. "Really, I do. Let me be selfish too and find out how you really taste."

He stopped resisting then, and relaxed against the headboard. "You're more than I've ever fucking deserved." His fingers stroked through my hair, gathering the strands away from my face. "Can I still touch you?"

I loved his hands on me, all his caresses and holds and kisses. But even then I felt the scars on my abdomen, a constant, unyielding reminder that I was not truly as beautiful as he found me. That despite his hard length right in front of my face, I still had the potential to completely turn him off.

"Just not under my T-shirt, okay?"

A flicker of an expression crossed his face, something

like disappointment, but it was gone in an instant. "Of course, darling. Only where you'll feel good."

He was so good, almost too good to be true. So protective and confident, but sweeter and kinder than any man I'd ever known. It only heightened my desire to please him, to give to him without taking anything for myself. He'd already given me so much.

My lips slid over his crown, my hand wrapping around the base of his shaft with a slight squeeze. Novak was already moaning as my tongue circled his head. I gave a few experimental strokes, listening to what kind of pressure and speed he liked best.

"Fuck, so good," he choked out when my hand twisted slightly just below his head. "Akra, fuck... your mouth. You're incredible."

His praise brought my confidence to a level I'd never felt before. I took more of him in my mouth, adding pressure with my lips and tongue to his velvety skin. Like a perfect gentleman, he held my hair back, twisted into a loose knot in his fist. The other hand caressed my neck and face. It was like he physically couldn't stop himself from touching me, from marveling at me. I was in the submissive position here, but it felt like he was the one worshiping me.

"So beautiful, you're sucking me so well." His voice became rough with a predatory edge. "Fucking Temkra, you're a vision. So fucking stunning, ugh, that mouth. So perfect, don't stop."

I built up to a steady rhythm, basking in his filthy, sweet words and eager for the reward of his release. He was solid and heavy, swelling even thicker with each stroke of my fist and tongue.

"I can smell how wet you are. You like sucking me that much, akra? Fuck, I want to touch you so bad."

His hand groped over my T-shirt, finding my breasts through the baggy material. I moaned with my mouth full of him and would have gasped if I could. He pulled and twisted the fabric taut, making it rasp against my achingly sensitive nipples.

"I want your bare skin on mine," Novak groaned. "I want these perfect tits filling my hands and no clothing between us when I finally fuck you. Is that selfish enough?"

That declaration should have sent alarm bells ringing, should have scared me into removing him from my mouth and backing away while telling him no, that would never happen.

But I just moaned agreement, leaning into the pressure of his hands and taking him deeper down my throat. Everything felt too good. I was swept away in the pleasure this was providing for me, not just him. His noises and needy, desperate touches, the heaviness of him on my tongue. All of it was proof of how I affected him, how sexy and irresistible he found me. That validation fed me like I was starving. For once in my life, I felt just a tiny bit powerful.

It would be over as soon as he came, like a broken spell. An illusion ripped away. I knew that I didn't *really* have power over him, that there were plenty of other women sexier than me, better at blowjobs than me. Novak didn't actually want to see me naked that badly. He probably already forgot that he said it. But for the moment, I could keep living in this fantasy of being the perfect woman of his wildest dreams.

"Akra, I'm so close." Novak's head was thrown back, the muscles of his throat working with each choked word. "You have me right there, you're going to make me fucking explode."

My jaw ached and my lungs burned from not taking a

deep breath for several minutes. I didn't want to stop and yet I still wanted to make him come, just to know that I could please him enough.

Novak released with a bellowing roar. His cock swelled almost to the point of cutting off my air completely before his salty release coated my tongue and throat. His hands went to his sides, clutching the sheets with a death grip while he shuddered stiffly.

I kept him in my mouth until he was completely spent and he pulsed softly from aftershocks. He grabbed my upper arms and hauled me upward the moment my mouth was free. When he leaned to kiss me, I backed away in shock. Surely he wouldn't want to taste himself on me?

With a rough growl, he held the back of my head and plundered my mouth with his own. I was still catching my breath and his deep, insistent kiss took me to a new level of lightheadedness.

His tongue tangled with mine and he sucked lightly at my lips like this was any other kiss. If tasting his own pleasure bothered him at all, he made no show of it.

A tiny prick of pain made me gasp, and then Novak licked gently at the wound. A shiver raced down my spine, all my erogenous zones pulsing with pleasure. He pulled back with a smirk, his exposed fang tipped with my blood.

"You're incredible, akra." He kissed the small wound on my lip, which was already closed and healing. Again, the pleasurable rush of sensations made me inhale sharply, and Novak made a low, approving noise in his throat. "Will you let me return the favor?"

A large hand caressed my inner thigh, kneading and stroking just outside of my panties. I squirmed under his touch, already sensitive and aroused from what I just did to him. Or rather, how he made *me* feel while I did that to him.

"With your hand?" I squeaked. It wouldn't take much.

"I meant with my mouth." His fangs trailed my neck. "But I'll please you however you prefer."

Having his mouth on me meant taking my underwear off. And him being down there would make it too easy for him to touch or see my stomach. Too risky.

Plus, the idea of asking for oral made me uneasy. I had asked for it that night Tom and I had been together, but he brushed me off saying he didn't enjoy the taste. I'd rather sink into the floor and disappear than see Novak react negatively to going down on me.

"Your hand," I said, wrapping an arm around his shoulders.

An expression crossed his face, something like skepticism, but then he was kissing me and pulling me into his lap. My thighs spread apart to straddle his, and then he nicked me again with a fang as he cupped his palm between my legs.

I had never had an orgasm so fast. Between his palm grinding small circles against my clit and his sips of my blood with each kiss, I was shooting into the atmosphere and seeing stars in under five seconds.

"You deserve all the pleasure in the world, Amy." Novak dragged a fang over my earlobe until he drew blood, then sucked at it while his hand commanded another orgasm out of me. "You deserve riches, the finest blood for your palate, every single thing you've ever desired."

"Only want you," I panted, not even fully aware of what I was saying. He was playing my body like a finely-tuned instrument, making me moan and sigh and clutch him for dear life.

"Oh darling, you have me." He gave me a moment of reprieve, taking his hand away. And then just as quickly slid it into my soaked panties. "You have me in the palm of your hand. I am wholly yours in every way."

Two fingers pressed inside me, his thumb heavy on my clit. He kissed me again, tongue flicking to catch another drop of blood. I came hard around his fingers, shuddering into oblivion as he curled those digits to draw out my pleasure.

"You deserve the life of a queen." Novak scraped a fanged kiss against the hollow of my throat and captured my blood with his lips and tongue, his fingers fucking into me with sloppy wet sounds as I rode them into another orgasm. "Nothing but respect, adoration, and worship for the most stunning creature I've ever set eyes on."

"Novak... " I was dead weight draped against him, barely able to hold myself upright. My lungs wheezed for air, every nerve spent and overstimulated. "I can't... can't come anymore."

"Mmm." He made sympathetic noises, petting my hair with the hand that wasn't knuckle-deep inside me. Gentle, fangless kisses rained over my forehead, brows, and eyelids.

When my breathing finally neared normal levels, he tilted my face up with a knuckle under my chin. "I think you can give me one more, can't you?"

His fingers curled inside me again, making me squirm.

"I don't know. It's too much."

"You can, akra. Just one more. For me." His teeth bared like a predator. "You wanted me to be selfish? This is what I want."

I didn't mean to laugh. I was still dazed from all the orgasms before, on top of the fact that it was absurd that *my* pleasure equated to *him* being selfish.

Out of nowhere, I was flying through the air and grabbed his shoulders for stability. In a mere second, I was lying flat on the bed with Novak hovering above me.

I looked at him with a mix of confusion and pure lust. God, he was so hot. How magical would it be to stare up at him like this on a regular basis? Watching his face, seeing the strength of his body as he moved inside me.

His fingers were still inside me, thumb circling around my clit hood without touching it directly. He knew exactly what to do to not overstimulate me to the point of pain, and the sweet consideration of that almost distracted me from the fact that he was moving down my body.

"Novak." I fought my wobbly limbs to sit up. "I said not your mouth."

He kissed the inside of my thigh before looking up at me, grinning. "You meant no oral, right?"

"Yeah."

"Good. Because I've been using my mouth on you this entire time."

His fangs sank into the artery on my inner thigh with lighting speed. He pulled a mouthful of blood at the same time his thumb returned to my clit and his fingers dragged along my inner walls.

It wasn't just one more orgasm. I lost count sometime after three.

Amy slept soundly after I truly wrung every last possible orgasm out of her. But even after she had pleased me so well, I couldn't relax.

I paced the bedroom, trying to convince myself to just run downstairs, stab my brother, then come back here and drag her warm body against me. It could all be over within minutes.

And yet every time I looked at the door, my feet felt cemented in place. Then I looked at the bed and could have flown across the room to be next to Amy. It was so much easier to stay in the comfort of this room, the comfort of her, and ignore the world outside.

When she stirred, I looked away from the window and toward the bed, not wanting to miss how adorable she looked when she woke.

"How long was I out?" she asked on a jaw-cracking yawn.

"About an hour." I went to the bed and rested my arm on the foot post. "How do you feel?"

She tried to hide her grin behind the sheet, but I saw the

apples of her cheeks and her eyes twinkling. "How do you think?"

"Tell me. I want to know."

Amy pushed the covers down and stretched with a groan. I heard bones popping, and then a massive sigh of satisfaction.

"Like a brand-new woman," she admitted. "I've never felt so... refreshed, and just so *good*. Like I've slept for a hundred years and I needed it."

My chest swelled with pride. "I'm glad to hear that." Not only had all the orgasms released pleasure from her, I hoped they released much of the tension and self-consciousness that she carried about her body. I had meant every word that I said to her as well, and hoped she took them to heart.

Amy seemed to notice something in my expression and her smile fell. "What's wrong?"

When I couldn't answer her right away, she crawled across the bed and came up to her knees in front of me. Her arms looped around my neck and mine automatically slid around her waist. As my head lowered, she kissed my brow before letting her forehead meet mine.

"I have to get this over with," I whispered.

She nodded, understanding. "Do you want me to come with you?"

I wanted to tell her no, that she should wait for me here. It would be safest, even though there was no risk of Evin escaping the basement. I didn't want the sight of him frightening her.

But more than that, I didn't want to give him the privilege of seeing her.

When he wasn't outright tormenting me, Evin's favorite pastime was seducing any female I got close to, even if we were just friendly. If I talked to anyone with romantic potential, he'd slap me on the back in congratulations then turn around and made sure I'd walk in on them fucking a week later. Usually in my room.

It was an irrational fear now, I knew. But if there was anything left of my brother in that monster, he would see how much Amy meant to me and even though he couldn't, he would *want* to use my feelings for her to hurt me. Maybe even more than before, considering I'd kept him prisoner for the last fifty years.

What I realized though, as I had paced the room and watched Amy sleep, was that I couldn't go down there alone. I needed her with me.

"Please?" My arms tightened around her waist. "Will you?"

She brushed a soft kiss, all lips and no fangs, against my mouth. "Let me get dressed."

I released her, watching her slide from the bed and walk barefoot to my walk-in closet.

My brother, my father—hell, anyone in my clan would have seen emotional support from a woman as weakness. The men of Rathka's Order saw any female as only good for blood, sex, and occasionally, children.

Naturally, that begged a question. If they were so strong and I so weak, why was I the only one left?

Survival was the ultimate measure of strength, was it not? In the end, everything came down to that, a simple binary of yes or no. You survived or you didn't.

I did. They didn't.

I had the power to shape my own life, to create my own legacy. They could only control me from the grave if I allowed it.

Tonight, I revoked that permission.

Amy returned wearing a different T-shirt and a pair of leggings. "Do you want to get dressed too?" she said, blatantly eying my bare chest. "Or has the shirt famine become even more dire?"

I laughed, grateful to her for breaking the tension as I reached for yesterday's shirt on the floor. "Things could get messy. I'd rather not get anything on my skin, so this one might become a casualty."

"How sad. We'll have to throw a funeral. For the shirt, not your brother." I chuckled while fastening my buttons and Amy winced. "I'm sorry. Was that too far?"

"No, it's okay. But I should do a death ritual in front of Rathka once it's done. He oversees death and the afterlife, the opposite of Temkra. She's all about life, vitality, fertility." I was rambling, stalling. "But anyway, I can't focus on any of that right now."

I finished with my buttons and then fiddled with my sleeves, rolling them so they were secure just above my elbows. Amy took my arm, wrapping her hand around my bicep while she stood calmly at my side.

"I know this isn't easy, but you're strong enough, Novak. You always have been." She gave my arm a gentle squeeze. "And I'll be right there with you."

Just like that, my fidgeting nerves left me. A resolute calm washed over me, like I had slipped beneath the surface of a glassy lake.

One final act of duty. One more sacrifice until I could wash away the stain of Rathka's Order and start anew.

"Let's go," I said, heading for the bedroom door.

———

THE SMELL ALWAYS HIT FIRST. Rotting leaves, rotting flesh. So much death and decay. I gave Amy a folded handkerchief from my pants pocket.

"Cover your mouth and nose with that," I said. It had traces of my cologne that would hopefully be easier on her senses.

A low, rattling growl came from the darkness, the noise startling Amy.

"He can't hurt you," I assured her before flicking the light on.

Evin was already pressed up against the bars of his cell. He probably scented Amy the moment she walked in. She was a fresh meal in his curse-stricken mind.

"Oh my God." Amy's voice was muffled from the cloth over her mouth. "He's...he used to be a vampire?"

"Not just any vampire," I said flatly. "The heir to Rathka's Order. A devastatingly handsome bachelor who had everything." I swallowed the lump in my throat. "And yet it was never enough."

The creature bared his teeth, long rows of jagged broken fangs, and let out a screech as he swiped a skeletal-thin arm through the bars. His claws were long, black, and filthy. Probably riddled with infection that had nothing to do with the Curse.

"He was your bully." Amy stated it matter-of-factly, all traces of fear gone from her voice. "Seems like his outsides finally match his insides."

She wasn't far off from a prevalent theory about Rathka's Curse. Many believed the sickness was divine retribution for all the harm they had caused. The biggest offense being forcing draitrium on lower-class vampires and sending them off in broad daylight to fight the werewolves centuries ago. Those who didn't burn from sun exposure became hopelessly addicted to the drug.

Some believed Rathka was so angry about this mindless slaughter of his sister's children, in his name no less, that his curse was simply a revelation of our true natures. He pulled back the curtain on our attractive features, our wealth, our pride, and genteel manners, and revealed Rathka's Order for the cannibalistic monsters they tried to hide.

I didn't fully buy into all that. My mother came from a different clan, and there were a few others not of my blood-line that were affected by the Curse.

But Amy was spot-on as far as my brother was concerned. He had been an awful, ugly person to everyone in his life, and now his exterior matched his personality.

That still didn't make him any easier to kill.

My hand went to Amy's shoulder and gently squeezed. "Don't come any closer than this."

"Okay." She grabbed my hand, holding on as I left her side until the last possible moment.

Evin snarled as I approached his cell, his twisted spine cracking as he followed my movement. A long black tongue licked his teeth, because he didn't have any lips to speak of.

I looked away only to grab the silver dagger from the shallow drawer of my work table. When I unsheathed it, Evin let out a long, wailing screech that made my eardrums ache. He grabbed at the bars and pulled, scrabbling as if to climb his way to escape, but it was no use.

"You know what this is?" I held out the blade, letting it catch the light. "So you are still in there."

The monster screamed again, chomping his jaws like he wanted to devour me right then. I had never seen him act this erratically before, and a knot of guilt formed in my gut.

After fifty years of observations, tissue samples, and examinations, I never truly attempted to communicate with him.

Amy seemed to sense my hesitation, her eyes catching mine from where she stood in the entryway. I saw no judgment there, only support. Even if I couldn't bring myself to use the blade, she would remain at my side.

The reminder of her quiet strength made me resolute. I held the dagger next to my thigh, watching the monster watch me.

"Even if I did try to communicate with you, what would we talk about?" I said. "You never said a single word to me that wasn't belittling."

His jaws clenched hard enough to crack some teeth, but those sunken eyes were dull, lifeless. Evin always had a glimmer in his eye, an arrogant light twinkling from his dark, filthy soul.

"I didn't think about what I should say," I admitted. "If saying anything would even get through to you." I tapped the blade against my leg. It wouldn't burn me as long as it didn't touch my skin. "For what it's worth, I don't hate you. Not even after everything you did. This... this isn't out of anger. Or revenge, or anything like that."

The creature quieted as if he were actually listening, his breaths making a soft, rattling whistle.

"I'm hoping that doing this is a kindness," I said. "I remember how you suffered in your final years of losing yourself as a vampire, how the hunger for flesh pained you. I can only imagine how you've suffered since. And I want to... apologize for my part in that. I've kept you down here for fifty years, with good intentions, yes, but... that doesn't make it right. No matter how much you enjoyed my suffering, I would never wish this upon you."

I brought the silver blade up to examine the metal surface, and the creature's breaths became low growls again.

"In some ways, I'm sorry I failed to find a cure. In other ways," I steeled myself with a breath, "I'm glad you never got a chance to come back."

Evin snapped his jaws with angry grunts and bellows, reaching through the bars to swipe at me again.

"I don't know if you deserved this curse or not. That's not my place to decide. But you're a danger to the outside world, and I won't condemn you to an eternity down here. So consider this your escape, brother."

"Novak, be careful."

Amy had edged closer, probably without realizing it, to move near me. At the sound of her voice, Evin pressed into the corner of his cell closest to her and slashed his claws through the air.

"Get back!" I cried.

She wasn't fast enough and those filthy claws snagged on her T-shirt, pulling her forward.

I moved without thinking. One moment I was yelling at her to stay back, the next, my silver blade was embedded to the hilt in my brother's neck.

Time stopped for an agonizing eternity. And then foul-smelling, black blood spilled from the wound in the monster's neck.

I released the handle and dragged Amy into my arms, pulling her away from the scene. "Did he touch you? Hurt you at all?"

Her shirt had ripped from his claws and I lifted the hem with a shaking hand to check for injuries. There was noth-ing, not even a scratch. Just clean, bare skin, thank fucking Temkra.

I was so relieved that I barely registered Amy snatching

her shirt from my grip and pulling it down over her stomach. I just hauled her to my chest, bringing my lips to the sweet-smelling hair on top of her head.

"Why did you get closer?" I demanded. "Fuck, akra, he could have killed you."

She had been tense but slowly relaxed, arms going around my waist. "I'm sorry. I was worried about you. The more you talked, the more agitated he seemed. Do you think he understood you?"

I sighed, resting my chin on top of her head. "I don't know. I guess it doesn't matter anymore."

A kiss grazed my throat. "How do you feel? Are you okay?"

"I don't know. I don't think it's sunk in yet."

My gaze drifted to Evin's lifeless form, crumpled in a heap in a corner of his cell. He was meant to die in old age with dignity, with his eldest son taking the helm of Rathka's Order. Either that or in a blaze of glory on a battlefield. But his death and the final years of his life had been... disgraceful. Unremarkable.

I couldn't look away, couldn't do anything but sink into the reality of what I had done while clutching Amy tighter to me.

Novak's eyes became vacant, staring past me at the unmoving body in his basement cell. His shirt and forearm were covered in his brother's blood. At least, I thought it was blood. All I knew was that it was thick as tar and smelled awful.

"Hey." I cupped the side of his neck. "You still with me?"

"It's done," he said softly. "My brother's dead. I killed him."

My chest squeezed with uncomfortable tightness. The shock of his actions must have been setting in.

"Come on. Let's get you upstairs and cleaned up, okay?" I took his clean hand and led him out of the basement. He was compliant, but his eyes never lost that thousand-yard stare.

Once in his bedroom, I left Novak by the door to start the massive four-headed shower. When I returned to him, he was looking down, seeming to notice the black sludge on his shirt for the first time. Tempting as it was, it wasn't the right time to make a joke about a shirt famine.

"Do you want me to help you?"

He didn't answer, so I gently steered him toward the shower and began undressing him. I wadded up the shirt when I removed it, careful to not let the dark stain touch anything else. There was no washing that thing. It probably had to be burned.

My hands shook slightly as I removed the rest of Novak's clothes. He let me take everything off without comment, even lifting his feet for me to remove his socks and shoes. When he was completely naked in front of me, all my sexual attraction to his body was overtaken by my concern for him. He was beautiful, statuesque, but also profoundly sad. His arms were limp at his sides, shoulders rounded forward, and his stare blank.

I tested the temperature of the water before taking his hand. "Come here. You'll feel better soon, at least physically."

I directed him to sit on one of the benches jutting out from the wall, and got to work on scrubbing him. The blood had only touched his forearm but I had a feeling he'd want the whole experience washed away. So I did my best to stay out of the direct spray of the water while washing him from head to toe. I even washed his hair, massaging my fingers into his scalp until his eyes closed softly.

After rinsing and then toweling him off, some life seemed to return to Novak. He embraced me, not caring that my clothes were soaked from staying fully dressed in the shower.

"Thank you, akra."

He sounded exhausted, weary, and I felt the same fatigue in my bones. Dawn had to be approaching soon.

"Of course. I can't imagine how difficult that was." I

reached on tiptoes to kiss under his jaw. "Let's get you into bed."

His arms around me tightened. "Are you staying?"

I didn't hesitate. "Yes. I just need to change into something dry and then I'll be right there."

After swapping out my wet T-shirt for a fresh one, and quickly texting Tavia that I was alive and well, I slid into bed next to Novak.

He embraced me from behind, molding his chest to my back and lining his hips with mine. All at once, his body relaxed with a massive sigh that ruffled my hair, and sleep overtook us both.

———

THE MOMENT I WAS AWAKE, I rolled over to check on Novak. His side of the bed was empty, the covers rumpled and pushed back. On my nightstand sat a steaming cup of coffee and two small cookies on a saucer. A slip of paper under the saucer read, *In the office. – N*

I sat up with a smile and popped one of the treats into my mouth, rolling my head around on my neck as I fully joined the waking world. The cookie was more like a miniature scone, buttery and flaky, and went down well with my first sip of coffee.

Rising from the bed with mug and second cookie in hand, I headed for Novak's office in nothing but my sleep shirt and panties. It was almost alarming how quickly I became comfortable in his house, but he didn't seem to mind.

The office door was open as I approached, with a flurry of movement within. Novak was surrounded by boxes and piles of papers on his desk. He sorted through notes and journals, organizing them into various stacks.

"Akra." A smile touched his lips when he looked up and noticed me. "How are you? Did you sleep all right?"

He was dressed down as well, at least for him. His slacks were unbelted, the top buttons of his shirt undone, along with his signature rolled-up sleeves.

"Definitely, I'm fine." I set my mug down on a side table before turning to him. "How are you?"

I reached for his face, relieved to find his warm red eyes alert and focused.

"I'm... good." He leaned into my touch, nodding as if confirming to himself that his words were true. "I am. Good, that is." His smile widened. "I'm free."

"You are." I stepped back to take in the boxes and piles of documents everywhere. "So what's all this? Are you tidying up?"

"Sort of. I'm finding all the clan decrees, everything referring to assets, customs, and clan laws of Rathka's Order. It's all going into this box." He pointed to the one sitting in the center of his desk. "And then it's all going into a fire. Because Rathka's Order is no more."

"And your brother?" I asked hesitantly.

"Yeah, I..." His voice took on a somber tone as he raked a hand through his hair. "I cleaned up downstairs and performed a death ritual. He's at peace now."

"And you're okay?"

"Yes." His expression softened. "I could feel Rathka taking him away and that gave me closure. I'm good, really."

I nodded, relieved. "So, what does this mean for you?"

Novak straightened to full height. "I'm starting a new clan. My own. I don't want any association with Rathka's Order anymore."

"You are? Wow. That's a big deal, right?"

He nodded. "And I want to align with Blood 'til Dawn. Nothing can erase what my ancestors did to them, but I want to atone for their losses if I can."

"Wow," I said again. "What's your new clan called?"

"I don't know yet." Novak caressed down my arm until his fingers reached mine. "I was hoping we could decide on a name together."

My gaze snapped to his. "Together?"

"Yes, akra." He drew me closer to him. "Because it won't just be my clan. It'll be ours."

Time stood still and I couldn't have heard him correctly. "What do you mean?"

"I mean it begins with you and me. Together." His forehead lowered to mine. "Just because I want an alliance with Blood 'til Dawn doesn't mean I'll let them keep you. I want you to myself."

My mind was connecting dots that seemed to make logical sense, but I still struggled to believe the conclusion I arrived at.

"I'm not sure I understand."

Novak turned abruptly and swept an arm across the surface of his desk, sending his neat piles and boxes of documents scattering across the floor. Before I could react, he grabbed my waist and lifted me in the air. Then he set my ass down on the center of his desk and spread my legs as he moved to stand between them.

"You understand, you just don't see yourself as I see you." Novak held a punishing grip on my hips, his fingers curling into my T-shirt. "You're my blood mate, akra. Your blood was made for me, and mine for you. I want you at my side for centuries to come, heading our clan, our descendants, together."

Desire, awe, and overwhelm swept through me in a maelstrom. His voice was strained, like he wanted this, wanted *me*, more than anything else. Humans called this marriage and children. Making our own family. But with a vampire, it was so much more. It was centuries of life, it was drinking blood and aging slowly.

Being with Novak would mean multiple human lifetimes of his fascinating mind, his sharp smirks and sweet forehead kisses. Centuries of being held and listened to, of being driven to orgasm within an inch of my life. He was the first and only man I ever trusted, and if he wanted to give me forever, how the hell could I refuse?

The rush of sensations and emotions overtaking me spilled out into four words.

"I love you, Novak."

He blinked in surprise, as if not expecting to hear that. "You're the first person to say that to me in centuries."

"You deserve to hear it." My arms went around his neck, legs squeezing around his hips. "You're amazing and you deserve to be loved." I let out a soft, deprecating laugh. "I'm not sure why you'd choose to start a new clan with me, but—"

"Because I love you too, Amy. Don't you see?" He pushed my hair off my shoulder, knuckles stroking my cheek as he did. "You deserve it too, far more than me. It's not even about establishing a new clan; I just want to see you every day. I never want the taste of your blood and your kiss to ever leave my mouth. I want your laughter and your curiosity filling up my home. I want the presence of *you* lighting up every dark corner of my life."

My breath was tight, my voice wavering with emotion. "You are saying very romantic things right now and I love that, but can you back up a second?"

His brow furrowed. "Back up to what?"

"We're actually blood mates? You're sure?"

He shrugged. "Pretty sure. We can test it by trying blood that's not each other's." At my grimace of disgust, he laughed. "Exactly how I feel." His forehead leaned on mine again. "We can have a priest of Temkra's Blood confirm it, do the whole ceremony if you want. All I know is your blood is the sweetest taste that's ever hit my tongue, and I can't stand to go a single day without it."

"I've never wanted anyone's blood except yours," I realized. "The idea of it disgusted me until I drank yours."

Novak's thumb nudged the corner of my lips, teasing one of my fangs. "You were also very new to being a brusang."

"Yes, and I hated what I was." My fingers stroked his neck and the ends of his hair. "But you never saw me as ugly or disgusting."

"Never," he agreed. "Not for a single moment. You're the most beautiful creature I've ever set eyes on." His lips curled on a growl. "And you're mine."

His kiss was all-consuming, a rough scraping of lips, tongues and fangs. He held my hips flush against his, the heat and pressure of his erection rubbing and teasing where I was most sensitive. If my panties weren't already damp, they would be in moments.

"I need you." The words dragged out of his throat on a rough whisper. "My blood is on fire for you. Tell me you need the same or I'm going to need an ice-cold shower immediately."

"Yes, Novak. I want you, need you." I was pinned against the desk, held in place with his hips and his hands. "But—" I grabbed his wrist when he reached for the hem of my shirt, about to lift it up. "But that stays on, okay?"

He pulled back with a growl that held a tinge of anger to it. With a dark look, he released me and planted his hands on the desk on either side of me. "No, akra. That's not going to happen."

Chapter 26

Amy

I started to withdraw, closing my legs and pulling them toward my chest, when Novak placed a hand on my knee.

"I'm not rejecting you, and I'll never force you. But I want to understand, Amy." His gaze was heavy on me, missing nothing like a microscope.

"I just don't like being naked, okay?"

Novak was never pushy about anything, and I was hoping he'd just drop it. But this time, he seemed unable to let it go.

"Why?" he asked.

"I don't need a reason, okay? I just don't."

"Amy." His voice gentled, and he separated my knees to stand between my thighs again. He held my face in his palms, making me look at him. "Do you trust me to take care of you?"

"Yes." My eyes closed on a shaky breath. "You already have, so well."

"Do you believe me when I say I love you?"

"Yes."

"Then you must know I already love every inch of you. Even the parts I haven't seen." His fingers trailed down my neck and over my shoulder. "Love doesn't feel like a strong enough word. My heart beats for you. I found the strength to free myself from my clan's expectations because of you. Every moment I look at you, hear your voice, taste your blood, touch your skin, they all feel like gifts I don't deserve."

"You deserve everything, Novak." I swallowed, my throat feeling on the verge of closing up. "I'm the one who's undeserving."

"And I want to run a silver blade through everyone who ever made you feel that way." His hands closed around my upper arms. "Because it's not true, akra. Everything humans told you about yourself is a lie." Novak brought my palm to his chest, pressing it flat against his heartbeat. "Believe *me*. Not them."

My heart felt heavy, both with how much love he poured into it and the fear of it shattering.

"I want to," I said, fingers curling into his shirt. "But I'm so afraid."

"Of what?" He covered my hand with his. "Let me dispel any fears you have. I'm happy to."

"Of disappointing you."

The silence that followed was deafening. Novak looked bewildered, like he couldn't fathom such a thing. But I knew disappointment all too well. It followed me everywhere back in Sapien. Every time I tried to help out with some task but got dizzy, or didn't have the strength, or had an asthma attack, disappointment was all around me.

It was the first thing I saw in Tom Harrison's eyes when he undressed me.

"What if I'm not everything you say I am?" I went on.

"What if you decide this isn't what you want in a few weeks or months?"

"We're blood mates," Novak answered as if the solution was so simple. "We are meant for each other."

I waved my hand in front of my face. "Forget about that for a second. There's more to our connection than just blood, right?"

"Yes, of course."

"So without that component, how do you know? How are you sure you won't hate my guts in a few months?"

Novak's face pinched with pain. "Because I could never hate you. I adore you. I cherish you."

My head fell back in frustration. "You're not getting it."

"I don't think *you* are," he retorted. "But it doesn't matter. If I have to spend every day of the next five hundred years convincing you that you deserve all I have to give and more, I'll do it."

I tried approaching it from another angle. "It's like with your family. Not to compare you to them, but you were never good enough in their eyes. They were wrong about you, obviously, but," I pointed to myself, "what if I'm actually not good enough, Novak? What if I can't be everything you need?"

His eyes narrowed and he went eerily still for a moment. I almost thought he wouldn't say anything, maybe storm off, when he said icily, "There's one major difference you're forgetting."

"What?"

"They had expectations of me that were always shifting. I could do something they would've been proud of one day, but the next day, the goalposts had shifted and that one thing was no longer impressive. It was a losing game no matter what I did. Even if I had found a cure for Rathka's

Curse and reversed the effects on everyone, they would have found reasons to be disappointed. There was no pleasing them, you understand?"

"Yes, I know." I brought a hand to my face. "I'm sorry I brought them up. That was a bad example."

Novak removed my hand from my cheek and replaced it with his own. "I have zero expectations of you, akra. Absolutely none. I want you exactly as you are. Your galaxy eyes, your kitten fangs, and this beautiful body you won't let me see. I wouldn't change a single thing about you, and I never want you thinking you have to impress me. I just want you here."

My tears began escaping, and he swept away every single one away with his thumbs. His lips came to my hairline and stayed there when my next words tumbled out.

"My body isn't beautiful. You saw my stomach."

"I did?"

"Yes, in the basement." I lifted my head to meet his eyes. "You saw my scars, so how can you say I'm beautiful?"

"Because you are." He looked confused. "I didn't see any scars."

I snorted derisively. "You might need your eyes checked. They're all right here." I placed my hand over my abdomen. "They're from the attack that... that killed me."

Novak looked thoughtfully down where my hand was. "My only concern at the time was if my brother had hurt you. When I saw you were whole and well, it was the biggest fucking relief of my life. I didn't notice them because I truly don't care if you have scars, Amy." His fingers laced through mine. "It doesn't change how beautiful you are to me."

"I hate them," I admitted. "I never look in a mirror when I change my clothes or get out of a shower. I hate that they're a permanent reminder of... of what happened."

Novak sighed, his breath trailing across my lips. "I am sorry the events leading to your transformation were so traumatic. I can't imagine the pain you were in, or how scared you were." His grip on my hand tightened. "But I'm not sorry that you're here, very much alive and lighting up my life." He cocked his head to the side, looking thoughtful again. "Would it help if you thought of your scars like your eyes and your fangs? As markers of your second life, symbols of what brought you to me?"

"I don't know," I admitted on a long breath. "I've never tried to reframe how I've thought of them like that."

"Would you be willing to try?" Novak traced the edge of my jaw. He was always touching me in small, caring ways. With such reverence and affection, like he truly could not get enough of me.

"How?" I asked, leaning into his touch.

"Reverse your thinking, akra." His thumb circled over the pulse in my neck. "Just see how it feels. What if you *do* deserve the world laid at your feet? What if you *are* perfect exactly as you are? What if your scars are part of what makes you beautiful?"

Our mouths met in a warm press that quickly ignited to a passionate frenzy. His fangs didn't draw blood, but their firmness against my lips mirrored the hard pressure of his erection between my legs. My thighs squeezed around his waist, pulling him closer for more. More friction, more heat, more of everything that was *him*.

Novak gripped the edge of my panties in one fist. I felt the tug of fabric drawn tight against my skin and then heard a ripping sound.

"Did you just... " The second half of my question died

as the front of his slacks pressed against my bare sensitive skin. The cool, hard metal of his belt buckle was a shock to my heated core.

"Anything to keep these legs wrapped around me." He gave me a wry smirk. "I'll replace your panties."

"Careful, or we'll have a shortage just like with your shirts," I warned.

"Oh no, how terrible," he murmured before kissing me again.

The panties were gone from my mind as I hurriedly pulled apart Novak's belt, and then the button and zipper of his slacks. Rather than fuss with his shirt buttons, he peeled the whole thing off over his head.

His slacks and underwear piled on the floor and he stepped out of them. My gorgeous vampire, a lean, lithe creature that for some reason, wanted a centuries-long life with me.

I ran my hands up his forearms first, feeling the corded muscles and prominent veins that I drooled over before I knew anything about him. My touch ran over the swell of his biceps next, and then his round, strong shoulders. He shivered when I stroked his neck, eyes heating to a fiery red when I explored my way down his chest, across the ridges in his firm abdomen, to the thick cock that jumped at my touch as if eagerly waiting for me.

"You're beautiful," I said as I gave him a long, leisurely stroke. "Has anyone ever told you that?"

"No," he choked out. Color darkened his cheeks and the sight of it delighted me.

I grinned as I stroked him, soaking up the blissed-out torture in his face. "I'll make sure to keep reminding you."

"Amy." Novak leaned over me, his fists gathering up my T-shirt. "You have me in the palm of your hand and I'll do absolutely anything for you. Please let me see you. I'm dying to love your whole body utterly and completely, so please don't hide from me."

It felt like staring out over the edge of a cliff. One simple step could ruin me beyond recognition, or lead me to the greatest freedom and bliss. I would never know until I fully placed my trust in Novak's hands and took that leap.

He waited for my answer with the patience of a saint, eyes rapt on my face.

"Okay," I said in a shaky whisper. "You can take it off."

The material lifted and I closed my eyes, unwilling to risk the chance of seeing disappointment in his expression. I lifted my arms to let the shirt, my shield, disappear, and then immediately brought them down to cover myself.

The next thing I felt were Novak's arms wrapping around my back, pulling me against his chest. He was so warm, like a life-sized space heater. Wherever the idea that vampires were cold came from had no basis in reality.

"You're so brave," he said, lips on my forehead. "And utterly stunning. You make me fucking *ache*, akra."

I unfolded from my defensive position just slightly, letting my head come to his shoulder and my legs dangle off the edge of the desk. His hands smoothed up and down my back, palms flat and fingers wide. I'd never had so much of my bare skin touched by another person before.

"Are you okay?" Novak kissed my temple.

"Yeah." My hands went around his waist, seeking more of his warmth. I was okay as long as he wasn't face-to-face with my scars. "This feels nice."

"That's good, but," his touch rounded my hips, running down my thighs. "I want you to feel better than *nice*."

One hand slid into my hair, curling into a fist at the base of my skull. He drew my head back and kissed me roughly, nicking the corner of my lip and sucking the blood that welled in the cut. While I was distracted by the pleasure pulsing through me, he slid one hand up my abdomen and kneaded a breast, plucking my nipple until I cried out.

"I'm going to spend centuries pleasing your body until you love it as much as I do," he promised with a growl. "It won't happen overnight but you will learn to love yourself, Amy. You will realize your worth, I swear to you."

I was wordless and panting, taken aback that this was *me* he was talking to. He leaned back to look at all of me, reverence and awe in his eyes like I was a work of art. And for the first time in my life, I didn't want to hide.

"So fucking stunning." Novak's gaze traveled down my body at a leisurely pace, not inspecting but appreciating.

His hands followed his eyes, running downward over me in loving caresses. I held my breath for a moment when his touch passed over my scars, but he didn't linger on them. Nor did he hurry past them. He simply gave them the same loving attention as the rest of me.

When he dropped to his knees between my legs and gazed at me there, I fought the urge to clamp them shut. Fought the chill of vulnerability telling me to cover up and scuttle away.

Novak's strong hands kneaded my thighs, working pleasure into my sensitive skin, then he quirked an eyebrow up at me. "If you deny me tasting you here, there's a strong chance you'll break my heart."

I forced out a nervous laugh. "We wouldn't want that, would we?"

His grin was predatory as he leaned in and licked a long stripe up the center of my core. I gasped at the sensation, but couldn't fully process the pleasure as he licked me again and again. Then his mouth covered me, lips sealing like a kiss while his tongue plundered and explored.

Before I knew it, my hands braced on the desk behind me, my head fell back, and my hips bucked against the face of my vampire lover. Novak held my thighs apart as he feasted on me, teasing me with swirls of his tongue on my clit until I shook with impending release, then he backed off to suck on my labia and slid his tongue inside me. He moaned against my skin, sending more vibrations to tease me toward orgasm but never enough to get me there.

I was desperate to come and never felt so wanton and uninhibited in my life. I didn't recognize myself like this, stark naked and sweating, head thrown back and breasts thrust in the air, getting eaten out on the edge of a desk.

"Novak… " My fingers tangled in his long silver hair, urging him up toward my clit to give me sweet release.

He answered with a moan that might have been my name, but resisted my pulling. The more wound up and desperate I got, the more he seemed to enjoy himself. When his mouth broke away and he began to stand up, I could have cried.

"Why'd you stop?" My fingers headed straight for my clit to take the edge off, but he stopped me, catching my wrist and returning it to my side.

"Because I'm taking this moment to be selfish." He licked his lips with a wicked grin, stepping in so close that his cock rested on my inner thigh, the skin warm and velvety around its thick weight. "I want to be inside you when you come."

"So what are you waiting for?" My thighs squeezed his waist, ankles locking at the small of his back.

"Nothing." He stroked my cheek and leaned his forehead on mine. "Just… savoring you."

He held my nape as our mouths came together in a kiss. This one was sweet, tender and unhurried. His hips shifted, and then I felt the heated kiss of his cock against my entrance. He pushed forward, and my body accepted him with a smooth glide and a sweet stretching that had me moaning into our kiss.

Novak pressed all the way in until our hips were flush and I was deliciously full. He paused there, forehead on mine.

"Fuck, you're perfect," he groaned. "Absolutely perfect. I could die right here."

"Please don't."

Our soft laughter turned into moans, sighs, and more kisses as he started to move. He went slowly at first, dragging in and out of me in long strokes with his attention rapt on my face.

"So beautiful when you take me," he rasped. "The bliss on your face, I love it."

"More," I begged, locking my arms around his shoulders. My legs drew him in to keep him closer, keep him deeper. "Please, more. Harder."

"Fuck..." His grip clamped down on my hips, holding me in place to take the full force of his thrusts.

His intensity and speed ramped up, crashing into me as my pleasure rose like a cresting wave. My head fell back again, awash in everything he was making me feel, when I felt his mouth on my neck. Fangs dragged a sharp path over my skin, adding to the anticipation of building pleasure .

"Yes." I leaned my head to the side, giving him full access. "Please."

"Bite me too," he groaned, his thrusts never stopping. "I need your fangs in me, need to give you my blood. Give you everything."

I reached for his shoulder on the opposite side, kissing the round muscle before dragging my lips to the side of his neck where his vein pulsed so beautifully. I kissed him there too, feeling the blood pump under his skin as he pumped into me.

We bit at the same time. I didn't know if it was instinct or coincidence, but no other feeling or sensation could describe that moment. It was completeness, perfection on a level I never thought possible. This connection through our blood, through the joining of our bodies was nothing short of divine.

I felt the orgasm physically, felt the pleasure in my body reach its peak and release through waves of sensation, but also on another plane. It was like my soul, my heart, was also singing in pleasure. And when Novak's release spilled while I swallowed down his delicious blood, bliss cascading over me while he drank mine, I swore our souls wound together like wires coiling together for eternity.

Chapter 27

Novak

I couldn't decide which was my favorite moment of last night. The first time, with Amy perched on my desk as we took each other's blood. Or when I convinced her to come outside on the balcony, and took her bent over the railing under the stars with the mountains in the distance. Then there was using the detachable showerhead on her clit while I had her again in the shower. She didn't think it would be strong enough, but she underestimated my water pressure.

And then there was crawling into bed with her, dawn moments away and the two of us completely spent, naked, and tangled in each other's limbs.

It was impossible to choose just one memory to relish in as I woke up the following dusk. Amy lay on her back next to me, still asleep for now, with the covers pushed down to her waist like she'd been hot as she slept during the day.

I couldn't stop looking at her, my beautiful blood mate. She was completely uncovered and seemed at peace, her face relaxed with her lips softly parted. The scars she'd been so worried about were pale, jagged stripes from her navel to just under her breasts. They flushed red when she was hot, but were otherwise slightly lighter than her normal skin tone.

And I loved them because they were part of her.

I loved the dip between her collarbones for the same reasons. As well as the freckle above her eyebrow, and the shape of her lips when she tried to hide a smile.

With a sigh, I propped my elbow on the mattress and rested my head in my hand. "I don't understand how anyone can look at you and not just... fall head over heels."

Amy started awake with a kick of her leg and a snort. "... what?"

"Sorry." I barely contained my laughter as I slid closer. "Didn't mean to wake you."

"Mmm... " She groaned and stretched, making her body a long, elegant arch. "Is it dusk already?"

"Yeah."

I brought my lips to her shoulder, running my hand across her ribcage as I resettled next to her. She didn't flinch at all when I touched the tops of her scars. It might have been because she was too sleepy to notice, but my heart swelled anyway.

"You got somewhere to be tonight?" I planted another kiss on her shoulder before nuzzling into the space by her neck.

"I should go see Tavia." Amy sounded reluctant, her hand coming up to rest on my arm. "Texts are one thing, but she'll be demanding proof that I'm alive at some point."

"I'll send her a picture of you holding today's newspaper."

Amy laughed, turning on her side to face me. "Now that won't be suspicious at all."

"Kidnappers are full of great ideas like that." I drew her

into me, already missing the full press of her body on mine. "But seriously, I understand. You should go see her."

A smile played on Amy's lips. "What should I tell her about... " She trailed off, running a finger down the center of my chest.

"Anything you want. Maybe mention that you're moving in with me."

Her finger stopped, eyes widening. "I am?"

"I want you to." My hand slid down her back, cupping a handful of her ass. "I want to wake up to this at every dusk."

"You mean it?" Her galaxy eyes filled with dark tears, lower lip trembling. "Seriously, Novak. You want me to live with you, like permanently?"

"Of course I do." I caught the tears, wiping them away before they ever touched her cheeks. "You're the love of my life, my blood mate, the co-leader of our new clan." I smiled wryly, remembering how we got distracted the night before. "We still need to come up with a name, by the way."

"Hang on." Amy sniffed. "Just so we're clear, this is... forever you're wanting with me? Partners for life. A new clan meaning we're a family who will... have children?"

"Yes." I thought last night was pretty clear but I would give her all the additional assurance she needed. "A thousand times yes, my darling. I want all of that with you."

"Really?"

"Yes." I kissed her forehead. "Yes," I repeated, kissing her nose bridge. "Yes, yes. Do you need me to actually say it a thousand times? Because I will."

She let out an excited sound and kissed me furiously, bringing her leg over my hip as she rolled to her back, pulling me with her. I settled over her with a groan, more than happy to sink into her soft heat first thing in the evening. Soon enough, I'd have her first thing *every* evening.

"No, wait." Amy dodged my next kiss with a sigh, pressing on my shoulders. "I'll never leave your bed if we start this now."

"It's *our* bed," I corrected, kissing her neck. "And I don't see the problem with that."

"Tavia. I should go see her first."

"We could always fall back on the newspaper idea."

Her laughter made my chest spark with emotion, even as I rolled reluctantly to my side, releasing her from under me. "Want me to walk you?"

"No, I'll be fine."

"You're sure?"

"Yes, there's no way I'm giving Blood 'til Dawn the chance to harass you again. I'll just rub it in their faces as I skip around the place."

"Don't gloat too hard. We want their allyship, remember?"

"Yeah, yeah. But I can't resist a *little* gloating."

I watched her get dressed, already anticipating when she'd return and I could peel those clothes from her again. "Hurry back, then. And text me when you get there, and when you're on your way back."

"All right, bossy man."

She leaned over the bed to kiss me, and I made that contact linger for as long as I possibly could.

"I'll have Jo make a meal for us. To celebrate."

"Ooh, yes." Her eyes brimmed with excitement. "I'll see if Tav has a new wine I can grab."

"Perfect."

I pulled on a pair of pants to walk her to the door, then after a few more long, lingering kisses, I let her go.

My own well of excitement was overflowing as I went up to my office. There was so much to do. I'd have Jo make the meal several courses, at least five, all aligned to Amy's tastes. We'd eat in the formal dining room, which I never used. There needed to be candles for a romantic ambiance. And over the meal we'd talk about plans for our future clan, our legacy, including when to start trying for a child. We had plenty of time, at least a century if she wanted to wait, but the overjoyed buzzing inside me could not be contained.

The thought was so overpowering that I had to pause tidying my desk and just bask in my imagination. Amy cradling a round belly, nourishing our child with her incredible body. The two of us as parents, giving our child all the love and validation and opportunities that neither of us ever had.

Fantasizing about our future made my chest and throat tighten with emotion. A family filled with love and acceptance was all I ever wanted and here it was, actually within my reach.

My gaze slid to the portrait of Temkra across the room. "Thank you," I mouthed to the image of the goddess. I'd have to thank her properly soon, with offerings and prayer. The gesture would hopefully have her look favorably on conceiving a child and a healthy pregnancy for Amy when that time came.

I spent the next couple of hours organizing documents, including the box of everything related to Rathka's Order that I would burn. Maybe Amy and I would do it together after dinner. She could burn something from her human life if she wanted. It could be a ritualistic cleansing of our pasts.

When a knock came on my doorjamb, I was so focused that I hardly looked up from my desk. "Ah, Lourna. Can you please give this to Jo? She has creative liberty of course, but these are a few ideas." I held out the slip of paper on which I'd scribbled down some ideas for dinner courses. "And if you'd be so kind as to set the dining room for a meal to be served, let's say three hours before dawn. Do we have candles in storage somewhere?"

"Yes, sir. Of course." She took the list from me and hesitated before speaking again. "You have visitors in the foyer, sir."

"Visitors?" My head lifted for the first time since she entered the room. "Amy and Tavia, I presume? They're welcome to come and go as they please. In fact, Amy will be moving in, so—"

"It's not them." My housekeeper interrupted me for the first time in both of our lives, her mouth a hard line. "It's Baros and Inessa of Carpe Noctem."

Everything went still upon hearing those names, including my breath and my heart.

"What are they doing here?" I asked, my voice hard.

"I don't know, sir. I said you were occupied and they insisted on waiting. When I asked what their business was with you, they said they wouldn't waste their breath on a human and to fetch you immediately."

"Fuck." I stood, my thoughts roiling. "I'm sorry about that, Lourna. I'll get them to leave, and they'll never speak to you like that again."

"Oh, it's fine. Don't worry about me." Her mouth hardened again. "Just be careful, sir. Baros seems to be in a good mood."

"I'll handle him. Thank you."

Lourna gave a curt nod as I rounded the desk, heading past her out of the office and down the stairs.

Fucking Baros. I should have killed our agreement for good on that phone call. He wasn't a problem that would just go away if I ignored him.

At least I knew who I was now, and where I stood. I had a blood mate, a partner I deeply loved. Baros could no longer hold Rathka's Order over my head because that clan was now extinct, a relic of the past that held no power over me. Maybe I could even convince him our deal was null and void since I no longer claimed that name.

Baros sneered as he saw me coming down the stairs. I was extremely dressed down, barefoot in slacks and a rumpled shirt that wasn't even tucked in. It wasn't like he could complain, calling on me unexpectedly like this. He was lucky I had a shirt on at all. I'd thrown it on just so I'd be able to make an inside joke with Amy when she returned.

"It's extremely improper to visit unannounced," I said when I hit the bottom landing. "I'm sure whatever you're about to tell me could have been a phone call."

"Not very proper to have your *human* staff try to needle information out of me," Baros returned.

"She was only trying to report back to me. That's the last time you'll disrespect her, by the way. You are not welcome here."

Baros's mouth lifted in a calculating smirk. "Is that any way to talk to your ally?"

"We're not allies." I crossed my arms. "Our deal is off. I will not be following through."

He didn't look surprised. "I thought you might say that. After that phone call, it sounded like you were trying to weasel your way out. But you can't just take back your word, Novak. You made an agreement with blood."

I shook my head with a scoff. "I did no such thing. You don't have my signature or my blood on anything binding."

"That is true, yes." Baros stepped aside, revealing his daughter standing quietly behind him. She wore a long cloak covering her from neck to foot, held by an ornate clasp at her throat. "But you took Inessa's blood."

"That means nothing. It was only to sample our compatibility." I turned to speak to her directly. "I am sorry you were a pawn in this. I do wish you the best and hope you find someone who... "

She unclasped the cloak as I spoke, letting the fabric pool on the floor around her. My words died not only because she was completely naked underneath, but also from the scent perfuming the air. The cloak must have suppressed her scent because moments after she took it off, that scent hit my brain like a stimulant, shooting blood, sensation, and desire right to my cock.

"No." I stepped backward, fighting all the lust suddenly driving me to grab the approaching naked woman and plunge into her, and promptly stumbled on the bottom stairs.

"We did the fertility ritual early," Baros said cheerily, as if his own daughter wasn't naked in my foyer and stalking toward me. "It turned out the timing aligned much better with her natural cycle. She arouses every nearby male who isn't a blood relative. But because you've already tasted her blood, the effect is much stronger on you."

"Stop. Don't come any closer." I tried to inject all of my will into my voice, but it came out sounding like a lusty growl.

I held my palms out toward Inessa, but quickly closed them into fists and drew them back into my body. If I touched her bare skin with all this unwanted desire in my system, I might truly do something I regret.

All my effort went into looking at her eyes, not the gentle sway of her breasts as she walked, nor the lines of her waist and hips. Staring at her face wasn't much easier. She was an attractive woman. And she was quickly encroaching on my personal space.

"Stop," I repeated. This time I had no choice but to put my hands on her shoulders, otherwise she'd rub up against me.

"You can't fight it, Novak," she said in a flat tone, leaning into my hold. "You're just making this harder on yourself."

"Please." I searched her red gaze, wondering if there was any sympathy in those depths or if she was just as cold and self-serving as her father. "I have someone, a blood mate," I whispered. "Please, I love her. Don't make me do this; it would destroy her."

There was a flicker of warmth in her expression, but it was gone before I could fully register that it happened.

"You think you're the only person who loves someone?" Inessa hissed under her breath. "Do you know what he'd do to me if I tried to be with the one I wanted?"

Hope broke through my lust-filled haze like moonlight through thick clouds. She didn't want to be doing this any more than I did. That was my only move, the only angle I could play. I glanced at Baros, whose attention was on his phone. Whispering in Inessa's ear would be risky to me, but I couldn't let him hear me. I leaned in close and held my breath as I spoke.

"I can help you," I said hastily, fighting the urge to suck at the curve of her neck. "I can get you out from under his thumb, keep you safe. Neither of us have to be beholden to him. You can be with your love, I can be with mine. Maybe we can... fake this right now, but don't make me do it for real. Please."

She stilled, quiet for a moment as if considering my words.

"Enough of this," Baros moaned. "Quit pillow-talking and get on with it. You don't need romance to get her pregnant. Just get it done."

Inessa's face hardened, like she was grimly determined to see this through. She went for the button clasp on my pants, but I stopped her with a hand on her wrist.

"Maybe we should go to a bedroom," I suggested, loud enough for Baros to hear. "For privacy and... comfort."

The last place I wanted to take this woman was the room where Amy and I had shared and learned so much about each other, but I had to stall. Had to convince Inessa to turn against her father, then maybe shut her in a room by herself so I could clear my head from her scent.

I had to call Amy and tell her to stay away until they were both gone. Carpe Noctem was too dangerous, and it was better if she remained under their radar.

"Comfort is fine, but there will be no privacy," Baros said with a long, eerie smile. "This child will be the heir of both Carpe Noctem and Rathka's Order. The conception must be witnessed by at least one head of a clan, and you don't count."

My heart sank, and with it, all of my hope.

Just when I thought I couldn't get any lower, a knock came to my front door. Baros cocked his head, curious, then went to answer it as if this wasn't my fucking house.

"Get away from the door!" I snarled, but that only made Baros gleefully quicken his pace. The door opened a moment later.

"Oh, hello." I heard the note of surprise in Amy's voice and wanted to scream. "Is Novak home?"

Chapter 28

Amy

I practically skipped my way back to Novak's place, swinging an overnight bag filled with toiletries and the few changes of clothes I had back at the Blood 'til Dawn compound. Tavia didn't seem all that surprised when I told her I was moving in, or that Novak and I were blood mates.

"I had a feeling," she'd mused. "In the beginning I was worried, but it makes so much sense now, looking back. Cyan and I chatted with him for a while, did he tell you that?"

"He did. He's a big fan of your wine. And he said Cyan doesn't seem like a bad guy."

"Such a high compliment." Tavia laughed. "Cy said the same thing about him. Very reluctantly, I might add." She watched me pack thoughtfully. "I do like him for you. It just kinda sucks that we'll live separately again."

"Oh please, I'm like a mile down the road." I zipped the bag closed, then turned to her. "It is different, but this is good. I need my own life, and you need yours."

Tavia nodded and I saw the emotion she tried to hide behind a tough face. "I'm really proud of you, you know."

"Aw, Tav." We clasped each other in a tight hug, the two of us sniffling.

"This is so dumb." She laughed into my shoulder. "You'll be so close, we can still see each other every day."

"I know. But I'm leaving your nest, mama bird."

She gave me one more squeeze before releasing me. "Text me when you get there. I'd insist on coming along, but I have a million wine bottles to fill."

"We'll have you over soon," I promised, shouldering the bag. "You and Cyan." Saying *we* felt presumptuous but also good. Novak made it sound like he would share everything equally with me.

Tavia snorted. "That'll be something."

I thought back to that conversation as I came to Novak's and knocked on his front door. He'd said his bed was ours. Did that also extend to the whole house? Did I have the right to walk in like I owned the place?

Someone opened the door before I could think more of it, and I came face-to-face with a man I'd never seen before.

"Oh, hello," I said in surprise. "Is Novak home?" He didn't mention having any other guests over.

This man looked obscenely rich, from his clothes—including the ornate crest pinned to his jacket—to the mild disgust at the sight of me on his clean-shaven face. He was handsome in a cold, severe way. He looked a decade or so older than Novak, with fine lines around his deep crimson eyes, but there was no telling how old he actually was.

"The heir of Rathka's Order is occupied," the man said after giving me a long, disapproving once-over. "What business does a brusang have with him?"

The way he said *brusang* made it clear he considered

me beneath any full-blood vampire. Confusion made a nervous laugh drift out of my mouth and I glanced around to make sure I didn't accidentally knock at the wrong door. Surely Novak wouldn't have a guest like this in his house? Not after he denounced Rathka's Order completely.

"Sorry sir, I feel like we're misunderstanding each other," I said as politely as I could manage. "Novak is expecting me. Can I just slip past you really quickly? Thanks."

The man's body angled just slightly and I took the opportunity to push my way into the foyer. My feet stopped dead in my tracks before I could even process what I saw next.

Novak stood against the banister of the main staircase, his shirt wrinkled with the sleeves rolled up and top buttons undone, one bare foot propped on the bottom step. A fully nude woman stood in front of him, her hand around the back of his neck in a comfortable, intimate way. She was tall, all long legs and slender curves, and able to reach him easily from a normal standing position.

It felt like I'd been punched three seconds ago, but time had frozen and I hadn't felt the full impact of the blow yet.

"Novak?" My voice was high and betrayed all the confusion I felt. "What's going on? Who's that?"

His eyes slid from her face to me, his expression cold. "Ah, you again. Just barging into my house now, are you?"

The delayed gut punch hit me right then, forcing all the air from my lungs. He'd never ever spoken to me like that, or looked at me like I was beneath him.

"What are you talking about?" I demanded.

The man at the door walked past me through the foyer. "Show some respect, brusang. She is my daughter, Inessa of

Carpe Noctem. You're barging into a sacred joining of two powerful clans, not that an undead human would know anything about that." He glared at Novak. "Who is this brusang to you?"

"No one."

The calm delivery of that statement killed any hope of him setting the record straight, of explaining why these people were in his home. In what I thought would be *our* home.

"Novak?" His name came out like broken, jagged glass. "How... how can you say that?"

"She's just a former blood pet who started having lofty demands, so I kicked her out." He never looked at me directly as he spoke. His gaze seemed to be traveling over the naked woman instead.

"Poor delusional thing," the other man said with zero sympathy. "This is why you can't fuck humans, pre-turned or after. They always want to mix with the pure vampires when it's not their place."

The woman turned slightly as if to see what all the fuss was about, and the front side of her, what Novak had been looking at, made me feel even worse. She was perfectly proportioned with utterly flawless skin, like a porcelain doll. Not a blemish or even a freckle in sight.

"Is the brusang going to watch us conceive an heir as well?" she asked as though my presence was incredibly inconvenient.

"Conceive a... " I was too stunned to finish the sentence, my mouth gaping open like a fish.

Confusion, hurt, and betrayal didn't scratch the surface of what I was experiencing. I felt like I'd stepped into a mirror world where everything looked the same, but in reverse. What else could explain Novak's disdainful tone now when he'd spoke with such love and affection earlier in the evening?

"Was any of it true?" I heard myself ask. "What you told me at dusk, and in your office last night? Did you mean a single word of what you said to me?"

His expression barely changed as he took the woman's hand from around his neck. He brought her fingers to his lips, and she let out a soft, surprised breath as he bit her fingertip. When he licked the resulting blood droplet where I could plainly see, he might as well had kissed her. Might as well have shed his clothing and penetrated her right in front of me, for how much it hurt.

What Tom Harrison did to me didn't hold a candle to how utterly fucking painful this was.

I thought I knew pain. I thought I knew heartache and constant rejection and never being good enough. Watching the vampire who I thought wanted a family with me, a life with me, who I finally believed had accepted and loved me, scars and all, drink someone else's blood was beyond heart-breaking.

I felt my heart die.

"You should go, Amy." It was a cold dismissal from the same mouth that asked me to move in with him just a few hours ago.

I was numb, empty. Still trying to figure out what the hell had gone wrong, but my body responded like an automaton. I turned and left the house. Someone must have opened the door, and then I was outside.

My feet moved but I had no sense of direction. I felt severed, exposed. Cut off from what made me feel safe and grounded, and now floating aimlessly through space.

"Amy?"

I didn't know how much time had passed before I heard my name. For all I knew, it could have been minutes or weeks.

My eyes focused on a familiar face with a harsh, concerned expression.

"Amy? Are you all right?"

"Man, look at her. Something's damn wrong."

Two voices. Male. Familiar. My brain processed this information incredibly slowly, like a computer from the last century. Their names came to me moments after their faces registered.

Thorne and Rhain.

The two Blood 'til Dawn vampires blocked my path, the size of them together practically surrounding me.

Rhain leaned over to meet my eye level. "Amy, why are you walking like a zombie? Are you hurt?"

"No." That one word seemed to take more energy than I had.

Thorne hung further back, but I felt his gaze on me like a weight on my shoulders.

"Novak?" He said it like he already knew the answer.

That name, *his* name, broke though all the numbness and sent my systems crashing. A broken, ugly sob left my throat, the sound a perfect reflection of everything I felt.

"Take her bag, Rhain." Something was removed from my hands, and then I felt a real arm over my shoulders, urging me gently to walk. "Let's get you home." Fingers squeezed sympathetically around my shoulder. "Guess you found out. I know we haven't talked much, but you're one of ours and I am sorry he played you."

I looked up at Thorne in surprise. "You knew?"

"About his deal with Carpe Noctem? Yes. I gave him the benefit of the doubt, hoped he'd tell you before things got serious. Guess he really is of Rathka's Order after all."

"Let me guess," I said bitterly. "Everyone knew except me."

"No, that's definitely not true. I just have eyes and ears inside every clan." He gave me another shoulder squeeze. "Novak's bloodline made an art out of betrayal and deception. Don't blame yourself."

"So fucked up," Rhain muttered, but otherwise kept silent on the walk to the compound.

I was mostly able to keep my composure until I saw Tavia. She didn't see me at first, too busy controlling the chaos in the kitchen. Wine bottles covered the central island. Buckets and carboys lined the counters with long tubes coming out of them. She employed Cyan, Laith, and Desmond to help bottle her latest batch, the three of them sanitizing, filling, and corking in a smooth assembly line. On top of all that, it looked like she had a test batch of something boiling on the stove.

"Put those with the crate going to Carnassian's, please," Tavia instructed. "Cy, don't overfill! I didn't bust my ass for this batch to give away free samples."

"Sorry, love. How's this?" Cyan held up a bottle for her inspection, his grin a mix of sheepish and adoring.

"Better, thank you." Tavia leaned over and kissed him, the two of them smiling, gazes warm and loving when they separated.

That was the moment my composure broke, when the brittle outer layer of numbness finally shattered to expose all of the raw, ugly hurt underneath.

Because I would never, ever have what they had. The easy, quiet *knowing* that you had your person, and knowing they were devoted to you like it was a basic fact of life. I'd never have that feeling of steadfast support, love, and desire. I'd never be special to anyone.

I thought I found it. I thought I was so close to my happily ever after. But I'd only been duped again. Silly, weak little Amy always fell for it.

"Amy? Oh my God!"

Tavia rushed over and crushed me in a protective bear hug. She smelled like grape juice. I must have been sobbing, but it felt like fighting for air against a saw slicing open my heart and ribs.

"What did he do?" She petted my hair while holding me to her like she always used to. "I'm gonna fucking kill him. Cyan? Thorne? I can do that, right?"

"Can't allow it, as much as I'd like to." Thorne sounded legitimately disappointed. "Being a two-timing piece of shit isn't a crime."

"What the fuck?"

I couldn't see with my face buried in Tavia's shirt, but I pictured the bewildered look that she and Cyan shared. They had shared a bottle of wine with Novak, had even begun to like him.

He fooled them too. He played us all. But for what?

That was the biggest piece that I couldn't make sense of. Why? Why tell me so many elaborate lies? Why start a friendship with me, pretend for weeks that he cared about me? Why convince me to show him my scars if he never wanted me in the first place? Just for the conquest?

I knew some people enjoyed being cruel, enjoyed the torment and humiliation of others. But not even Tom Harrison tried *this* hard to make me trust him.

"Come on."

Tavia turned me around, leading me through the great room toward the underground apartments.

"I'm gonna burrito you up in a blanket, you're gonna drink as much wine as you want, and you're gonna tell me what happened, okay?"

My only answer was a shaky, rattling breath.

Chapter 29

Novak

Even after Amy left, I had to be careful. I had to make sure she got far enough away that Baros would forget about her. Out of sight, out of mind. If he saw her, he might get curious again and see if he could use her to torment me.

She was safest far away, even though it killed me to speak to her like that. And watching her go, with the heartbreak plain on her face, killed me all over again.

Baros turned to his daughter and me at the base of the stairs, seemingly having already forgotten all about Amy.

"Now," he made ushering motions with his hands, "get on with it, will you? You'll probably have to fuck a few times before dawn."

Inessa's expression barely changed, but I saw the slight clench in her jaw. She hated being used in her father's schemes, she had to. If only I could have a real conversation with her without Baros hovering.

She wrapped her arms around my neck, leaning in to brush her mouth against my ear. "That was your blood mate?" The question was so soft to avoid Baros's detection, she made barely any noise besides breath.

I leaned my head back as if in pleasure. "Yes... "

Her nose drifted along the side of my neck. "You're no longer affected by my scent?"

Her blood that I'd tasted from her finger still sat inside my cheek. It tasted so damn foul, so much unlike Amy, that I couldn't bring myself to swallow. My erection was gone and my head was clear. Tasting the blood of someone who was not my mate made me stone-cold sober, as I'd hoped it would.

I just hated that Amy had to see me do it.

"Yes," I confirmed.

Inessa gave a tiny, imperceptible nod. "Fine. You owe me, Rathka's Son."

My hand went to her shoulder in what looked like a possessive grip, but it was truly a show of gratitude. "My word is my bond. I will help you."

"Push me away," she whispered against my neck. "Kick us out and make a scene."

"Have your butler contact my maid," I answered before shoving at her shoulder, just hard enough to make her stumble back. "Enough of this." I glared at Baros. "You won't seduce me into a deal I no longer want. Both of you need to leave."

Baros looked stunned. Maybe I should have acted like I was still affected by the fertility ritual, but I was fucking sick of pretending. I needed them gone and Amy back.

"It's too late to back out, Novak," he warned.

"I disagree." I bent to pick up Inessa's cloak and shoved the bundle of fabric at her chest. "Leave now before I remove you."

"Don't be stupid. You're the last of your line with no

heir. Our clans are the only two worth a damn in Sanguine. You have no other options, Novak."

"No." I pointed an index finger at him. "*You* don't."

"I beg your fucking pardon?" Baros blustered. He had tried to hide his desperation, but it was crystal clear to me now.

"You need me far more than I need you," I said, crossing my arms. "And I'm not interested in what you have to offer."

He was grinding his jaw, still trying to gain the upper hand. "Your father would be *so* disappointed in you."

"Fuck him."

Baros didn't know how to respond to that. His mouth gaped open like a fish.

"He was disappointed in me my whole life. What do I care?" My shoulder lifted and lowered in the laziest of shrugs. "Fuck my whole damn bloodline while I'm at it. Might as well let it die with me."

"You... you're bluffing," Baros spat. "You can't possibly give up thousands of years of such a proud legacy."

I cocked my head. "Or can I?"

He forced out a laugh. "This is out of... what, spite? Jealousy? You always were jealous of Evin, I could see it since you were a juvenile. Well this is the chance to prove yourself, son. Rathka's Order will be glorious again because of you! No one will remember your father's name once we get rid of Blood 'til Dawn. The streets will hail Novak of Rathka's Order; just imagine it! You'll finally have the glory that was always out of your reach."

My mouth hardened. "I'm done listening to your pathetic attempt at a power grab. Get the fuck out of my house."

"Be reasonable, Novak—"

A snarl erupted from my chest and I saw my hands curl

around the lapels of Baros's jacket before I'd even realized I moved toward him. The fear in his eyes was satisfying. His clan had raised him to be soft, spoiled and pampered. Rathka's Order was a warrior clan and, despite being bookish and studious, I was confident I could tear him limb from limb.

The only thing that stopped me was a hand on my forearm. I still had Inessa's foul-tasting blood in my mouth and her touch made me recoil.

"Put him down," she said.

It turned out that I had lifted Baros a foot off the floor by his lapels and pressed him against a wall. I opened my hands, not caring about his abrupt drop and stumble.

"The next time I see your face," I gritted out, "it'll be you coming at my call. Not the other way around."

"You're a disgrace," he sputtered. "You're nothing, just like your father always said you were. Tell yourself whatever excuse you want but the truth is, you're too fucking weak to lead a clan."

"Best not waste your precious time in my presence, then."

I held my arm out toward the door and after a long, lingering glare, he finally left. Inessa followed him out, and when the door closed, it felt like I could finally breathe for the first time.

I went to the kitchen and spat out Inessa's blood, gagging when it hit my tongue. After quickly rinsing my mouth with water, I raced up the stairs to my office and grabbed my phone. My heart pounded a furious beat as I hit Amy's number and brought the phone to my ear.

"Pick up, akra. Come on." I paced around the office, nearly tearing my hair out as I listened to it ring. She had to be a safe distance away by now.

The call went to voicemail, so I dialed again. This time, I got her voicemail after two rings. So I called a third time, and then a fourth.

On the fifth attempt, she picked up.

"Amy." I breathed out her name on a huge sigh of relief. "Listen, I—"

"Stop fucking calling, asshole," Tavia growled into the phone and hung up.

When I tried to call again, it went straight to voicemail.

I thought back to the entire exchange between me, Amy, and Baros. There was no time to come up with a plan, no way to give her a signal that she needed to get away for her own safety. I just needed her gone before Baros figured out she meant something to me.

I knew it looked bad, that my actions would hurt her, but once I got the chance to explain, she'd understand. There was just no time.

But thinking from her perspective, she saw a naked woman standing in front of me, touching me, and I had dismissed her so callously. I drank another woman's blood, right in front of her.

I did more than just hurt her.

I confirmed her worst fears and all her deepest insecurities.

"Oh, fuck." I brought my fists to my temples, the full weight of what I'd done hitting me like a brick building. "Oh no, no, no. Oh... fuck! What have I done?"

Dawn was approaching but this couldn't wait. I raced back down the stairs, shoved my feet into the first pair of shoes I found and popped the door to my garage. Within another minute, I was on my motorcycle and speeding toward the Blood 'til Dawn compound.

———

THE BUILDING WAS CLOSED up when I arrived, all doors shut and security lights on. I parked in front of their warehouse door and left my bike running as I walked up and pounded on the metal door with my fist.

"Yeah, I know you can see me," I said, making eye contact with the camera lens fixed to the corner of the building. "Come on out."

Nothing happened for several minutes, but I refused to be ignored. I circled the large square building, pounding on every outside door that I passed. The eastern sky was lightening and I felt the first prickle of warning instincts on my skin. Were they waiting to see if I'd stay out past dawn? I wouldn't put it past them.

"I just want to talk to Amy," I said to yet another camera lens. "Please."

A side door opened after another long minute and two vampires emerged, one that could have been from my bloodline with pale blond hair, and another with the typical darker complexion of Blood 'til Dawn. They stood in front of the door, arms crossed and looking pissed off. Not a great sign for me.

"Learn to take a hint, for Temkra's sake," the blond said.

"I only need a few minutes to talk to Amy, please." Neither of their expressions changed, so I elaborated. "The brusang, Tavia's friend."

"We know who Amy is, Rathka's Bastard," spat the other one, revealing one blunt fang when he snarled. "She's one of ours, and she doesn't want to talk to you."

Fuck, I'd misstepped badly and assumed Blood 'til Dawn, like my clan and Carpe Noctem, did not see brusang as full-on clan members.

"I just want to apologize." Desperation crept into my voice, just like the creeping heat on my skin as the sky lightened with dawn's approach. "Please. I only wanted to protect her. I didn't mean to hurt her."

"Yeah, yeah, we've heard it all from you." The blond stared at me coldly. "Every word from a Rathka's Order mouth is bullshit. It's too bad Amy had to learn the hard way."

"I'm fucking serious!" My composure was slipping, desperation taking over in full force. "This isn't clan shit, this is just between me and her. Please, I only need a few minutes to talk to her."

"You're not getting it, fancy pants." The blunt-fanged vampire looked seconds away from swinging at me. "*She* wants zero minutes with *you*. If she's really that important to you, you'd respect her wishes."

"But it wasn't like what she saw! I didn't mean what I said... "

My hope dwindled. There was no chance they'd let me see her, no chance for me to explain. That was my whole justification for sending her away like I did. I'd assumed I'd be able to set things right once Baros had left. Now I was robbed of that opportunity and Amy truly believed she meant nothing to me, when it was the exact opposite.

"Go home and cry into your silk sheets about it," the blond sneered. "You've done enough already."

"Or you could stay here and wait for the sun to take you," the other suggested. "That would do us a huge favor."

Giving up on being with Amy was not an option. But there was nothing I could do here, so close to dawn and with these two in my way. Even if I managed to get past them, fight and claw my way into enemy territory as my instincts urged me, I'd never reach her. And if I harmed anyone from

Blood 'til Dawn, that would not bode well for my future plans.

A future that included Amy at my side, and this clan as our ally.

So I straightened, took calming breaths, and fell back on the lessons of courtesy and decorum that had been beaten into me since birth.

"I don't take your insults personally," I began.

The blunt-fanged vampire snorted. "Well, you should."

I ignored him. "My clan has indeed done terrible things to yours, and I sympathize with your anger toward my bloodline. I apologize for my behavior and the disruption."

The two vampires exchanged an eye roll and the blond stuck a darakt cigarette between his lips. "Yeah, whatever."

"Before I go, I want to thank you for your steadfast protection of Amy." That got a surprised look from both of them, as I'd hoped. "Especially now, while I, for the moment, cannot protect her myself. You're good vampires and I'm sure your entire clan is proud to have your loyalty. Good day to you both."

I turned and headed for my idling motorcycle without waiting for a reply. A muttered, "What the fuck?" was all I heard before my engine drowned out all other noise.

A huge, painful breath left my chest as I sat motionless on my bike. It killed me that I was leaving without Amy. It hurt beyond anything that she wouldn't even hear me, but I had only myself to blame.

And only I could fix it.

Chapter 30

Novak

A human waitress in a slinky, short dress approached me with a tray. "Can I get you a blood cocktail, sir?"

"No, thank you."

She slipped away just as demurely as she'd approached, leaving me alone in the VIP loft of Pulse Point nightclub, one of Blood 'til Dawn's many businesses. I glanced at my watch, knowing full well that their lateness was a power move. As if they didn't make me jump through enough hoops just to set up this meeting. All I could do was grit my teeth and show that I was willing to play ball.

At long last, three dark figures ascended the stairs, red smoke of darakt wafting all around them like a cloud. Thorne's face became clear in the dim club lights first, shadows making his cheekbones and jaw more pronounced. He was flanked by Rhain and Cyan.

I didn't get up to greet them and they showed no expectation of it, taking seats on the sofa across from me. Blood 'til Dawn, with its humble roots, was not a clan of formalities and social gestures even after taking the ruling seat. Secretly, I'd always admired that about them.

"So, are congratulations in order?" Thorne had already finished his first darakt cigarette and lit up a fresh one. "Have you knocked up Carpe Noctem's daughter yet?"

On either side of him, Rhain and Cyan tensed. If it was possible for Blood 'til Dawn to hate a clan more than mine, it was definitely Carpe Noctem. Cyan especially looked like he was holding himself back from throttling me.

"Nothing came of that deal," I said. "I had a change of heart and broke it off. Permanently. There's nothing Baros has that would benefit me."

Thorne's brows lifted slightly. Whether it was genuine surprise or his usual sarcasm, I couldn't tell. "So you've lost the chance for an heir *and* the brusang who fell in love with you. Must be rough."

"You still made the deal in the first place," Rhain pointed out. "You had intentions of challenging us, of taking property that is rightfully ours. Who's to say you won't change your mind again?"

I straightened in my seat, folding my hands in front of me. "You're right. I did make that deal, fully intending to work with Carpe Noctem and challenge you for ruling clan once we claimed the Crown region and gathered enough support. The heir I would have made with Inessa would have tied me to Carpe Noctem for the long haul."

"And you changed your mind because... ?" The question came from Cyan, scowling like he didn't expect a real answer.

"Because of Amy," I said, looking at him squarely. "I didn't just fall for her. I found out she's my blood mate."

Cyan narrowed his eyes. "That's not possible."

"It is possible and the truth."

He shook his head. "It's too rare to happen again this soon. Tavi and I are the first blood mate pairing in almost twenty years."

I shrugged. "Maybe Temkra has blessed both of you, and us by association."

Cyan glared daggers at me. "I'm nothing like you, Novak. You kept your deal with Carpe Noctem hidden from her. Who betrays their blood mate like that?"

My head cocked to the side. "I seem to remember you having a colorful reputation before settling down with Tavia. You didn't exactly discriminate where your blood sources came from, did you?"

A twitch of his mouth was the only warning before Cyan shot up and lunged at me. Rhain, moving impressively fast for his size, stopped him with a hand to his chest.

"Easy," the bigger vampire said. "He's trying to get under your skin. Don't give him that."

Rhain all but forced Cyan back to his seat. The mated vampire was huffing and puffing with anger, but stayed put.

"Do you need to step out?" Thorne asked, barely looking at him.

"No, I'm good," Cyan said.

"You sure?"

"Yes." Cyan's glare was molten on me. "I'll stay civil as long as he does."

"My apologies," I offered. "I should've known you'd be... sensitive about your past."

"Watch your mouth," Cyan hissed through his teeth. "You know who's sensitive? Amy. Nothing wrong with it, but you hurt someone who feels pain very deeply. My mate wants to string you up by your balls, said it would ensure you never get that heir you desperately wanted. Honestly, I don't see why I should stop her."

I almost nodded my agreement. Tavia was fiercely, almost violently protective of Amy. With how badly I fucked up, I was relieved to know she still had support. A friend and the entire ruling clan to help her.

But what I planned to offer was hopefully more useful than my mutilated genitals.

"Did you demand this meeting for an actual reason or just to poke Cyan's bear?" Thorne stubbed out his darakt cigarette and lit up another. Cyan lit up too, eager to take the edge off his temper. The human waitress came by with a drink on her tray and set it in front of Rhain.

"I no longer claim Rathka's Order as my clan," I said. "I want to remove myself from that lineage, and everything associated with it."

This time, Thorne's eyebrows lifted in genuine surprise. "You want to renounce your clan?"

"I understand it's unprecedented, but I'm willing to cooperate with whatever methods you decide to make this official and legal." I reached inside my jacket and pulled out a folded letter, placing it on the low table between me and the three of them. "That's my formal renouncement. In that letter, I've also condemned the cruelties and abuses that my ancestors committed upon yours. I've listed out the ones I know of. If there's more you'd like me to add, I'd be happy to."

Thorne said nothing as he unfolded the letter, his two clansmen leaning in to read over his shoulder. When he reached the end, the slightest smile quirked his mouth as his gaze lifted to me.

"Novak, formerly of Rathka's Order, now extinct." He read aloud my signature at the bottom.

"I haven't chosen a new clan name yet, but I can amend the letter when I do."

"You're really willing to let the proud name of your ancestors die out? Our memories are long, Novak, but everything that dies is eventually forgotten."

"Yes, I am."

"Why?" Thorne demanded with narrowed eyes.

I shifted in my seat, at first unsure of how personal I should get, but then remembered Amy's bravery. Not only in showing me her physical scars but trusting me enough to let her guard down and be vulnerable. I ached without her presence in my cold, lonely house, but I could still draw on her for inspiration.

For her, I had to lay it all out on the line.

"I spent my whole life trying to live up to the standards of Rathka's Order, even after they all wasted away from the Curse," I said. "Countless hours running tests, trying to bend magic, science, and medicine to my will so that I could cure them. Because surely a cure would elevate me past a useless second son in my father's eyes. And if I had an heir on the way, even better. The clan would surely be restored to its former glory, and I would have the love and respect of my family."

My gaze fell to the table. "Amy made me realize I was trying to win the approval of ghosts, that I was stuck in the past like an insane person, doing the same thing over and over again while expecting different results. The truth I didn't want to face was that my family never cared. The first two hundred years of my life proved that. It didn't matter that I had three doctorate degrees, learned to read and write faster than my brother, and brought our clan out of the dark ages with modern technology. No matter what I did, I was never good enough for them. So you see, Thorne," I lifted my head, meeting the gazes across from me, "I was never truly part of Rathka's Order to begin with.

And I'm happy to let a cruel, abusive legacy become extinct."

Thorne leaned back, his expression pensive. Rhain also looked thoughtful, his gaze cast to the side. Only Cyan regarded me with suspicion.

"So you want the go-ahead to start a new clan and renounce your old one," he summarized. "Anything else?"

"No, but I would like to offer a few tokens of good faith. In the future, maybe we can consider ourselves allies."

"Don't get ahead of yourself," Thorne scoffed. "What does a now clan-less vampire have to offer us?"

"Amy mentioned you took blood samples of the Marrowers who attacked Sapien," I said. "I have the equipment to analyze blood for draitrium and other substances."

"We already know they were on draitrium," Rhain growled.

"Yes, and I can get a much closer look at the molecular structure of the drug in the bloodstream. I've already identified four different varieties in the tests I've run. If I can match your blood to one of them, I can probably tell you where it comes from. At least, which dealers."

Thorne's fists closed on his knees, his lips flattening. I knew he felt responsible for the attack on Tavia and Amy's old community. As head of the ruling clan, he was tasked to protect it. Finding out who drugged the Marrowers and set them loose would go a long way toward preventing another attack.

"Is there a way to verify that your tests aren't bullshit?" he asked after long consideration.

"I'm the only one in Sanguine who knows how the equipment works. But you're welcome to come watch me run the tests. I can explain everything step-by-step."

Rhain crossed his arms. "I don't like it. Renouncing

Rathka's Order is a nice gesture, but we still don't know if we can trust you."

"I understand." I leaned forward, resting my forearms on my knees. "So I have one more thing to offer. It's simple in concept but will be very complex in terms of execution."

"Please," Thorne drawled with a barely concealed eyeroll. "I'm shaking with anticipation."

A weighted breath left my lungs. "I'll convince Carpe Noctem to release Kalix."

Silence filled the loft. The three vampires stared at me in abject disbelief. Cyan went pale. If I had my facts straight, he'd been the closest to Kalix, and might have even been present when Kalix murdered Baros's father, the former head of Carpe Noctem.

"You're full of shit." Cyan spoke first. "You're not going to ally with us by promising pie-in-the-sky shit that's not possible."

"I'm completely serious," I said, hoping he could hear the earnestness in my voice. "It won't be easy, but if we handle this carefully, it is possible."

"Nobody knows if he's even alive." Cyan's voice cracked with emotion and Thorne placed a reassuring hand on his back. "And even if he is, Baros must be pissed you broke off the deal, so how do you expect to pull this off?"

"He is alive. I have a source inside Carpe Noctem who's helping."

"Who?" Rhain demanded.

"I promised to keep them safe. Their identity getting out could—"

"It's Inessa, the daughter." Thorne casually lit up another cigarette.

Rhain and Cyan's heads whipped to face him while I stared in shock.

"What? How do *you* know?"

"She's my source too. Been slipping me information about Carpe Noctem for about a decade. We've been talking about breaking Kal out for the past year." Red smoke wisped from the corners of Thorne's mouth. "She was actually gonna help me ruin you if you went through with the deal." His heavy-lidded gaze slid over to me. "Good thing you had a change of heart, didn't you?"

"I'm still not convinced," Rhain cut in before I could respond. "Why test the blood? Why try to free Kalix? It just sounds to me like you're trying really hard to convince us that you're good and trustworthy." He took a long sip of his drink, eyeballing me over the rim. "And I don't trust ass-kissers."

"Consider it a small retribution for everything my ancestors did to yours," I said. "I never condoned what they did, especially with the draitrium and the werewolves. It wasn't just wrong, but horrific to treat other vampires like that. Aligning myself with you won't undo what happened, but I do hope it can lead to healing and collaboration between my new clan and yours."

Thorne gave a slow nod, like he was intently absorbing everything I said.

"Honestly," I rubbed my jaw, "I've always held a secret admiration for Blood 'til Dawn. I could never tell my family of course, so I kept it to myself. You've fought and scrapped and bled for every ounce of power you have. From what I've seen, you do your best to wield it responsibly. And," I sighed, feeling the weight of grief and despair settle over me, "you're Amy's clan, the family protecting her. I miss her more than I can express, but I respect the lengths you're going to in order to keep her safe. Even if she and I don't work out, you're a good clan that looks out for your own and she's lucky to have you."

The silence from the other side of the table was contemplative now, not quite as tinged with suspicion or shock.

"What will you do without her blood?" Cyan broke the silence with an intense expression. "As blood mates, you'll both suffer if you cannot feed from each other."

I nodded, grinding my teeth and hating the thought of Amy suffering like the first day I met her. "If she's done with me for good, maybe one of you can broker extracting my blood for her. I'll give it freely. I don't need her blood in exchange."

Cyan cocked his head with a skeptical look. "It's hell, drinking blood that's not your mate's."

"I know." My gaze held his. "I'll suffer through it, but she doesn't deserve to."

His chin lifted, his expression one of muted surprise, but he didn't comment further.

Thorne stubbed out the last of his cigarette and stood up. "We'll be in touch after discussing this with more of our people."

I rose to my feet after the other two vampires did. "Thank you for meeting with me."

Thorne let out a dry huff of breath. "We'll see. Until next time, Rathka's Order. Or whoever you are now."

With those parting words, the three of them turned and left.

Chapter 31

Amy

Under the crushing weight of depression was a familiar place I never hoped to be again. But really, what did I expect? This was me after all.

The only difference was that I had Tavia to lean on again. Instead of pushing her away, I rested my head in her lap while sobbing over Novak. She didn't hold back on the wine or the disparaging words toward him, although she pulled back on the insults when I requested it. For some reason, I still felt the urge to defend him and never wanted to hear anyone speak of him badly.

That was only for me to do, privately. Under my breath, drunk off my ass, or while sobbing into a pillow.

The anger was new and unexpected. It wasn't the first time a guy had hurt me, but before, I had always put the blame entirely on myself. It was my fault for falling short of what Tom Harrison had wanted, my fault for being so agreeable, gullible and naive.

With Novak, something in me had shifted. Maybe I held onto some of the confidence he gave me in the beginning, or maybe it had to do with my turning. But I *knew*, as well as I knew my own name, that I was not at fault for this outcome. *He* was.

Sure, I had the bad luck of trusting the wrong people. But trusting in itself wasn't a shortcoming. *He* chose to discard me, chose to build me up with lies before tearing it all down. He was the only person to blame for this hurt in my heart, not me.

But that didn't make it hurt any less.

It didn't make any of his sudden change in behavior less confusing. And it definitely didn't stop my head from replaying that sight of him tasting the naked woman's blood, over and over again.

Days and nights blurred into each other. I barely ate, sticking to a steady diet of wine instead. The mere thought of tasting someone else's blood made me physically ill.

Tavia was around frequently, but Cyan less so. She said he was dealing with clan politics whenever I asked.

She was a true friend, almost like old times but not quite. She never pushed me to move on or talk about it, just offered support, a listening ear, and gently encouraged me to eat. If we were still simple humans living in Sapien, she would have hunted Novak down with a baseball bat over her shoulder, but she kept that violent side in check now.

I was trying to make myself useful one day, tidying up the apartment instead of rotting away in bed, when a knock came to the door. When I answered, it was Laith, Des, and Rhain each carrying large black plastic totes.

"Hey, Ames." Laith invited himself inside first, followed by the other two. Each vampire set their containers down on the coffee table in front of the couches.

"Hi, guys." I eyed the large totes and the men who brought them in. "What's this?"

"Delivery for you." The three of them were already heading out of the apartment, their task efficiently done.

"Delivery of what? From who?"

"No idea, we're just the messengers. But hey," Des shot me a heartfelt grin with that chipped fang, "you're looking better. You should come out with us tonight. Hit the clubs, get some drinks and let loose. We're good bodyguards; we won't let anyone bother you."

"Rhain will even dance with you." Laith patted the big vampire's shoulder, who looked at him incredulously.

"I will?"

"Thank you guys, but maybe another night." I gave them the best smile I could muster, which still felt strained.

"For sure. Whenever you're feeling up to it. See ya, Ames." Laith waved before closing the door after them.

I spun to face the totes the moment they were gone, feeling incredibly wary of this random delivery. Was it a prank? Some kind of taunt?

I ran a finger along the lidded edge of one container, circling all the way around, and found nothing suspicious. Gripping one edge, I lifted to find the tote surprisingly heavy.

"What the hell are you?" I checked the lids and weights of the other two to find them similarly heavy and most likely not sprung with booby traps.

The safest option was to wait for Tavia or Cyan to come home, but my curiosity was too great. I popped the lid off of one container and held my breath while I peered inside.

It was full of books, all stacked neatly with care. Not just any books, but romance paperbacks. The kinds I'd been obsessed with and would read cover to cover late into the night. Some of the titles looked familiar, but I had never read most of these. They definitely weren't my old collection from Sapien.

I picked up one pristine paperback and opened it to the title page. *Fire of a Lady's Dragon* by M.J. Nance, but the title wasn't the most interesting part. There was some kind of mark or seal embossed into the paper. I brought the book directly under a lamp and angled the page to see better.

The embossed seal was of three intersecting swords circled with the words, *From the library of Dienna, Rathka's Order.*

I almost dropped the book with how hard the realization struck me. This had belonged to Novak's mother. It was from the glass case in the library at his house.

I ran to the opened tote and pulled out another book, which had the same embossing on the title page. My hands were a shaking blur, grabbing paperback after paperback to find the same thing on every single title page. I ripped the lids off of the other two totes and handled the books as carefully as I could to confirm what I already knew.

Novak had sent me his mother's entire romance collection.

But why? Was this his cruel way of mocking me? I wanted to believe he had kinder intentions, perhaps an apology, but his callous, uncaring words at the very end remained stuck in me like splinters.

While flipping through one of the books, I spotted one of those sticky, colored annotation tabs and paused to read the marked sentence.

Her laughter is the sweetest music, her smile the force that drives my icy heart to beat.

It was from the hero's point of view in a passage of him expressing his feelings for the heroine. Flipping through more pages, I found another sentence marked with a tab.

She cannot be caged, nor reduced to a mere accessory on my arm. Her beauty shines brightest when she is free and wild.

I picked up another novel and found similar excerpts marked with the same tabs. Every single one was of the hero confessing his love, or thinking of the heroine in an admiring way, whether about her beauty, her spirit, or whatever it was that drew him to her and made her unique.

After going through no less than twenty books and finding multiple tabbed sections in all of them, I sat abruptly on the floor and tried to make sense of it all.

There was no way Novak read through all of these books and marked all of these passages for me to find, was there?

His mother could have tabbed the books. She embossed her collection, after all. Marking her favorite parts with colored flags wasn't that far-fetched. But Novak had said she died a long time ago, when he was still a juvenile. Had sticky tabs even been invented at that point?

I grabbed a novel at random and opened it, flipping to the closest tab between the pages.

To be loved by her would be the greatest privilege of my life.

With a frustrated groan, I slammed the paperback closed and let it drop to the floor.

"What the fuck do you want?" I asked the empty totes and stacks of books, fresh tears brimming my eyes.

Hours later, there was a gentle knock at my bedroom door, almost whisper-quiet. I wiped the tears from my cheeks and said, "Yes?" in the most normal voice I could muster.

"Hey Amy, it's Cy," came the voice from the other side. "Tavi's doing something in the kitchen and she wants you as a taster."

Oh, there had been a *lot* of wine tasting over the past few days. Tavia was certainly letting me indulge in drowning my sorrows.

If I was being honest, it was getting to be too much. I craved the emotional numbing from a full bottle after flipping through all those books, but stopped myself. It would only make me feel worse later.

"Thanks, Cy, but can you let her know I'm not feeling up to it today?"

A long pause preceded his answer. "It's not wine this time. She's... cooking. And she really wants your opinion. It won't take long, promise."

I heaved out a sigh. It really didn't take much for me to cave to Tavia. Especially when I knew she was trying to get me out of my room and eat something. To live life and stop wallowing.

Being alive isn't the same as living. Novak's words when we first met came back to me in a cruel sense of irony. I hated that, even now, he wasn't wrong.

"Fine. I'll be right out," I called.

"Sounds good. I'll let her know."

I rolled out of bed, feeling about as lively as a sack of potatoes, and did my best to make sure my face and clothes were decent. There wasn't much to be done about my puffy eyes, but Tavia wouldn't hold them against me.

Cyan leaned against the wall next to the front door of the apartment, typing something on his phone. "Hey, I'll walk up with you," he said, barely looking up as he held the door open.

"Um, okay."

He shoved his phone into a pocket and met my eyes, his gaze sympathetic. "How've you been holding up?"

I shrugged, and he acknowledged the gesture with a nod.

"What's Tavia making?" Anything to get the subject off of me as I walked past him into the corridor.

"I don't know." Cyan closed the apartment door behind us. "Something to do with uh, goldfish crackers, I think."

I stopped at the bottom of the stairs going up to the main level, turned and stared at him. "What?"

He grinned sheepishly. "No idea. It's an adventure." Gesturing to the stairs, he added, "After you."

The seed of suspicion had been planted when he waited and offered to escort me up to the kitchen. It was growing even more now as I climbed the stairs.

Cyan opened the door for me at the top landing, and I walked into a mostly empty great room.

Empty except for Novak.

My breath got stuck in my chest and did not seem to remember the right way out.

Novak looked as fucking dapper and handsome as ever, in gray slacks, a waistcoat, and those goddamned shirt sleeves rolled messily past his elbows. His hands were shoved in his pants pockets, making the blood vessels and lean muscles of his forearms pop.

One of those hands revealed themselves, extending toward me with long fingers that I once loved to feel running over my skin.

"Please, Amy. Just give me ten minutes to speak with you. That's it. If you want me gone afterward, I'll never reach out to you again. But please. I have never needed anything more than these few moments right now."

Shocked and dazed, I looked over my shoulder at Cyan, who hovered near the door.

"You can tell him no, and we'll kick him out," my friend's mate said. "Or if you do want to hear him out, we'll give you the room. No one will eavesdrop or interrupt."

Looking back at Novak, the desperation was plain on his face. Now that his presence had sunk in, I realized he did not look his best. He looked thinner, paler, and like he hadn't been sleeping.

Had he been suffering this last week as well? Did he miss me, and regret what he'd said that night? What was the point of sending me those books? Those were only a few of the questions that had been running on a loop in my mind.

I was done being foolish and reckless with my feelings. But if he had any answers, I wanted to hear them.

"Yes," I said, sounding calmer than I felt. "We can talk."

With my focus entirely on Novak, Cyan's voice registered behind me. "We'll be nearby if you need anything."

Then the door closed and we were alone.

"Why?" I said after the first beat of silence.

"Amy." Novak's face contorted with agony, his shoulders slumping forward. "I am *so* fucking sorry."

"That doesn't answer my question. *Why?*"

"None of what I said in front of Carpe Noctem was true. I swear to you, I didn't mean any of it."

"I will yell for Cyan to come back in here if you don't stop making fucking excuses and tell me why–"

"To protect you!" he cut in. "I needed you to leave. I needed Baros to believe that you meant nothing to me, so he wouldn't use you to manipulate me. That's why I lied and said those terrible things. I had no time to think of anything else, or a way to tell you what was happening."

I stared at him, genuinely not expecting that response. My confusion only heightened. "That doesn't explain why his daughter was standing naked right in front of you. They said you were going to make an heir, and you... " I couldn't even choke out the rest, that he looked at her flawless, perfect body like he wanted her. And that he took her blood.

Novak lowered his gaze, unable to look at me directly. "I did make an arrangement with Carpe Noctem to produce an heir with her, but after developing feelings for you, I tried to end it. I knew they would cause trouble for me when I wanted to go back on it. They're a dangerous, powerful clan. But I still should have tried harder. That's completely my fault. I should have told you, so you wouldn't have been blindsided. I regret so, *so* much, Amy."

"Why was she naked?" For some reason, that was the detail I was hung up on. "Did they expect you to see her and just drop trou immediately?"

He winced. "Yeah, pretty much. She did a fertility ritual to increase the chances of pregnancy and her scent was... overpowering." His eyes snapped up to mine, serious and intense. "I responded to her physically only because of biology. I did *not* want her, and I still don't. You are the only woman I've wanted more than I want air to breathe."

"But you *touched* her," I hissed through hot, angry tears. "You drank her blood! I saw you."

"You're right, I did." Novak's jaw clenched. "And her blood tasted disgusting. It cleared my head of her scent and I was no longer physically aroused. Because I found you, my blood mate, and my body is only yours to command."

"So what happened after I left?"

"Nothing. I swear to Temkra, you saw the worst of it. What I said to you, and tasting her blood. I kicked them both out not long after you left. I just had to make sure Baros forgot about you and wouldn't go after you to retaliate against me."

He looked at me again, eyes full of sorrow. "But there are no excuses for the hurt I caused you. I will always regret that, because my sole priority has been to make you feel safe. I broke your trust and I will never regret anything more."

Emotions swirled through me so fast, I could hardly grasp any of them. But somehow I was able to wipe my tears and keep my composure.

"You made... an arrangement for an heir? What, like you were going to donate sperm or something?"

"Or something," he echoed bitterly. "Humans call it an arranged marriage. It would have been a loveless union to cement allyship between our clans. Outside of producing an heir, there was no relationship expected between her and me."

I shook my head in disbelief. That sounded nothing like the affectionate, romantic Novak I'd gotten to know.

"Why would you do something like that?"

"Because I thought it was my only option at the time," he said. "The whole idea made me uncomfortable from the start, but Baros had been pushing it on me for months. Because of my clan's name and all the speculation about Rathka's Curse, I thought it was my only chance at some kind of family. A future." Novak's gaze held mine. "Until I started falling for you, and realized I could have something real."

I broke eye contact, forcing myself to stay strong against

the sadness in his eyes. "You never said a word to me about any of that."

"I know. I should have. You deserved to know the truth. I just... thought I could handle it. Make it go away like it never existed so it wouldn't affect our happiness." He crossed his feet at the ankles, shoving his hands back into his pockets. "I also didn't want you to worry about Inessa. I was never interested in her like I was with you, and I didn't want you to think I was somehow... conflicted between two women. There was never any comparison in my mind. I only ever wanted you." His head fell back, his gaze focused toward the ceiling. "I realize keeping this from you only made it so much worse. It's my fault you walked in and saw that with no prior context. I wish more than anything that I could undo the whole stupid arrangement just so I could prevent the hurt I caused you."

On a small level, I almost felt insulted. He thought I was so fragile and insecure that he couldn't tell me about a loveless, political marriage he hadn't wanted or even sought to consummate? At the same time, I had to acknowledge he was probably right. My crush on him was nearly all-consuming before we'd ever gotten physical. I would have been jealous if there was even a whiff of another woman in the picture. And if I had known what Inessa looked like? Yeah, I definitely would have been concerned.

"Have you slept with her before?" I asked.

"No," he answered quickly, then got a hesitant look. "But—"

"Oh, do go on." I crossed my arms, facing him squarely.

"No, I didn't mean... Nothing like that!" Novak brought his hands together and huffed out a quick breath. "Nothing romantic or sexual has ever occurred between Inessa and me. But she is working with Blood 'til Dawn and me, indirectly, to dismantle Carpe Noctem. We're trying to free a prisoner, among other things, but she and I are communicating through our household staff, strictly about these plans. She wants to escape her father, so Thorne and I have agreed to help her if she'll help us." Novak spread his hands. "That's all. I'm never hiding anything from you again, so I'm just letting you know that she and I are in contact. Nothing more."

"Okay, that's good to know, I guess." I rubbed my forehead, as if that would make all my feelings and thoughts make sense. "Why did you want to tell me all this?"

"So that you would know the truth," he said. "So that you would know that my feelings for you never changed, even though I made terrible choices that made you believe otherwise. Whether you believe me or not, you are my blood mate and I will love you until my last breath."

"The books," I said, suddenly remembering. "What's the deal with the books?"

He shrugged. "You love them. I thought you should have them."

"Did you mark all of those excerpts with the tabs?"

"Yes."

"Why?"

There was another shrug as he looked down at his hands. "I'm not a writer. I only have so many words to express how much you mean to me. Each one of those marked passages is a description of love that I never could have come up with." A mirthless huff escaped him. "And still, none of it compares to the bliss of waking next to you before I fucked it all up." He glanced quickly at his watch. "I've said my piece and taken more than ten minutes of your time, so I'll leave you be."

"Wait," I said, my chest tightening in despair at the thought of him leaving.

Novak paused on his way to the door. "Yes?"

I forced the words out through a tight throat and a thundering heart. "Do you... do you want us to be together again?"

"More than anything," he answered quickly. "But I'm not arrogant enough to ask for a second chance. I've already hurt you enough, and I will never put that pressure on you. You know my feelings and where I stand. If you'd like to try again"—a shadow of his playful smirk emerged as he turned to leave—"you know where I live."

Chapter 32

Amy

A few days later, after lots of thinking around in circles and talking to Tavia, I headed out to Novak's house to give him my answer.

I smelled the fire before I saw it. When I saw the tall plume of smoke in the direction of his street, panic overtook me and I started running in that direction.

No one else seemed concerned, and that was crazy to me. House fires were devastating in Sapien. A person could lose everything, even loved ones, in a blaze that spread out of control.

But when I saw the dead end and the curving retaining wall that marked Novak's courtyard, my running steps slowed. A fire was indeed ablaze, but contained.

A pile of wooden furniture was on fire, with cardboard boxes and crumpled pieces of paper stuffed in various spots for kindling. I couldn't tell what the furniture had been, possibly armchairs or a desk.

Novak sat on the steps leading up to his front door, his arms resting on his knees, a lit darakt cigarette dangling in his hand as he watched the fire. He didn't move, didn't seem to hear me or my heartbeat over the crackling wood as I stepped closer.

"I've never seen you smoke those before."

He startled at my voice, eyes blinking and going wide as he looked at me, like he couldn't believe I was there.

"Guess I'm not feeling like myself lately." He tossed the cigarette into the bonfire. "Don't like the taste of those anyway."

A long moment of awkwardness passed, like neither one of us was sure what to say or do.

"What are you burning?" I asked finally.

"My father's favorite armchairs," he said. "And all documents and records pertaining to Rathka's Order. That clan is ash on the wind now."

"Good," I said. "Good riddance."

"Agreed." Novak sighed.

"Have you thought of a new clan name?"

There was a long pause before he answered. "No, not yet."

I took a deep breath and swallowed. "I... had an idea for one. If you'd like to hear it."

He gave me a long, lingering look. "Sure. What've you got?"

"How about," I swallowed again, "Blood and Truth?"

Novak looked toward the fire again and nodded slowly. "It's a good one. I like it."

"Thanks. I thought you would."

The next awkward moment felt like a canyon neither of us knew how to cross.

"Novak, I—"

"Amy—"

We started talking at the same time when the silence became too much, and when the smile crossed his face, I knew mine looked similar.

"What would Blood and Truth mean to you, as a clan name?" I asked. "What does it signify?"

Novak folded his hands, looking pensively at his linked fingers. "It means trust, not just within the clan but any agreements made outside of it as well. It means integrity, standing by your word. It means forging strong bonds, creating honest relationships. Blood and Truth to me sounds like an honorable clan, one whose strength comes from the ability to be honest. Even if, *especially* if, the truth is unpleasant. Such a clan doesn't shy away from ugly truths, but leans on each other to weather those storms. Because they're a clan that trusts in each other."

He glanced at me, a hint of that sheepish smile returning. "How'd I do?"

"Good." I could barely choke out the word with my throat so tight with emotion. "Great, even. And you know what?"

I went to stand in front of him and reached for one of his clasped hands. The bonfire was a bank of heat at my back, flames casting dancing shadows across Novak's face. A face that wore an expression of heartache and longing.

"You embody everything Blood and Truth stands for. Everything you just said can be used to describe yourself, Novak. You are someone worthy of trust." I let out a shaky breath. "And forgiveness."

His face barely changed. Only a flicker of emotion passed over his features, but his hands wrapped around mine with an iron grip.

"Amy," he rasped, his voice thick. "Does this mean... "

The tears fell freely as I nodded. "I believe that you

were trying to protect me from Carpe Noctem. I believe that your feelings never changed and you didn't intend to hurt me as badly as you did."

"No, darling. Not ever." His knuckles grazed my cheek, already wiping my tears away. "But I did hurt you, I know that. And I'm so sorry."

"I know, and I had to process that." I sniffed and a little laugh escaped me. "Laith keeps telling me to feel my feelings. He says it's in some self-help book he read."

"Hmm. He should probably switch to romance novels."

"Right?" Another laugh bubbled out of me, this one brighter and happy. "Thank you for all those books, by the way. I can't believe you read and marked them all."

"I just couldn't stop thinking about you." Novak pulled me closer to stand between his legs. "Couldn't believe how badly I fucked up when I love you so much. I wanted you to *know*, to never have a single doubt about how I feel."

"I do know." My hands went to his shoulders, running through the long strands of silvery blond hair. "I understand you made a mistake. And it's because of you that I'm able to pick myself up from this." I laced my fingers at the back of his neck, bringing my forehead to his.

"You made me stronger and more confident than I've ever been in my life. You've helped me to understand myself and even love myself. No one else has ever given me such a gift. I love you, Novak and I never want you to doubt me either."

His breath fanned across my lips and I thought he might kiss me.

"Let the first vow of Blood and Truth be this: I will never keep another secret from you. I will never cut you down with my words or actions. I will do everything in my power to lift you up and support your dreams and desires. I give you my blood and my body freely and will cherish yours in return."

"Yes, agreed," I sniffed, the tears returning. "Ditto, all of that. Fuck, I can't top that, you romantic jerk."

With light laughter, Novak finally ended my misery and kissed me. It felt like falling into a soft, warm bed after a long time away from home. He tasted like everything I'd been without, and all that I needed.

It didn't take long for my fangs to lengthen and throb, for the burning ache between my legs to rival the heat of Novak's bonfire, and for my thirst to make itself known.

We'd both gone without each other's blood for nearly two weeks.

"I need you." My lips were already finding their way down his warm neck to the perfect spot.

Novak stood with a groan, lifting me up with him using a strong grip under my thighs. "I've never needed a single fucking thing as much as I need you right now."

He turned us toward his front door, pushing inside with a firm nudge of his body.

"Shouldn't we keep an eye on the fire?" I watched the dancing flames over his shoulder.

"We can from in here." He carried me into the front sitting room just off the foyer, lowering us onto the couch, back to the first place he'd ever laid me down. "I need you so fucking much, I can't even bother going upstairs."

Novak pressed me down into the sofa with another kiss, with his whole body fitting against mine like a long-lost puzzle piece. I tugged on his lower lip, sinking my teeth until I tasted blood. He shuddered, groaning into my mouth as I licked and soothed the cut.

"Trying to make me come in my pants again?" He smirked, lifting away to remove his shirt and undo his belt.

"If it gets you to use the shower head on me again." I lifted my hips, allowing him to slide off my jeans and panties.

"Oh, we can absolutely repeat that adventure." He let our discarded clothing fall to the floor.

The firelight was softer through the windows, but it made him no less beautiful. Lights and shadow played over tan skin, lean muscle, and his gorgeous hair.

Novak lowered himself to me, fitting his hips between my legs as he kissed me tenderly this time. I could feel how much he was holding back, the slight tremble of need not yet unleashed. I still had a T-shirt on, and he gripped the hem in a fist, his kisses long and languid.

"Will you let me take this off?" he whispered. "So I can see and love all of you?"

The fear that once ruled me was still there, just as a whisper when it used to be a roar. I had forgiven him, but my emotions were still raw. Everything that happened remained fresh, and that tiny jolt of panic at him seeing me was not yet snuffed out.

But I had chosen to trust him, to forgive him. And with time, maybe I could truly see myself as he saw me. With Novak, real confidence and self-love didn't feel like a far-off fantasy anymore. It could be a reality, if I allowed it to be.

If I faced that fear and didn't let it win.

"Yes," I said.

I pressed up and let him peel the shirt over my head. But he didn't lay me back down. Instead he grabbed me around the waist and hauled me into his lap until I strad-dled him while he sat in the center of the couch.

"Gorgeous." His hands ran reverently all over me, ruby eyes dilated and taking me in everywhere. "So stunning and perfect."

I found myself stretching, arching, loving the attention he paid me. At the same time, my fangs ached and I felt the dizzying buzz of going without his blood for so long.

"Novak," I whined, leaning forward to nuzzle the side of his neck.

"Yes, akra. Take what you need from me."

His head fell back, giving me access. While my lips skimmed over the strong pulse in his jugular, his fingers stroked between my legs. The moment my fangs sank into him, he sank into me.

Pleasure rushed through me so fast, I was drowning in it. His blood was hot and refreshing at the same time. More than refreshing; revitalizing. He was the smoothest, silkiest wine on my tongue. With each swallow, he drove his fingers into me, stretching and caressing me from the inside while his thumb pressed a matching rhythm on my clit.

I didn't feel control over my body as my hips bucked and ground against his hand. My nipples dragged against his chest as I drank from him. I was pure sensation, chasing more pleasure, more friction, more contact with my blood mate.

"That's it, ride my hand," Novak whispered in my ear. "You're going to ride my cock just like that."

His filthy words tipped me over the edge, lightning zipping through me as my pleasure crested and crashed.

"Open your eyes, darling."

I must have stopped drinking from him at some point, and found myself blinking and meeting his adoring gaze.

"I missed these galaxy eyes so much." He palmed my nape, stroking my cheekbone with his thumb. "Can't bear to not see them."

My head turned to nibble the tip of his thumb. "You're

ridiculous." The words came out lazily, everything soft and dreamy in the aftermath of my orgasm.

"About you? Yes." Novak grinned. "I missed these kitten fangs gnawing on me too."

I released his thumb and leaned forward to lick the bloody mess on his neck that I'd left. The skin looked torn, as if my teeth had ripped away from the force of my orgasm. "Sorry about this. Did I hurt you?"

"No, love," he said on a soft groan, head falling back again. "Did you get enough?"

"Think so." I lapped and kissed at the wound to speed up his healing.

"Good. My turn."

That was the only warning I got before his fist wrapped in my hair and yanked down, sending my neck and entire spine into a long arch. He kissed my throat first, making me squirm in anticipation. At the same time, his hips shifted below me, the hard heat of his cock sliding through my wet, sensitive flesh. I could only hold onto his shoulders as his head found my entrance and he pressed inside me in one long, fluid stroke.

My moan reached the ceiling at that first thrust, and I barely got to relish how good it felt when Novak's fangs sank into the base of my throat.

His forearms braced around my lower back, loose enough only to let me rise and lower onto his cock. He made hungry, animalistic moans as he drank from me, low and growling like a possessive predator.

I let gravity and instinct and need take over, my hands finding the back of the couch to bring myself down harder. Novak's hips lifted to meet me, the force of every crash together making me see stars.

It felt like too soon when he pulled his fangs from my

neck, swiftly licking the wound closed despite my riding him like my life depended on it.

"No, don't stop," I begged. "Take more from me."

"Oh, I am," he growled, lifting one breast in his hand as his mouth fell to it.

He teased my nipple for a tortuously long time, sucking and grazing it with his teeth until the peak ached. Then his fangs sank in just above it, his mouth sealing over and tonguing my nipple while he took more of my blood.

My left breast was red and tender by the time he finished with it. When he pulled away to repeat his ministrations on the right side, I was on the knife-edge of another orgasm.

"Novak," I moaned, grinding against the base of his cock with every thrust, desperate for more friction. "Novak, Novak…"

"Amy…"

A strong forearm came around my waist and the world spun. My back hit the couch and Novak's weight hovered over me. His mouth fell to mine in a rough, biting kiss. We bit each other, blood filling my mouth and his as our teeth clashed and our tongues tangled.

Through the hard kisses, he fucked me just as hard, driving into me with all his male power and strength as he chased his own pleasure.

The orgasm shook me like an earthquake. My body clasped around Novak's length and his punishing thrusts grew wild and frenzied. He swelled within me, turning as hard as iron and growling out my name with those final drives into my body.

Feeling his release made my orgasm roll directly into another. My arms and legs locked around him, refusing to ever be apart from him again.

We only untangled well after becoming limp and spent. Post-orgasm Novak was achingly gentle. He lightly kissed away any lingering cuts on my lips and neck, making me shiver with aftershocks.

"I want to live in this moment forever," I sighed, running a hand down his back. "Everything about this right now is perfect."

"We'll have centuries' worth of these moments." Novak kissed my forehead. "Time is very much on our side for plenty of this and... other moments."

I lifted an eyebrow quizzically. "What kind of other moments?"

"Well." He turned on his side, stroking a hand down my body. "If I may confess something."

"Please do, Novak of Blood and Truth."

A smile touched his lips, his hand pausing to rest on my abdomen. "I really want to make a baby with you, Amy of Blood and Truth."

Emotion overwhelmed me to the point of feeling like my heart would leap from my chest. "You do?"

"When you're ready, of course. Like I said, we have centuries of time. But yes, I want to create the family you and I never got to have." His eyes met mine with shy reservation. "What do you think?"

"I think... " I was grinning so hard, my heart so full of love and hope, that it was difficult to speak. "I think we should do that much sooner than centuries away."

Novak blinked, his eyes lighting up as a grin split his face to match mine. "Really?"

"Yes, really. Although I have no idea when I'll be fertile. Bea was saying it can take a couple of years for a brusang to have a regular once-in-a-year cycle like a vampire."

"That's no problem. Once you have an idea of your

window, we can do a fertility ritual if you'd like. Or just see what happens."

"That works for me." I wrapped an arm around his neck, drawing him down toward me. "In the meantime, we can get lots of practice in."

"Oh yes," he agreed with a husky murmur, settling between my legs again. "Lots and lots of practice."

Epilogue

Laith

One month later

I rushed down the street toward the party in Novak's courtyard. The celebrations spilled out beyond his residence, with neighbors and strangers talking excitedly as they drank, ate special meat dishes prepared by Novak's chef, and smoked their best darakt.

It seemed as though I missed the blood mate ceremony, and the after-party was in full swing. I hoped Amy wouldn't be too upset with me. I didn't mean to miss her ceremony, just the first and most boring part of the evening where Thorne gave his stamp of approval on the formation of a new clan.

They were now Amy and Novak of Blood and Truth, blood mates bonded and blessed in the eyes of Temkra and the ruling clan, Blood 'til Dawn. Great stuff; I was happy for them. But it wasn't exactly the most pressing issue on my mind at the moment.

I slid through the crowd, looking for Des, my best friend.

"Where the hell have you been?"

"Rhain." I spun around, coming face-to-face with the big hulk of a vampire. "You seen Des?"

"He's over there with Tavia and Cyan." Rhain gestured with his drink hand, eying me suspiciously. "You missed the ceremony."

"I know." I cringed. "Is Amy mad?"

"I don't think she noticed. She's only got eyes for Rath—I mean, fuck. Blood and Truth. It's gonna take a while to get used to saying that. But anyway, where were you?"

"Had to make a stop at the blood bank." That wasn't a lie; it just wasn't the full truth.

Rhain took out his phone and glanced at the time on the screen. "And that took you two hours? Did you drink from a syringe?"

"Yeah, how'd you know? Didn't have any people, so I had to drink from a gerbil without killing it. Tiny blood vessels, it was highly inconvenient. Anyway, I gotta find Des. Enjoy the party!"

I pressed through the crowd before he could call bullshit on my, well, bullshit. Near the curved retaining wall, Des was talking animatedly to Tavia. Next to her, Cyan and Novak were engaged in conversation, the two of them looking jovial and almost brotherly.

It was quite a sight, but Des was my target. I zeroed in on him, dropping my arm on his shoulder while smiling apologetically at Tavia. "I'm sorry, Tavi. Can I steal him for a quick minute?"

"Hey!" Cyan barked. "Watch what you call her."

Fucking Temkra and her possessive, mated males. Couldn't even call a female friend by a nickname if her mate claimed ownership of it.

"Sorry, Cy. Tavi-*ah*, may I?"

The human woman nodded and rolled her eyes. "Sorry about him," she whispered, jerking her head toward Cyan.

"All good," I said tightly. After what just happened at the blood bank, I was beginning to understand that possessiveness.

I patted Des's back and beckoned him to follow me to a quiet area just outside of the courtyard.

"What's up? Where you been?" Des stuck a darakt cigarette between his lips and thumbed his lighter.

"I'm pretty sure I just drank from my blood mate," I said in a harsh whisper. "At the fucking blood bank."

Des's dark brows furrowed, and then relaxed. "No way."

"Yeah way. My usual didn't come in for the appointment, so they paired me with a human who just happened to show up. And Des, I'm telling you." My head shook slowly, recalling the sweet, silky flavor that ran over my tongue and quenched a deep thirst I didn't know I had. "I've never tasted a human, vampire, or anyone like this."

"That good, huh?"

"Yeah. Better than good. It was... everything." I looked toward the party just in time to see Amy and Tavia wrap each other in a hug, their vampire mates watching them with quiet love and adoration. "Now I see why those dummies risk it all. That taste... it's unreal."

"So what happened?" Des asked. "Who is she? Where is she?"

"That's the thing, dude. I don't know." I laced my hands on top of my head, blowing out a breath. "The donation process has to be anonymous, I get that. But after it was done, she wouldn't tell me her name. She just left. And the blood bank staff knew something was up, so they kept me in that room so I wouldn't follow her. By the time they let me out, I couldn't trace her scent or her blood. She was just fucking gone."

"Damn." Des's face crumpled in sympathy. "So she could be anyone."

"Yeah, literally. Gimme one." I held my hand out for a cigarette and he tossed the whole pack to me. "I don't even know if she's a regular donor or just a one-off who needed some cash."

"And you don't even know what she looks like." Des handed me his lighter. "That's rough, man."

"She could be as big and toothy as a Marrower and I wouldn't give a fuck. She's mine." I lit up, took a long drag, and exhaled it slowly. "But I do know she's human. Caucasian, I think. She had purple nail polish on and a weird tattoo on her wrist."

"Weird how?"

"It was just like lines and a bunch of shapes. Really clean and simple, but nothing I'd ever seen before."

Des gave me a knowing look. "Sounds like you need to do some serious searching among the humans. Maybe even try a bunch of different blood sources."

"Fuck." I scratched my eyebrow with my thumb. If I really did drink from my blood mate, life would be utter misery until I found her again. Now that I'd tasted the perfect blood chemistry for me, my brain would not be satisfied by anything else. All other blood sources would be nausea-inducing by comparison.

But if Cyan and Novak's dopey faces of happiness were proof of anything, it was that finding your blood mate was worth it.

Resolute, I finished my cigarette, flicked the remains to the ground, and crushed it under my boot.

"Guess it's time to become one with the humans then."

Whoever this woman was, she was meant to be my one and only blood source.

And I was meant to find her.

———

Thank you so much for reading Taste of Death! I hope you enjoyed Amy and Novak's love story.

Laith's romance with his mysterious blood mate is coming next! Read his POV of meeting her for the first time in **this free bonus scene when you sign up for my newsletter.**

———

If you haven't already, make sure you read Tavia and Cyan's romance in **Taste of Fate, Vampires of Sanguine Book 1.**

Glossary
Sanguine clans and vampiric terms

Vampire Clans

Blood and Truth: a newly formed clan created when Novak of Rathka's Order renounced his clan to start anew

Blood 'til Dawn: Current ruling clan of Sanguine

Carpe Noctem: A previous ruling clan, longtime rivals of Blood 'til Dawn

Marrowers: Clan and subspecies of vampires with a diet rich in bone marrow and preference for living underground

Rathka's Order: A now-extinct clan that succumbed to an unknown illness causing madness and cannibalism

Temkra's Blood: Clan and religious order with a strong focus on the vampire's primary deity, Temkra

Vampiric terms

Akra: A term of endearment similar to darling or sweetheart. It can be used for familial affection, but is most often used between lovers.

Blood mate: Someone whose blood is considered chemically and nutritionally perfect for the recipient. Once tasted, a bond is created in which all other blood tastes foul and rancid. Can be one-sided or between two parties.

Blood pet: Someone who provides their blood to a vampire in exchange for care and protection. Generally expected to be an exclusive arrangement on both ends, unless both parties agree otherwise. Can be platonic or a sexual/romantic arrangement.

Brusang: A human who has been given vampire blood near or soon after their death. They awaken after 2-3 days with blackened eyes and adopt vampire traits such as the need for blood, accelerated healing, an 800-year lifespan, and an aversion to sunlight.

Darakt: A mixture of dried blood and herbs crushed to a fine power, usually rolled in paper and smoked like cigarettes. Provides a brief, euphoric high like nicotine to humans.

Draitrium (drae): A mineral found in the dragon shifter territory that allows vampires to walk in daylight unharmed. Also a highly addictive drug with terrible side effects.

Half-Century Selection: Event in which the human community of Sapien gives one of their own as a blood pet to the ruling vampire clan every fifty years. In exchange, no vampires are permitted to feed from Sapien citizens

Rathka: Temkra's younger brother, an impulsive trickster deity prone to violence. Patron deity of the clan, Rathka's Order.

Sapien: The last remaining human-only compound in Sanguine.

Temkra: primary deity of vampires, thought of as the mother of the species. The territory of Sanguine is believed to be the remains of her body when she laid down to die. This is why the regions of Sanguine are divided into body parts (the Heart, the Ribs, etc.).

Verakt: A vampire or brusang who claims a blood pet. Responsible for the blood pet's care, comfort, and protection. Generally expected to be an exclusive arrangement on both ends, unless both parties agree otherwise. Can be platonic or a sexual/romantic arrangement.

Acknowledgments

Taste of Death, and the entirety of Sanguine itself, would not have been possible without all of the vampire stories and lore that came before it. Charlaine Harris, J.R. Ward, Annette Curtis Klause, Anne Rice, and of course, Bram Stoker, all wrote stories that impacted me long before I decided to become a writer. I would be remiss to not mention the great vampire authors who shaped the genre.

I must, as always, mention my incredible family who has supported me every step of the way along this author journey, especially my husband. Thank you for always talking about my books to your barber and your coworkers, even if it is a little embarrassing. ;)

A huge shout-out to my team of beta readers who were the first to read Taste of Death. Marti, Jamie, Jackie, Kasondra, Samantha, and Edie, thank you so much for invaluable feedback and helping me make this book the best it could possibly be!

And finally, thank *you* for reading this book! Whether this is your first time reading me or you've read everything I've written, I deeply appreciate your support.

Until the next book!

All my love,
Sophie

Also by Sophie Ash

<u>Gods and Myths</u>

The Minotaur

<u>Howling Death MC</u>

Traitor Wolf

Enemy Wolf

Cursed Wolf

About the Author

Sophie Ash is a USA Today bestselling author from Northern California, writing paranormal romances with plenty of bite, as well as passionate retellings of myths and folklore.

When she's not writing, she's probably reading, gardening, vacuuming up cat hair, or enjoying a craft beer in the sun.

Sign up for Sophie's email list and get a free standalone novella as a thank you gift: https://BookHip.com/KBRCFWN

facebook.com/Crystal.Sophie.Ash.Books

instagram.com/crystalsophieash

amazon.com/author/sophieash

bookbub.com/profile/sophie-ash